Some Welcome Home

Some Welcome Home

An Elizabeth Pepperhawk/Avivah Rosen Mystery

Sharon Wildwind

Five Star • Waterville, Maine

First Edition
First Printing: February 2005

Published in 2005 in conjunction with Tekno Books and Ed Gorman.

Set in 11 pt. Plantin.

Printed in the United States on permanent paper.

ISBN 1-59414-275-0 (hc : alk. paper)

Dedication

To the patients, doctors, nurses, and corpsmen who were a part of ward Six-A, Womack Army Hospital, between July 1971 and June 1972, especially Top, Big Dave, Little Dave, Tony, the two Ricks, Murphy, and the Mouse. I still remember what you taught me about courage and about recovery and getting on with life.

To my wonderful husband, Ken, who is a maddeningly accurate proofreader, has a vast military knowledge, almost unlimited patience, and a terrific sense of humor.

Acknowledgments

On July 4, 1971, at approximately 1800 hours (6:00 p.m. for those not familiar with the twenty-four hour clock) I signed into the Normandy House Transient Officers' Quarters at Fort Bragg, North Carolina. There was no body on the bed in my room, and I had no idea, at the time, that the cool, dark room and white bedspread would open this book some thirty years later.

This book is, in part, a tribute to the men and women I served with during the late sixties and early seventies. My only regret is that we never kept up with one another over the intervening years.

Some of the officers and enlisted soldiers in this book are drawn in an unflattering light. I served with far more honest, decent men and women than those with bad habits, but, in order to make a mystery you need villains. I apologize to any serving or former military personnel who served in the same capacities as my not-so-nice characters. Perhaps next time I can make one of your own the hero or heroine.

It's a funny thing about memories: sometimes the created ones seem more real than the remembered ones. My thanks to the following people who helped me accurately recreate the summer of 1971 at Fort Bragg. Gene Moser, Lieutenant-Colonel (retired) for advice about Army brats and general support. Fred Fuller, Reference Librarian, Throckmorton Memorial Library, Fort Bragg for helping me reconstruct details of what the post was like thirty years ago. Betty Dickson, Executive Director, Mississippi Nurses Association, for assistance in verifying Pepper's nursing education. Ellen Brodsky, Nancy Cohen, and Jill Grundfest for pointing out inconsistencies in Avivah's character. Rick Blanchard, Ken Bugg, and Randy for advice about the NASCAR circuit in the 1960s. Joe Grau for Civil War information and how to restore cars.

Thanks to Avivah Wargon, who allowed me to borrow her first name, and to Pat Gladding, who taught me the writing game that produced the name Elizabeth Pepperhawk one night as I worked one very dull midnight shift in a small emergency room.

Thanks always to my agent, Janet Benrey, for believing in me and to Bill Crider for a wonderful editing job. I'm grateful to Tekno Books and Five Star Publishing for allowing Pepper, Avivah, and Benny to go out into the world to seek their fortunes.

And a thank-you I cannot fully express to the late Elizabeth Daniels Squires who inspired me to write mysteries in the first place and who patiently tracked down the order of worship for a funeral that might be held in Marshall, North Carolina. I miss you, Liz, and I wish you had lived to read this.

Chapter 1

Through the slit in the closed drapes, a thin bar of afternoon sunlight fell across the soldier's chest, highlighting the dark, small bullet hole. Captain Elizabeth Pepperhawk watched his chest for a full minute. No breath. She crossed the room and shook his shoulder, more out of habit than a sense she could do anything.

"Sir, sir, wake-up, sir." It was the automatic line she learned in CPR class.

Her fingers located the angle of his jaw and slid down to where a pulse should be. His skin was cold. No pulse. He'd had green eyes. Green eyes and dark black hair. Pepper was relieved to note his fixed, dilated pupils because she could forget CPR. She'd done enough meaningless CPR in the past year.

The hotel room door stood open, her key still in the lock. She removed the key, closed the door, and turned the bolt lock, then sat in an armchair and looked at the body. She took great pride in being a captain, an experienced emergency room nurse, and a Vietnam veteran. She wouldn't go screaming down the hall of the Transient Officers' Quarters just because she had found a body.

Pepper looked around the room. The solid hardwood floor gleamed under her feet. Heavy green drapes covered the windows and a thick, cotton spread covered the double bed. Pepper was glad the blood had soaked into the bed under the body. She'd seen enough blood.

Nothing was out of place in the room except her small overnight bag sitting just inside the door with her purse on top of it. And a dead soldier on the bed. She noticed now that his hair wasn't cut short enough for a soldier. Maybe he wasn't a soldier; maybe someone had dressed him in a uniform. But there was something about him, even in death, that said soldier. He was one of us, Pepper thought regretfully.

One of us. A soldier? A Vietnam veteran? He looked the right age, late twenties, a little older than she was. He could have been over in '67 or '68. Damn, she thought, he'd come home and died. She pushed her tongue hard into the roof of her mouth. That always kept her from crying in the emergency room in Qui Nhon.

Then she noticed his uniform. Green wool Ike jacket, wool pants, polished jump boots. The patch on his shoulder was the double "A" of the Eighty-second Airborne. There was no insignia, no indication of rank. The dead man wore a World War II Army uniform and that war had ended over a quarter of a century earlier. Confused, Pepper leaned back in the armchair.

Some welcome home, she thought. She wasn't going to have a leisurely supper at the Officers' Club, after all. It was time she called someone. She left her bag and purse in the room and locked the door behind her.

A plastic-coated index card taped to the wall over the lobby phone gave the number for the military police.

"MilitaryPoliceSpecialistRamerezMayIhelpyou?"

She hated it when enlisted men strung the words together so fast. It made her feel stupid because she couldn't sort out the person's name from his unit. "This is Captain Elizabeth Pepperhawk, Army Nurse Corps. I've just discovered a dead body in my room at Normandy House. I think you'd better send someone over."

★ ★ ★ ★ ★

A few minutes later, Pepper sat in the lobby, where she could see both the desk clerk and, through the large windows that formed one wall of the lobby, the street in front of Normandy House. When a military police jeep pulled up outside, she watched, with some small amusement, the look of alarm on the desk clerk's face. A man, wearing an MP helmet and side arm, and carrying a walkie-talkie, hurried through the front door, letting the screen bang behind him.

He demanded of the desk clerk. "Which room belongs to Captain Pepperhawk?"

The clerk, a thin, young woman in a black skirt and cream blouse, pointed in her direction. "That's Captain Pepperhawk. She came down here about five minutes ago and told me not to go to room 106. Is there a problem?"

Oh, yes, Pepper thought, there is definitely a problem. The man crossed the small lobby toward her. She stood.

"I'm Specialist Ramerez. You called us? Something about a body?" It was a Mexican-American accent, probably Texas border country.

"This way, please. I assessed him to see if CPR would do any good, but he's quite dead, pupils fixed and dilated." Pepper realized that she was using the same tone she would use to show visitors to a patient's room. He must think she was crazy. Maybe she was, but she wasn't going to break down. She'd seen bodies before.

The two of them walked to the end of the hall and she took the key out of her sundress pocket.

"I locked it. I hope you don't have to keep my overnight case and purse. I left them inside. I've already touched the doorknob a couple of times, so I guess it won't matter if I touch it again," she rambled as she unlocked the door, pushing it out of the way so that he could see into the room.

11

"Oh, shit," Ramerez said, under his breath. He went into the room, took several seconds to verify what Pepper had said, then took the key out of her hand and locked the door.

"Unit 1 to dispatch," he keyed into his walkie-talkie.

"Go ahead, Unit 1," a woman's mechanical voice responded amid static.

"Find Captain Rosen and tell her to get over to Normandy House. Now!"

"You need backup?"

"Affirmative."

He released the button on his walkie-talkie. Positioning himself at parade rest in front of the door, he said, "Please stay where I can see you, ma'am."

Pepper didn't let the slightly spread legs, the hands behind his back fool her. Ramerez could move in an instant if he needed to.

There was no chair, so Pepper stood where she was and tried to not think about being thirsty. The long drive through July heat, even in an air-conditioned car, had made her feel hot, gritty, and dry. At least, not being on official business, she could travel in civilian clothes instead of her uniform.

She heard the screen door in the lobby slam again and a muffled conversation. A tall woman with short black hair and a confident gait strode down the hall. She wore a summer duty uniform, military police insignia, a gun, and a black arm band around her right arm that said SOD: Staff Officer of the Day. Staff Officers of the Day were drawn from a pool of lieutenants and captains from all the units throughout the post. That a military police officer had drawn SOD duty on a day there was a death confirmed Pepper's belief that the Army was full of coincidences.

"What's going on, Ramerez?"

"This is Captain Pepperhawk. She discovered a dead body in her room." Ramerez unlocked the door so the woman could look inside. "I checked him. CPR isn't going to help."

The arrival of four military policemen, their polished helmets gleaming, confirmed that Ramerez's backup had arrived. The captain signaled for them to come down the hall.

She had a northern accent, possibly New York. "I want a guard on this room and someone on all the exits. No one in, no one out. Ask the desk clerk how many other guests are registered and find all of them."

"You going to call criminal investigation?" Ramerez asked.

"I'm going to cover my tail on this one. Criminal Investigation Division, the Field Officer of the Day, the Medical Officer of the Day, and the Public Information Officer."

Ramerez looked confused. "Why the PIO?"

"You want to explain another MacDonald media fiasco to the general?"

Pepper wondered who MacDonald was and why they were afraid of another media fiasco.

Ramerez commented, "Captain Delaney is on CID call tonight."

The tall woman shook her head. "Figures. That should make it an interesting evening."

She walked over to Pepper. "Captain Pepperhawk, I'm Captain Rosen, military police. You understand that you can't leave. It may be a long evening."

Pepper looked around the hall. "I understand. Do you want me to stay here?"

"I'd prefer it if you waited in the lobby."

She escorted Pepper back to the lobby and pointed to

the chair Pepper had been sitting in half an hour earlier. "Stay in that chair, please."

The *please* didn't fool Pepper. Captain Rosen had ordered her to stay put.

At least, she had a good seat to watch what came next. More military police arrived and scattered from the lobby in different directions. One took up a post blocking the front door. An Army ambulance arrived and Pepper was glad to see something familiar, even if it was just a box on wheels with a big red cross painted on it. The military policeman let in the Medical Officer of the Day and pointed to the office behind the desk, which Captain Rosen had entered several minutes before.

A crowd, mostly men, gathered across the street. A few were in uniform, but most in shorts and casual shirts. Through the open windows in the alcove, Pepper heard repeated questions of "What's up?" "What's going on?"

Another jeep arrived, this one carrying a major who wore infantry insignia and an arm band like the one that Captain Rosen wore. This one said FOD: Field Officer of the Day. He was also admitted and directed to the office.

The desk clerk asked Pepper if she would like coffee. Pepper asked for a soft drink and the woman brought her one. She drank it down at once, savoring the sweet, stinging taste on her tongue.

A man in his forties, with a grey crewcut and bushy eyebrows, arrived. He wore captain's bars, military police insignia, and his nametag said "Delaney." That would make him the Criminal Investigation Division officer. Pepper was curious to see why he should make for an interesting evening. He went into the office and Pepper had to restrain herself from giggling. She imagined people continuing to arrive and each one entering the small office, until they had filled it up, like college students stuffing a telephone booth.

Pepper shivered. Giggling was a sign of delayed shock. She pulled her arms tighter and wished she could get a sweater from her car.

The lobby was crowded now. Captain Delaney came out of the office and asked the clerk for a key. The clerk unlocked a door on the other side of the lobby.

Captain Delaney directed the group, "Wait in here."

Pepper and the eight men filed into the lounge. They were all in civilian clothes, so Pepper had none of the familiar clues of rank or insignia to tell who they were. They milled around, finding seats on the chairs and sofas, introducing themselves to one another, and asking what was happening. Pepper pulled a large wingback chair into a corner so that she could sit with her back against the wall and still see the lobby front door. The desk clerk brought a tray of coffee in Styrofoam cups. Pepper wished for another cold drink, but she didn't want to bring notice to herself by asking for one.

The lobby door opened. A tall man with dark blond hair and deeply tanned skin joined the group. He wore a knit shirt and a pair of dark blue pants. Captain Delaney did not look pleased to see him.

"Colonel Tyler, what are you doing here?"

"That's what I'd like to know. The mayor's wife had served me a lovely, medium-rare steak minutes before Captain Rosen requested a Public Relations Officer. We don't get many emergency calls, especially on the Fourth of July." His Virginia accent flowed like honey.

The PIO, Pepper thought. He certainly looked the part of public relations. His hair was not just cut, but styled; his tan was perfect. He looked at the curious faces staring at them from inside the lounge. Before he closed the door,

15

Pepper heard, "Perhaps we could discuss this in a more *private* place?"

The officers in the lounge knew that if the Criminal Investigation Division and the Public Relations Officer were involved, something bad had happened. The tension in the lobby rose. Fifteen minutes later, everyone turned as the door opened. The Public Relations Officer gave a wide, reassuring smile to the room in general. He walked straight to the two oldest men—colonels, Pepper guessed. The three men bent their heads together in private conversation. The two older men nodded in unison.

Turning toward the group, the man said, "Ladies and gentlemen, I'm Colonel Tyler from the Public Information Office. I regret to inform you that a body has been discovered here in Normandy House."

"Any possibility this is related to the MacDonald killings?" one of the men in uniform asked, uneasily.

There was that name again. The tension in the room was palpable.

Colonel Tyler made a conciliatory gesture with his hands. "The investigation is just beginning, but I can assure you that this has no similarities to the MacDonald killings."

Pepper wondered how he knew that.

One of the men asked, "When can we leave?"

"Each of you must give a statement before you will be allowed to leave. The police have sealed off this building, so you won't be able to stay at Normandy House tonight. After you have been questioned, a military policeman will escort you to your room to pick up what you need for the night. If you need transportation to a civilian motel, we will provide that."

One of the younger men asked, "I've already paid for tonight. Will I get my money back?"

Colonel Tyler turned on his charming smile. "Of course. Any of you who have paid Normandy House will be re-imbursed and the Public Information Office will pick up your motel tab for tonight. And coffee and sandwiches will be arriving for you shortly."

Pepper took a deep breath. "I'd like a soft drink, if it's not too much trouble?"

He nodded in her direction. "Of course, Captain Pepperhawk," he said in his honey voice. Captain Rosen must have told him who she was. Pepper blushed.

Colonel Tyler circulated for a few minutes, shaking hands, meeting people individually, offering reassurances. Captain Delaney, Captain Rosen, and Specialist Ramerez came to the lounge. The specialist took out a notebook and began circulating, taking down everyone's name.

Captain Delaney turned to Captain Rosen. "Did you search Captain Pepperhawk?"

"There was no need."

"Do it. Now." Several of the men glanced between the two women, looking uncomfortable. Captain Rosen just looked angry. We're getting to the interesting part, Pepper thought.

Captain Rosen took her to a room in another wing from her room. "Consider yourself searched. You might as well take advantage of the privacy and use the john. It's going to be a long night," she said, as she locked the door.

"You aren't going to search me?"

"I don't have to. You couldn't hide anything in that sundress. You have short hair. You're talking, so nothing is in your mouth. I don't think either of us want me to search the other possible orifices. Besides, you had thirty minutes between the time you checked in and when you called us. If you had something, you've already hidden it."

"Why did you bring me in here?"

"Because Delaney wouldn't be satisfied until I did."

Pepper sat on the bed. "This isn't bad-cop, good-cop, is it? Did you and Delaney cook this up so I'd feel comfortable with you and start talking?"

Captain Rosen made a disgusted face. "If you are going to play bad-cop, good-cop, you have to play it as a team. Thomas Delaney is *not* a team player. He did it to embarrass you. And me."

"Why would it embarrass you?"

Captain Rosen ran her fingers through her short hair. "Some men think that every woman in uniform is a dyke. A lesbian," she said, as if Pepper hadn't understood the word *dyke*. Pepper hadn't. Now the men's uncomfortable looks made sense. "Half of them out there probably think I'm copping a feel. If you don't want to use the john, I do."

Pepper took her turn after Captain Rosen had finished. "Is this long enough to cop a feel?" she asked, coming out of the bathroom.

"I wouldn't know," Captain Rosen said, unlocking the door. Pepper went before her out into the hall. When she reached the lobby, she pretended to be smoothing her dress down. She gave Captain Rosen the coldest look she could muster and had a feeling the other woman was trying very hard not to smile.

She sat beside the officer who had asked when they could leave, but he immediately moved to sit somewhere else. One of the military police brought them hamburgers and fries. Evening lengthened into night. One by one—according to no pattern Pepper could see—the men were called to give statements. As the room emptied, Pepper took over a comfortable easy chair and laid her head back, napping for small intervals. She had not slept well the night before and the driving, the irregular meals, and the heat made her tired. Finally all of the men had gone and she was alone in the lounge.

"Captain Pepperhawk."

She followed Specialist Ramerez to the small office.

There was a desk and a side table, a filing cabinet, and a small sink with a coffee maker. Captain Delaney sat behind the desk. Specialist Ramerez sat at the side table. Captain Rosen stood in a corner, her back against the wall. Captain Delaney indicated that Pepper should sit in the straight-backed wooden chair on the other side of the desk. He advised her of her rights under the military code of justice, finishing with, "Your statement will be transcribed and you will be required to sign it. Do you understand this?"

"I understand."

"For the record, state your full name, rank, and branch."

"Captain Elizabeth Ann Pepperhawk, Army Nurse Corps. Or maybe I'm Army Nurse Corps Reserve. I never keep that straight." She said it honestly and was surprised that Captain Delaney looked irritated.

"What's your address?" he asked sharply.

"My military address or my home of record?"

"Your military address."

"I don't have one. I'm in transit." Captain Delaney began to fidget, picking up a paper clip out of a holder and unbending it. Out of the corner of her eye, Pepper could see that Captain Rosen looked amused, but she couldn't figure out what was funny.

"Transit from where?"

"Sixty-seventh Evacuation Hospital, Qui Nhon, Republic of Vietnam."

"To where?"

"Womack Army Hospital, Fort Bragg, North Carolina."

"You arrived today?"

"Yes, about 1800 hours."

"From where?"

"Asheville, North Carolina."

The clock behind Captain Delaney's head said 2300 hours. Pepper really wanted sleep.

"Tell me everything you did in the last twenty-four hours."

"I left my aunt's house in Bat Harbor, Tennessee, about 1400 hours yesterday. Drove to Asheville, reached the Grove Park Inn about 1830 hours. I checked in, ate supper, and spent the rest of the night in my room." Pepper almost faltered. That wasn't exactly true. Now that she had said it, she didn't want to go back and retract it. It probably wouldn't matter anyway.

"This morning I woke up about 0900 hours. I had a shower and packed. I checked out, had breakfast in Asheville, and drove from Asheville to Fayetteville. I drove straight here, registered, and got the key to my room."

Captain Delaney relaxed and sat back in his chair. "Did you stop anywhere while you were traveling?"

"Once for gas, at an Esso station, and twice to get something to drink, both times in a fast food restaurant on the highway."

"Was anyone with you?"

"No."

"Did you pick up any hitchhikers?"

"Certainly not."

"What happened when you went to your room?"

"I opened the door. The room was dark, the lights were off, and the curtains drawn. I saw a man lying on the bed and thought I'd gotten the wrong room. Then I realized the man had been shot. I performed an evaluation to determine if I should start CPR and decided resuscitation would be of no use."

"What made you think that?"

"The skin was cold. The pupils were fixed and dilated."

"Then what did you do?"

Pepper remembered that Captain Rosen knew about the gap between when she had checked in and when she telephoned the military police. She assumed Delaney knew, too.

"I sat in a chair and looked at the body." Then she was back in the room again, sitting in the chair, staring at the dead soldier. She hadn't noticed at the time that she smelled blood, but she remembered it now. It reminded her far too much of the emergency room in Qui Nhon. She was tired and still thirsty and cold. It had been a horrible evening—no, it had been horrible ever since she checked into the Grove Park Inn yesterday. She just wanted to be alone. "I thought what a shame it was that he'd made it through Vietnam and come home to die," she said slowly, faltering, looking down at her hands in her lap.

Chapter 2

In spite of very little sleep, Captain Avivah Rosen roused herself out of bed Monday morning at her usual time. She made breakfast, then brought in the morning paper, wondering how bad the headline would be. She found it on the first page, a short piece, with no photograph.

Body Discovered at Fort Bragg

(Fayetteville, July 4) The body of a young man, in his mid to late twenties, was discovered in the Fort Bragg Transient Officers' Quarters early Sunday evening. The Criminal Investigation Division is treating the death as suspicious. An autopsy is being conducted today to determine the cause of death.

Captain Thomas Delaney, of the CID Office, stated that officials at Fort Bragg and at Pope Air Force Base are trying to account for all personnel, a task made difficult because many soldiers are on leave for the July fourth holiday. He did not rule out the possibility that the man may have been stationed at another military installation or may not have served in the military at all. The victim's fingerprints have been sent to Washington.

According to Captain Delaney, there is no indication that this death is connected to the MacDonald murders.
(See page 2)

22

Avivah didn't have to read the story on page two. The MacDonald case still provided an example of how not to do an investigation. Thank God she'd called in Colonel Tyler right away. The story was certain to get into the papers, but Tyler had managed to convince the *Observer* to tone down what they could have printed.

Leaving her breakfast dishes in the sink, she dressed in sweatpants and a T-shirt, and threw some clothes, her swimsuit, a couple of towels, and her toilet case into a gym bag. At the gymnasium, she stowed her bag in a locker, and went outside to run.

She loved her early morning runs around the post and, this morning, the post looked especially pretty, a holdover from the cleanup done in preparation for the Eighty-second Airborne reunion this past weekend.

She ran past terra-cotta houses with red slate roofs in the senior officers' section, the stone buildings of the old post where the military police office was located. The white wooden buildings, built as temporary structures during World War II, were newly-painted. Thick, manicured lawns surrounded all of the buildings.

A special forces class from Smoke Bomb Hill was also out for their morning jog. Avivah joined the group, thinking about her special forces neighbor, Sergeant Kirkpatrick, who would grumble about a woman running with the berets. She paced the group for a few minutes, just for fun, just because she could.

The sergeant chanted, "I want to be an airborne ranger."

The groups, including Avivah, chanted in response, *"I want to live a life of danger."*

"I want to go to Vietnam."

"I want to fight the Viet Cong."

"Sound off."

"One, two . . ."

When they turned to go back to Smoke Bomb Hill, Avivah ran in the other direction—toward post headquarters and around the flagpole, then back to the gym. She paused, leaning over, hands on her thighs, catching her breath and walking around slowly to cool down. She had to run more often. Her officer efficiency report would come up in September. She knew she could pass the obstacle course, but she always liked passing it with high marks. A high score left no doubt that she could do the physical part of the job as well as any man.

Inside the locker room, she peeled off her sweat-stained clothes and changed into her bathing suit. The pool would be empty for thirty minutes before swimming classes began. The only swimmer, Avivah eased herself into the water, shivered, and began swimming with long, smooth strokes. Within a few minutes, she fell into an easy rhythm, freeing her mind to think. She could not think while running.

Elizabeth Ann Pepperhawk. What an odd duck. Delaney finished questioning her after midnight and, Avivah had to admit, Captain Pepperhawk looked exhausted. She had taken pity on the woman, retrieved her overnight bag, and escorted her to a motel on Bragg Boulevard.

Avivah flipped over into a backstroke. Kicking herself through the water, she admitted she was jealous of Captain Pepperhawk. All a nurse had to do was ask, and she got orders for Vietnam. She'd asked three times and been turned down each time, just because she was a woman. It wasn't fair.

"Are you Captain Avivah Rosen?" one of the gym attendants yelled at her.

Avivah stopped swimming and began treading water. "Yes."

"There's a phone call for you from the military police. A

Specialist Ramerez. You can take it in here." She pointed to a wall phone.

Avivah stood, dripping onto the concrete floor, drying her face and hair with one hand and holding the phone with the other. She squinted at the pool clock. "Ramerez, why are you at work at 0845? We're the evening shift, remember?"

"I got some paperwork I had to do. I saw you out for a run, so I figured I'd catch you at the pool or the weight room."

"Now that you've caught me, what do you want?"

"I've got something. I thought I might check with the civilian police to see if anyone reported a World War II uniform stolen. On Saturday, a man named Curtis Butterfield reported his uniform stolen to the Anson County Sheriff's Department. I found Mr. Butterfield and he's sitting in the waiting room right now. I thought you might want to interview him."

"I would *love* to interview him, but he belongs to Captain Delaney."

"Well, I told Captain Delaney that a man in the waiting room said he had a vital clue about the murder. I might have hinted he wanted to confess. Captain Delaney waved me away, told me to take his statement, and not bother him with every crackpot that walked in the office."

"I'll be right over."

Avivah kept a spare uniform at the office because more than once—usually after breaking up a brawl in a bar—she had to change in the middle of a shift. Twenty minutes later, dressed in her uniform, she found Ramerez poised on the edge of her desk, notebook in hand.

"Give it to me from the top, Ramerez."

"Curtis Butterfield. Forty-five years old. Owner and operator of the Ruby O'Day Mine in Franklin, North Carolina. Member of the Eighty-second Airborne in World War II. Saturday afternoon he reported to the Anson County Sheriff that his World War II uniform had been stolen."

"Go get him."

"Incidentally," Ramerez said as he started for the waiting room, "Captain Delaney has some questions for Captain Pepperhawk, if he can find her."

"She's disappeared?"

"It looks that way. First thing this morning Captain Delaney sent someone over to the motel to bring her back for more questioning. She'd checked out and no one has seen her. She hasn't reported in to the Chief Nurse. Delaney is thinking about putting out a warrant for her arrest."

"Why did Delaney want her first thing in the morning?"

"He sent her description to the Asheville City Police. They interviewed the desk clerk, the bellboys, the waiters at the Grove Park Inn. They remember her checking in. She made quite a scene in the lobby, almost like she wanted to be noticed, then she walked out of the lobby and disappeared."

Damn. She'd been so cocky about not searching Captain Pepperhawk. So much for sisterhood.

Curtis Butterfield followed Ramerez into the office. A rangy man, about five feet ten inches, with a white crewcut, he wore a knit shirt and an American Legion cap, covered with Legion friendship pins. Avivah watched him look her up and down. His gaze stopped for an instant on her captain's bars. She waited for him to say something about a woman in the military police, but he just shook her hand, and took the seat she indicated. He took his cap off carefully and laid it on the desk.

"Mr. Butterfield, I understand you had your uniform

stolen. Could you tell us about that?"

"It was my pride, that uniform. Issued to me in '43, just before we left for England. It was in my kit when I jumped into Normandy. Had it with me all through France and Germany. Kept it real nice after I got out, all clean and wrapped in tissue in my wife's hope chest."

Avivah didn't mention that he probably had been required to turn the uniform in when he left the Army.

"We're more interested in how it disappeared," Specialist Ramerez interrupted. Avivah held up her hand. She had met witnesses like Butterfield before. They would tell their story in their own time. "Just keep telling it the way you want."

"There were six of us from Franklin. Used to be a dozen or so, but half of them are either dead or moved off. We enlisted together in '43, trained together, went to England together, jumped into Normandy together."

She sat back in her chair, squinted a little, and tried to imagine Curtis Butterfield in 1944. At forty-five now, he would have been eighteen when he jumped into Normandy, almost a decade younger than she was now. Probably always one of those stringy types, lean and tough, never been out of the Smoky Mountains until the day he and his buddies enlisted. She knew he could tell them more details about jumping into Normandy than about his uniform disappearing two days ago. She wondered if his experience matched the old newsreel films about World War II, the parachutes blossoming from C-47s against a dark sky. Mr. Butterfield digressed into a complicated story about a French farmer, a bicycle, and an attempt to use the French phrase book the Army had provided. Ramerez assumed a look of patient boredom.

She let Mr. Butterfield finish his story, then quickly interrupted before he began a second one. "How did you decide to come to Ft. Bragg this weekend?"

"Commander Harold Green of the Marion Legion Post one-o-eight got this letter around Easter time from General George S. Blanchard, the commander of the Eighty-second Airborne. I came home from the meeting where he read it into the minutes and I said to my wife, 'Dottie, I don't care if it is Fourth of July weekend, I'm going to that shindig. The Fourth is the middle of the tourist season, you see.' "

"You run a ruby mine, I believe?"

"That's right. Fine little mine. Real easy to salt. Keeps the tourists happy. Anyway, like I said, I told Dottie I wanted to go real bad. And she said, 'Curtis, you got to go. I can see to the tourists for one weekend.' She knows I don't like her doing that. Sometimes these city folk think they're going to get rich, you know, find a big stone. And they get a little angry when it gets to the end of the day and all they've found is gravel stones. But I figured we could get one of the high school football players in to help her. No one's going to mess much with one of those big guys. So that's what we did."

"And the uniform?" Ramerez, seated in a chair beside Avivah's desk, tried one more time, this time a little more desperately.

"I'm getting to that, son. Anyway, everybody else left on Thursday so they could be here in plenty of time for the welcome party on Friday. Fred had to work the night shift Thursday night at the paper mill in Canton and one of us had to stay behind to give him a ride. So I picked Fred up first thing Friday morning."

A gleam entered Ramerez's eye as the story finally progressed. "And you came straight on to Fort Bragg?"

"Well, not right off. Fred insisted we get breakfast.

Night shift makes him hungry. Besides we only had to get as far as Wadesboro. That's not more than a four-hour drive. I've got a sister in Wadesboro and we'd planned to see her on Friday and come on in early Saturday morning."

Avivah asked, "What time did you get to Wadesboro?"

"A little before noon. We checked in to the motel, and I called Sadie to tell her we were there. She and Nolan came over to the motel for dinner with us."

Avivah made notes on a legal pad. "Your uniform was in your motel room?"

"Lord, sister, I wish it had been. It was in my truck. I've got one of those pickups with the little space behind the seat. The guys figured it would be better to hang the uniforms up instead of putting them in suitcases. We put a hanging rod up there and hung all the uniforms, all neat, so they wouldn't get wrinkled."

"Could you keep an eye on the truck?" Ramerez asked.

"Nope. Had to park in the back because there was some kind of a meeting in the motel. Those women who sell those pink cosmetics. Dottie's always buying that stuff. Can't see much in it myself. She's right pretty just the way she is. Anyway, the front parking lot was full. I could show you better if'n I had a piece of paper."

Ramerez gave him a piece of paper and a pencil. Curtis drew a U-shaped motel, complete with a kidney-shaped object that Avivah took to be the swimming pool.

"Our room was here," he said, making an X along one side of the motel. "The restaurant was here. And I had to park way back here behind the building in this little side parking lot."

"Was anyone else parked back there?"

He shrugged, "Couple of cars. Nothing to take any notice of." Avivah reflected again that he could probably tell them a good deal more about Normandy on the night of June 5, 1944.

"So you all went to lunch at the restaurant?"

"Yep. They got a real good chicken fried steak platter there. Two fried steaks, gravy, double serving of mashed potatoes, biscuits, and vegetables. Coffee and pie included."

Avivah felt her arteries close, listening to the menu. "It sounds like you took your time in the restaurant?"

"Must have been over an hour or more. We got to razzing Nolan. He was in the Navy during the war." No need to identify which war, Avivah thought. For Curtis and the other members of Legion Post one-o-eight, it would always be The War.

"Anyway, we bragged about how the Army was doing right by us, inviting us back, having us march in the parade and all. Then we started swapping stories about the war and we kept going. Must have been almost two in the afternoon by the time we paid the check."

"Is that when you discovered your uniform was missing?"

"No. That was later. We told Sadie and Nolan we'd be at their place after supper to pass the evening with them and went back to our room. Fred, he was kind of tired, so he lay down to take a nap, and I went to the pool."

Right after chicken fried steak, all the trimmings, coffee and pie—and in July heat. Avivah shuddered.

"I took a swim and came back, real quiet-like so I wouldn't disturb Fred. The parking lot was empty then, so I went to move my truck. The uniforms were all mussed up, not hanging straight on the rod; mine was missing. I woke Fred, but he didn't know anything about my uniform. We called the sheriff."

Avivah opened the folder on her desk and rifled through the eight-by-ten pictures.

"Mr. Butterfield, I want to show you a picture of a man who's been killed."

"That man they found in Normandy House? I read about it in the paper this morning."

She handed him the photo of the dead man. "That's right. This is the man. Did you see this man while you were at the motel? Take your time."

"Don't have to take much time, sis. I recognize him all right. He was sitting in the booth next to us."

"While you were talking about coming to Fort Bragg?"

"Yep."

"Did you mention you had uniforms in your truck?"

"I was bragging how I could still fit into mine. Nolan can't fit into his Navy uniform any more, you see."

"Did this man seem to be listening to your conversation?"

"Not particular. He was nervous-like, drinking coffee. Figured he was a hippie."

"Why?"

"Way he was dressed. Jeans and one of those shirts with the spots of color all over it. You know, the kind hippies wear?"

Avivah guessed. "Tie-dyed?"

"Yep, that's what they call it. Kind of a purple splotchy color. And a blue bandana tied around his head."

"Did you talk about where your truck was parked?" Ramerez asked.

"Didn't have to. Dottie had painted up this real nice poster, with the Eighty-second patch and all. She does all the Sunday school posters, you know. Anyway, she'd done this big poster that said, 'Fourth of July Eighty-second Airborne Reunion, Fort Bragg or Bust.' We taped it on the side of the truck. Figured if we passed anyone who was also going to the reunion, we'd get a wave or something."

Avivah leaned forward. "Mr. Butterfield, this is very important. Would you be prepared to swear that the man you saw in the restaurant and the man in that picture are the same man?"

"Yep. I'm sure they're the same man. And I got a good memory for faces. You have to in my business. Folks take it real kindly when you remember them from year to year."

First piece. Avivah knew where John Doe was on Friday about noon.

Curtis looked at Ramerez. "Think there's any chance I'll get my uniform back?"

"I'm afraid not, sir. It's evidence in a murder case. We'll have to keep it."

The man sighed. "I suppose after twenty-seven years, maybe it's a good idea to let go of some things. At least they didn't get my medals. I don't think I could of stood it if they got my medals, too."

"You had them in your suitcase?"

"Had them in my gem safe in the truck."

"Thank you, Mr. Butterfield. We'll want you to tell your story again to a stenographer, then have you sign it."

"Even with losing my uniform, I had a fine time this weekend. Met General Blanchard hisself. He shook my hand, and thanked me for coming. Told me not to forget to put my name on their mailing list so I'll get their newsletter. Even met a few soldiers who'd been at Camp Gordon in 1917 and went to France with the original Eighty-second Division. I was real proud to meet those doughboys. Gave them all pins from our post and told 'em if they were ever in Franklin, the Legion would have a do for them—barbecue, clogging, the whole works. Course, they're getting a bit on in years. I don't imagine they travel much any more."

Avivah stood. "I imagine they don't. Now, you go with the specialist here and he'll arrange for someone to type up your statement."

"Come this way," Ramerez said as Mr. Butterfield picked up his cap. "We'll take you to Specialist Osborne. And you make sure you tell Specialist Osborne the whole story. Don't forget the part about the French farmer. Specialist Osborne will be especially interested in that part." He led him out and closed the door behind them.

Specialist Osborne, the newest member of the brigade, still endured the office's practical jokes. Avivah remembered her first weeks at Fort McClellan and reminded herself she had once been as green as MaryLynn Osborne. She sat, meditating on a much younger Curtis Butterfield and on parachutes coming down against a dark sky. We were all that young once, she thought.

Chapter 3

Pepper started her Monday at 0600 hours, because she had been awake at that time almost every morning for the past year. She ordered breakfast and a copy of the Fayetteville *Observer* from room service.

The story about the body was on page one. Pepper read it as she idly stirred her grits. She turned to the additional story on the second page.

MacDonald Murders Remain Unsolved

(Fayetteville) Anyone who was in the Fort Bragg area on February 17, 1970, will remember the brutal murders of the wife and children of Dr. Jeffrey MacDonald, a Special Forces physician. At 3:30 a.m. that morning, a Fayetteville operator received a call from Dr. Jeffrey MacDonald. Military police were dispatched to the doctor's home.

There they discovered MacDonald's pregnant wife, Collette, twenty-six, and their two daughters, Kimberley, five, and Kristen, two, dead of stab wounds and repeated blows to their heads. Doctor MacDonald had been stabbed and required CPR twice before reaching the hospital.

MacDonald contended that his family had been attacked by three men and a blond woman. Both the Army's Criminal Investigation Division (CID) and the Federal Bureau of Investigation (FBI) investigated the

34

murders. William Ivory, chief investigator for the CID at Fort Bragg, did not believe MacDonald's story and the investigation focused on the doctor. He was eventually charged with the murders.

Dr. MacDonald's Article Thirty-two proceeding (the Army's equivalent of a preliminary hearing) began on July 6, 1970, and was initially open to the public and the press. During the trial, testimony showed that the crime site had not been well controlled and evidence may have been either incorrectly collected or, in some cases, ignored. After this evidence was presented, the hearings were closed to the press and public.

Freddie Kassab, Collette MacDonald's father, and Bernie Segal, MacDonald's attorney, both believed Helena Stoeckley had been an eyewitness to the murders. Miss Stoeckley, the daughter of a retired Army officer, was reported to be involved in both the drug culture and the practice of witchcraft. The court dismissed Miss Stoeckley as an unreliable witness.

After six weeks of hearings, the Army reluctantly dropped the charges against Dr. MacDonald on the basis of "insufficient evidence." Captain MacDonald subsequently left the Army and is believed to be living in California. The police files on this case remain open.

Pepper had been a second lieutenant, stationed in Kansas when the MacDonald murders happened. She hadn't even seen the story in *Stars and Stripes*, the weekly military newspaper, though she was sure it must have been there. She must have been working night duty that week. When she worked night duty, the rest of the world went away. She understood now what Captain Rosen had meant by not wanting another MacDonald fiasco. The

Army had messed up badly on that one.

According to the weather report, the day was going to be hot and partly cloudy. Pepper sighed. She was going to bake in her uniform, but if she was going on post, she had to wear it. She debated whether to keep the motel room for another night and decided to check out. She would be in her own quarters by evening.

An hour later, sweltering in the heat, she located the Fort Bragg Housing Office. A clerk, with the rank of specialist-four, rose slowly from his desk, looking reluctant to move out of the small breeze offered by his electric fan.

"Can I help you, ma'am?"

Pepper took her orders out of the large manila envelope and handed them to him. "I've come to be assigned to quarters."

He read the orders. "May I see your in-processing checklist?"

"I don't have it, yet. I'm not really due here until a week from today, but I arrived early." She started to tell him about the body she discovered, but remembered that Captain Rosen had cautioned her against discussing it with anyone. "I thought I would take some time to move in and get settled before I reported for duty." He handed her orders back.

"Well, ma'am. First of all, I can't assign you to quarters until I see your in-processing checklist and, second, unless your commander gives me some special reason, you're not going to get quarters on post. We have enough trouble housing the married officers with dependents."

This wasn't at all what she'd expected and she didn't know what to do. "Where am I going to live?"

He reached under the counter and pulled out a Xeroxed map and a typewritten list. "You'll have to find off-post quarters. This is a list of apartments that may have vacancies. We don't guarantee anything. You'll have to look them over yourself."

"Look," she said, "I just got back from Vietnam. Surely you could do something."

The specialist smiled at her and Pepper realized that people came to Fort Bragg from Vietnam all the time. Having been in a war zone conferred no special privilege. She thanked the specialist, and took the map and list. As she opened the screen door, the heat hit her like a wall. It was a different kind of heat, not hot and wet like Qui Nhon, more of a dry heat, a sandy heat, a pine-tree-smelling heat. She walked over to the brief shade of a small tree, sat on the blistering hot seat at a picnic table, and looked at the list.

Getting settled had been so simple in Kansas. Forty-five minutes after she arrived, one of the nursing supervisors shepherded her to a two-bedroom apartment and introduced her to her roommate. She began to resent Fort Bragg: heat, sand, a murder, and, now, no place to live. She turned back to the printed list, deciding to begin her search with the most promising apartment on the list. According to the information the specialist had given her, it had a swimming pool, tennis courts, and a recreation room "suitable for parties and family gatherings."

It also had a rent she could never afford. Plus, they wanted first month's rent, last month's rent, and a damage deposit. She lowered her sights.

Lowered them too far, she decided, after looking at the next place on the list. The rent was affordable, but she had no desire to share her apartment with cockroaches and a large hole in the kitchen wall.

By one o'clock, she was hot and sweat matted her hair. Her wet, wrinkled uniform clung to her body. She ate a late lunch at a fast food drive-in. After lunch she changed into jeans and a sweatshirt in the drive-in's bathroom, consulted the "to rent" ads in the newspaper, and spent the next four hours looking at apartments, duplexes, and trailers. By five she gave up and checked into a cheaper, but clean, motel.

As she rinsed her uniform out in the bath tub and hung it to dry, Pepper decided what she needed was a leisurely supper at the officers' club. She tried to remember what the dress code for the officers' club had been in Kansas. It was summer and the weather was hot; she'd take a chance that her rose-print sundress and clunky white plastic jewelry would be all right.

When she reached the club, she was startled to realize that it was just across the street from Normandy House. She vaguely remembered seeing it before she had checked in yesterday. The police tapes were down and Normandy House looked quiet and open for business again.

The water sprinklers were on, moving a fine spray over the green lawn and flowers in front of the club. She heard children splashing in the swimming pool. Muted traffic noise reached her from the road outside the post. A solid line of pink stucco houses with red tile roofs lined the streets. Senior officers' country. Along those private streets lived generals, colonels, perhaps a senior major or two. *They* sure didn't have to worry about finding quarters off-post.

Two officers came out of the club as she entered. One of them held the door open for her. She stood in the blissfully air-conditioned lobby for a moment, read the directory, and tried to decide if she wanted the dining room or the lounge.

"Good evening, Captain."

She turned to face Colonel Tyler, the Public Information Officer, dressed in a white knit golf shirt and tan trousers.

38

"Good evening, Colonel."

"Are you meeting someone?"

"No, I just came for supper. I was debating if I should try the lounge or the dining room."

"Definitely not the lounge." He took her arm. It didn't register at first that he had touched her, but a moment later she decided she didn't mind.

"Why not the lounge?"

"Junior officers with too much time on their hands, stale pretzels, and Monday night football."

"You're right, definitely not the lounge."

"Besides, the food in the dining room is better."

The maitre d' nodded to them. "Good evening, Colonel Tyler."

"Good evening, Harold. Two for dinner."

She waited until the waiter had seated them at a table near the window. Heavy drapes shielded them against the summer sun. The linen-covered table had a small bowl of red, white, and blue carnations, with a candle in the center. A waiter approached their table and lit the candle.

"Drink?" Colonel Tyler asked, looking at the wine list.

She started to say a soft drink, then said, "White wine."

"Sweet or dry?"

"You choose."

He turned to the waiter. "Johannisberger for Captain Pepperhawk. I'll have a Manhattan."

The waiter nodded and left.

"Please, call me Elizabeth."

He took a package of cigarillos and a gold lighter from his pocket. "Gardner."

"That's an unusual name."

"Old family name. Do you mind if I smoke?"

She did mind, but part of the game was that a good

Southern lady never denied a man his pleasures. "Feel free."

He blew a thin stream of smoke into the air. "Pepperhawk is an unusual name, too."

"It used to be Pffieferhagen in German. When my grandfather entered New York through Ellis Island, Pepperhawk was what the immigration officer heard and that's what he wrote on the papers. My grandfather thought that was the way things were done in America. You came to a new country and got a new name. He was very proud of his American name."

Their drinks arrived and the waiter disappeared again without asking if they were ready to order. Pepper took a sip of wine, rolled it around in her mouth and let it slide down the back of her throat. It tasted wonderful and she realized it had been over a year since she had wine. In Qui Nhon, she always drank beer or whiskey.

Gardner asked, "Is something the matter?"

She swallowed the rest of the wine and patted her mouth with her napkin, noting the wonderful cloth texture against her lips. "Oh, no. The wine is wonderful. Is it something special?"

"It's the house wine," he said, looking superior. "We could order something special, if you like."

"This is fine."

It had been a long time since she had a meal, with a man, in a dark, air-conditioned dining room. In the rough-and-tumble atmosphere of the Qui Nhon club—really just a quonset hut with a homemade bar and black lights—she'd gotten out of the habit of small talk. Colonel Tyler looked equally uncomfortable with starting a conversation.

"You don't sound like you come from New York," he said finally.

She found his tone interesting, halfway in between making conversation to a fellow officer and speaking to a servant. She'd bet the Tyler family, or the Gardner family, or both, had money. Real money. Old money. Not like an upstart German-American family, only three decades in this country, and with an artificial name to boot.

"Biloxi, actually. Grandfather spent the winter of 1920 in New York and decided that one winter there was enough. He started south and didn't stop until he reached the Gulf of Mexico." She leaned back in her chair, looking at him over the rim of her wine glass. "How about you?"

He waved the cigarillo with a dismissive gesture. "My family has been in Virginia so long, we've forgotten how we got there."

Carpetbagger, Pepper thought to herself. No, that's being unkind. It must be the wine. She wasn't usually this catty. Better to stick to military careers and leave families alone.

"How did you become a public information officer?"

"I studied pre-law at William and Mary. My father died just before I graduated and we were not as well off as I'd been led to believe." A touch of bitterness there. "I'd done ROTC. The Army offered me a commission."

"When was that?"

"Nineteen-fifty-four."

Fifty-four. The Korean War was over and Vietnam hadn't begun. Peacetime must have been a nice time to come into the Army. She thought of her own university and how the Army Student Nurse Program had paid part of her expenses.

"Surely the Army would have helped you go to law school?"

He shrugged. "Actually, I never really wanted to be a

41

lawyer. Our family sacrifices the first son on the altar of Hypocrites and the second to Blind Justice."

"And your brother is?"

"Dr. Singleton Tyler, one of the better sports medicine doctors in Atlanta."

She was right. Old money. Big money.

"Where were you stationed before Fort Bragg?"

"Vietnam. I was aide-de-camp to a general in three corps. Public relations is a family tradition, too. My great-grandfather was aide-de-camp to Confederate General Gilbert Sorrel during the Battle of the Wilderness." Mentally Pepper apologized for thinking his family might have been carpetbaggers.

The waiter stood a discrete distance from the table.

Colonel Tyler picked up the menu. "Are you ready to order?"

Pepper looked at the menu. "What's good? I've never eaten here before."

"Allow me." He turned to the waiter. "We'll both have the sautéed chicken breast with wild rice and asparagus." He closed the menu with a decisive snap. "We'll decide about dessert later."

She waited until the waiter had left, then leaned closer to Colonel Tyler. In a low voice she said, "I saw the article in the paper. You did a good job of getting them to downplay the murder."

He nodded. "I had to call in favors."

"So, is there any news? Something not in the paper?"

Gardner Tyler smiled indulgently at her. "I'm not at liberty to say."

All in all, it was a most pleasant meal. They ate in companionable silence, talking occasionally in the small pleasantries of two officers comparing past assignments.

Pepper returned to her car at dusk, just as shadows darkened over the terra cotta buildings. Water sprinklers made quiet swishing sounds over the green lawns. She stood beside her car for a few minutes, listening to the soft water sounds and the occasional cricket chirping. It had been nice to have a dinner with a man, to laugh and drink wine, nice to be able to stand in the gathering dusk and not look at barbed wire, not worry about mortar attacks. She unlocked her car door and, then, without warning, tears rolled down her cheeks.

Chapter 4

On Tuesday, the heat wave remained unbroken. Avivah ran, showered and did errands before reporting for her shift at 1500 hours. When she asked Major Plauche, the day shift officer, about the murder investigation, he shrugged and said, "Captain Delaney isn't asking us to play in his sandbox."

She was vaguely aware of the background noise of people being waited on at the counter and the occasional bursts of chatter from the dispatching office, the usual sounds of the office early in the evening. Specialist Ramerez circled her desk like a satellite, filing, posting papers on the bulletin board, checking something from a folder on the desk next to hers. Every time she caught his eye, he jerked his head a little in the direction of the lot behind the building, where the duty jeeps parked.

Avivah finally got the message. She took her hat from the desk drawer and said, "Specialist Ramerez."

He looked at her with complete innocence and she realized again why the nickname "Cherub" suited him so admirably. "Yes, ma'am?"

"I'll need you to drive for an hour or so." She hoped whatever he wanted could be done in an hour.

He shoved the filing cabinet drawer shut energetically. "Yes, ma'am."

The late afternoon enveloped her as soon as they stepped outside. Dark purple thunderclouds built towards

44

the east. Avivah hoped if the thunderstorm developed, it would be big enough to cool the day and not just turn it into a steam bath.

Ramerez hardly started the jeep before he announced, "The *National Enquirer* has the story. Front page this week, 'GI Abducted from Omaha Beach Found Dead at Fort Bragg.' Accompanied by a drawing of a guy going ashore at Normandy, a spaceship, and a ray from the ship sucking him up. My source says the post commander is livid."

His *source* had to be the civilian switchboard operator at headquarters, a woman Ramerez dated. "I'll bet. Anything else new besides the *National Enquirer*?"

"Captain Delaney's been over at headquarters twice today. He's not very happy with you."

"With me?"

"The first time he was there, he told the general we didn't know anything about the uniform. About three hours later, he found Mr. Butterfield's statement in his in-basket. He had to go back and confess we'd known since yesterday where the uniform came from. He thinks you suppressed evidence."

"Captain Delaney should clean out his in-box more than once a week," Avivah muttered. "What else did you find out?"

"There's no ID yet from Washington. Delaney's mad about that. He acts like the Fourth of July was on a Sunday just to slow down his investigation."

"Maybe the victim doesn't have prints on file."

"His prints are on file," Ramerez said, with the air of one who has a secret he doesn't intend to keep. "I know the results of the autopsy report."

"I thought Captain Delaney wasn't playing shares."

"He isn't. Private Osborne isn't too familiar with the

copier yet. Sometimes extra copies get made by accident."

"I do not want Private Osborne in harm's way. Do you hear me, Ramerez?"

"I hear you. It's okay. I also gave her a lesson on the shredder. *Madra dea,* did you see that? That guy ran the red light. And he's speeding."

Ramerez reached for the switch for the light mounted on the jeep, but Avivah's hand covered the switch. "I do not want to play traffic cop right now."

"You can't let him get away with it. He's seen us."

"All right, just pace him. No siren, no lights."

Ramerez put his foot on the accelerator and caught up with the car. The car slowed. Ramerez slowed, keeping a car's length behind. They followed, until the man turned into a driveway in the married quarters, stopped, and got out of the car. As they passed, Avivah gave him a shake of her finger that clearly said, "Next time you won't be so lucky."

She caught the odor of a barbecue being lit. A man dressed in shorts and tattoos mowed his lawn. Two women stood on the drive separating their lawns, garden hoses in their hands, talking and looking at the clouds overhead. The older row houses looked so peaceful, Avivah thought, even though she knew that peace was an illusion. Come payday, or Saturday, or too many hot days in a row, and the military police would be responding to a string of domestic disturbances in these same peaceful houses.

Ramerez turned back toward the main part of the post. "It's Tuesday, your turn to buy the shift doughnuts."

"You know I hate going into a doughnut shop in uniform. Cops in a doughnut shop are the worst stereotype we have."

Ramerez asked, grinning, "Worse than bright-light interrogations and rubber truncheons?"

"You know what I mean. Okay, I'll buy but you have to go in for them."

"I'm in uniform, too."

"Yes, but it doesn't bother you."

"Okay, but we're going to that place by Kmart. They're fresher there." He swung the jeep toward Bragg Boulevard and called the dispatcher to say they would be off-post for about half an hour.

"So give, before I go crazy. What did the autopsy show?"

"Our corpse had malaria."

"He had malaria when he died?"

"No, he'd had malaria. Past tense. I guess when you've had it, there are these little things that stay in your blood. He had them."

"Don't jump to conclusions. There are a lot of ways he could have gotten malaria. Maybe he traveled in a foreign country."

"Maybe he was in the Peace Corps."

"Maybe he was in Vietnam," they said in unison, knowing it was the most likely explanation for a man in his late twenties to have malaria. "His prints have to be on file."

"That's what I think."

"What else did the autopsy show?"

"Time of death between 0900 and 1500 hours. The doc can't pin it down any closer because the air-conditioning was on full blast in the room. You remember how cold the room was."

Avivah did remember and, in spite of the hot afternoon, she shivered. "Cause of death?"

"Probably the gunshot wound to the chest."

"Probably?"

"The guy was hit over the head, then shot while he was unconscious. Doc said the blow might have killed him, but he didn't think so. Once he was unconscious, he was laid on the bed and shot at close range. The murderer probably wrapped the gun in a blanket and held it right against the victim's chest. There were blanket fibers in the wound and a blanket is missing from the room. Single shot, right through the heart. Died instantly."

He pulled into a parking spot in front of the doughnut shop. "Dozen chocolate-covered okay?"

"Sure, and a large coffee, black." She gave him money.

On the other side of the concrete island that separated the doughnut shop from Kmart, a security guard walked idly from car to car in the parking lot. He was an older man, maybe in his seventies. Even in the heat, his pants and shirt were pressed and his shoes shined. Retired military, Avivah thought, probably retired about the time she was born.

A hot, muggy wind blew through the jeep. She took off her hat and pulled her uniform shirt from her hot skin, blowing down her front to try to cool her skin.

This was her third murder. The first had been a death in a civilian bar in Germany. Two soldiers on cocaine had gone at one another with knives. One died; the other was now in Leavenworth. The second death was the result of a domestic dispute, in the Fort Leonard Woods married quarters. The neighbors listened to the escalating violence for almost an hour before someone called the police. By the time they arrived, the husband was dying on the floor, and his wife was standing over him with a kitchen knife. She had been convicted of manslaughter, in spite of Avivah and some of her neighbors testifying that the man had been violently abusive towards her. It still bothered Avivah that the woman had been convicted. To distract herself, she took a small notebook from her shirt pocket and made a list:

1. Premeditated? Did the gun belong to the victim or the murderer?
2. Door was locked. How did they get in?
3. Would a blanket cover the sound of a gunshot?
4. What time did the Fourth of July parade start?
5. What time did it pass Normandy House?
6. Was the room empty? Who had it last? When did they check out?

Ramerez kicked the side of the jeep, startling her. She took two Styrofoam coffee cups from him, freeing him to put the cardboard box carefully behind the seat. He opened it and took out two doughnuts, handing her one. The dark brown icing was still warm. The thick odor of chocolate surrounded them. Ramerez juggled doughnut and coffee and looked at the notebook in Avivah's lap.

"I can answer the last one," he said, his mouth full of doughnut. "The last occupant of the room was a Navy lieutenant. He was on his way to Pensacola Naval Air Station with his wife and baby. They checked out at 0630 hours."

"That's awfully early."

"Desk clerk said they told her they wanted to get on the road before it got too hot. The day desk clerk sent the maid to clean room 106 as soon as she got there at 0800. The maid finished about 0815, locked the door behind her, and apparently no one went in there until Captain Pepperhawk found the body. Incidentally, she surfaced again."

"Who surfaced?"

"Captain Pepperhawk? She reported to the chief nurse this morning. I guess she just took yesterday off."

"Wouldn't you if you'd just come back from Vietnam and discovered a body?"

Ramerez shrugged. "I guess."

"Did Delaney question her?"

"Didn't get a chance. The chief nurse sent her off to in-process before she telephoned us. But Delaney figures she has to report for her shift tomorrow. At least now he knows where she is."

Avivah lost interest in her doughnut and tossed the remaining piece on the concrete beside the jeep. A flock of sparrows flew down to investigate and began pecking at it. A sudden breeze, heavy with rain, blew across Avivah's face. Ramerez hurriedly finished his doughnut.

"Better get back. It smells like it's going to rain buckets."

He started the jeep and began to back out. "Hold on there," a voice called out. "Hold on there, Sergeant." It was the security guard, jogging toward them across the parking lot.

Avivah knew she must be right about him having retired a long time before. He didn't recognize that Ramerez wore specialist rank, not sergeant stripes.

"What does he want?" she muttered. "We're not even in his parking lot."

"Old times, maybe. Bet he was a policeman. Probably wants a doughnut."

Avivah steeled herself for whatever the man's reaction to her might be. She would almost bet there hadn't been any female military police officers when he served. The man stopped beside the jeep, breathless, his face red. "Afternoon, Sergeant," he said, a little breathless. He leaned over so he could see Avivah. "Afternoon, sir . . . ma'am . . . Captain," he faltered.

"Good afternoon, Mister Cook," she said, reading his nametag on his uniform. "Can we do something for you?"

He hesitated. "I'm not sure. I been trying to decide if I should call someone. You know about the murder at the post this past weekend?"

Ramerez answered. "Yes, sir, we know about it."

The man rubbed his fingers over his clean-shaven chin. "I saw the drawing in the paper this morning, asking people to come forward with information. I think I might know something."

Oh, good, Avivah thought. Just what we need. She'd figured that after the drawing of their victim appeared in Tuesday morning's paper, the people who thought they had information would start to come out of the woodwork. At least the Fayetteville *Observer* was less likely than the *National Enquirer* to bring out the truly kooky witnesses. By this time next week, they'd be up to their ankles in people who believed in UFOs, or had seen the murder in a crystal ball, or been transported to an astral plane to converse with the dead man.

Specialist Ramerez said politely, "Tell us what you know. We might be able to tell you if it's worth reporting."

"I can show you. It's over on the other side of the parking lot."

They made room for Mister Cook in the jeep. Avivah didn't want him collapsing from another jog across the parking lot. He directed them to pull in beside a blue car. A few drops of rain fell as they got out to look at the car.

"I was working extra on Sunday morning. People could park here and take a shuttle to the post, for the reunion parade. This guy pulled in about 0945. I noticed him right off because he was wearing a World War II uniform—Eighty-second Airborne. I could tell he wasn't old enough to have been in the war, so I thought he might be someone's grandson, you know, come for the parade in his grandpappy's memory. I was going to ask him about it, but there was a shuttle bus pulling out right then and he got on it before I could talk to him."

"And you're sure he looked like the drawing in the paper this morning?"

"Pretty sure. It was kind of hard to tell because I only saw him for a minute or two. And the paper never said anything about him being in a World War II uniform. Guess they would have mentioned that if it was important."

It was a detail the military police held back. Avivah got out and did a slow walk around the dusty car with Michigan rental plates.

"You say it's been here since Sunday?"

"Yes. There's not supposed to be any overnight parking, but well, sometimes, I let it go, especially if it's out here at the end of the parking lot. But I saw your jeep parked across the way there and that got me thinking about the story in the paper. I thought I should show you before I called a tow truck."

Ramerez put his hand on the man's shoulder. "We appreciate that. This may be a very valuable clue." He walked over to where Avivah was peering in the windows.

"You want me to have a look in the trunk?" Avivah didn't have to ask him how he was going to get into the trunk. Ramerez picked up a variety of skills in Brownsville, Texas before a judge suggested he was old enough to join the Army.

"Captain Delaney should be sitting down to supper about now. I think we should call him," she said, pointing to the purple tie-dyed shirt and jeans on the back seat. A large clap of thunder rolled overhead and the rain fell.

Chapter 5

Pepper stood three paces in front of the chief nurse's desk and gave a sharp salute, which Colonel Norton returned. "Captain Pepperhawk reporting."

Handing across her personnel file, she sat across from the stocky colonel, who had blue eyes and blond hair done in tight waves that Pepper associated with pictures from the 1940s.

The colonel placed her hands on her desk and leaned forward. "Where have you been, Captain?"

"Should I have reported at the beginning of day shift this morning? I wasn't sure."

"You should have reported *yesterday* morning."

"But my orders said for me to report next Monday. I thought I was early."

"Captain Pepperhawk, when the military police question you about a murder, you should report that fact to your commanding officer immediately. I did not appreciate never having seen you, nor having any idea of your whereabouts, when the CID questioned me."

Oh, shit. She knew immediately how much trouble she was in. A fine way to start a new assignment. "Yes, ma'am. I understand. I apologize for the inconvenience."

Pepper sat very still while the colonel studied her folder.

"Honor graduate at basic training, I see."

"Yes, ma'am."

"Emergency room experience in Qui Nhon."

"Yes, ma'am."

"Then this should be a change for you. You're going to be head nurse on ward Six-A, a male orthopedic unit. Please complete your in-processing today and report to the current head nurse, Captain Paxton, on Six-A tomorrow morning at 0645." She stood to indicate that the interview was over.

Pepper stood. "I can't report for duty tomorrow morning. My white duty uniforms are in storage with my household goods."

"My sergeant will find you loaner uniforms until your stored goods arrive."

Colonel Norton's sergeant took her to a small, window-less uniform room that smelled like starch and scorched cotton. White uniforms in plastic bags packed circular metal racks. Dust covered the frayed plastic bags on the rack where nurses abandoned their uniforms when they left the Army. Pepper found three that she thought would fit. In a cardboard box, the sergeant located a stiff white cap. Pepper held it up to her head and looked in the chipped mirror on one wall. The regulation duty cap—so different from the combat fatigues and boonie hat she'd worn for the past year—made her look like she had a white ball growing out of the top of her head. She remembered how much she hated Army nursing caps. This was going to take some getting used to.

The sergeant pointed to a laundry bag on wheels. "Throw your dirty uniforms in that bag. There is a three-day turnaround for the laundry."

She thanked him and took her uniforms to her car. While she waited for the blistering heat inside of her car to cool, she looked at the handful of papers the sergeant had given her. In-processing was like a scavenger hunt. Collect all the signatures and win a prize—the right to report for duty, in a heavily-starched uniform and an ugly cap, at an ungodly hour, to an unfamiliar ward.

Pepper began with the housing office. The specialist there was happier to see her now that she had official paperwork. He still did not have a place for her to live. She had a brief vision of herself as a Flying Dutchman, going from motel to motel until she had stayed in every one that Fayetteville had to offer.

By early afternoon she'd had papers signed at the medical clinic, post locator, vehicle registration, library, and several other buildings scattered across the huge post. Off-post, in a service station bathroom, she changed from her damp and sticky uniform to shorts and a halter top. There was a health food restaurant across the street from the service station. Pepper ordered a cheese and avocado sandwich on whole wheat bread and a glass of iced mint tea. While waiting for her food, she looked at bulk food and herbs and at the bulletin board, covered two deep in posters. She expected to find anti-Vietnam propaganda there, but, at least in here, natural remedies and alternative healing workshops pushed the war off the bulletin board.

We're all tired of this war, she thought, as she savored the squish of the ripe avocado and tangy taste of sharp cheese. We're so tired of this war and just want it to go away.

The sandwich and tea made her feel better and Pepper realized how much she needed more meals like this, a regular schedule, more exercise. At least she'd beaten the booze. Then she remembered Saturday night in Asheville. Okay, so maybe the booze still snared her, but at least she lasted days now, instead of hours, between drinks. Life would right itself once she stopped living out of motel rooms and her car.

The official list from the housing office hadn't helped. Neither had newspaper ads. If Fayetteville were a small town, like Bat Harbor, Tennessee, where her Aunt Corabell lived, Pepper would never have relied on newspapers or lists to find a place to live. Her aunt would telephone a friend, who had a sister, who knew someone who had a place going vacant at the end of the month. Small towns—and the Army was a small town—worked because of whom you knew.

Who did she know at Fort Bragg? Colonel Tyler, Colonel Norton, Captain Delaney, and Captain Rosen. Pepper couldn't imagine either of the colonels or Captain Delaney helping her find a place to live. That left Captain Rosen.

In the telephone book, she found phone numbers for two Rosens. No one answered at the A. Rosen number. At Samuel Rosen's residence, she spoke to an elderly woman, with poor hearing. She'd try the A. Rosen address. What did she have to lose?

The address turned out to be a three-story block of utilitarian apartments, about five miles from Fort Bragg's main gate. Faded turquoise aluminum panels hung on the railings surrounding the open breezeways and metal stairs. Huge trees surrounded the property.

Pepper checked the mailboxes and found A. Rosen's apartment on the third floor. Drawn, dark drapes covered the living room window. Pepper knocked, waited, and knocked again.

A young man came up the stairs, carrying a laundry basket heaped with clean clothes. "I think she's at work."

"I'm looking for Captain Rosen, the military police officer."

He opened the door of the apartment across the breezeway, and depositing the laundry basket inside on the floor. "That's Avivah. You a friend of hers?"

"An acquaintance. I just arrived at Fort Bragg, and I hoped Captain Rosen might help me find an apartment."

He extended his hand. "I'm Mister Levy."

"Elizabeth Pepperhawk. Is that 'Mister' as in civilian or as in warrant officer?"

"Warrant Officer. Wobbly Two, actually."

"Helicopter pilot?" Only helicopter pilots referred to their rank as wobbly.

"One of the best."

Pepper laughed. "All helicopter pilots say that."

"But in my case, it's true."

"They say that, too."

He pushed the door open and stood aside so she could enter his apartment. "Come on in."

Mister Levy was obviously going somewhere. A green nylon flight bag and piles of neatly-folded clothes covered the furniture. He moved a stack of shirts so that Pepper could sit on the couch.

"Can I get you something to drink?"

She started to ask for beer, then remembered Saturday night. "Something cold and nonalcoholic, if you have it. Water if you don't."

The apartment seemed huge after her ten-foot-square room in Qui Nhon. Mr. Levy didn't have much furniture, just an oatmeal-colored couch and chair, a big television on a cheap stand, a glass-topped coffee table, and a small dining table with matching chairs. An intricate collection of flat-black stereo equipment, with spring-loaded glass doors protecting the dials, slides, and buttons, dominated one wall. Above the stereo hung a huge black-and-yellow Air Cavalry flag.

Pepper recognized the stereo setup from the *PACEX Catalogue*, a mail order post exchange through which soldiers stationed in the Pacific purchased electronic equipment and other items at a reduced price. She took the glass of soda from Mr. Levy. "Did you buy that while you were in Vietnam?"

"Okinawa."

She waved her glass-filled hand in the direction of the green nylon suitcase. "Are you on your way back there?"

"Nope, going temporary duty to Fort Huachuca, Arizona for three months," he said, tossing two pair of pants over the clothes already in the suitcase. "Where are you coming from?"

"Vietnam. Sixty-seventh Evac Hospital at Qui Nhon."

"Nurse?"

"Yeah."

He hesitated a minute, his face serious. "You gals do good work. . . . Do you smoke?"

"No," Pepper said, puzzled.

"Good. It's not good for the stereo, even if I do plan to lock it up. So, the deal is this. Four months' rent in advance, in four post-dated checks. You don't do any damage, I tear up the fourth check. You pay the utilities and the telephone while you're here and you're out by September fifteenth. Leave me an address and telephone number where I can reach you."

"I beg your pardon?"

"You came about the apartment, didn't you?"

"No, I came to see Captain Rosen."

"You're not here because I asked Avivah to help me find someone to sublet while I was away?"

"No."

"I'm sorry. I thought that when you said you knew

58

Avivah, and were looking for an apartment, that she had mentioned me to you."

Pepper said, "Let me get this straight. I've been looking for a place to live for two days, without any luck, and I've just wandered into an apartment that I can have?"

Mr. Levy scratched his short, curly hair. "Looks that way. Do you often blunder into the unexpected?"

Pepper thought of the body on the bed. "It does seem to be the pattern since I got here. I mean, this is great. Can I see the rest of the apartment?"

He showed her the bedroom, the bath, and the kitchen, then took her downstairs to show her the self-serve laundry, the mailboxes, and the picnic tables in the green space.

Coming back up the stairs, she asked, "What about your stuff? Furniture and all?"

"Part of the deal. That's what the fourth check is for. You're welcome to use everything except the stereo. I'm locking that away in the pantry. It's not that I don't trust you, but I'm very particular about that stereo. I'd never be able to afford another one like it."

Pepper nodded. "I feel the same way about my camera. Like I don't want anyone else to even touch it."

"You got furniture?"

"Some household stuff, dishes and clothes, that the Army has stored away for me. I don't know when it will arrive."

"Where are you staying tonight?"

"A motel, I guess."

"The living room couch makes down into a bed. If you want to spend the night here, fine with me."

Sleeping space had been at a premium in Qui Nhon. Many mornings Pepper returned from night shift to boot a stranger out of her bed before she crawled in. She had no qualms about spending the night in Mr. Levy's living room. "That would be great. I'm tired of motels."

She wrote four checks to Pembrook Levy. He helped her unload her car and then finished packing while she did a load of laundry and took a long bath. They ordered pizza and sat on the couch for a long time, talking mostly about flying. Just before going to bed, Pepper helped Pembrook move his stereo into the pantry. By midnight she was asleep on the couch, unaware of Avivah opening her apartment door across the breezeway, and equally unaware that Captain Delaney was most anxious to question her.

Chapter 6

The next morning, Pepper broke starch before dawn. The sleeves of her borrowed uniform—heavily starched and flat pressed while still wet—stuck together so hard that her fingers couldn't separate them. She slipped the tip of a butter knife into the sleeve and slid it up, then across. The sleeve came apart with a pop. She forced her captain's bars, nursing caduceus, and black plastic nametag through the stiff cloth. Then she pried apart the rest of the uniform and stepped into its starched confinement.

She'd forgotten how the back of the stiff collar chafed her neck. Maybe one of the nurses could lend her some baby powder to rub on her skin. At least she'd brought a pair of white duty shoes with her, but after wearing combat boots for a year, her feet felt cramped.

She protected her white duty cap with a plastic bag and settled the green outdoor garrison cap on her head, then looked at herself in the mirror. With the starched cotton uniform, the green cap, and black leather purse, she looked like a nurse from the 1950s. She wanted her fatigues and combat boots back.

Driving to work in the cool and sweet dawn, she admired the way the post looked newly-washed after yesterday's thunderstorms. At the hospital, other nurses and corpsmen crowded into the elevator with her. Pepper instantly felt that she had her bearings. She was an Army nurse in an Army hospital, with her rank on her collar and her nametag on her uniform. The day slipped into place.

Green metal doors with reinforced glass panels opened into Ward Six-A. A wide hall, with half a dozen doors on either side, ran from those doors to the large wards at the end of the wing. The ubiquitous military hospital paint job—cream on the ceiling and the top of the walls, green on the bottom—covered the walls. Pepper peeked into the patients' day room. Oblivious to the background noise of the television, four patients in blue pajamas played cards. One of them spotted Pepper and leaned over to whisper to the other three. All turned to look at her.

She smiled and waved at them. One of them gave her a thumbs-up sign.

Her shoes made small squeaking sounds on the black and green rubber floor. Pepper stood in the empty nurses' station, looking at the two grey metal desks, chairs, and a steel chart rack on wheels, filled with aluminum chart holders. A tall black man came from the ward, holding a coffee cup. "Captain Pepperhawk?"

"Yes."

He held out his hand. "Dave Willett. I'm your wardmaster. How do you take your coffee?"

A few minutes later, Captain Paxton, Pepper, two more day nurses, the night nurse, the wardmaster, and three corpsmen crowded into the treatment room for change-of-shift report. Pepper thought they looked very formal: the nurses in white starched uniforms and white caps, the corpsmen and wardmaster in white pants, white T-shirts, and white medical jackets. In Qui Nhon they sat on a concrete floor for report. She found it a struggle to balance her coffee cup, a notepad, and still keep her knees covered with the slightly-too-short uniform.

After report, Captain Paxton handed Pepper a fistful of

small white cards. "Could you please give meds today?"

Pepper and the night nurse counted the narcotics in the double-locked cabinet. The count was correct and the nurse handed Pepper the narcotics keys. From habit, she tried to hang them on her fatigue's shoulder epaulet. The keys clattered to the floor. Pepper sheepishly picked up the key ring and put it in her uniform pocket.

As she caught up with the group making walking rounds, Captain Paxton leaned into the day room. "You know the rules, Sergalis. No TV before breakfast."

With a bored look, the patient who had given Pepper the thumbs-up sign picked up a crutch, and used it to reach the TV's off button. In a few days, when *she* was head nurse, the rules would change. She'd let the patients watch television any time they wanted.

As they moved through the dozen private and semiprivate rooms lining the hall, the four-bed ward across from the nurses' station, and the six bays in the main ward, the sight of so many casts, crutches, braces, wheelchairs, and missing limbs overwhelmed Pepper. She hadn't thought much about consequences in the emergency room. Just keeping men alive filled her day. Here, her job would be to help men live. She wondered if she would be any good at this kind of nursing.

They finished rounds, and Captain Paxton turned to the group. "It's Wednesday, so everyone try to finish up by 1300 hours." She looked out one of the large ward windows, at the bright blue sky. "It looks like good jump weather."

The staff scattered. Captain Paxton asked Pepper, "Count correct?"

"Yes, ma'am."

"Better get your 0800 meds ready. Don't hesitate to ask

me or Specialist Willett if you have any questions."

"Could you explain the connection between Wednesday and good jump weather?"

Captain Paxton smiled. "The Eighty-second Airborne does parachute jumping every Wednesday afternoon and, about 1400 hours, we're likely to get three or four new patients."

Pepper went to the medication cabinet, a small alcove wedged between the nurses' station and the treatment room. She sorted the medication cards, took out the cards for the preoperative medications, and set them aside on a small metal tray, wondering why there were only three cards when there should have been four. She found Captain Paxton talking to one of the patients.

"I thought we had four people going to surgery?"

"We do."

"I've only got pre-op cards for three."

"Sergeant Doan doesn't get a pre-op."

Pepper wondered why, but the captain looked busy and she didn't ask.

She hadn't poured medicines for a ward in a long time. It took a while to read the card, find the medicine, and double-check the card against the bottle label. The breakfast carts arrived just as she finished setting up her medication cart. Then she began her first long trek through the ward, pushing the cart before her. Some of the patients asked her where she had come from. When she said, "Sixty-seventh Evac, Qui Nhon," they nodded and said, "That's all right then," as if she passed some test. Other patients seemed oblivious to her. One patient, his leg in traction, held his hand out at the precise moment she approached his bed with his paper cup of medicines. He poured himself a glass of water, took the pills, and dropped the empty cup into the wastebasket beside his bed, without looking up from his paperback book.

She and Lieutenant Aileen Forbes went to second coffee. Downstairs, in the officers' dining room, there were more introductions and handshakes, then the talk settled into a familiar routine of hospital gossip.

"Oh-oh," one of the lab officers said, looking up from his cinnamon bun. "Here comes trouble."

Pepper turned. Captain Delaney stood in the door, flanked by a military policeman who carried his polished helmet under his arm. Delaney scanned the room, then came to their table.

"Captain Pepperhawk, come with me."

Pepper pushed her coffee cup away and stood up, facing the CID officer. "No, Captain Delaney, I will not come with you. I am on duty. If you would care to accompany me to my ward, I will report off to Captain Paxton, so she knows where I am and so my duties can be reassigned to another nurse. Then I will come with you." Her heart pounded as she walked out of the dining room, her head high, trying to ignore how conversation stopped as two policemen escorted her through the main dining room.

Captain Paxton went with Pepper and the two policemen to the chief nurse's office and handed them over to Colonel Norton. The chief nurse accompanied them to the hospital commander's office. Shaking and scared, Pepper tried to tell herself she hadn't done anything except find a body.

Pepper, Colonel Norton, and the military policeman sat in the waiting room while Colonel Granger, the hospital commander, saw Captain Delaney alone in his office. The colonel's voice carried. He told Captain Delaney exactly how he would conduct himself in the future if he wished to interview an officer in hospital command. Pepper felt like she was fourteen again, waiting outside of Mother Mary Immaculata's office. She sat uncomfortably in her chair, wishing that the borrowed uniform covered her knees better.

Eventually, Colonel Granger ushered them into his office. Two flags flanked his desk, an American flag on his right and a Womack Army Hospital flag on his left. The commander's chest was covered with rows of ribbons. Pepper immediately spotted the two campaign ribbons for Vietnam on the colonel's chest. She and Colonel Norton stood side-by-side and saluted. That unity of movement, standing there with a fellow officer in front of a colonel who wore the same overseas service ribbons she had, comforted her. She might be in trouble, but the Army would see that she didn't face trouble alone.

Everyone seated himself around a conference table on the other side of the room. Pepper sat directly across from Captain Delaney. Colonel Norton sat on her left and Colonel Granger on her right. The military policeman sat at the far end of the table.

Colonel Granger said, "You may begin."

Delaney again explained her rights under the military code of justice and indicated that the military policeman would take her statement, which she must sign.

"Captain Pepperhawk, we have been unable to verify your story about where you were on Saturday, July third. Tell me again where you were?"

"Exactly where I told you I was. I left Aunt Corabell's house about 1630 hours and drove to Asheville. I checked in at the Grove Park Inn about 1800 hours."

Delaney took a small notebook out of his pocket and consulted it. "Yes. Made quite a show of it, didn't you? Had hysterics in the lobby?"

Pepper looked down at her hands and took a deep breath. "I suppose I did."

"And then, after that, poof." Delaney opened his hands in a magician's gesture, as if the pigeon had just disappeared. "No one remembers you. You did not order from room service. You did not eat in the dining room. You did not speak to anyone at the desk, not even to check out. Where were you on Saturday night and Sunday morning?"

She was acutely aware of the colonels flanking her. She could smell Colonel Granger's aftershave. Colonel Norton sat beside her, her uniform heavily starched, her hair in perfect Marcel waves. Pepper could not tell these two senior officers that she had been drinking Saturday night and into Sunday morning.

"I'm sorry no one remembers me, but that's not my fault. I was where I said I was."

The interview continued for half an hour with Delaney asking for exact details about her stay in Asheville. What was her room number? She couldn't remember. When she checked out, was the desk clerk a man or woman? She hadn't noticed; she had left her key in the quick check-out box. Where did she have supper? In her room. Why wasn't there a record of room service? She lied. Because she had a cooler of food with her. Finally, when he began to repeat questions, Colonel Granger looked at Colonel Norton.

"What do you think?"

"The child is telling the truth," Colonel Norton said.

Pepper managed to hold her tongue and not snap that she was neither a child nor telling the truth.

"This interview is over," Colonel Granger announced. "If you wish to question Captain Pepperhawk at a later time, please let me know." He and Colonel Norton stood and Pepper took that as a sign that she should stand, too.

After Captain Delaney and the military policeman left, the commander turned to Pepper. "I don't think he will bother you again. You do understand that either Colonel Norton or myself are to be present if he interviews you again."

"Yes, sir."

"Have you a lawyer?"

"No, sir. Do you think I need one?"

"Not unless he contacts you again. You know about Legal Assistance Officers?"

"Yes, sir. We had a class on it at Fort Sam. The instructor talked about how not to get swindled in contracts and things. I don't think she mentioned murder."

The two colonels exchanged glances that said how green and naive they thought her. Colonel Granger sighed, a very small sigh, but none the less audible.

With the evident patience of talking to a child, Colonel Norton said, "Come and see me if you feel you need a lawyer."

Pepper felt her cheeks flush. "Yes, ma'am."

"You may return to your ward."

As Pepper closed the office door behind her, she heard Colonel Norton say, "Harry, they're letting children fight this war." She did not hear Harry's reply.

Pepper felt she owed Captain Paxton an explanation for the police interest. "I'm the one who discovered the body in Normandy House on Sunday night. CID wanted to double-check some details of my story. The 'Where were you on the day in question?' thing."

"Murder makes people around here nervous."

"I read about the MacDonald murders in the paper. Were you stationed here then?"

"I was. The whole post was afraid. People didn't know who to trust. I've heard some of the patients talking this morning. This murder has them upset."

"What do we do about it?"

"Tell them the truth," Captain Paxton said. "I can do it or you can."

Captain Paxton and Dave Willett went with her to the middle of the large ward.

The wardmaster bellowed, "Captain has an announcement." A couple of the patients turned off bedside radios. One patient, talking on the wheeled bedside phone, said, "I'll call you back."

Pepper took a deep breath. "I'm Captain Pepperhawk. I've met most of you today and you already know that I'm the new head nurse. Knowing how the hospital grapevine works, you probably also know that the CID escorted me out of the dining room this morning. This is not a good beginning for a new head nurse."

Several patients laughed.

"Sunday night, I discovered the body in Normandy House. Also not a good beginning for a new head nurse."

Fewer patients laughed. Stop trying to be funny. Don't push it. Just get it over with.

"The CID questioned me today as part of their ongoing investigation. I am not, as far as I know, a suspect. I am definitely not—I'm sure of this—involved in this murder in any way. We all know how gossip works and that gossip isn't good for a unit. Squelch the rumors. Don't let this get blown out of proportion. That's all."

A couple of the patients nodded. One man turned the radio back on. Pepper heard the sound of a gurney being wheeled down the hall and a voice called, "Surgery up."

A few minutes later, David Willett came into the nurses' station, carrying a chart. "Doan's back from surgery."

Captain Paxton took the chart. "Is he throwing up?"

"Right on schedule. I told them to put him in one of the private rooms temporarily."

"All right. Pepper, Cody Doan's body doesn't like anesthetic. He's sick as a dog every time he has surgery."

"Has he had it often?"

"This is number six." She handed the chart to Pepper. "Give him seventy-five milligrams of Gravol and fifty milligrams of Demerol."

Pepper prepared the syringes and took them to Doan's room. Sergeant Doan, a tall, thin man with brown hair, wore blue hospital pajama pants and no shirt. A plaster half-splint immobilized his right foot and ankle. The room smelled like wet plaster. When Pepper entered, Sergeant Done retched, holding a metal basin under his chin.

She checked his arm band. "Cody Doan?"

"Yeah, that's me."

"I have a shot for you."

"Is it Demerol?"

"Yes."

"Hell, that won't do any good."

Pepper hesitated. After six surgeries, Sergeant Doan knew what would or would not work. Captain Paxton entered the room, carrying his chart. "Take it or leave it, Doan. It's our best offer."

He glared at her. "All right. I'll take it."

Pepper gave him the shot, wondering why her hands shook. Cody Doan frightened her. She had never felt that way about a patient before.

A few hours later—toward the end of the shift—the two captains relaxed in an empty room with the door closed.

Captain Paxton unpinned her cap and laid it on the neat bed. She ran her fingers through her short hair and loosened the knots in her shoelaces. "Get comfortable and call

70

me Nancy. Dave will call us if he needs us."

Pepper laid her cap on the bed and took her shoes off so she could massage her feet. "Most people call me Pepper." She groaned. "I wasn't this tired after twelve hours in the emergency room."

"You had an unusual first day."

"Thanks for all your help. Are you sure you don't want to stay and be head nurse?"

"Absolutely not. Two years is long enough. I want out."

"What are you going to do now?"

"Start a family. My husband finished his pediatric residency last month. We've had a long-distance marriage long enough. Monday morning, I'm leaving for California."

Pepper wondered what it would be like to have a husband with a medical practice waiting in California. It sounded about as far removed from her life as she could imagine. She wasn't ready yet for that much civilian life.

Nancy Paxton pursed her lips. "You think I'm a hard-nose, don't you?"

Pepper looked for more diplomatic words. "You've been doing this for a long time. You must know what's best."

"But . . . ?"

"But how come patients can't have the TV on before breakfast?"

"Couple of reasons. First, these guys look healthy, but some of them are frail. They need rest. We try to keep the ward quiet until at least 0700. Second, it's a matter of discipline. We have to remind them that—hurt or not—they are still soldiers. Soldiers obey rules. If you have to make a rule, make it because it has some sense behind it. Then expect them to follow it."

Pepper changed her mind. The rule about no TV before breakfast would stay.

"You were pretty tough with Sergeant Doan."

"Cody Doan has an addiction problem. For him, the choice is to hurt for a little while today, or go through withdrawal in a couple of months." She looked at her watch. "It's been a couple of hours since you gave him the shot. Dave and I have been checking on him every half hour. This time, you go."

Reluctantly, Pepper put her cap and shoes back on and walked down the hall to Doan's room. He lay on his back, his hands behind his head, staring at the ceiling.

"You okay?"

"Yeah."

"Need anything?"

"Not anything you've got. . . . Sorry. That didn't come out right. Surgery makes me cranky. I don't mean anything by it. It's just a hard day." Pepper heard the soft Blue Ridge accent in his voice. It was the way people talked where Aunt Corabell lived.

"I know something about hard days."

"I heard."

Pepper closed the door again, thinking that the grapevine penetrated even behind the closed doors of private rooms.

Nancy had found cold drinks for both of them. She handed one to Pepper, who wasn't convinced that Doan wasn't still in pain, but not saying anything because no one would listen to him.

"I guess he's okay."

"It's hard to say no to them, especially if they've been to 'Nam. You figure they've been through enough."

"This is the other end of the line from the emergency room. I thought about that this morning during rounds. Do you ever think we saved some that we should have let go?"

"Occasionally, not often. I guess part of it is that we don't get the bad casualities."

Pepper thought of the patients with the broken and crooked bones, the missing arms or legs. "They look bad hurt to me."

"Most med-evacs, we'll get two or three guys that are going to get well and get out of here. We get the fractures, the joint problems, the single amputees. If you break a few bones or lose a bit of an arm or a leg, you still have a lot left. The multiple amps, who have lost two or three limbs or the guys missing everything from the waist down, they're sent to the special rehabilitation programs. Places like Fitzsimmons Hospital in Denver."

"How often do the med-evacs come in?"

"Once, maybe twice a week. The chief nurse's office calls in advance to let you know one is scheduled."

"What happens if we get a med-evac and a jump on the same day?"

Nancy laughed. "Have one of the nurses bring you a sandwich from the mess hall because you will be running your tail off."

"I guess that's a tough day, too, getting them back from Vietnam?"

"It's tougher two or three days later, when the families come to visit for the first time."

"We never had to think about families in Qui Nhon."

"You'll think about them now. At least the relatives of the guys back from 'Nam are mostly grateful to have their son or husband home. It's the relatives of the patients who cream themselves on a motorcycle or have a bad back that drive me crazy. Sometimes I think that all active-duty families are dysfunctional. I spend a lot of my day making nice with angry wives." She looked at her watch. "Time for change of shift report. Go count and check out early. Tomorrow we'll do the staffing roster."

"How many staff do I have?"

"Not enough. We're always shorthanded over the summer. They keep telling us it's because the staff are needed in Vietnam."

Pepper laughed. "When we were short-staffed in Qui Nhon, they told us it was because the corpsmen were needed back on the block."

Nancy repeated, "Back on the block, back in the world, I've heard guys say both of those things. What do they mean?"

Pepper laughed. "I never figured it out. I told a corpsman once that I didn't come from a block, I came from a neighborhood. He looked at me like we were from different planets, which maybe we were."

"He was black?"

"Yeah, from Detroit."

"Honey, you *were* from different planets."

Pepper thought of the months of racial tension between black and white soldiers in Qui Nhon. "What about Dave? He's black."

"Dave's a good head. He's not into dapping and that power shit. I respect him and he respects me."

The racial tensions had run too deep in Qui Nhon. Pepper couldn't help feeling dealing with Dave wasn't going to be that simple.

By 1515 hours, the day shift was filing out of the ward. On her way to the elevator, Pepper detoured to the uniform room. After spending a day holding her skirt over her knees every time she sat down, she wanted longer uniforms.

A wardmaster in the uniform room looked nervous, idly fingering clothing, almost pacing in the small space. His nametag said *Carter*. She nodded to Wardmaster Carter and he acknowledged the nod, but he didn't speak. As Pepper looked more closely at him, she decided he wasn't as old as she first thought. The grey hair sprinkled among the brown, and the deep bags under his eyes, fooled her at first. He looked like a boozer. The longer Pepper looked at uniforms, the more nervous Wardmaster Carter became.

She found two uniforms that might do, nodded again to Carter, and went to the elevator. The doors opened and a major in a nurse's uniform got off. For a moment, Pepper tried to place the woman's blond hair and familiar face. Then it came back to her as a warm and gentle memory.

"Excuse me, Major Buckner, I know you probably don't remember me. I'm Elizabeth Pepperhawk, part of the August '69 class at Fort Sam. You were our class advisor."

When sixty new military nurses arrived at Fort Sam Houston, Major Buckner was waiting at the reception desk to answer their questions. She helped them make sense of their schedules, taught them to march and salute, explained the intricacies of getting uniforms made at Sugarman's Tailors. Jane, as she told them to call her, had been a part of their late-night gabfests, their speculations about future postings, and the pros and cons of volunteering for Vietnam. On their last day at Camp Bullis, when, hot and exhausted, they finished their compass and map course, Jane Buckner was waiting for them with a brass band. Pepper had a snapshot of her pretending to lead the band and mugging it up for the camera.

She hoped that Major Buckner would remember her, would say something like, "Of course I remember you. You were one of the top five graduates of that class." Or at the very least, she would notice the captain's bars and say, "You've done well, I see."

Instead the woman shook Pepper's hand in an absent-minded way and, in a perfunctory manner, asked Pepper what assignment she had.

"I'm the new head nurse on Six-A. Yourself?"

"Evening supervisor."

"I won't keep you," Pepper said, uncomfortable with the woman's unexpected coolness. "I'm sure you're very busy."

Flustered, Pepper pressed the elevator button several times, as if she could hurry the elevator along the more times she pushed. In the mirror beside the elevator, she watched Major Buckner enter the uniform room and close the door, then heard the sound of a lock being turned. Why was Jane Buckner meeting a boozy wardmaster in a locked uniform room?

Chapter 7

Avivah settled herself into a metal folding-chair in the front row of the small classroom and wondered what had pulled Captain Delaney's chain. Something had. He'd posted notice of a briefing for junior officers. Normally, Delaney felt no need to interact with ordinary human beings.

Major Gilbert Plauche, the day supervisor and Avivah's mentor when she first came to Fort Bragg, came in, looked around, and took a seat behind her. "You see the *National Enquirer* this morning?"

"Oh, yes."

"The murder made *Stars and Stripes,* too, though they didn't feature the alien abduction angle." *Stars and Stripes,* the official military weekly newspaper, reached around the world to all active-duty personnel. It was bad enough to be featured in a tabloid, but to let your fellow soldiers know there had been another murder in your own back yard hurt even more.

Captain Delaney entered and put a sheaf of papers on the desk at the front of the room. "Good afternoon, I'm Captain Thomas Delaney of the CID." He looked directly at Avivah and Gil Plauche. "I'm afraid you might find this a rather basic briefing. I'd intended it for junior officers."

Plauche tinted his voice with a heavy Cajun accent. "We can all learn something. Me, I'll raise my hand if I don't understand, no."

The barefoot bayou pose didn't fool Avivah. Gil had

joined the Army with an eighth-grade education and a better command of Cajun French than of English. He'd bootstrapped himself through a high school diploma and into a commission.

Delaney nervously adjusted his tie. "Let's begin, shall we? As you know, a murder victim was discovered on-post Sunday. I thought it would be a useful exercise to discuss the progress the CID has made to date."

Right, Avivah thought. Delaney did not do "useful exercises." What else was going on?

"When there's a murder, the Criminal Investigation Division collects evidence as any civilian police force does, or for that matter, the way detectives do in murder mysteries. We gather scene-of-crime evidence, request an autopsy, interview witnesses."

For God's sakes, this was kindergarten stuff for military police officers. From the sound of shuffling bodies around her, the rest of the officers felt the same way Avivah did.

"In this case, we began with the autopsy report, which showed that the deceased died from a single gunshot to the chest, between 0900 and 1300 hours, on July 4. The medical officer can't pin the time down any closer because the room's air-conditioner altered the body's cooling rate. A witness saw the victim alive at 0945 hours, boarding a shuttle bus that disembarked passengers on-post at 1007 hours."

A witness she and Ramerez had found. Avivah raised her hand.

"Captain Rosen." In just two words he managed to convey "might as well let the dear thing ask a question."

"The Eighty-second Airborne Fourth of July parade passed Normandy House between 1045 and 1055 hours."

"Your point is?"

"A brass band would hide the sound of a gunshot."

"Yes, but that would suppose that the murderer knew the exact time the band would pass in front of Normandy House."

"Begging your pardon, sir, but it would be obvious when a brass band was passing outside your window."

Captain Delaney gave a small, pained smile, but everyone else in the room laughed.

Avivah pictured the distance between the spot where the shuttles dropped off passengers and Normandy House. If the victim was alive at 1007, when he got off the shuttle, and dead by 1055, that left only forty-eight minutes for him to meet someone, cross the post to Normandy House, enter unseen, and be killed. Who had met him at the shuttle bus?

A lieutenant raised his hand. "What about the room's previous occupant?"

"Well away from Fort Bragg by the time in question."

Though she already knew the answer, Avivah bated Delaney with, "How many doors are there into Normandy House?"

"Three."

"Were they locked?"

"No, they are never locked during the day."

"But the door to room 106 was locked, wasn't it?"

"It was."

"Who had a key?"

"The key given to people when they check in was in its slot at the front desk. The maid and the maintenance man have master keys. The maid was on duty July 4, the maintenance man wasn't. Frankly, we're still working on how the body got into the room." Delaney looked annoyed that he had to admit he hadn't figured that out yet.

Gil whispered in Avivah's ear, "Do you think he checked

to see if a key to room 106 went missing?"

Avivah whispered back. "Don't know." She playfully took Gil's wrist, as if she were going to raise his hand for him, "You ask him?"

He wrestled his arm out of her grasp. "Behave, *ti chou*." Little cabbage. It was the name he teased her with, just like he teased his teen-aged daughters. Avivah sat back and concentrated on what else Delaney had to say.

Another hand. "What about the murder weapon?"

"It was a .32 caliber pistol. So far, we haven't located it. Now, to continue, we have reason to suspect that the victim was or had been a soldier, possibly serving in Vietnam. However, Washington could not identify his fingerprints and that stumped us. But even without an identification, we managed to trace his movements. We know, for example, that he rented a car in Detroit on June thirtieth, using a Quebec driver's license issued in the name of Doucette Hebert, with an address and telephone number in Montreal."

Ramerez and I gave you the car, too, Avivah thought with some satisfaction. And the World War II uniform, which she noticed Captain Delaney hadn't mentioned.

Captain Plauche's hand rose in a lazy motion. "Did he have a Quebec accent?"

"As a matter of fact, the clerk at the rental agency said he had a Southern accent."

The second lieutenant's hand was up again. Captain Delaney nodded at him. "What about the Montreal address?"

"It's a car wash. No one there recognized the picture we sent to the Montreal police."

He picked up a stack of photocopied pages and began to distribute them. "I think it's time to share my real coup."

Avivah sat up straighter. Here it came, whatever had pulled Delaney's chain.

"At first we assumed Washington had problems identifying the victim's fingerprints because of staff shortages after the long weekend. Logically, we asked initially for non-deceased matches. When I thought to ask for all possible matches, Army records identified our previously unidentified victim as Specialist-Four Dermid Hagan, who died in Saigon January 20, 1969."

Amid the general hubbub, Delaney looked pleased with himself. Avivah took one of the photocopies. Dermid Hagan. Engineering Specialist. Home of record: Marshall, North Carolina. Last assignment: Engineering battalion near Long Bien. Deceased: January 20, 1969. Cause of death: Motor vehicle accident.

Hands went up all over the room, but no one waited to be recognized. "How was he identified in Saigon?" "Who identified him?" "What happened to the body?" "Could it be a mix-up in fingerprints?" "Could he have a twin?"

"You see our problem, gentlemen. A real puzzler. First of all, we don't know how or who identified the body in Saigon. We've asked for the accident report. The Army sent the body home to North Carolina. Dermid Hagan was interred, with full military honors, on February 18, 1969." He turned to the second lieutenant, "And no, he didn't have a twin. At least his parents said he didn't and they should know." The lieutenant's face turned pink.

Avivah's heart constricted for the parents. How horrible to have been told that their son died in Vietnam, to go through the burial and the grief, only to be told eighteen months later that a terrible mistake had been made. Unless, she thought, sitting up a little straighter, someone in the family knew all along that Dermid wasn't dead. The

Hagans of Marshall, North Carolina, greatly interested her.

Major Plauche didn't bother to hold up his hand. "Whose body did the Army send home?"

Delaney opened his hands in a questioning gesture. "We don't know. I'm in the process of applying for an order to exhume the body."

The second lieutenant in the back of the room had been sitting quietly, chewing on his fingernail. Hesitantly, he raised his hand.

"Lieutenant?"

"I know this is an odd suggestion, but is there any possibility the CIA or military intelligence is involved?"

General laughter filled the room.

"Now we shouldn't discount any possibilities," Captain Delaney said with a kindness that Avivah knew was acting, "no matter how far out they sound. I don't think this is a likely possibility, Lieutenant, but I will follow up on it. Thank you for your suggestion."

The lieutenant looked relieved. "Thank you, sir."

Bingo. Delaney's favorite hobby horse: conspiracy theories. Ramerez once described Delaney as "CID with delusions of CIA." Even Delaney couldn't just telephone Langley, Virginia, and ask the CIA, "Have we stumbled into your patch?" Now a very green lieutenant would be credited with giving him the idea. Avivah didn't believe for a minute that this death had any CIA connection, and she was infuriated that while Delaney went off to chase spooks, the real murderer would get away.

Captain Delaney looked at his watch. "That's all the time we have. Thank you for coming. I hope you've found it helpful to have this kind of session. I'll try to have more of them in the future."

Yeah, Avivah thought as she got up, the next time you're stuck for a straight man.

Specialist Ramerez sat like a vulture on the edge of a desk just outside the classroom door.

Avivah passed him at a fast walk. "Come on."

He jumped down from the desk. "Where are we going?"

"Fishing."

A few minutes later, the desk clerk at Normandy House sighed as Avivah and Ramerez approached the desk. "More questions?"

"How many keys do you have for each room?"

"Four. One for guests, one for the maid, one for the maintenance man, and the original locked in the safe."

"Who can open the safe?"

"The manager."

"Where was he on July 4?"

"She," the desk clerk said pointedly, "was in Charleston. She left Thursday at noon and was back on Monday morning."

"Do you keep a record of any lost keys?"

"Oh, yes, we're required to for insurance, you know."

"Have you ever lost a key for room 106?"

She dug in a desk drawer and came out with a small bound ledger. "We had to duplicate that key in June of this year."

"Who was the guest?"

The woman ran her finger along a line in the ledger. "Colonel Frances Euston; her home address is in Langley, Virginia."

Avivah felt a hint of panic. Please, please, she thought, don't let Colonel Euston have anything to do with the CIA or military intelligence. She couldn't bear for Delaney to be right. "Do you have an address for Colonel Euston?"

"I'll get her registration card. Here it is. Colonel Frances Euston, Army Nurse Corps, Washington, D.C."

Avivah relaxed. Nothing could be further from the CIA than the Army Nurse Corps. She noted that Colonel Euston had checked in on June 8 and checked out on June 10. On the back of the card was a note that she had reported her key missing on the afternoon of June 9. Avivah copied the colonel's home address and telephone number and returned the card to the clerk.

"You going to call her?" Ramerez asked as they climbed into their jeep.

"Don't know. I have to think about it."

She and Captain Delaney disliked one another from a long way back. Avivah thought him the sloppiest investigating officer she knew. He didn't think women made good police officers. Fortunately, because the military police and CID worked separately, they had very little contact with one another. Until now.

That she had been Staff Officer of the Day when Dermid Hagan's body was discovered irritated him. He'd been downright angry with her for calling in Colonel Tyler. Delaney did not like to work with other people looking over his shoulder.

Delaney wasn't in her chain of command, so he had no direct ability to discipline Avivah. In the Army, there were other, more subtle ways to affect an officer's career—particularly if that officer was a woman—and Avivah had the good sense to know she definitely did not want Captain Delaney as an enemy.

It took several hours before curiosity won out over common sense. Avivah finally reached for the telephone and dialed the Langley, Virginia number Colonel Euston had listed as her home number.

"Good evening. Frances Euston speaking."

It was an older voice, a New England voice, which Avivah imagined belonged to a tall, thin woman, who knew exactly what she wanted.

"This is Captain Rosen, military police at Fort Bragg. I'm calling in regard to a death that happened on post last Sunday."

"The young man I read about in the *Stars and Stripes?*"

"Yes, ma'am. He was an ex-soldier from here in North Carolina."

"Someone I knew?" Her voice tightened a little, as if fearing bad news.

Delaney hadn't said the corpse's identity was confidential. "Specialist Dermid Hagan. An engineer."

"No, I don't recognize the name." She sounded relieved.

"I called to ask about the key you lost during your visit to Fort Bragg."

"Oh, my. Was he found in the room where I stayed?"

"I'm afraid so."

"I'll be glad to answer any questions, Captain."

"I'll need to have a stenographer take down your statement. Will that be all right?"

"It will."

Avivah cupped her hand over the mouthpiece. "Osborne," she yelled toward the reception area.

Specialist Osborne popped into the doorway like a jack out of the box. "Yes, ma'am."

"Can you take dictation?"

"Yes, ma'am."

"Get your pad. I need you to take a deposition."

Avivah introduced the colonel to Specialist Osborne and told her that she would be taking her statement and that a copy would be sent to her for signature.

"Colonel, for the record, please state your name, rank, and current posting."

"I am Colonel Frances Laverne Euston—that's Frances with an 'e', Specialist Osborne, and Colonel with a bird," she said, pride in her voice. Avivah suspected that Frances Euston had been a full colonel about as long as she had been a captain. The newness hadn't worn off yet.

"My current posting is Special Assistant to General Anna Mae Hayes, Chief of the Army Nurse Corps and I am stationed at General Hayes' office in Washington, D.C."

"Please describe your visit to Fort Bragg earlier this year."

"I arrived Wednesday, June 8, at approximately 1600 hours. Colonel Norton, chief nurse at Womack Army Hospital, met me at Pope Air Force Base. She escorted me to the Transient Officers' Quarters—I believe you call it Normandy House—where I checked in and changed clothes. Then Mary Melissa and I went to supper. We were together until approximately 2100 hours that night."

"A business meeting?"

Colonel Euston laughed. "Absolutely not. Mary Melissa and I have been friends since we were both lieutenants in Korea."

"Why didn't you stay with her?"

"That would have been . . . inconvenient. In any case, she escorted me back to Normandy House about 2115 hours."

"You had your key then?"

"Yes."

"What did you do Thursday?"

"Colonel Norton picked me up at 0600, we ate breakfast together, and I spent the rest of the day meeting with nurses."

"About what?"

"Uniforms. Have you noticed, Captain, that military nurses' uniforms haven't kept pace with changes in civilian hospitals?"

"I noticed."

"In about eighteen months, you will see significant changes to Army nurses' duty uniforms. On behalf of General Hayes, I am making a series of trips, to different Army hospitals, to discuss preliminary design sketches with the nurses."

Actually consulting nurses about new uniforms. The New Army, Avivah thought unkindly, then felt ashamed. Colonel Euston sounded honestly pleased with the coming changes. "What did you do after the meetings?"

"I toured the hospital and medical holding company. General Hayes expects anyone from her office, when they travel, to be her eyes and ears. I brought her greetings to both the staff and the patients."

"What did you do after the tour?"

"Taped an interview at a local television station about opportunities in Army nursing."

Avivah looked at the notes she scribbled. The places a key might have been lost looked impossibly long. She doodled the word *Korea,* calculated the colonel's estimated age, and, with a start, realized Colonel Euston could be younger than her own mother. Somehow, Avivah pictured an aging woman with grey hair.

"After I finished the interview, my escort took me from the station to the Transient Officers' Quarters. That's when I discovered my key was missing. I looked through my purse and finally went to the front desk. They let me in with a master key."

With the toe of her shoe, Avivah pulled open her bottom desk drawer and looked at her own black leather purse. All the women in the service carried the same kind of purse, a black leather shoulder bag, with a snapped flap and side pocket.

"You were in summer greens?"

"That was the uniform of the day."

"Black leather purse?"

"Of course."

"You tossed the key in the side pocket?" She always threw her own keys and spare change into the side pocket because it saved opening the flap. In the side pocket, the key would have been visible to even a casual passerby.

"I'm afraid so. You know how it is."

"Yes, ma'am, I do. While you're redesigning the uniforms, maybe you could redesign the purse, too? And that nurses' hospital cap?"

The colonel chuckled. "We may always hope for miracles, Captain."

"Did you check to see if anyone had found your key?"

"I called the hospital and spoke with the evening supervisor. She promised she would have the hospital and medical holding company searched. I also called the television station. The evening supervisor phoned me back. The television station did not." The tone in the colonel's voice said that indicated the difference between the military and civilians.

"Do you remember the evening supervisor's name?"

"Of course, Major Jane Buckner."

"Why did you say *of course?*"

"I discussed her at length with Mary Melissa during my visit."

The negative tone made Avivah sit up straighter. "Why?"

The colonel hesitated. "Mary Melissa thinks highly of Jane Buckner. She's a remarkable young woman. Came from a disadvantaged background. Put herself through nursing school. In eight years in the Army, she completed two tours of duty in Vietnam, earned a bachelor's degree in nursing, attended staff college, and taught at the Medical Field Service School at Fort Sam Houston. Mary Melissa asked me to do what I could to push through a posting in Washington, so that Jane could attend graduate school at Georgetown University."

"Begging your pardon, Colonel, but I sense some reservations about Major Buckner?"

"I am equivocal. Standing alone, Major Buckner's record looks outstanding. Her relationship with Mary Melissa concerns me."

Avivah waited a long time to give the colonel an opportunity to volunteer more information.

Colonel Euston finally spoke, tentatively at first. "Mary Melissa retires next month. She wants to leave a legacy to the Corps. Originally, we talked about a bursary in operating room nursing—Mary Melissa was a fine operating room nurse—but instead she decided to act as Jane Buckner's mentor and sponsor. Several months ago, she invited Major Buckner to share her house."

"Is that why you stayed at Normandy House?"

"As a representative of the chief nurses' office I must not only *be* impartial, but *appear* to be so. Since I recommended that Major Buckner be permitted to jump the queue for a Washington posting, I needed to keep my distance."

"You did recommend her?"

"Eventually."

"Sorry, ma'am, but I have to ask you one other question. Where were you on July 4?"

"In the morning I shared the parade review platform with General Hayes. In the afternoon, I sailed on the Potomac with my three nieces from noon until after the fire-works."

"Your nieces would be willing to testify to that?"

"If necessary."

"Thank you. I should warn you that you might have to answer these questions again. I have to turn your statement over to Captain Delaney of the CID. He may be a little more . . . forceful in his questions."

"Captain, my calendar tomorrow includes meetings with two senators, a general, and a delegation from the International Congress of Nursing. I may have the skills to find my way through an interview with your Captain Delaney."

"Yes, ma'am, I think you might."

Chapter 8

Standing at the counter in the military police office, Pepper handed Captain Rosen an index card. "I came to give you my new address. It shouldn't be hard for you to remember; it's across the hall from your apartment."

Captain Rosen glanced at the other people in the office. Pepper recognized one of them as the policeman who responded to her phone call. Opening a gate in the desk, Captain Rosen said, "Ramerez, I'm on break. Come this way, Captain Pepperhawk."

My, aren't we formal, Pepper thought, as the two women walked down a narrow corridor and out a back door. An Army-issue, green canvas tent filled a corner of the parking lot. Inside, a string of pale yellow bulbs illuminated a beat-up picnic table and a barbecue. In the close, hot evening, the tent smelled musty. Captain Rosen swung her long legs over the picnic table bench and Pepper wiggled in on the other side.

Captain Rosen used a voice that reminded Pepper of Captain Delaney. "Tell me about finding this apartment."

Pepper recounted her search. When she finished, Avivah did not look pleased. Pepper traced concentric circles around a knothole in the table. "What was my mistake, getting the apartment next to yours or coming here tonight to give you the address?"

"A little of both. How would you feel if a patient showed up on your ward and announced, in front of your corpsmen, that he'd rented an apartment across the hall from you?"

"I'd be wary. Why did he do that? Would my corpsmen think there was something between us? At least your staff can't think that with both of us . . . being . . . Oh my."

Avivah grinned. "I didn't think you were that naive."

"I'm sorry. I just wanted to tell you that we were neighbors. I thought you might give me a few tips, like what's a good bank?"

Pepper liked the honest way Captain Rosen sat back and appraised her. Take a chance on me, Pepper wished. I make a good friend and I could really use a friend.

Captain Rosen held out her hand. "Call me Avivah." Her handshake was warm and firm.

"Most people call me Pepper."

"Are you working this weekend?"

"No."

"I'm not either. I'll show you around: groceries, a bank. I know a great dry cleaner. He's a retired first sergeant. You tell him you want creases, you get *creases*."

"Thanks."

Avivah looked around the tent. "Remind you of Vietnam?"

"No. I don't know why everyone thinks Vietnam resembles that movie about the Army hospital in Korea."

"*M*A*S*H*?"

"That's the one. I never saw a tent the whole time I was in Qui Nhon."

"What was the hospital like?"

"It had been converted from airmen's quarters at one end of the Qui Nhon airfield. Two-story concrete barracks, with big wooden porches on one side. The nurses lived in a wooden building, arranged around a quadrangle. Like . . ."

She faltered for an image. "Like the fishing camps my dad likes. One of those down-at-the-heel places with all the buildings painted the same color. Half sand and half weeds covering the ground. An old rowboat sunk by the dock, where minnows swam. The smell of dead fish, except in Qui Nhon, we couldn't see the ocean from the hospital and the place smelled of av-gas and hot tarmac."

Avivah laughed. "In the Adirondacks, we had camp gardeners and the whole camp smelled like lilac bushes."

"Sounds expensive."

"We got by."

Pepper tried to imagine Avivah as a rich, New York, Jewish lesbian, but instead she saw just another fellow officer.

Avivah returned Pepper's appraising look. "How are you doing?"

"As a witness, a suspect, or as your neighbor?"

"Not a suspect, no matter what Delaney thinks. As my neighbor, I guess."

"They made me a head nurse."

"That's bad?"

"It's a lot of responsibility. I only graduated two years ago. What's your assignment?"

"Evening shift supervisor."

"Oh, wow, like Major Buckner. That's even more responsibility than a head nurse."

"You know Major Buckner?"

"She was our class advisor at Fort Sam Houston."

"What's she like?"

Pepper shrugged. "Right after basic, I'd have said she was funny, smart, friendly, and a great officer. She's changed. I talked to her yesterday and she acted like she wished I hadn't recognized her. How come you're interested in her?"

"Her name came up."

"About the murder?"

"You know I can't answer that."

"I guess not. How long have you been evening super-visor?"

"Four months. I was assigned right after I got my cap-taincy."

Pepper counted backwards on her fingers. "I got my cap-taincy about four months ago, too. March fifteenth."

Avivah grinned. "I have date of rank on you by two weeks. Mine's March first."

"You going to make it a career?"

"Don't know. How about you?"

"I'm having trouble thinking beyond tomorrow."

"What happens tomorrow?"

Pepper rolled her eyes. "At the end of day shift, Ward Six-A belongs to me. My first command."

"Don't let it go to your head."

The two women sat for a moment, then Avivah asked, "Does your aunt live in North Carolina? I'm interested in a little town called Marshall."

"Bat Harbor and Marshall lie about fifty miles apart, Bat Harbor on the Tennessee side of the Cherokee National Forest and Marshall on the North Carolina side."

"The murder victim was from Marshall."

" 'Nam vet?"

"Yes."

An incredible sadness rose inside of Pepper. "I knew it. Grunt?"

"Engineer."

"When was he there?"

"Part of '68, part of '69."

"The bad times." Almost everyone she knew in the Army considered 1968 and 1969 the worst years to have been in Vietnam. Pepper felt distressed that this soldier survived, only to come home to die. She wished she could do something for him.

"When I was nine, my aunt took me to Marshall. It's one of those little mountain towns with a downtown two blocks long. French Broad River, railroad track, Main Street." Pepper moved her hand in three precise lines to show that the river paralleled the railroad tracks and the railroad tracks paralleled Main Street. "The Daughters of the Confederacy dedicated a plaque to the memory of Robert E. Lee on the county courthouse lawn."

"You remember pretty well for being nine."

"When I was nine, Robert E. Lee figured prominently in my daydreams."

"What would a man from Marshall be like?"

"How much money did his family have?"

"I don't know."

"If he was like Aunt Corabell's family—not rich, not poor—his family and his church, probably a Baptist church, would have been important to him. I imagine he spent a lot of time out-of-doors. Before he joined the Army, the longest trip he'd ever taken was likely a school trip to Washington, D.C., or Atlanta. Why? Does this help?"

Avivah rubbed her fingernail against her teeth. "Anything you can learn about the victim helps."

Chapter 9

Friday morning, as she listened to change-of-shift report, Pepper tried not to stare at Corpsman Pinna. He sat across from her, on the edge of the treatment table, swinging his legs back and forth. Beneath his starched white trousers, he wore bright red socks.

Maybe Pinna hadn't had any clean black socks this morning. That didn't matter. Dress regulations said black socks. Pepper resolved to speak to him privately, but firmly, immediately after report.

The night nurse closed the stiff holder that held patient information. "That's it."

Pepper looked at her notes. "We've got fifteen going on weekend pass and only two for surgery, so things should be quiet by noon. Captain Paxton's going-away party begins at 1400 hours."

Food filled the ward refrigerator and colored decorations peeked out of a brown paper bag behind the red-socked Pinna.

"I'll have the assignments up in about twenty minutes. Rock and roll, ladies and gentlemen, rock and roll."

The customary shuffling that normally followed report stopped. A couple of the corpsmen, who had been in Vietnam, stared at Pepper. "Sorry," she said, blushing. "Old habits die hard." She wondered how many other things that seemed so natural in Qui Nhon stood out here in the States.

David Willett stood up. "Pinna. In my office. Now."

Pinna reappeared half an hour later, wearing black socks.

Pepper took David Willett aside. "Was Pinna testing me or was it just the party atmosphere?"

"A little of both. He's a short-timer, with only a month left in the Army. He knows that as long as he sticks to small infractions, there's not much we will do to him."

"Was I supposed to discipline him? I mean, you didn't step in because I'm new, did you?"

"The corpsmen are my responsibility."

"You will let me know when it's something I'm supposed to handle, won't you?"

"Yes, ma'am, I certainly will do that."

Cody Doan came out of the ward, swinging himself down the hall on his crutches.

"Good morning, Sergeant Doan."

"Humph," Doan grunted at her, a response barely this side of insubordination. The relationship between him and Pepper hadn't improved since their initial confrontation over pain medication.

A blue tag beside Doan's name on the patient list indicated he had a weekend pass. Pepper almost asked the doctor to cancel the pass order, but the doctor would have asked her why. What would she have told him? Doan didn't look right. Too skinny for his tall frame. Too tired. Too pale. Too burdened. It was nothing she could explain to the doctor or even to herself. She just felt like Doan needed to be watched.

He stopped at the desk outside the nurses' station and picked up the morning paper. His face paled and he almost collapsed, swaying heavily on his crutches. Now what, Pepper wondered as she hurried toward him. Before she could reach him, Doan righted himself and went barreling down the hall, at a pace she had not imagined he could do.

She called after him, "You don't look well. I don't think . . ." He paid her no attention. "Sign out to say you're off the ward," she called lamely after him. He disappeared through the ward doors.

Just to keep the record straight, Pepper wrote his name, the time, and "off ward" in the spiral notebook kept at the desk.

David Willett came up behind her. "What's with Doan?"

"I don't know. Follow him. Make sure he's all right."

Willett hurried down the hall after their patient. Pepper looked at the front page of the paper, wondering what Doan had read.

Murdered Ft. Bragg Soldier Identified;
Mystery Deepens

"Rest in peace, Dermid Hagan," she murmured as she read his name. Then she read further into the article and lost herself in the mystery of the man who had died twice.

David Willett came back in a few minutes, carrying a milkshake. "Doan went down to the private telephone booths on first floor."

"Did he see you?"

"Maybe. I walked past the telephone booths and kept going into the canteen. He's really upset, pounding on the phone booth door while he talked. What set him off?"

Pepper showed him the article. "Mean anything to you? Was Dermid Hagan ever a patient on this ward?"

"I can't remember everyone. I'll look in the ward log. When would he have been here?"

"Before '68. He was in 'Nam in '68 and '69. It says he supposedly died in Saigon in January 1969."

David read the article. "Sixty-eight was before my time here, and we don't have logs going back that far. We toss them after two years."

Pepper had things to do and she never saw Doan come back to the ward. By noon, the two patients for surgery had gone, come back, and, with the resiliency of the young, were now sitting up, eating lunch. Most of the patients going on pass had already left. On her way to lunch, Pepper walked down the hall, closing doors to empty rooms, aware of how quiet the unit had become. When she checked the pass book, she saw Doan had managed to leave on pass without her seeing him. She hoped he would be all right.

David Willett handed her a chart. "Lieutenant Batta's liver profile is still elevated. Want me to call the doc and tell him?"

"Might as well. I'll go have one more look at him, not that it will do any good."

Lieutenant Batta presented, as he had all week, as an extremely tired young man for whom no reason for the tiredness could be found. After she had examined him, Pepper wandered down the hall, studying his chart for answers that weren't there.

"You're looking powerfully puzzled, Captain."

She looked up, expecting to see one of her corpsmen. Instead, she found herself speaking to the wardmaster she met in the uniform room.

"I'm Harlan Carter," he said, coming down from the ladder, where he had been stringing crepe paper streamers from the light fixture. "I'm the wardmaster in the medical holding company. Most of my boys left on weekend pass, and Dave said he'd appreciate it if I could give ya'll a hand decorating."

For an instant, Pepper doubted this could be the same

man. She finally realized this was the same man: cleaned up, sobered up, and polite as could be.

Leaning against the ladder, he said, "You look like you're puzzling on a mystery."

"The mystery of Lieutenant's Batta's liver."

"What's wrong with the lieutenant's liver?"

"That's what we'd like to know." Pepper hesitated. "I'm not sure I should be discussing one of the patients with you."

"It's all right," he said leaning toward her as if they shared a confidence. "I'm one of you. Top of my class in ninety-one-Charlie school."

Ninety-one-Charlie school graduated licensed practical nurses for the Army. He recounted his achievement like a proud little boy. In spite of her reservations, Pepper felt charmed.

"May I, ma'am?" Wardmaster Carter asked, pointing at the chart. Against her better judgment, Pepper gave it to him.

"His liver function tests are all out of whack, and he's mightily tired all the time." *Mightily tired.* Carter had her talking in that same soft drawl he had.

"Jaundice?"

"No. Just tired all the time. A broken leg shouldn't account for the fatigue. He's negative for malaria, negative for hepatitis, says he's a teetotaler and I believe him." She blushed a little, embarrassed to mention drinking. Wardmaster Carter did not appear to notice.

"Drugs?"

"Not Lieutenant Batta. He's the kind of officer who would report anyone he suspected of using drugs."

Carter sat down on one of the vinyl sofas under the paint-by-number picture of two deer drinking at a forest pool. The afternoon sun came in at a slant through the window, making his graying hair look ragged. He looks like he needs a couple of weeks off, some square meals, and a good cuddle, Pepper thought.

He thumbed through the chart, read all the laboratory results, and stopped at the original history and physical. "So the lieutenant was standing in Chu Lai, watching a football game, when three guys ran out of bounds and knocked him over an iron pipe."

"That's the story."

"You think he was popular with his men?"

"I doubt it. He strikes me as the kind who should never have been commissioned, only he had a degree, so the Army made him an officer. He was in communications. Ran a telephone exchange."

"How long did he have left in-country when he was hurt?"

"About two weeks."

Harlan stroked his clean-shaven cheeks, as if thinking. "You know about black syph?"

"Oh sure. That's the mythical venereal disease that can't be cured. If they find you have it, you never come home. They keep you on this secret ship in the Gulf. One of the sillier rumors in Vietnam."

"You and I know that, but what about the lieutenant? He's a little young?"

"Yes."

"A little gullible?"

"Yes."

"So if he's not too popular, a real prig, and scheduled to come home soon, what do you think would happen if people told him he had black syph? Would he believe it?"

"He'd believe it."

"He wouldn't want to go on sick call, so he'd treat himself with antibiotics from the black market."

"He's not the boom-boom type."

She saw an amused look in Carter's eyes. "Probably not, but he sounds like the kind who could be convinced you caught black syph from a toilet seat. My guess is he took himself down to his supposed black market agent, and bought himself a bunch of pills. God only knows what those pills contained. The lieutenant's got himself a little liver damage from some high-octane contaminants. Six or eight weeks from now, he'll be right as rain." He closed the chart and handed it to her.

"You make a very good detective."

"Aw, shucks. Wasn't nothing. I did a stint at the Third Field Hospital as wardmaster in the medical ward. I've seen that pattern of lab results a whole bunch of times."

Pepper left him to decorating the day room. She wrote a note for Lieutenant Batta's doctor, put the chart in the rack, and went to look for Dave. She found him at his tiny desk in the supply room. Pepper closed the door behind her.

"That man who's putting up the decorations, Wardmaster Carter. Do you know him?"

"Yes."

"Does he drink?"

"Damn. I was sure he was sober today."

Pepper waived her hand. "Relax. He's sober, but I met him in the hall a couple of days ago and he didn't look sober then."

"Harlan's a binge drinker."

Like me, Pepper almost said. So far she had been able to arrange her binges so no one noticed. Or thought she had. Maybe Harlan thought he was hiding his drinking as well as she thought she hid hers. The memory of Harlan's appearance a couple of days ago scared her so much that she sat down in the chair beside David's desk so he wouldn't see her shake. She did not want to end up like Harlan Carter.

"Why isn't anyone trying to do something for him?" she asked angrily, thinking, why wasn't anyone trying to do something for her?

"We are. About a year and a half ago, his drinking got out of hand. Patsy and I tried to talk to him, but he didn't want to talk, so we did what we could to help his wife and kids." David's wife, Patsy, a civilian licensed practical nurse, worked on the labor and delivery ward.

"A couple of months ago, the wardmasters sponsored a picnic. Harlan and Betty had a horrible fight. After Patsy took their kids and our kids home together, Harlan took a beer out of the cooler. Betty tried to take it away from him, and he pulled back to hit her. I don't think he realized he had the bottle in his hand. Fortunately, I swatted the bottle out of his hand before it connected. It fell on the concrete pad and exploded.

"Harlan broke down crying. We had to call an ambulance. For the first time, Betty pressed charges. He spent time in the psych ward and almost ended up with an Article Fifteen for public drunkenness and attempted assault."

An Article Fifteen was a disciplinary measure just short of a court-martial.

"How come they didn't give him an extended sick leave or something?"

"Psychiatrist's idea. Betty said the psychiatrist told her that Harlan had a poor self-image and that to put him on sick leave would only increase his sense of failure. He was transferred from wardmaster in coronary care unit to the medical holding company. As far as I know, until last weekend, Harlan hadn't had a drink for two months."

"What happened last weekend?"

"Memories. During his first tour in Vietnam, Harlan served as field medic with the Eighty-second. He has a Silver Star."

The Silver Star recognized uncommon bravery in combat.

"I took our kids to see the parade on Sunday. When we left, I saw Harlan and a couple of other Eighty-second medics getting into a car. They'd obviously been drinking."

"Did you talk to him?"

"No. Patsy and I try to protect our kids from drunks as much as possible. Besides, they were tired of soldiers. They wanted ice cream."

Just before two o'clock, Nancy Paxton arrived, wearing civilian clothes. She walked through the ward, saying good-bye to each of the remaining patients, hugging them, telling them to work on getting better. Work stopped completely.

The nurses, corpsmen, and patients crowded into the day room for a big, noisy party. Colonel Norton and Major Buckner attended to represent the chief nurse's office, and Colonel Granger presented Captain Paxton with a plaque thanking her for her services. Pepper expected Harlan to be there, but the wardmaster never reappeared. She had more curiosity than ever about his meeting with Major Buckner in the uniform room.

When the party was winding down, she noticed one of the patients, standing in the hall. He was nineteen and had been shot in the shoulder by a sniper. Until his cast came off, the doctors wouldn't know how much nerve damage he had or if he would regain any use of his right arm. Pepper thought him incredibly young and her heart ached every time she looked at him. An older couple stood with him, each of them carrying brown paper bags.

Nancy put down her punch cup and excused herself. Curious, Pepper followed her.

"I'm Captain Paxton and you must be Mamaw and Papaw. He talks about you all the time. I'm glad to meet you."

Damn, Pepper thought, she does that so well. Would she ever learn to be that gracious with families?

The man spoke, "Excuse us for interrupting your party."

"They just come for the punch and sandwiches. They'll hardly miss me." She pulled Pepper forward. "This is Captain Pepperhawk. She will be taking over from me as head nurse. Could I get you something, coffee or punch? We've plenty of food."

"No, thank you. Tony wants us to take him out for pizza."

The young man was practically bouncing up and down. "Could we see you, in private like, for a minute?"

"Let's go to the treatment room," Nancy said, leading the party in that direction. Pepper hoped no one would mind if she came along. Something was happening here and she wanted to find out what. "Did you have a nice trip?"

"It was tolerable fine," the woman said.

When they were in the treatment room, Papaw nodded. "Go ahead, son."

He pulled himself up, like a child reciting before a class. "You've been so nice to me, I wanted to give you something. Mamaw, she makes the best mayhaw jelly around, but you can't make mayhaw jelly in July. At least Mamaw says you can't. But she makes loads of other good stuff, don't you, Mamaw?"

"I brought you some strawberry jam instead. I hope it pleases you." She fished in her bag and brought out a small jar.

Nancy took the jar. "Oh, thank you."

Papaw cleared his throat. "When he went to Vietnam we did a lot of praying that the Lord would keep him safe. We're sorry he's come home hurt, but that's the Lord's plan, and we're just waiting for His guidance. We're grateful to you, and the rest of the doctors and the nurses, that he's come home at all.

"I carve toys," he said shyly. "They're not like store toys, but children likes them. My grandson says you and your husband are fixing to have a family." He reached in the bag and took out a perfect miniature wooden wagon. "I thought maybe a wagon. If you have a boy, he can play wagon train with it, and if you have a girl, she can take her dolls for a ride in it."

Nancy put her hand up over her mouth. "Oh, my," she finally managed to say. She looked the wagon over carefully, put it back into the brown paper bag, then hugged everyone. "I'd love to hear from you, know how he gets on when they take his cast off. Would it be imposing if I gave you our address?"

"That would be fine," Mamaw said. "And when the mayhaws get ripe, I'll make you up some jelly."

"Let's go help gather up his things. I'm sure he wants to go get that pizza." The two women walked down the hall, talking together like old friends, with the two men walking behind them. Pepper watched them go, thinking how wrong she had been to think that families were in the way.

Lieutenant Forbes came from the nurses' station and handed her the ward keys. "You okay, Captain?"

Pepper hefted the keys, feeling their weight, thinking about young men and their families. "I'm fine. I feel like I've just inherited the keys to the kingdom."

Chapter 10

Saturday afternoon, Pepper lay on her living room couch, dropping cold, sticky globs of ice cream and Oreo cookies into her mouth. Thanks to Avivah, she now had a bank account, groceries, and a dry cleaner she trusted. The weekend stretched before her without any commitments.

A fist pounded on her door. "Pembrook, open this goddamn door. I'm ready to party."

Pepper stuck the spoon straight up in the ice cream, cradled the bowl in one arm, and opened the door. "May I help you?"

A balding, stocky man, dressed in jeans and a loud tropical shirt, paused with his fist raised to strike the door again. He looked at the number beside the apartment door, then back at Pepper.

"Where's Mister Levy?"

"Gone temporary duty to Ft. Huachuca, Arizona. Who are you?"

"Sergeant First Class Benjamin Kirkpatrick, John F. Kennedy Special Warfare Center. Who are you?"

"Captain Elizabeth Pepperhawk, Womack Army Hospital."

Sergeant Kirkpatrick took the bowl of ice cream. Around a gooey mouthful, waving the spoon in Pepper's direction, he asked, "What are you doing in Pembrook's apartment?"

"None of your business."

She heard a chuckle. Avivah stood in her open apartment door, leaning against the door jamb.

"Good for you, Pepper. I see you've met Benny the Beanie."

The man shoved the bowl back into Pepper's hands, grabbed Avivah, and swung her around. "Avivah, I'm even glad to see you."

Avivah beat playfully on the man's shoulders. "Put me down, you animal. He's like this every time he gets back."

"Back from where?"

Benny set Avivah down. "Jungle survival school. I've just spent two months in the Panamanian jungle, up to my ass in snakes, leeches, and fungus. I want a meal I don't have to kill first and a gallon of beer. You two want to join me?"

"Yes."

"No. Pepper, let me warn you about the Beanie here. He teaches jungle survival, so he's gone for months at a time. This is good. Then he comes back with a new shirt. This is bad." She appraised the electric blue and tangerine flowers. "Not as bad as last time, Benny. Did you buy this shirt with your eyes open?"

Benny's round, smooth face contorted as he made a face at Avivah. His green eyes had a tired, frantic quality about them. Pepper remembered the same look in her mirror in Qui Nhon.

"Anyway," Avivah continued, "he comes back with a new shirt, bouncing off the wall because he hasn't been in civilization for months. He's impossible until he runs out of energy. We let Pembrook deactivate Benny—like an un-exploded bomb—and give him back to us when he's safe. Goodness knows what we're going to do since Pembrook isn't here."

Benny swept Avivah into his arms again and danced her around the balcony. "You will love me, and cherish me, and go Texas two-stepping with me."

Avivah pushed him towards Pepper. "You want him? He's yours. *Mazel tov*."

Benny, singing, "I Could Waltz Across Texas with You," danced Pepper and her bowl of ice cream across the narrow concrete balcony. "Phone Pembrook. Find out what he does," she called to Avivah as Benny tried to dip her over the balcony railing.

"Maybe feeding him would help."

They sent Benny for take-out, thinking the intense midday heat might wilt him. No such luck. He came back an hour later with fried chicken, potato salad, coleslaw, rolls, and beer. Sitting at Avivah's kitchen table, the three of them went through the food, the beer, and several hours of nonstop storytelling before Benny ran out of energy. Pepper wrapped herself in his stories. Listening to him felt just like being back in Qui Nhon, when the helicopter pilots told "No shit, there I was" stories. Benny finally leaned back against his chair and blew out a long breath. "I feel like I've been run over by a truck."

Avivah put the last of the garbage in a plastic bag. "You look like it. When did you come out of the jungle?"

"Wednesday night. In the middle of the worst goddamn rainstorm I've seen. We swam the last fifty yards to the trucks. We debriefed Thursday, had a party Thursday night, and then spent eighteen bone-jarring, earsplitting hours in a military transport plane. I got in at 0300 hours this morning, took a shower, and fell into bed."

He leaned forward, resting his chin on his hand. Without the frantic expression, he now just looked tired. "So who are you, Captain Elizabeth Pepperhawk, and how do you come to be here?"

A lump caught in Pepper's throat. She'd heard that same

line, with variations, too many times in the officers' club in Qui Nhon.

"If you mean, how do I come to be in this apartment, I'm house-sitting for Pembrook. I'm the new head nurse on Ward Six-A, and I came here by way of Fort Sam Houston, Fort Riley, and the Sixty-seventh Evac in Qui Nhon."

"Been back long?"

"Six weeks."

"You okay?"

Every day she was on leave, her parents asked her if she was all right. They meant, was she likely to go crazy and embarrass them? They read about people who had been to Vietnam and went crazy after they came home. People asked her Sunday night if she was all right. All right after finding a body, they meant. Captain Paxton asked her if things were all right. Was she settling into the work? Benny asked the question as one Vietnam veteran to another, the way no one ever asked her the question before. Looking for the one answer she didn't know. She began to cry.

"I think so. I don't know. Do I look all right?"

"You look terrific." He took her hand and kissed her palm. "Welcome home, pretty lady."

Pepper bent her head. Long wracking sobs shook her body. Benny pulled her to her feet and held her. Avivah and her kitchen disappeared so that Pepper's whole world became Benny's arms around her. "I should never have come home," she sobbed into his shoulder. "I should still be in Qui Nhon where I understood what was going on."

Even as she said it, she remembered how, three weeks before she left Qui Nhon, she sat in a deserted corner behind the hospital and cried because she couldn't stand being in Vietnam any longer.

"I don't belong anywhere. Not there, not here. There's no safe place any more."

He stopped hugging her and pushed damp hair out of her eyes. "There never was. We just thought we were safe."

Pepper slid her hands off his shoulders and over his chest, stopping suddenly as her fingers touched deep scars that spread out, covering his whole right side like a map of a river delta.

He removed his shirt. "Plei Girang. An A-camp near Pleiku. June 12, 1968. We were burning perimeter ground cover. I got too close to a flame thrower."

Pepper reverently traced the scars. "Stupid thing to do."

"The sappers on the other side of the ground cover distracted me."

"You okay?"

Benny shrugged, "Most days." He put on his shirt and buttoned it. "You will be, too. Want some coffee?"

"Sure." Embarrassed, Pepper dried her eyes and turned to apologize to Avivah, but her chair was empty. Pepper found her on the couch, thumbing idly through a magazine.

"I'm sorry. I don't know what happened."

"It's okay."

It wasn't okay but Pepper didn't know why it wasn't. She washed her face in Avivah's bathroom, and tried, unsuccessfully, to sort out her feelings. She almost thought Avivah was jealous, but that didn't make any sense. Pepper was certain Avivah and Benny were just friends. Why would it matter to Avivah if she and Benny hugged? When she came back to the living room, Benny handed her a coffee cup.

"Want to talk?"

"Not much to talk about. When you called me *pretty lady*, something hurt. Did you ever run into a special forces

111

major named Darby Baxter? Solid, blond, good-looking. north Georgia accent."

"I know Baxter."

She turned to Avivah. "He taught us compass and map reading at Fort Sam Houston. He always called the nurses *pretty lady*. A lot of us had a crush on him. All kinds of stories circulated about him. What's the truth, Benny. Was he a hero or did he screw up?"

"You'll have to ask him. You had a crush on Darby Baxter? God help us."

Pepper dribbled a spoonful of coffee into the cup, over and over. "Some welcome home. I got an assignment I'm not sure I can handle, I started off on the wrong foot with my chief nurse, and the first thing I did here was discover a body."

Benny took his coffee and sat in the recliner. "What kind of body?"

"A dead one. In Normandy House. He'd been murdered. Oh, yeah, you wouldn't know any of this. I guess it didn't make the Panama papers."

"Wouldn't matter. No papers in the jungle. What's shaking, Avivah?"

Avivah recounted the discovery of the body and a summary of what had been in the paper the past week.

Benny listened as if he had a personal stake in Dermid Hagan's death. When she finished, he asked, "Any connection to the MacDonald murders?"

"I don't think so."

Benny relaxed. "Thank God. Special forces got enough bad publicity out of that one." He turned to Pepper. "You know about the MacDonald murders?"

"I do now, but what I don't understand is why everyone freaked so much over the whole MacDonald thing."

Benny looked at his coffee cup as if he expected to find the secret to the universe there. "One way or another, we failed Jeff MacDonald."

"What do you mean?"

"Either he was an abusive, drunken officer who built a head of steam and murdered his family, or he wasn't. If he was, then no one cared enough about him and his family to get him help in time. And if he wasn't, then he went through a horrible time and no one lifted a hand to help him. Either way, we haven't taken care of our own, and special forces prides itself on taking care of its own. Every time someone mentions MacDonald, I want to sneak off and hide. A lot of berets feel the same way."

"Did you know him?"

"Saw him around a couple of times. Never even spoke to him. He was still family. Thank God this Dermid Hagan wasn't a beret, too."

"I forgot to tell you, Avivah, but I think you'd better talk to one of my patients. Sergeant Cody Doan must have known Dermid Hagan."

Avivah sat up straighter. "What makes you think that?"

"When he read the newspaper article Friday morning, he almost fainted. Then he went downstairs and made an angry phone call. I looked up his home of record on his chart. He's from Marshall, too."

She reached for the phone. "I'll send someone over right away."

"He's on weekend pass."

"You let him leave?"

"I don't have the authority to keep people from pass unless there's a medical reason. You can talk to Doan on Monday."

"If he comes back."

"He'll be back."

The two women stared warily at each other.

Benny took a set of keys out of his pocket. "How about a movie, ladies?"

He bundled them into his truck and drove Fayetteville streets as if they were jungle roads in Panama. Benny parked outside the John F. Kennedy Special Warfare Center.

"I thought we were going to the movies."

"Private showing."

Avivah looked dubious. "Not a porn film, I hope?"

The idea never occurred to Pepper. Her face turned red.

Benny's round face assumed an injured puppy look. "I am shocked and disturbed that you would even suggest that. What we're going to watch comes straight from Hollywood. Wait here. I have to deactivate the door alarm."

Pepper wandered across the parking lot to look at the seven-foot bronze statue of a special forces soldier. His beret sat firmly on his head, and his arms bulged under tightly-rolled fatigue sleeves. Pepper realized his sleeves fell into the same easy creases as hers had. The statue's left arm extended toward her, his eyes focused on the future. Pepper wondered if he saw peace or war.

Benny came up behind her very quietly, but she knew he stood there. "Captain Pepperhawk, meet Bronze Bruce."

He sounded like he was reading a pamphlet. "His left hand is extended in friendship. Note that his foot rests on a rock and there is a snake under the rock. His heel is on the oppressor's head; that's what the snake is supposed to represent. His weapon is ready, but his finger is off the trigger and the safety is on. He'll fight only if he can't find another way. Don't take him too seriously, Pepper. We don't."

"Yes, *you* do." She laid her hand on his arm. "Thank you. For what he means."

114

Benny took her hand and squeezed it. "You ever know any special forces in Qui Nhon?"

"No."

"Pity. I think you might have liked them. I know they would have liked you."

"Is it true that people who have been in Vietnam go crazy around loud noises, have flashbacks, or something?"

"Some do. I've been under a table more than once when a car backfired. Are you having flashbacks?"

"I'm not sure. Have you ever been to the Grove Park Inn in Asheville?"

"No."

"It's a fancy place, expensive. While I was checking in, a woman, who dressed like she dripped money, pushed her way to the front of the line and argued with the desk clerk about her room. He didn't even look at me when he took my registration form and money. He slid a room key across the counter toward me and it went too far. It fell off the edge of the desk and I bent down to pick it up."

Pepper stopped and put her hands together, her thumbs pushing into the corners of her eyes. "There were some kids in the parking lot with firecrackers. They went off as I was picking up the key. I dove for the floor. A couple of bell-hops tried to help me up. I pulled them to the floor and yelled, 'Incoming. Get down.'

"I guess they thought I was having a fit. The desk clerk insisted that he was going to call a doctor and I screamed at him that I didn't need a doctor."

Benny smiled. "No, Pepper, you screamed at him that you didn't need a goddamn doctor, or was it a mother-fucking doctor?"

Pepper smiled. "It was one of the two. Finally, they let me go. I managed to get to my room before I started crying.

I couldn't stop crying. Was that a flashback?"

"No. That was a reaction to a loud noise. What did you do?"

"I bought some cold drinks from a vending machine and I had a bottle of bourbon in my suitcase. I cried, shook, and drank all evening, trying to remember every detail about Vietnam. I've only been gone six weeks and I've already forgotten some of the small details. What if I forget it all, Benny? What if I spent a year there and, by next year, I can't remember any of it?"

"Believe me, pretty lady, you won't forget."

"Sunday morning, I was so ashamed, I snuck down to the lobby and left my key in the quick check-out. That's why no one from room service or anywhere else remembers seeing me after I checked in. When the CID asked me about Saturday night and Sunday morning, I was too ashamed to tell the truth, that I'd been drunk out of my mind. I guess I'll have to tell."

"I guess you will."

"What do I do about the drinking?"

"How many times have you been drunk since you got home?"

"Just that one night. I also drank a glass of wine at dinner the night after I got here, and some champagne at my aunt's."

"Are you fighting it all the time, like you want to drink, but won't let yourself?"

"Mostly I worry about if I've got a drinking problem or not."

"Hell, Pepper, the first time I came home from 'Nam I was drunk for a month. If you think you have a problem, get help. The Army isn't as blind to that kind of situation as you may think."

Pepper remembered Harlan Carter. "I guess they aren't."

"Come on, Avivah is waiting."

"Benny, what's with her? It's like there is something eating at her."

"There is."

"You going to tell me?"

"Like I said about Darby Baxter, you'll have to ask her yourself."

After a few minutes, Benny waved generously at the thirty-seat theater. "Take any seat in the house, ladies. I have to thread the projector."

Pepper and Avivah took seats in the middle of the auditorium. There was a whirr from the projector and the screen flashed. Benny came out of the projection booth, turned a light dimmer, and climbed over several rows of seat backs as the lights in the auditorium slowly dimmed. He wedged himself in between the two women, making Avivah move one seat to the right.

"This, ladies, is Hollywood's latest attempt to portray the green beret as he really is. A little piece called *Billy Jack*. Released in a limited number of theaters last month."

"How come you have a copy?"

"A Hollywood connection. A very special lady. I'd tell you, but I'm not sure you have the right security clearance. Shhh, it's starting."

They watched the movie, taking turns making *sotto voce* comments from time to time. When Tom Laughlin took his shoes off, Benny sank down into his chair and moaned.

Pepper whispered to him, "What's wrong?"

"We survived Robin Moore. We survived *The Ballad of the Green Berets*. We survived John Wayne. I suppose we'll survive *Billy Jack*, too."

"Shhh," Avivah said.

Pepper looked at Avivah's face. Her expression of jealousy filled the space between them. She wants to go to Vietnam, Pepper realized, wants it so bad that she can taste it.

Chapter 11

Avivah lay awake Sunday night, thinking about whether Cody Doan might have an important clue for her murder investigation. *Her* investigation. The proprietary feeling surprised her. She dug deeper, trying to find out what was behind her sudden decision that Dermid Hagan's murder was her case.

All right, she was jealous of the way Pepper and Benny connected. She'd met Benny the day she moved into her apartment. The first time Benny hugged her, Avivah realized he had burn scars, but she'd never seen them. Until today, Benny never took off his shirt in front of her.

But he did for Pepper. That Benny allowed Pepper to touch him startled Avivah. Even if he had shown her his scars, she would never have traced them in the intimate, almost indecent way Pepper did. Benny had allowed her to explore to her heart's content.

What had Pepper said to him when they stood looking at Bronze Bruce? Standing by Benny's truck, Avivah had watched Pepper touch Benny's arm, and saw the way he responded, as if Pepper touched something deep inside him.

Avivah felt left out and angry with the Army. It wasn't her fault she hadn't gone to Vietnam. She'd repeatedly volunteered, and been turned down each time because she was a woman. If she couldn't have Vietnam, then she wanted to solve this murder as a consolation prize.

Monday morning, after very little sleep, she showered,

dressed, and arrived at Captain Delaney's office by 0700 hours, only to discover that Delaney had left for Marshall. She cornered Gilbert Plauche and laid out what she knew about Cody Doan. "I want to be in on that interview."

"Get your hat."

After hearing Pepper complain about how she didn't know if she would make a good head nurse, the calm, professional air her friend displayed on duty surprised Avivah. "Sergeant Doan is in a six-bed bay. I don't imagine you want to interview him there."

"Do you have an empty room we can use?"

"Not today. We've got loads of patients going to surgery and a med-evac due in any minute. Every room is spoken for."

"We'll take him down to the Brigade office."

"The chief of orthopedic surgery put Doan on strict bed rest this morning, and told Doan if his feet so much as touched the floor, he'd personally Article Fifteen him for self-inflicted injury. Why don't you wait in the day room? I'll phone his doctor."

Two patients stopped playing cards when the military police officers entered the day room. They wheeled themselves out without saying a word. The police make people nervous, Avivah thought.

Gil wandered over to the window and looked at the grey, wet day. Heavy summer rain beat against the windows. "I don't like hospitals. They make me nervous."

The double doors next to the day room swung open to admit a parade of four stretchers, pushed by hospital staff. This must be the med-evac. The stretchers passed the day room so quickly that Avivah managed only a brief impression of young faces, dark blue blankets, and bright green plastic bags resting on each man's chest. Two of the men wore body casts. The third had an arm in a cast, held at an odd angle by a metal platform. The fourth man had only one leg-shaped bulge under the blankets.

She watched the parade stop in front of the nurses' station. Pepper came out carrying four clipboards. She read the evacuation tag attached to the first man's pajama shirt, said something to him, and they both laughed. She patted his shoulder, balanced one of the clipboards on his chest, and waved the stretcher on toward the ward. For someone who didn't think she wanted this assignment, Pepper looked very much at home.

A man in his late twenties, dressed in the ubiquitous, blue Army pajamas, wheeled himself from the ward. His right leg rested on a pillow on top of a plywood extension laid over the wheelchair seat. As he came closer, Avivah saw that his right foot bent forward as if he couldn't straighten it. The skin over the swollen ankle looked shiny and red.

The man wheeled himself into the room. "Head nurse said you wanted to see me."

Avivah closed the door behind him, moved a straight-backed chair under the door knob, and pulled the orange and green drapes across the glass windows.

Major Plauche turned from the window. "Are you Cody Doan?"

"Yeah."

This guy had attitude before he ever joined the Army. Being wounded hadn't knocked it out of him.

Major Plauche scowled. "Sergeant, the correct response is 'Yes, sir.' "

Doan drew himself up in the wheelchair, as close as he could come to attention. "Yes, sir. I'm Sergeant Cody Doan, sir."

Plauche indicated that Doan should wheel his chair to

the table. "We want to talk to you about Dermid Hagan."

He sat across from Doan. Avivah sat in one of the vinyl-covered chairs near the door and took a notebook out of her pocket. The rain beat steadily on the window.

Major Plauche explained to Sergeant Doan that this was a formal statement, which he would be expected to sign. "To begin, state your name, rank, and current duty assignment."

Doan nodded in Avivah's direction. "What's she doing here?"

"She is a military police officer."

Doan made a little movement with his mouth. "My name is Cody Terrance Doan, Sergeant, currently assigned to the Medical Holding Company, Womack Army Hospital."

"Were you acquainted with Dermid Hagan, the man whose body was discovered in Normandy House eight days ago?"

"I knew someone named Dermid Hagan, but I don't know if it's the same person. Maybe the dead guy was a different Dermid Hagan."

Major Plauche leaned across the table. "Son, where do you want to spend the next few days? In bed, like your doctor ordered, or in a cell?"

Doan tried to outstare Gilbert and lost. "How did you find me?"

"You were very upset when you read the murdered man's identity in the paper."

"Bet that bitch of a head nurse told you that. She should mind her own business."

You are her business, Avivah thought, and you're lucky that you are.

Cody Doan shifted uneasily in the wheelchair. "All right. I knew Dermid. We grew up together in Marshall."

"Did you join the Army together?"

"I was drafted. Dermid, he enlisted. We told him he was crazy. He had a deferment to go to tech school."

"Did he tell you why he enlisted?"

"He said he missed us, but I never believed him. Dermid always had an angle. I thought he'd gotten some girl pregnant, but my sister never wrote me about any misbegotten babies; maybe I was wrong."

"You said, 'He missed *us.*' Who's us?"

"Me and Boyd Ramsey."

"Who's Boyd Ramsey?"

"A friend of ours."

"Where's Boyd now?"

"If it's a good day, he's on the street. If it's a bad day, he's locked up in the nut ward in the Veterans' Hospital in Asheville."

"How come?"

"Because a hootch roof fell on him during a mortar attack. It permanently scrambled his marbles."

"The three of you stayed together in the Army?"

"Yeah, odd, isn't it?"

"Did Dermid have an angle on that?"

Doan chuckled. "Not even Dermid could fuck the Army. Usually they take three guys who've been together all their lives and send one to Pennsylvania, one to Texas, and the third to Alaska. I guess the person in charge of screw-ups had the day off when our assignments were handed out. We all ended up in an engineering company outside of Long Bien."

"When?"

"I got there in May of '68. Dermid and Boyd arrived in June."

"When was Boyd hurt?"

"January 10, 1969."

He remembered the exact date, probably even the exact

hour. Just like Benny did, Avivah thought.

What did she remember the exact date, the exact hour of? May 20, 1961, 5:00 p.m. She and her mother sat on a couch in the front room of a small frame house in Montgomery, Alabama. Avivah remembered the embroidered butterflies with their yellow-gold wings on the antimacassars. A man came to the living room door and said, "It's time."

She stood up. "I'm going. I have to." Her mother nodded, and hugged her, whispering a Jewish blessing in her ear.

She understood how Cody Doan could remember the exact date his friend had been wounded. She pulled herself back to his story.

"Our compound took incoming. The hootch roof collapsed before Boyd made it to the bunker. When we pulled him out, he had a hole in his head. Blood covered everything. When I loaded his body on that Dustoff chopper, I figured he was already dead."

Avivah tried, unsuccessfully, to imagine what it would be like to load a friend's body on a Dustoff chopper. Benny would know. Pepper might know. Jealousy nibbled at her.

"So the next afternoon, the chaplain tells us that Boyd's got a real bad brain injury. They'd evaced him to the Third Field in Saigon. He asked us if we wanted to pray for him, so we knelt down and he said a few words and we said some prayers."

Major Plauche consulted a piece of paper he'd taken from his pocket. "That was the same month that Dermid supposedly died?"

"It was a shitty month all around. Dermid had leave coming. I bet him he wouldn't get it; they were canceling leaves because of Tet. I didn't figure rightly on Dermid. Almost everybody else had his leave canceled, but he got to go. He called me from Saigon. Said Boyd was in a coma and they didn't know if he'd ever wake up, but, if he survived a little longer, they were shipping him to Japan."

"When was this?"

"January 19, 1969. The day before Dermid's accident. That's the last I heard from him in Vietnam."

Avivah expected Gilbert to pounce on those two last words, but he didn't interrupt Doan's story.

"The next day the chaplain's back, telling us Dermid was run over by a bus in Saigon. Dermid was dead, Boyd was a vegetable, and three months later, I stepped on a mine. End of story."

Except, Avivah thought, that Dermid wasn't dead. It was far from the end of the story.

"How did Dermid behave just before he went on leave? Did he seem bothered or preoccupied?"

Doan shifted in the chair, rearranged his leg on the pillow, and grimaced. "The gooks started Tet early. We worked sixteen-hour days repairing the roads, the airfield, the water supply they blew up every night. For days, I'd been too tired to say more to Dermid than, 'Pass the fucking ketchup.' "

"When did you learn Dermid didn't die in Saigon?"

"I had a letter from him at the end of April of this year."

"That must have been a shock."

Doan smirked. "What do you think?"

"Did you notice the postmark on the letter?"

"Montreal, Quebec."

"How did he know where to mail the letter?"

"I thought at first he'd talked to my family. I hinted around, asking if any old buddies called. I couldn't just fucking come out and ask if they'd had a call from a dead man. But they said no one asked about me. I finally figured out he must have seen *60 Minutes*."

"The television program?"

"Yeah, they did a bit on the history of the Eighty-second Airborne and the upcoming reunion. I got to show Harry Reasoner our jump site."

"Engineers aren't usually airborne-qualified."

"I jump-qualified after I got back from 'Nam." He rubbed his thigh. "Between the first and second times that I hurt my leg. The producers weren't too interested in details. I wore an Eighty-second patch on my shoulder, I'd been to Vietnam, and I limped. Made for what they call a good visual."

"What makes you think Dermid knew where you were from the television program?"

"The envelope was addressed to me, care of the Eighty-second Airborne, Fort Bragg. He could have gotten that much from the television program. I guess he trusted the post locator to find me."

"How soon after the program was shown did you get the letter?"

"They showed the program on April 11 and the letter arrived April 30."

"What did the letter say?"

"Said he wanted to come home."

"Did you keep it?"

"No. I thought at first it was a fucking sick joke, but I was curious. I sent a letter back asking for a reply to general delivery, Fayetteville, saying that, before I'd believe he really was Dermid, he'd have to tell me what we won in Mr. O'Byrne's class. All the next letter said was 'five hundred dollars and autographed pictures of Richard Petty.' That freaked me because only Dermid or someone from Marshall would have known that."

"Did you hear from him after that?"

"I wrote him back, asking for a phone number, so I could call him. He wrote saying he was moving around and didn't have a permanent phone, so I sent him my phone number and told him to call me. Then my ankle acted up and I've been in and out of the hospital for the past three months. I wrote him a couple more letters. They weren't returned, they weren't answered. I fucking went crazy, trying to figure out what the scam was."

"Did you ever hear from him again?"

"He called me three days before he died. Said he was coming to Fort Bragg. Asked me to pick a public place to meet him Sunday afternoon. I gave him directions about how to get to the Fayetteville cemetery."

"Was it Dermid's voice on the phone?"

"It was him. I'm sure of that."

"Why meet at the cemetery?"

"Fucking good joke, meeting a dead man in a cemetery." When Doan saw that Gilbert Plauche wasn't laughing, he shrugged. "The tombstones are short. Good field of vision all around so no one can sneak up on you. It was a place to talk and not be overheard. We were supposed to meet at 1500 hours, but he never showed up. I spent Monday calling every fucking motel in town."

"Why didn't you contact us when the article was in the paper asking for information? Did you recognize Dermid as the man in the drawing?"

"I didn't see that paper. I checked into the hospital Tuesday for surgery on Wednesday. I didn't feel good for a couple of days after surgery and I didn't look at a paper until Friday morning. There was his name, screaming at me from the front page."

Avivah asked, "Who did you phone after you saw his name?"

Dermid glared at her. "That bitch of a nurse did have me followed. Not that it matters, but I called my sister in Marshall."

"Why?"

"She's family. I don't need a reason to call my sister. I was worried about Mrs. Hagan, Dermid's mother. She was good to the three of us. I wanted my sister to go see her. And I wanted her to look up Boyd, see if he'd heard Dermid was dead. Hell, I wasn't able to handle the news, and I had all my marbles. I didn't know how Boyd would understand it all."

Gil looked at Avivah. "Any more questions?"

"What was Dermid like? Before you went to Vietnam?"

Cody shrugged. "He was just this guy I grew up with. We went fishing and hung out and worked on cars."

"You said he always had an angle going? Was he honest?"

"Hell, yes. Not that he wouldn't work a situation to his own advantage, but he never did anything against the law. Well, except maybe drive a little too fast and pass a bottle now and then at a high school dance, but we all did that."

"Did he drink?"

"No more than the next guy."

"Did he do drugs?"

"Not much: a little pot, some pills, just like everyone else."

"Can you think of any reason that someone would want him dead?

"None."

"What I don't understand," Gil interrupted, "is why he reappeared after being missing for two years."

Doan shifted his weight again. "I told you, it was in his letter. He was homesick. He wanted to come home."

Chapter 12

Avivah phoned Captain Delaney in Marshall with a report on Cody Doan's interview. He dismissed her with, "I'll look at his statement when I have time." His tone said that he clearly thought what he was doing in Marshall was more important than anything she could possibly do.

From what Doan said, Avivah guessed right about Dermid's background. Fishing. Cars. Hanging out. Nothing in his background gave her a clue why, on January 19, 1969, Specialist Hagan left Long Bien for a leave he'd requested months earlier, stopped to see his friend in the hospital, phoned back to his unit, and then, twenty-four hours later, faked his death and disappeared.

Before she went to Germany, Avivah had been stationed at Fort Leonard Woods, the home of Army Engineers. She tried to remember what she knew about engineers and combat units, but all she could remember was that some companies were combat units and some weren't. Doan talked about mortar attacks, but he'd also sounded like they weren't an everyday occurrence.

All special forces soldiers cross-trained in two specialties. Benny graduated from both engineering and communications schools. She dialed a number from memory.

"Special Warfare Center, Sergeant Kirkpatrick."

"Benny, it's Avivah. How can I tell if an engineering company in Vietnam was a combat unit or not?"

"Depends on where they were stationed and what they were assigned to do."

"Stationed in Long Bien and assigned to build a water supply and repair roads and the airfield."

"Probably not a combat outfit, but that's just a guess."

"Why would someone disappear in Vietnam?"

There was a small chuckle, then a full minute of silence.

"Benny?"

"I'm here. I'm just trying to think of how to answer that. You're not talking about someone disappearing in combat, are you?"

"No, someone going on leave to catch a plane in Saigon, and just falling off the face of the earth for year and a half."

"Sounds like desertion."

"Why would a man desert?"

"Fear, or exhaustion. Maybe he'd received orders for an assignment he couldn't face. Maybe he'd shacked up with a Vietnamese girl. Maybe alcohol or drugs clouded his judgment. Maybe he knew too much about the black market and disappeared for his health. Maybe . . . remember that line in the movie where Billy Jack told the young boy about moral toughness?"

"Yes?"

"Maybe he lacked moral toughness. How long had this guy been in country?"

"About six months."

"First tour?"

"Yes."

"Black? White? Hispanic?"

"White."

"How old?"

Avivah quickly pulled the information on Dermid from the folder on her desk. "Just turned twenty."

"Anything unusual happen to him before he disappeared?"

"Nine days before he deserted, their compound took incoming. One of his best friends received a severe head injury. They didn't think the friend would survive. Would you consider that unusual?"

Another long silence, a different silence in which Avivah heard the gulf of experience between her and Benny.

He spoke slowly, like he would explain to a child. "Yes, Avivah, I consider that unusual."

"Don't patronize me."

"All right. Cool down. Was their compound frequently shelled?"

"I don't think so."

"For the average soldier, an occasional shelling and seeing a friend wounded doesn't sound like enough to make him desert. Look for something else going on."

If Dermid had deserted, she wanted to know what was going on inside his head. Remembering Pepper's unabashed confidence in touching Benny's scars, Avivah took a chance on asking him a question she'd never dare ask otherwise. "Did you ever think about deserting?"

"Yes."

"You did?"

"Everybody gets the urge, Avivah. It's just some of us figure out you can't solve things by running away."

"How would you have done it?"

"Found a way to get to Bangkok or Singapore. It's easy to buy a fake passport there."

Sergeant Ramerez came out of the communication room carrying a sheaf of papers. He stopped in front of Avivah's desk and exaggeratedly waved them, like they were on fire. Avivah held up one hand with the fingers spread apart and silently mouthed *five minutes,* pointing to the phone. Instead of leaving, Ramerez sat in one of the vacant desk chairs and rocked back and forth. Avivah tried to remember the last thing Benny had said.

"Wouldn't a fake passport be expensive?"

"It costs."

"And wouldn't you need contacts? You know, like James Bond has."

"It's easier than you think. I've known a couple of guys who managed it."

"Where did they go?"

"Canada or Sweden."

"Why Canada?"

"There's an underground railway for draft dodgers and deserters. They'll set up the person some place with a fake identification."

"Someplace like Montreal?"

"Quebec has a large ex-American community."

"Thanks, Benny. I've got to go. Yes, Ramerez," she said, hanging up the receiver.

"We just received the accident report filed in Saigon."

"So give. You're acting like this solves the whole mystery."

He handed her three pieces of paper. "A bus hit Dermid Hagan, or someone the Army thought was Dermid Hagan, about 1400 hours local time, Monday, January 20, 1969. The two GI witnesses to the accident are both out of the Army by now. Don't hold your breath that we can find them."

He picked one page out of the stack of papers he carried. "Look at this. Another GI didn't witness the accident, but showed up minutes later and tried to render first aid. He identified the body as Dermid Hagan."

Avivah looked at the name. "So?"

"About two months ago we were called to the picnic area over by the lake. One of the wardmasters from Womack went off his nut and tried to take a swing at his wife with a beer bottle. An ambulance carted him off to the psych ward. I thought I recognized the name so I pulled the file from that call. Harlan Carter, both of them."

"Could be two guys with the same name."

Ramerez held the two pieces of paper side by side. "Harlan Carter, Wardmaster, Third Field Hospital, Saigon. Harlan Carter, Wardmaster, Medical Holding Company, Fort Bragg. Same name, same rank, same military occupational specialty. My bet is same guy. I called to see if he was on duty right now, but he signed off duty at 1515 hours. What do you figure the chances are he's at home right now?"

Avivah took her military police helmet off the corner of her desk. "Let's go have a talk with Wardmaster Carter."

It took them five minutes to reach Carter's address, a duplex in the married enlisted men's quarters. Two men, chatting as they coiled lawn sprinklers, stopped talking and eyed the military police jeep as it parked at the curb. Neighbors were always curious when the police arrived.

No lights shone in either side of the duplex. The driveway on the right and that half of the duplex looked deserted. The grass on that side had not been mowed recently and the yard had none of the usual detritus of children's toys, bikes, or flowers associated with the lawns in the married quarters. Avivah knew Fort Bragg had too much of a housing shortage for half a duplex to stand empty.

Ramerez checked the address. He pointed to the part of the duplex with close cropped grass. "Left side."

A green garden hose coiled neatly beneath the faucet and

an older model car, in poor condition, stood parked in the concrete driveway. From habit, Avivah loosened the flap over her service pistol. They went to the door, knocked, waited, knocked again. The duplex remained dark and quiet.

"Let's try the back."

They walked around the side of the house, looking in windows as they walked. Drapes were drawn over all the windows. The back door faced into a common area, where, in the twilight, several children played on a set of playground equipment. The smell of barbecue smoke and cooked meat drifted across the grass. Ramerez knocked on the back door. No answer.

Two black girls in shorts, T-shirts, and pigtails jumped off the swing and ran over to them.

"I know you," the taller one said, looking up at Ramerez. "You came and talked to us at school." In a singsong voice, she recited, " 'Before you cross, look left and right. Take someone's hand and hold it tight.' " She pointed to the other little girl. "This is my friend, Jennifer. She hasn't had street safety yet 'cause she won't be in the first grade until this year. She's a lot younger than I am."

Avivah, amused, tried not to show it. "And your name is?"

"Rosa."

"Well, Rosa. We're looking for the man who lives here. Do you know him?"

"Yes."

"Did you see him come home tonight?"

"Yes."

Jennifer joined in. "He had a gun."

Ramerez said, squatting down so that he was closer to the children's height, "A what?"

"When he came home today, Specialist Carter had a gun. My daddy says I have to call him Specialist Carter. I can't call him Harlan like the adults do. He used to have kids, but they moved away. I miss them."

Avivah squatted down as well. "Jennifer, this gun. Was it like this one?" She half-drew her side arm out of her holster.

"No, it was a big one. This big," she said, stretching her arms wide apart. "It's the kind you break," she said, pantomiming breaking a stick. "That's so it's safe," she said to Rosa to show her that, even without first grade, she knew something about safety. "My daddy showed me how he does it when he goes hunting. And it's got two eyes, like this," she said, holding her fingers in two circles around her eyes.

"Double-barreled shotgun," Ramerez said under his breath, as they both stood up.

Suicide weapon of choice for males, Avivah thought. She looked at the ominously dark house.

"My daddy has a key to this house," Rosa said, trying to regain the upper hand in the conversation. "He and Harlan are friends." Apparently she wasn't under any compulsion to call him Specialist Carter.

"Is your daddy home right now?"

"Yes."

Avivah looked at the backs of the duplexes that circled the commons. "Do you live around here?"

"On the next block."

Jennifer pointed to the duplex next door to Harlan Carter's. "I live here."

Avivah took the child's hand and lead her away from the dark back door. "Let's go see your parents."

"You can see my mama, but not my daddy. He's doing a night jump," the child rattled on, as Avivah knocked on the back door. A thin black woman came to the door, drying her hands on a dish towel.

"Yes."

"Captain Avivah Rosen, Military Police. This is Specialist Ramerez. Could we come in for a moment?"

The woman's hand went to her throat in a protective gesture. "Is it Jim?"

"Who's Jim?"

"My daddy," Jennifer said, taking her mother's hand and leaning her head against her thigh.

Families always thought the military police brought bad news, Avivah thought. Sometimes they did.

"No, ma'am. Your husband is just fine, as far as I know. We're trying to reach your neighbor, Harlan Carter."

The woman relaxed. Avivah saw her lips move in what she guessed was either a prayer or a curse. "Come in."

They stepped into a small kitchen, painted yellow and white, heavy with the smell of spaghetti sauce. A pot of sauce was bubbling on the stove and another pot, full of water, had just begun to boil. The table was set with three places. An infant about seven or eight months old, dressed in a faded yellow sleeper, sat in a high chair examining an arrowroot cookie. He looked up briefly as they entered, then went back to his cookie.

"I haven't seen Harlan for several days. It's not Betty, is it? I mean she hasn't come back. Something hasn't happened to her, has it?"

"Why are you worried that something might have happened to her?"

She looked down at the two girls. "Go and play in Jennifer's room, please."

When the girls had gone, the woman closed the swinging door to the living room.

"They had terrible fights before Betty and the kids went to her mother's. Jim went over several times and calmed things down."

And put himself at risk, Avivah thought. He should have called us. She let the lecture pass undelivered. "We knocked on Specialist Carter's door, but there wasn't an answer. Your daughter tells us that he brought a shotgun home this afternoon. You don't happen to have a key to his place, do you?"

"No."

"What about the people on the right side of his duplex? Would they have a key?"

"They've been gone on leave for three weeks. They're due back Sunday night." That explained the semi-deserted look and unmowed yard.

The woman looked toward the closed door behind which children's laughter could be heard. "You don't think . . . anything has happened?"

Ramerez shifted a bit. "We just want to make sure."

"But we would have heard. Oh, my," she said, as her hand went to the throat again in the same protective gesture.

"What's wrong?"

"There was a loud bang just about the time I started the spaghetti sauce. I thought it was a car backfire."

Avivah and Ramerez looked at one another. "Could you take the children to Rosa's house? And ask her father to come back with his key."

The woman already had her purse and was taking her son out of the high chair. He took the cookie with him. "I told Jim, after that terrible MacDonald thing, that he should ask for a transfer. He said this was as safe a place as any. Jennifer, Rosa. Come with me. Right now. We're going over to Rosa's house."

"I'm hungry," Jennifer whined, coming in the door.

Rosa put her arm around her friend. "It's okay. My mom can fix us bread and jam."

Ramerez walked them to the car. The woman backed the car hurriedly out of the driveway. Avivah turned the stove burners off and moved the pot of sauce to a cold burner, putting the lid on it. No sense spoiling good food. Ramerez came back in and reached for the telephone.

"Backup?"

Avivah held up her hand. "Wait. Let's just calm down. I think Jennifer is an accurate historian. She probably did see him bring a gun home this afternoon, and it sounds like a shotgun. But we're just stringing together a whole bunch of what may be coincidences. Let's just get inside the house first."

They sat at the table. Ramerez played nervously with a knife, turning it end over end. Avivah leaned back and closed her eyes. Tires squealed on the driveway and a man hurried through the back door without knocking. Avivah recognized the wardmaster from Pepper's ward. The circle got tighter all the time.

"What's this about Harlan shooting himself?" he said without preamble. Then, "You're one of the policemen that were at the hospital this morning."

She held out her hand. "Captain Avivah Rosen. This is Carlos Ramerez."

"David Willett," he said, shaking hands with each of them in turn.

"All we know is that Specialist Carter is reported to have brought a shotgun home this evening. We understand that he had a psychiatric episode about two months ago and that his wife subsequently left him. We've tried knocking on both the front door and the back door without response.

His car is in the driveway. His neighbor heard a loud noise that may or may not have sounded like a gunshot. We would like your permission to use your key to enter his premises."

He dug in his jeans pocket. "Sure, but let me go in first. I used to be a combat medic."

"And I am a military police officer."

Ramerez interrupted. "Begging your pardon, ma'am, but he's right. If Specialist Carter is in there with a gun and he hasn't pulled the trigger yet, he's less likely to be frightened by someone he knows."

It galled Avivah that she hadn't thought of that. She was more upset than she realized. "All right, but you have about three minutes, then we're in behind you."

By now the sun had set. A single light in the center of the commons cast shadows from the swing set over Harlan's door. Avivah stood beside the back door, looking carefully to see if there was anyone in the commons. For a moment, she regretted not having called for backup.

Avivah and Ramerez stood on either side of Harlan Carter's back door and both drew their service pistols. What were they going to do, Avivah wondered, shoot a man to keep him from shooting himself?

David Willett unlocked the door and pushed it open a little. "Harlan, it's Dave. You in here, Harlan?"

No answer. Willett felt for the light switch and turned it on. A dusty bulb threw a dim glare over the room. "Harlan," he said, walking into the kitchen. Avivah and Ramerez waited a few seconds for an answer, and when there was none, also stepped into the kitchen. This kitchen, Avivah noted, could use cleaning and a fresh coat of paint. Cobwebs hung in murky blue corners. A single plate, cup, frying pan, and some silverware were stacked in a plastic dish drainer, but otherwise, the counters stood empty. The house felt deserted.

Avivah followed the sound of Willett's voice as it moved down the hall, through the living room, up the stairs to the bedrooms on the second floor. Finally Willett called, "He's not here. The place is empty."

Ramerez closed his eyes, blew out a breath, and reholstered his sidearm. Avivah did the same, though without the sound effects. Her sigh was all inside, a sense of letting go of tremendous tension. This could have gone so bad. They walked through the kitchen into the living room, where they met David Willett coming down the stairs. He raised his hands in a bewildered gesture.

"He's not here, but I found the gun." He led them upstairs to a hall closet. Inside a rifle rack was mounted high inside the closet, on a wall. There was a rifle and shotgun chained to the rack. A repair tag from a Fayetteville gun shop dangled from the shotgun.

"There's your shotgun," David Willett said. "Harlan's had it for years. Betty made him keep it in the hall closet under a double lock because of the kids."

Ramerez shook his head. "It's crazy to have guns in a house where there was drinking, domestic violence, and children."

Willett nodded. "I agree. I've been after Harlan to get rid of the guns for a long time."

"So what the neighbor heard was a backfire."

"Looks like," Avivah said. She felt a little sheepish now. They had built a case on scattered bits of evidence and the conversation of children and they had built it wrong. She knew how lucky she was that David Willett had a key and had let them in. If they had broken into the house on the scant evidence they had, they would have been in serious trouble.

Willett looked at his watch. "Do you need me for anything else? Rosa is pretty upset. I want to go home and talk to her."

"No, thanks for coming."

They went downstairs and out through the kitchen door, turning off lights and locking the door behind them. David Willett backed his car out of the driveway. Half a dozen people had gathered across the street, closely watching the military police officers get into their jeep. Avivah wondered what Specialist Carter would think when his neighbors told him that the police had been in his home. In violation of the military code, she'd entered an enlisted man's home on very flimsy evidence. It hadn't seemed flimsy at the time, but, in retrospect, she knew she and Specialist Ramerez could be in a lot of trouble. She was the officer in charge. She'd decided not to call for backup; she'd decided to enter the house. Whatever happened from this, it was her responsibility, as an officer, to protect Ramerez from any fallout. Before her shift ended, she completed a report, and left it in the middle of Major Plauche's desk.

Chapter 13

Avivah's telephone rang at 0650 hours. "This is Gilbert Plauche. Be in my office in twenty minutes. In uniform."

"I fucked up, didn't I?"

"You did."

Her report sat squarely in the center of his desk. Outside his window, the sun rose, touching the red slate roofs with fire.

After she was seated in front of his desk, Gil shoved the report at her. "Give me your version of this. Not the written version you're going to give your commander, but what it felt like to be the officer on the ground."

He listened without comment as Avivah went through the details. The longer she talked, the more his expression said she was in deep trouble.

When she finished, Gil leaned forward. "The Military Code of Conduct gives enlisted men very specific rights. On the word of two children, you entered an enlisted man's quarters, without a warrant, and without his permission. You caused his possessions to be searched. You gave his neighbors reason to believe he might be a danger to himself and to them, possibly harming his reputation in the military community. What did you think you were doing?"

"Following up on a murder investigation."

"You don't normally overstep boundaries like this. What's gotten into you, Avivah?"

"I want to go to Vietnam."

"If you were a guy, this would be the way to do it. Cause a commotion and you'd be on the next plane."

"If I were a guy, I wouldn't have been turned down every time I volunteered. But since I'm not a guy, and the Army isn't going to send me to Vietnam, I want a consolation prize. I want to help catch this killer."

"Police work is not about prizes. If Specialist Carter decides to press charges, you could be about this far away from disciplinary action." The two fingers he held up were not very far apart. "Let's hope you and I can handle this without it going to the colonel."

"What about Ramerez? If I go down, I don't want to take him with me."

Gil flipped through the report. "You've done a good job of covering his tail, I'll say that for you. Legally, he's in the clear. Where he will suffer is in the barracks, with the other enlisted men. If this gets out, they are going to be less likely to trust him in the future, and there's not a damn thing you can do to prevent that."

If the first rule of military leadership was accomplish the mission, the second was to care for your men as much as possible. Avivah didn't feel proud of herself on either score.

Gil crossed the room and opened the office door. "Come in, please."

A tall man, dressed in hospital whites, entered. His lined face and grey-streaked brown hair could put him at any age between thirty-five and forty-five. The woman with him looked younger. She wore a perfectly-tailored summer uniform with gold oak leaves on her shoulders.

"Captain Rosen, this is Specialist Carter and his supervisor, Major Buckner."

Major Plauche provided chairs for everyone. When they

were seated, he asked Avivah to tell her version of the events the evening before.

For the second time, Avivah repeated her story. She found herself softening the details, emphasizing her concern for Specialist Carter's safety. When she finished, Major Plauche reviewed the Military Code of Conduct and informed Specialist Carter that he could, if he chose to do so, press charges of entering private quarters without due course, invasion of privacy, and conduct prejudicial to the reputation of an enlisted man.

Specialist Carter looked at Major Buckner, then at Plauche. "Could I talk to Major Buckner in private before I make a decision?"

Plauche stood up. "Certainly. Come with me, Captain."

He closed the office door behind them and they stood in the hall. The venetian blinds opened just enough that Avivah and Gil could see the two people.

Avivah muttered, "Convenient how the blinds are open at just the right angle."

Gil remained silent.

Specialist Carter sat with his knees spread apart, his hands clasped between his knees and his head down, looking at the floor. Major Buckner sat upright, half-facing him. He said something and she began to tick items off on her fingers like a parent trying to be reasonable with a recalcitrant child. Specialist Carter nodded his head each time, usually agreeing with her, once shaking his head no. When she had finished ticking off three or four items, he sat up, turned to her, and nodded yes. Then they both sat up and assumed the positions they had been in when the door was closed.

Plauche waited a few more minutes, then knocked on the door. "Do you need more time?"

Specialist Carter rubbed his hands on his white pants

and cleared his throat. "I'm not going to press charges. The lady here was concerned about my safety. I can't fault her for that."

Avivah hadn't realized she was holding in so much tension until she let it go.

Major Plauche nodded. "That's very generous. You understand that I'll still need to interview you about the traffic accident in Saigon?"

"Yes, sir." He glanced at Major Buckner. "I'll answer any questions I can."

"Could you both wait outside for a few minutes while I locate a stenographer to take your statement?"

Gil Plauche escorted them to the door and, after they left, readjusted the blinds so they closed completely.

"That was close, *ti chou.*"

"I know." She hesitated. "Would you have done last night different?"

"I don't second-guess another officer who was on the ground. Avivah, get over this Vietnam thing. Even without it, you've got a fine career ahead of you."

"It took me seven years to make captain. Pepper did it in two. Tell me that having a tour in 'Nam didn't help when you came up for promotion to major."

Gil opened his hands in a what-can-I-say gesture.

"I don't suppose I can stay while you interview Specialist Carter?"

Gilbert Plauche smiled. "Get out of here and don't come back until your shift begins."

Avivah went home, put on her sweats, and tried to run. A small detail, hovering out of reach, bothered her. As she rounded the corner by the newspaper box in front of the apartment building, it came to her. She turned around, cut across a lawn, and ran back to her apartment. Inside, she

145

paused long enough to find a towel and a cold beer before settling on the sofa with the telephone beside her.

"Ward Six-A. Corpsman Pinna speaking. May I help you?"

"Is Captain Pepperhawk available? It's Captain Rosen."

"Yes, ma'am. Wait one."

Pepper came to the phone a minute later. "Avivah?"

"Yeah, it's me. I've got a question. Who is the supervisor for wardmasters?"

"The hospital chief wardmaster and the chief nurse or, by her delegation, the day supervisor."

"Not the evening supervisor?"

"No. The wardmasters work days. Why?"

"Tell you later. Thanks."

She hung up and found her notebook, then phoned Pentagon information for the number of General Hayes' Office.

"Colonel Euston, it's Captain Rosen, with the military police at Ft. Bragg. We spoke last week."

"Yes, I remember. And you were right."

"Right?"

"Your Captain Delaney is very rude."

"He called you?"

"He did."

"I'm sorry," Avivah said, uncertain why she apologized. "Colonel, I need a favor."

"I assume that since you haven't mentioned taking my statement that this conversation is off the record?"

"Sort of. I'm not really asking for a statement, just some information; I could get it from records, but it would take longer than this phone call."

"Go ahead."

"Since you considered Major Buckner for a position in

your office, you must have a copy of her service record. I need some dates."

"All right. It will take me a few minutes to find her file. Shall I call you back?"

"Yes, please."

The colonel called half an hour later. "What was this about dates?"

Avivah consulted her notes. "You mentioned Major Buckner had done two tours in Vietnam. What were the dates and locations of those tours?"

"Her first was September 1964 to September 1965. She was a staff nurse at the Twelfth Evacuation Hospital in Chu Chi. Then she did a second tour, May 1968 to May 1969, as a head nurse at the Third Field Hospital in Saigon."

It fit. Major Buckner would have been in Saigon when Dermid disappeared. Avivah sat forward and ran her fingertip around the beer bottle.

"Would she have worked on the ward that took care of patients with severe brain injuries?"

"I don't think so. This says she was on a medical ward. A severe brain injury would have been in surgical intensive care."

"Could she have pulled some shifts for another nurse in intensive care?"

"Captain, nurses aren't interchangeable widgets. A head nurse on a medical unit would have had very different skills from an ICU nurse. Besides, head nurses are too busy to pull extra shifts."

Avivah bet Jane Buckner and Boyd Ramsey connected in some way. She thought about it for the rest of the day without any fresh ideas.

When she reported for work, there was a manila envelope on her desk, with a note in Gil Plauche's handwriting. "I'd like your analysis of this by tomorrow morning."

147

Transcript of Interview

Military Police Brigade Office; Ft. Bragg, North Carolina

13 July 1971

Interview begins at 0815 hours. Interviewee has been advised of his rights with the writer present.

Interviewer: Major Gilbert Plauche, Ft. Bragg Military Police Brigade, Ft. Bragg, North Carolina

Interviewee: Specialist-Seven Harlan Carter, Wardmaster, Medical Holding Company, Womack Army Hospital, Ft. Bragg, North Carolina

Plauche: Please enter into the record that this interview is being observed, at Specialist Carter's request, by Major Jane Buckner, from the Office of the Chief Nurse, Womack Army Hospital. Specialist Carter, for the record, state your name, rank and current duty assignment.

Carter: My name is Harlan William Carter. Rank: Specialist E-seven. Current duty assignment: Wardmaster of Medical Holding Company, Womack Army Hospital, Ft. Bragg.

Plauche: What was your assignment in January 1969?

Carter: I was Wardmaster on a medical ward at the Third Field Hospital in Saigon, Republic of Vietnam.

Hello, Avivah said. Major Buckner was head nurse on a medical ward in Saigon. Was there more than one medical ward at the Third Field? Probably. That didn't matter. Carter and Buckner would have known one another in Saigon; possibly Major Buckner had been Specialist Carter's head nurse.

Some Welcome Home

Plauche: Do you remember witnessing a traffic accident on January 20 of that year?

Carter: I didn't exactly witness it. I was inside a shop, buying a vase for my wife, so I didn't *see* the accident. I heard brakes, then a thud, and I ran out into the street. There were a lot of people milling around, mostly Vietnamese, and there was a body partially under a Vietnamese bus.

Plauche: What did you do?

Carter: I pushed through the crowd, yelling. *"Bac Si. Bac Si."* It's their word for doctor. I figured they'd recognize *"Bac Si"* as someone who could help. They were trying to pull the man from under the bus, I stopped them, and crawled under the bus to assess the casualty.

Plauche: Your assessment showed?

Carter: The bus rolled over the man's neck and chest. First aid wasn't going to help.

Plauche: Was the man in uniform?

Carter: No, sir, civilian clothes.

Plauche: Can you describe the clothes?

Carter: A short-sleeve shirt, pants. Both light-colored. I'm sorry, it was a long time ago.

Plauche: What did you do after you crawled under the bus?

Carter: I helped pull the body out. Several of the bystanders moved the body to the sidewalk. Somebody found a piece of plastic and I put it over the body. I yelled at a couple of GIs standing at the corner to find a military policeman, then I began to direct traffic.

Plauche: Did you know then that the man was an American soldier?

Carter: No, sir. As I said, he was in civilian clothes.

Plauche: If you didn't know he was a soldier, why did you send for military police?

Carter: He didn't look like a gook. Pardon, I mean he didn't look like a Vietnamese. I thought he might be a reporter or one of the civilian contractors. I thought the military police would be more efficient than the civilian police.

Plauche: You're listed on the accident report as the person who identified the victim. How did you do that?

Carter: From dog tags and an ID card he had in his pants pocket. And because I knew him.

Plauche: You knew this man? Before the accident?

Carter: Yes, sir.

Plauche: In what context?

Carter: He had been a patient at the Third Field Hospital several weeks previously.

Plauche: On your ward?

At this point Specialist Carter asked permission to consult with Major Buckner in private. The interview resumed five minutes later.

Buckner: Specialist Carter is concerned about violating a patient's right to the privacy of his medical information. But I believe that since this man is dead, and this is a murder investigation, I have advised him that it would be permissible to provide relevant medical information.

Carter: He was on my ward with malaria.

Plauche: How long before the accident was he on your ward?

Carter: Three months.

Plauche: How many patients had you had on your ward in those three months?

Carter: Several hundred.

Plauche: Could you remember them all?

Carter: No, sir.

Plauche: Could you remember most of them?

Carter: No, sir.

Plauche: Then was there something special about this patient that caused you to remember him?

Carter: I lost fifty dollars to him.

Plauche: How?

Carter: Playing poker.

Plauche: While he was a patient on your ward?

Carter: Yes, sir.

Plauche: Wasn't it against regulations to gamble with the patients?

Carter: Yes, sir. But we did it all the time, I mean, when things were slow. But not on the ward. We'd play in the evening in the Red Cross Recreation Room. Me and some of the corpsmen and some of the patients.

Plauche: So were all the patients invited to play poker with you and some of the corpsmen?

Carter: No, sir. Just the . . . ones who looked like they might enjoy it.

Plauche: You mean the ones who looked like they might lose?

Buckner: Captain, it was quite common in hospitals in Vietnam for there to be card games. Command was usually aware of it and, as long as there weren't any complaints, they ignored it. It was for penny-ante stakes and it helped pass the time for the patients.

151

Plauche: Thank you, Major. I'll keep that in mind. So you played poker with Dermid Hagan and lost fifty dollars to him. Over how long a period of time?

Carter: Approximately a week.

Plauche: Had you seen him since he left the hospital?

Carter: No, sir. Not until the accident.

Plauche: Did you recognize him?

Carter: Not right away.

Plauche: When did you recognize him?

Carter: After I'd pulled him out from under the bus, I looked for identification. I found an ID card and dog tags. I recognized his name. It was rather an odd name.

Plauche: There was no doubt on your part? You were certain you recognized him?

Carter: Yes, sir. I mean as well as I could. There was a lot of blood all over his face, and his face had been chewed up on the road, but yes, I believed, at the time, that the man was Dermid Hagan.

Plauche: Then how do you account for Dermid Hagan's body being found in Normandy House last week?

Carter: I can't say, sir. I believe now that I made a mistake in identifying him.

Plauche: It appears that you did.

Buckner: Captain, Specialist Carter made an honest mistake in a very emotional situation. The Army neglected to make further confirmation, such as fingerprint check. Specialist Carter was not at fault.

Plauche: In the year and a half since the accident, did you ever have contact with Dermid Hagan or with anyone who claimed to be Dermid Hagan?

Carter: No, sir.

Plauche: In April of this year there was a *60 Minutes* segment about the Eighty-second Airborne. Were you in it?

Carter: Just in a crowd shot, some of us looking at a scrapbook in the museum. They didn't interview me or anything.

Plauche: How did you come to be included in the filming?

Carter: There was a notice posted on the bulletin board at the NCO club. They were looking for people who had service with the Eighty-second for crowd scenes. I'd been a medic with them the first time I was in Vietnam.

Plauche: And, after that program, did you ever receive any telephone call, letter, or any other communication from Dermid Hagan?

Carter: No, sir.

Plauche: When Dermid's name was in the paper last week, did you recognize the name?

Carter: Yes, sir. I realized at the time that I had probably made a mistake in the identification.

Plauche: Why didn't you call CID and tell them that you had been the one to identify the body in Saigon?

Carter: I'm an alcoholic, sir. I've only been going to AA about two months. I'm not very far on the program, but I have been told that alcoholics sometimes don't make good decisions. That's why I went to a meeting last night, to ask the guys if I should get involved.

Wonderful, Avivah thought. I was invading this guy's house and he was at an AA meeting. That would have looked great in the paper. She owed Gil one for saving her tail before the colonel got wind of what had happened.

Plauche: These guys at the meeting, they'll tell me the same story?

Carter: I believe they would.

Plauche: Tell me their names.

Carter: I'd rather not, sir.

Buckner: Captain, Specialist Carter is dealing with a very difficult personal problem. Surely you respect the confidentiality of Alcoholics Anonymous? Perhaps, Specialist, you could tell these other men that Captain Plauche needs some verification of the events last night and they could choose if they wanted to contact him?

Carter: Yeah, okay. I guess we could do it that way. But it's up to them if they want to call you or not. Look, I've told you everything I know about Dermid Hagan. He was a patient on my ward, we played poker, I never saw him after he left the hospital until I made a mistake in identifying him as the victim of the bus accident. That's all I know.

Plauche: Does the name Cody Doan mean anything to you?

Carter: Sergeant Cody Doan is assigned to medical holding company, but he's in the hospital right now.

Plauche: Did Sergeant Doan mention Dermid Hagan to you at any time?

Carter: No, sir.

Plauche: Did he ever show you letters he received from Hagan?

Carter: No, sir.

Plauche: Did he ever mention the accident or that he knew the murdered man?

Carter: No, sir.

Plauche: Does the name Boyd Ramsey mean anything to you?

Carter: No, sir. As far as I know, I've never heard that name before.

Plauche: Do you remember someone from General Hayes' office visiting the hospital and the medical holding company in June of this year?

Carter: Yes, sir. A Colonel. I don't remember her name.

Buckner: Colonel Frances Euston. She's a special assistant to General Hayes.

Plauche: Thank you, ma'am, but I would prefer Specialist Carter to answer the questions. Do you remember Colonel Euston's visit?

Carter: Sort of.

Plauche: Sort of?

Carter: I told you I am an alcoholic, sir. Sometime I can't remember things. I'd been drinking at the time the colonel visited.

Plauche: Were you aware that Colonel Euston lost a key while visiting the hospital?

Buckner: This is a question I should answer. When Colonel Euston telephoned me to say that her key was missing, I contacted the wardmasters of all the units she had visited and asked them to search their wards or areas for the key. Specialist Carter was one of the wardmasters I telephoned. I can check the evening log if you would like the names of all the wardmasters I contacted.

Plauche: Yes, ma'am, that might be helpful. So Major Buckner telephoned you? When was this?

Carter: I don't remember, sir. I had been drinking heavily that day.

Buckner: It was between 1630 and 1700 hours. I remember because I'd gone to last supper and was paged while in the dining room. I telephoned all of the wardmasters and all of them, including Specialist Carter, telephoned me back by 2100 hours to say that no key had been found.

Plauche: After Major Buckner telephoned you, did you go to the medical holding company to look for the key?

Carter: Frankly, sir, I was drunk. I called the sergeant on evening shift to have a look around, then call me back.

Plauche: What is this sergeant's name?

Carter: Vincent D'Acosta.

Plauche: Can you tell me how you spent Sunday, July 4 of this year?

Carter: Not all of it, sir. I remember very little after Friday night, July 2.

Plauche: Tell me what you remember.

Carter: I met three of my buddies from Vietnam Friday night. We went out for steak and beer. I only planned to have a couple, but we all got drunk. I stayed in the motel with my buddies Friday and Saturday nights.

Plauche: No one missed you when you didn't come home?

Carter: My wife and I separated in June. There wasn't anyone to miss me.

Plauche: What did you do on Saturday?

Carter: Went to the bar-be-cue for the Eighty-second reunion.

Plauche: And on Sunday?

Carter: Watched the parade Sunday morning.

Plauche: You didn't march in the parade?

Carter: We weren't in good shape. We thought it wouldn't look very good for the Eighty-second if we stumbled over our own feet when we tried to march.

Plauche: What did you do after the parade ended?

Carter: Went back to the motel so the guys could pack and check out. After I said goodbye to them, I went home and slept until noon Monday.

Plauche: You didn't report for duty Monday morning?

Carter: I had previously requested leave for that day.

Plauche: Did you see Dermid Hagan at any time on Sunday, July 4?

Carter: No, sir.

Plauche: Were you in Normandy House or anywhere near it on July 4?

Carter: Not to the best of my memory.

Plauche: I'll need the names and addresses of the men you were with over the weekend.

Carter: All right, sir.

Plauche: The stenographer will type up this interview and ask both of you to sign it.

Carter: Yes, sir.

Buckner: Yes, sir.

The interview ended at 0905 hours.

Avivah looked at the two signatures on the bottom of the statement: Carter's scrawl and Major Buckner's careful *Major Jane S. Buckner, BSN, ANC.* She pulled a clean sheet of paper out of her desk drawer and wrote on it:

Major Buckner *is* *not* Specialist Carter's supervisor. She is an evening supervisor, and wardmasters are supervised by the day supervisor.

I have reason to believe that Major Buckner was Specialist Carter's head nurse at the Third Field in Saigon in January 1969. If so, Dermid Hagan was her patient, too.

Get a copy of that *60 Minutes* program. See if the production company kept a list of everyone who appeared in it.

She paper-clipped the note to the statement, sealed it in the envelope, and put it in Major Plauche's inbox.

Chapter 14

Benny and two small boys stood at Pepper's open apartment door.

Benny pointed first to the older of the two boys. "This is Randall. This is Mark. Come on, guys, what do you do when you meet a lady?"

The boys took off their baseball caps and two voices piped, "I'm pleased to meet you, ma'am."

Mark looked up at Benny as if to ask, did I get it right? Benny put his hand on the boy's shoulder.

Pepper smiled. "What can I do for you gentlemen?"

"We're going for burgers and ice cream. I thought you might want to come with us."

"At four o'clock in the afternoon? Won't it spoil their supper?"

The younger boy, Mark, nodded. "You sound just like my mother. She told Uncle Benny, 'Don't fill those boys up with junk food.' "

Pepper hid another smile. "Sure. I'll come. Let me just get my purse and lock up."

"Go wait in the truck, guys. Miss Pepperhawk and I will be along in a minute. Right, Miss Pepperhawk?"

"Right, Uncle Benny." Pepper went into her apartment for her purse. "They are adorable. Who are they?"

"The sons of the woman I love. Their dad went

159

missing in Na Trang province three years ago."

"Beret?"

"Yes."

"I'm sorry."

"Me too. Come on, those boys don't wait well."

An hour later, she and Benny sat on the bleachers beside a small park, watching the boys play in the late afternoon sun. Benny opened the first couple of buttons on his shirt—today it was orange and yellow hibiscus—leaned back, closed his eyes, and groaned.

"I'm too old to keep up with children."

"This is the same person that follows green berets through the Panamanian jungle?"

"No, ma'am. This is the same person that *leads* green berets through the Panamanian jungle."

"How come two small boys are too much for you?"

"Teaching guys jungle survival is different from teaching two boys about life."

"How did their dad go missing?"

Benny took a slow drink from his milkshake. The boys tired of the swings and began to play follow the leader across climbing equipment made of old tires and wooden platforms.

"His team called for an extraction out of a tight spot. Just before the chopper arrived, he took a bad chest wound. It was hot a landing zone, no one could get across the clearing to him, and the chopper took off without him."

"Do you think he's alive?"

"Nope. I've talked to every member of that team who is still alive. They all said that even if he survived, the Viet Cong don't have the kind of medical care Randy would have needed."

"But it's not enough, is it? To know for certain he's dead, I mean."

"Some days it is and some days it isn't. Lorraine is more convinced than I am that he's dead. That's why she won't marry me. If Randy could go missing, I could, too. She says she can't go through this again."

Pepper suddenly felt chilled. "You going back to Vietnam?"

He looked at the two boys climbing over the playground equipment. "I hope not. I've got nine years in and two tours of 'Nam and I'm due for another overseas rotation. But if I don't go to 'Nam, I'll go to some other place."

Benny swung his legs through the bleacher steps so that his back faced the sun. He folded his arms on one of the higher bleacher levels and rested his chin on his arms.

"What other places?"

"Places we don't talk about."

Pepper studied him for a minute. "Do you have fruit salad?"

"Some."

"You're not holding out on me, like you have the Medal of Honor or something?"

Benny made a noise under his breath. "Not likely."

"What do you have?"

"Including service medals and unit citations?"

"No, just the good stuff."

"In order of date awarded or order of precedence?"

"Quit stalling, Benny."

"The *good stuff,* as you so charmingly put it, is an Army Commendation Medal for valor, a Purple Heart, and a couple of Bronze Stars."

"Are the Bronze Stars for valor?"

"Yes." He turned his head to look at Pepper. "You look

like you're waiting for me to say something else."

"Isn't this where you say, 'That and fifty cents will buy you a cup of coffee'?"

He chuckled. "Take it as read, okay?"

"You going for twenty years?"

"I don't know. If Lorraine would agree to marry me, I'd be in the chaplain's office requesting a hardship discharge so fast it would make your head spin. If she really won't marry me, then I'll probably sign up again."

"If you got out, what would you do?"

"Go to technical college, then open a radio and television repair shop next to my dad's hardware store."

"Sounds boring."

"Sounds settled. Lorraine and I could use a little settled."

"Why not just go into the hardware business with your dad?"

"My sister has already made it known that she plans to inherit the business."

"No brothers?"

"No brothers interested in hardware. My younger brother is a folk musician, living in Ireland right now, and my older half-brother works for a commodities trading firm in Chicago."

"How old is your sister?"

"Seventeen. She's taking loads of high school business courses, and driving my father crazy about adopting modern business practices. Last time I talked to him, he wanted to know if special forces would take a man his age."

"What does your mom do?"

"Holds office in the Grange when she feels like it. Makes stuff for their Christmas bazaar. Works part-time."

Pepper eyed Benny suspiciously. "Are you sure you

aren't making this up? It's just too, I don't know, too Frank Capra. Small town hardware store, mom who does the Christmas bazaar."

"You mean, like does my dad have a secret drinking problem or is Joseph covering IRA gunrunning with his folk festivals?"

"Is he?'

"God, I hope not. Granddad left County Monahan because of the Irish Republican Army. Sorry, Pepper, we're just a typical Missouri family. Well, okay, my mom came from Alaska and she's a certified welder and pipe fitter. She and my dad met building the Canol Road in the Yukon during World War II. When I said she worked part-time, you figured she was a secretary or a teacher. Actually, she mounted a portable welding shop in the back of a pickup and services farm equipment. For bazaars, she makes those horrible welded-chain, rural mailboxes. We love her anyway."

Pepper fell sideways laughing. "Stop, stop. I can never trust you to tell a straight story."

"I *am* telling you a straight story. My mom and dad *did* meet on the Canol Road. In fact, I was born in a truck on the Canol Road. Cross my heart," he said, making a crossing motion over his heart with two fingers.

An Irish-sourdough, Pepper thought. That explained a lot about Benjamin Kirkpatrick.

He stood up and buttoned his shirt. "Come on, my scars are starting to itch. I promised Lorraine I'd have the boys home for supper. Want to come and meet her?"

"Won't she mind you bringing a stranger to supper on short notice?"

"That's one of those woman things, isn't it?"

"Yes."

"We'd better call her."

He put two fingers in his mouth and gave a sharp whistle. The two boys stopped playing and looked in their direction. Benny pointed to his truck and gave a hand signals for *Rendezvous. Five minutes.* Randall responded with hand signals for *Understood. Rendezvous. Five minutes.*

Pepper laughed. "Did you teach him hand signals?"

"I didn't have to. When Randall was about three, his dad took him to the commissary. The sergeant waiting behind him in the check-out line tapped Randy on the shoulder, and said, 'I think your trooper wants your attention?' There was Randall beside some cereal advertised on television, signaling *Form up immediately on my position.*

"Where did he learn it?"

"The playground. The day care. Who knows? They're Army brats. They pick up all kind of military customs. Come on, let's phone Lorraine."

Chapter 15

Avivah sat in a dark room, watching the *60 Minutes* segment for the fifth time. On the yellow legal pad in front of her, she wrote:

> *Cody Doan—identified by name—interviewed at drop site—on screen for one minute and fifteen seconds. He had been a healthier-looking Cody Doan, not as skinny, face not drawn in pain. He walked with a cane and had a slight limp.*
>
> *Harlan Carter—name not given—in group looking over Eighty-second memorabilia—on screen for thirty-five seconds. No surprises there. He looked like the tired, rumpled man that I saw the day before in Gilbert Plauche's office.*
>
> *Jane Buckner—name not given—standing beside a bed, with the hospital commander and the chief nurse, while an Eighty-second Airborne soldier in Womack Army Hospital received a Purple Heart and Silver Star— on screen for forty seconds.*

Dermid Hagan, in Montreal, watching American television, saw three people he might have recognized. Cody Doan said that his letter came with only his name and Eighty-second Airborne. Avivah rewound the tape to the brief segment that showed Harlan Carter. Carter was in summer uniform, not hospital whites. There was no way to identify he belonged to the hospital. Perhaps Dermid wrote him a letter as well, addressed with his name and Eighty-second Airborne on it. The company clerk looked at the letter, found no Harlan Carter listed on his roster, and returned it to the dead letter office, marked "Not in this unit." Avivah wondered if a third letter, addressed to Jane Buckner at the hospital, reached her.

"Osborne," she yelled through the open door.

"Yes, ma'am?"

"Call information for Marshall, North Carolina. Find phone numbers for all the funeral homes, call them, and find out when and where Dermid Hagan's funeral is."

Specialist Osborne returned in fifteen minutes, and tore a sheet from her steno pad. "Bowman Funeral Home. The funeral is at 1300 hours, Friday, July 15, at his family's church with burial in the church graveyard. They're Baptist. I got directions to the church. And Captain Delaney wants a list of everyone who asks about Dermid Hagan."

"How do you know that?"

"Because the secretary at the funeral home asked my name. She said it was a very small church and they needed a list of everyone who was going to be at the funeral. Only I'd never said I was coming to the funeral, only that I was asking when it was."

"What did you tell them?"

"I gave them a false name. I hope that was okay. I said that I'd known Dermid in third grade and that I hadn't seen him since my family moved away. That I'd seen his name in the Fayetteville paper and wanted to send flowers. I kind of gave them the impression that I was one of those people who do anything to claim a connection to a story in the paper."

"Uh, very good, Specialist Osborne. Quick thinking."

"Thank you. How much shall I spend on flowers?"

"What flowers?"

"I told them I'd send flowers. If Captain Delaney is monitoring the calls, he might get suspicious if this person called and didn't send flowers. I thought I'd put on the card, 'A friend from school.' "

Avivah dug in her purse and handed Specialist Osborne money. "Don't use the post florist."

"No, ma'am. I've got a nice civilian florist picked out of the phone book. Do you think I should wear dark glasses?"

"No. Go as yourself, keep it low key."

"Yes, ma'am."

Avivah wondered if Specialist Osborne read spy novels in her spare time.

Wednesday afternoon, Pepper found Avivah sitting at the picnic table outside the apartment.

"Why aren't you at work?"

"Occasionally, I have a day off. Come over for supper."

Avivah did not do *subtle* well; her body held too much pent-up energy. Curious about what she wanted, Pepper accepted the invitation. "Let me shower and get out of this uniform."

When Pepper arrived an hour later, Avivah had her head stuck inside the refrigerator. The small light highlighted her sharp features and black hair. "We have ground beef, green onions, bell pepper, a few old mushrooms, and some anchovies. What do you want on the pizza?"

Pepper sat at the counter dividing the kitchen from the living room. "I don't know. You can't eat fish and meat at the same meal, can you?"

Avivah came out of the fridge carrying several containers and shut the door with her foot. "That's meat and dairy and only if I keep kosher, which my family doesn't." She opened a plastic container, made a face, and dumped the shimmering green contents in the garbage pail. "Pepper, have you ever known a Jew?"

"Sure."

"Did you ever have one for a friend? Go to their home? Have them to your house?"

"When I was in seventh grade, I liked a boy named Isaac. Mom said we couldn't have him over because he had to eat special food and use special plates. Then his dad got transferred to Milwaukee and he moved away the next year. I hope he's all right."

"Why wouldn't Isaac be all right?" She pronounced it Itzak.

"Vietnam. I can't think of the boys I grew up with without wondering if they were drafted, if they came home safely. Especially when I was in university, I saw the fear in their faces during final exams. A couple got up halfway through the test and walked out. They knew they'd be drafted if they lost their educational deferment. They looked like they were going to a firing squad."

Avivah opened the oven door, looked inside, then turned it on. She put a bowl and cookie sheet on the counter and handed Pepper a knife and a cutting board. "Dice everything into small pieces." She began to make the crust.

"I graduated in 1964. We worried more about getting blown up in the Cuban missile crisis and about how safe it was to bus to the South or to register black voters or if a church would be firebombed while we were inside."

"You were part of the civil rights movement?"

"Yes. Remember the first Freedom Ride in '61?"

Pepper hoped she did subtle better than Avivah. She didn't want Avivah to know how her stomach turned over just thinking about civil rights confrontations. "I was only fourteen."

"I turned nineteen the month before the ride started. My mother had a lot of friends in the movement. She debated going on the bus with them, but her friends convinced her that the first ride would be too dangerous for a white woman, so she planned to go to New Orleans to welcome them at the end of the ride. Of course, they never reached New Orleans."

Pepper couldn't remember why not or where they had ended up. She hoped Avivah didn't expect her to know this stuff just because she came from the South.

"My mother went to Montgomery, Alabama instead. My birthday present was that she allowed me to go with her."

Pepper could not imagine her own mother allowing her to be involved in something like that. She couldn't imagine her mother involved in a confrontation at all.

"I was inside the church in Montgomery, where Dr. King was preaching, when white demonstrators surrounded it. For a while, we didn't think we'd get out alive. About three in the morning, Robert Kennedy persuaded Governor Patterson to declare martial law. The state police and National Guard rescued us."

Pepper stopped, her knife point in the air. "You met Martin Luther King?"

"Yes, and Robert Kennedy, Bella Abzug, Barbara Jordan. Don't look at me like that. It wasn't a big deal. When you went to school in New York City, you didn't have to go looking for the world. The world came to speak to you."

"Nobody ever came to speak at our school, except football coaches and Southern writers. Well, nobody that I would have felt safe going to hear. What was Dr. King like?"

Avivah laughed. "He was a very dedicated and determined man."

Pepper pushed bell pepper bits around on the cutting board. "I don't want you to think I'm a segregationist, because I'm not. My parents said if blacks just let things alone, change would come at the right time. They said rosaries for peace. In university, during the demonstrations, I hid in a closet. Literally. I closed my curtains and locked my door and hid in a closet. I couldn't stand the violence, the hate. The anger. The dogs. The black men marching and the white men yelling obscenities."

"Both black and white women marched, too."

"I never noticed. I was too busy being afraid of the black men. My mother told me that if I were ever alone with a black man, he would rape me."

Avivah put the dough in a bowl and covered it with a damp towel. "Your wardmaster is black. How's that working out?"

"In Qui Nhon, we did CPR on a black electrician who was electrocuted. Every time I breathed into his mouth I knew that my mother would die if she knew what I was doing. We used to talk about it in nursing school, like what would you do if a black man needed CPR? There I was doing it. A lot changed for me in those fifteen minutes."

"Did the guy live?"

"No."

Avivah worked shreds of dough off her fingers. "My family comes from a long line of social activists. My grandmother was a union organizer with miners and textile workers in the South. Papa's a juvenile court judge in Schenectady; my mom is a social worker. She specializes in unwed mothers."

Pepper transferred the contents of the cutting board to a

bowl, scraping the wood with the back of the knife. "When I went to basic training at Fort Sam Houston, my sister told her friends that I had gone to a home for unwed mothers because she was too embarrassed to tell them I was in the Army."

Avivah finished arranging the toppings on the pizza. "At least your family was still talking to you. Get us something to drink, will you?"

Pepper set two sodas on the counter. Avivah poured hers into a glass, pulled up a stool, and they sat side-by-side.

Pepper took a long drink. "Your family stopped talking to you?"

"For a while."

"Why?"

"In my family you don't become a policeman, especially a military policeman."

"Because you're a woman?"

Avivah ran her finger around her glass until it made a squealing sound. "Because I'm a Jew. Soldiers and policemen conducted pogroms against Jews for centuries."

"What's a pogrom?"

Avivah stared at her and shook her head. "I thought you'd been to university?"

"Nursing students didn't study world history."

"Pepper, the world is going to come as a great surprise to you one day. A pogrom was a massacre where Jews were systematically hunted down and killed."

"That's terrible."

"It's unspeakable. According to my mother, it was also unspeakable that her daughter would become not only a soldier, but a policeman as well. She thought I'd betrayed everything she and Grandmother believed in."

"Why are you doing it?"

171

"Two women. One was my grandmother. She said you could never know something from the outside, you had to do something before you could understand it. I couldn't have understood the civil rights movement if all I'd done was read about it in the paper, or seen it on television. The other woman was a policewoman, a beat cop in New York City. She spoke to one of our sociology classes about being a woman in law enforcement, how she felt like she made a difference for other women, not just the women she protected, but an example for other women."

"Wouldn't she have helped you get into the New York City Police?"

Avivah paused. "About three weeks after she spoke to our class, her patrol car blew a tire during a high-speed chase. The car hit a bridge abutment. She died at the scene and her partner died of his injuries a few weeks later."

"I'm sorry."

"My dad came to this country when he was three; he's very proud of being an American. He served in the Judge Advocate's Office during World War II. If I wasn't going to law school like he wanted, I thought maybe being an officer would be a little substitute."

"Your family sounds so interesting. My dad's just a mechanic for the Southern Pacific and my mom works as a dental clinic receptionist."

"What do they think of Captain Elizabeth Pepperhawk, Vietnam veteran?"

"I don't know. We never talk, we only fight."

"How come?"

"I caught my mother screening my telephone calls. She told everyone that 'I was just exhausted' and could not come to the phone. When I blew up at her, she said, 'Well, dear, you have been in a war. You can't expect a normal life.' How come you've never put in for Vietnam?"

"I have, several times. When I was in military police school, I got Germany. When I was in Germany, I got Fort Leonard Woods. When I was a Fort Leonard Woods, I got Fort Bragg. If you're a woman, and not a nurse or a doughnut dolly, you're not going."

"That's stupid. Vietnam isn't that big of a deal, at least if you aren't in combat. I saw lots of military police at the hospital or riding around the airfield. They weren't doing anything you couldn't do. How come you want it so bad?"

"How come you did?"

"I came in under the Army Student Nurse Program. I knew I had a chance of being sent to Vietnam, but it was a trade-off to get money to finish nursing school."

"That what you told your parents?"

"Pretty much."

"How about a little truth and honesty here? What didn't you tell your parents?"

"You remember those guys who left the testing room in university?"

"Yes."

"Guys my age were dying. I couldn't do anything about the war, but I could do something about individual men dying or, if I couldn't, at least they didn't die alone. Sounds kind of stupid, doesn't it."

"No. I watched you on the ward with guys on the med-evacs. You care about them."

Pepper played with her soda. "I guess I do."

"Tell me about Cody Doan."

"He almost lost his leg when he stepped on a mine. They should have amputated then, but they put him in a cast and shipped him home. He got well enough to go back to duty, then he decided to go airborne. He broke his leg again in a bad jump and about a year ago he developed osteomylitis. That's a chronic infection in the bone."

"Why don't they discharge him from the Army and let the Veterans' Administration take care of him?"

"The doctors use him as a guinea pig, thinking of new ways to save his leg. He's bored silly, he hurts, he can't get a straight answer out of the docs, and he's mad at the whole world."

"What's going to happen to him?"

"He'll either lose his leg or he won't."

"If you could do something to help him, would you?"

"What did you have in mind?"

"Go to Dermid Hagan's funeral in Marshall day after to-morrow."

Pepper felt confused. "Why me? How will my going to a funeral help Sergeant Doan?"

Avivah took a piece of mushroom out of the bowl and nibbled at the end of it. "I can't talk about that."

"Cody Doan did not kill Dermid Hagan. I saw the expression on his face when he read Dermid's name in the paper."

"Killers have been good actors before." She tossed the mushroom in the sink. "Oh, hell, Pepper, I believe you. I don't think Doan is our killer, but you remember Captain Delaney, don't you?"

"I'm not likely to forget him."

"There's no way to know what kind of a crazy theory he will come up with. Once he gets an idea, he's like a bulldog worrying at a bone. The more I know about Dermid, and about Cody Doan, the more I might be able to protect Doan. As for going to the funeral, you're ideal. You have an aunt in Bat Cave."

"Bat Harbor."

"Whatever. You could bring them a casserole, you speak their language. I sound like I belong in a New York Hadassah more than in a Southern Baptist church."

"I wouldn't bring a casserole. That would be presuming too close a connection to the family. If I were family or a member of the church congregation, I could bring food. Even if I were a member of the community, but didn't know the family, I could bring brownies or peanut butter cookies. But as a stranger . . . What are you staring at?"

"My sister pays good money to take cultural anthropology and learn what you know as a matter of course. Okay, if not a casserole, what?"

"Flowers, something small, not ostentatious. And I should sit in the back of the church, not be too noticeable."

"That would be ideal. It would give you a chance to watch everything. We need to know more about Dermid, his family, what he was like before he joined the Army. I'm looking for clues in his past that will tell me what kind of a person he was."

"You're forgetting something; the funeral is Friday. I work Friday."

"Take a day of leave."

"What kind of reason am I going to give?"

"You don't have to give any reason. Officers take a day of leave all the time, especially in the summer. Just say you have personal business."

"I suppose I could."

Chapter 16

Marshall, North Carolina, hadn't changed in fifteen years. The waters of the French Broad River still ran green and deep under high summer clouds. The single railroad track still paralleled the river, and Marshall's Main Street, lined on either side with flat-topped, red brick buildings, paralleled the railroad track. The plaque to the loving memory of Robert E. Lee stood to the left of the concrete walk that led to the courthouse.

Granny Lee. His soldiers idolized him.

Pepper laid her hand on the warm bronze. "War's different now," she said to the figure on the plaque. "You'd hardly recognize it, except, too many men with Southern accents still fight . . . Men and women," she amended, wanting General Lee to realize she had been there, too.

The bas-relief of Lee, seated on Traveler, had no answers for her.

She went into the small café next to the courthouse.

The waitress cutting pie slices behind the counter thought a moment. "Flowers. You'll want Miz Lilly Bell for flowers." She gave directions.

Half an hour later, Pepper spotted the hand-painted sign, *Lilly Bell Flowers*. A further message, *Lilly Bell Payne, Prop.*, hid in the middle of the colorful flower bouquet painted under the business name. Pepper slowed as her car rocked over the Texas gate.

Pepper knew the waitress would have called ahead.

"Stranger coming your way. She *says* she wants flowers."

A large woman, with a neat bun of grey hair, came out of the modest frame house, wiping her hands. She wore a print dress with a cotton apron over it.

Pepper got out of the car. "Came to buy some flowers for a burying."

The woman looked her up and down and Pepper was glad that she'd taken time to buy the right clothes for a summer funeral. A navy-blue dress with white piping, white shoes, white purse.

The heavy smell of flowers—more than could be accounted for by the six white-painted tires used as yard planters—hung in the air.

The woman extended her hand. "I'm Lilly Bell."

"Elizabeth Anne."

"You're not from around here?"

"Fayetteville."

"Family here?"

Pepper inclined her head in the general direction of Tennessee. "Out Bat Harbor way. Maybe you've bought chickens or a turkey off of my Aunt Corabell's poultry business?"

The woman reached down and plucked a few dead blossoms from a tire filled with blue and purple flowers.

"I get my poultry and eggs off of Jimmy Teague in Walnut. But I've heard speak of your aunt. You said something about a burying?"

"They're burying Dermid Hagan this afternoon."

The woman nodded. "Tilda and Dicey's boy. Real sad, that."

"Real sad."

"Dicey used to go hunting years ago over Bat Harbor way when he was a boy."

"Afore my time." God, Pepper thought, she was already slipping into the dialect.

"I guess so, you wouldn't even have been born then."

Pepper knew she had to establish a reason to attend Dermid's funeral, since it was obvious she didn't know the Hagans. "Guess that's why my aunt remembers him. Aunt Corabell said, since I was in the neighborhood today, I might bring the family some flowers."

"Nice of your family to remember Dicey and Tilda in their sorrow."

She turned towards the back of the house and Pepper knew she'd passed some kind of test. She followed Lilly Bell along a dirt path through a large vegetable garden. Deep red pods of the tall scarlet runner beans showed clearly against dark green leaves. Neat rows of carrots and onions alternated with huge cabbages larger than basketballs. At the far side of the garden, green plastic netting covered a dozen tomato plants, heavy with fruit. A black-and-white cat stepped cautiously among cucumber vines, bounding after a monarch butterfly it scared from under one of the massive leaves.

Pepper suddenly longed for a meal of fresh vegetables and corn bread. "You sell vegetables, too?"

"Just flowers, vegetables go to the family. You hungry, child?"

Lilly Bell's voice sounded concerned. Hospitality wouldn't allow a visitor to go away hungry.

Pepper would have given anything to sit down to dinner in Lilly Bell's kitchen. "I'm fine, but thank you for offering."

As the path crested a small rise, Pepper saw a field of flowers, moving gently in the summer breeze. Bright blobs of red, orange, yellow, white, purple, and blue covered the field. Tall, spear-like flowers barricaded the north end and the plants sloped downward, by size, towards the south, with the most southern row being more a patch of ground cover than flowers. The two women stopped beside a small wooden building, made of scrap lumber.

Lilly Bell took a cotton bonnet off a nail. "What kind of flowers?"

"Aunt Corabell didn't signify. What do you think?"

She tied the bonnet under her chin, and picked up a peach basket and a set of flower shears. "Tilda likes daisies, had some in her wedding bouquet. We'll build a remembrance bouquet."

Pepper followed Lilly through the garden, stopping to bury her face in the fragrant round head of a many-blossomed pink flower, and to admire the almost polka-dot effect of some small red and white flowers. She lost herself in the celebration of color and fragrance, and in the antics of the black-and-white cat now rolling itself in a shallow, dusty depression at the end of a row of flowers. A streak of yellow pollen ran across the cat's nose. Pepper wanted to spend the entire afternoon here, lose herself in the colors, move from the scent of one flower to another, nuzzle the cat's soft underbelly against her face. For the first time in weeks, she felt alive.

Lilly Bell rose from kneeling in front of a patch of deep blue flowers. "That should do it."

Pepper peered in the basket. "Red, white, and blue."

They walked back to the potting shed. "Soldier's colors, for him being in Vietnam." Lilly Bell pronounced it differently, emphasizing 'Nam and rhyming it with jam. She pointed to a spiky purple flower. "And a sprig of lavender for remembrance."

She set the basket down on the rough wooden shelf and

began to expertly strip unwanted leaves from the stems.

Pepper rested her back against the cool wall of the shed. "You know the Hagans well?"

"Nodding well." It meant that they would speak if they met on the street, but they didn't socialize. Avivah would have been lost in the mountain codes. "James—that's my husband, James Payne—he knows Dicey better, working on the volunteer fire department with him."

"People must find it strange, burying Dermid twice and all?"

Lilly Bell wrapped the flowers in a piece of green florist's paper. "My great-great uncle had two funerals. Went off to the War Between the States. His folks got a letter saying he'd died. Held a service for him. The date's written in our family Bible. A few years later he came home right enough. Lived another thirty-five years. Had another funeral for him in 1897. That's in the family Bible, too. Sometimes it happens in a war." She tied the paper lightly with a piece of string and handed it to Pepper.

After she'd paid, Pepper turned for one last look at the flower field, wondering at the equanimity with which Lily Bell accepted a man who died twice. She wondered if many people around here felt the same way. Or did someone know Dermid hadn't died in Saigon?

Fifteen minutes later, Pepper made the second-to-last turn indicated on Private Osborne's written directions. Immediately after the turn, two Madison County Sheriff cars were parked nose to nose to form a roadblock. A deputy waved for her to stop. She rolled down her window, feeling the hot air rush into the car.

The deputy touched the brim of his hat. "Afternoon, ma'am. Where are you going?"

"Dermid Hagan's funeral."

"Name, please?"

"Elizabeth Pepperhawk."

He consulted a clipboard. "I don't find your name here."

Captain Delaney's head appeared, bent over, peering in the car. The sun glinted on his polished captain's bars. "Captain Pepperhawk, you're a bit far from Fayetteville, aren't you?"

Pepper put both hands on the steering wheel and stared straight ahead. "I believe I have as much right as anyone to go to a funeral."

"Family and invited guests only. Pull over there."

Pepper pulled over to a dirt road, where two sturdy iron gates attached to stone pillars made a natural crowd control area. She parked in tall summer grass on one side of the road. The funeral started in thirty minutes. She and Avivah should have guessed this might happen.

Frustrated, Pepper rolled up the car window and turned the air-conditioner up to full. A knock on the window startled her. Colonel Tyler wore a white linen suit, a shirt with pale blue and yellow stripes, and a pale blue tie. Pepper rolled the window down.

"Delaney is about to throw you to the wolves." Tyler looked at the surrounding hills. "I assume there are wolves around here."

"What are you doing here?"

"I've been assigned to smooth things over with the family. Army's condolences. Please excuse us, we made a tiny mistake telling you your son was dead. Actually, he was a deserter. Delaney says you want to go to the funeral. I can't imagine why."

"Because I'm having a post-Vietnam flashback. Instead of going up in a tower and shooting people, I thought I'd bomb a funeral." She pointed to the bouquet on her back seat. "Those aren't really flowers. They're plastique, cleverly shaped to look like flowers. The daisies are the detonators."

Tyler pointed to a sleek silver car parked on the highway. "It would be my pleasure to escort you to the funeral."

"I'd rather drive myself."

Tyler bowed. "As you wish. Turn around and follow me. Don't dawdle. I'd prefer not to be late."

Any port in a storm. Pepper waved to Delaney as she passed him. She would have preferred to give him another gesture.

The small white wooden church, long and narrow, stood at the top of a little rise. The carved wooden sign hanging next to the road said *Freewill Baptist*. Another sheriff's deputy directed them to park at the end of a gravel parking lot beside the church. Pickup trucks and older cars filled the small lot. Colonel Tyler's shiny silver car almost looked embarrassed to be parked among them.

Pepper straightened her skirt and picked up the flowers from the back seat.

Tyler bent to smell the flowers. "Red, white, and blue, how appropriate. I'd planned to bring flowers, but I couldn't find a florist in Marshall."

Pepper held the bouquet towards him. "These could be from both of us." She wanted to take the words back as soon as she had said them.

"I couldn't take your flowers."

Southern games. Pepper said, "I insist," because he expected her to say that.

Colonel Tyler took the bouquet.

At the church's door, a man in his forties, with grey hair beginning to highlight his temples, took Pepper's hand. "Colonel Tyler, nice to see you again. How nice to meet you, Mrs. Tyler. I'm Reverend Pretcherd."

Colonel Tyler didn't bother to correct the preacher's misconception. As they entered the church, he took Pepper's arm and whispered in her ear. "I have to talk to the family. Pick a seat in the back. I want to leave as soon as I can."

Plenty of seats stood empty in the back of the church. Pepper started for one, then walked up the right side aisle to a half-vacant pew second from the front. Tyler could follow her there, if he wanted.

She tapped the shoulder of the young man sitting at the end of the row. "May I sit here?"

"Have to . . . have to s-save a s-seat on the end," he stuttered. "You can s-sit beside me on the other side."

He stood up to let Pepper into the pew. She seated herself and looked around for Tyler. He crouched beside a woman in the front row, on the other side of the church, his hand resting on her hand. Pepper's flowers lay in the woman's lap. That must be Dermid's mother.

What had Lilly Bell said her name was? Tilda, probably short for Matilda. Tilda Hagan. The man sitting beside her, in the slightly tight suit, had to be her husband, Dicey Hagan.

Tilda Hagan cried and nodded as Colonel Tyler said something to her. He patted her hand, stood up, and looked around until he spotted Pepper. She smiled and indicated the empty seat beside her. He scowled and walked to the back of the church, where he sat alone in the very last row.

Pepper looked around the church. A woman in a flowered black-and-white dress played the piano softly. Instead of an altar, a raised platform filled the front of the room. A lectern stood in the center of the platform, flanked by three stuffed armchairs. An American flag hung on a standard to the right of the chairs and a white flag with a red cross in a blue field in one corner hung on the left side. Behind one of the chairs, a hand-carved wooden board said *Register of Attendance and Offering*. Thirty-seven people attended last Sunday.

Beside the attendance board hung a printed, framed poster.

We engage to maintain family and secret devotion; to religiously educate our children; to seed the salvation of our kindred and acquaintances; to walk circumspectly in the world; to be just in our dealings, faithful in our engagements and exemplary in our deportment; to avoid all tattling, backbiting, and excessive anger; to abstain from the sale and use of intoxicating drink as a beverage; and to be zealous in our efforts to advance the kingdom of our Saviour.

Saviour, not Savior. The old British spelling. People in the Appalachians didn't make changes lightly.

Dermid's simple, brown coffin, with gold-painted handles, rested on sawhorses in the middle aisle, between the varnished pews. She wondered what Dermid's coffin had been like for his first funeral. Who had been buried in it? Buried out of this same church, with the same people in attendance. She suspected the church had been full to overflowing that time. The rest of the country might be demonstrating against Vietnam, but the people in these mountains still respected dying for your country.

The young man beside her fidgeted and turned around frequently. Suddenly he grinned and slid towards Pepper to make more room at the end of the pew.

Cody Doan, wearing his summer uniform, maneuvered

both of his crutches into his right hand and worked his way into the pew. He looked over and saw Pepper.

"Shit," he said, a little too loud. "Half the fucking hospital is here."

The woman behind him tapped him on the shoulder with her paper fan. "Cody Terrance Doan, you will show respect. You are in the house of the Lord."

"Sorry, Miz Davis." He started to stand, but Pepper stopped him. "Wait, Doan."

She maneuvered her way to the side aisle, leaned over, and whispered in his ear. "I am so sorry. I should have realized that you would be here."

"I was on the pass list."

"I left after day shift yesterday. I never saw the pass list."

He motioned for her to come closer until his voice was wisps of sound in her ear. "What the fuck *are* you doing here?"

"I'm the one who discovered Dermid's body. I came to say good-bye to another veteran."

Doan looked at the floor. "You've earned that right."

"I'll stay out of your way. I'm so sorry to have made this more difficult for you."

Pepper retreated down the side aisle to another pew as Reverend Pretcherd came down the center aisle, Bible in hand, and mounted the platform.

Chapter 17

After an opening hymn, the congregation composed itself in silence. The fan in the middle of the ceiling creaked in slow circles, moving warm air around the room. Pepper picked up one of the paper fans with which some of the ladies fanned themselves. Mounted on a wooden stick, the worn cardboard square contained a colored picture of a river and a flowered-covered bank. Under the picture Pepper read:

"Shall We Gather at the River"
Freewill Homecoming and Revival Meeting
August 7–9, 1970
Supper on the grounds

She waved the fan in front of her face. It moved just enough air to keep her from sweating.

Reverend Pretcherd laid one hand on the Bible on the lectern. "I was called to be with Dicey and Tilda eight days ago, after they received the news about Dermid. Dicey met me at the door and said, 'Dermid wouldn't desert his country. My son was not a coward.' "

The middle-aged man in the front pew, who Pepper took to be Dicey Hagan, bowed his head. A man seated in the pew behind him leaned forward and laid a hand on Dicey's shoulder, then lifted his face in the direction of the ceiling fan. Pepper hoped he wouldn't start testifying or whatever they called it. The man remained silent.

"I prayed with them that afternoon, kneeling on their living room floor, seeking guidance and comfort from the Bible. We found our comfort talking about the friendship Dermid shared with Cody Doan, and Boyd Ramsey. You remember how it was with them. I don't have to tell you that story." He paused and took a sip of water from a glass on the lectern.

But you're going to tell it, Pepper thought, because people love stories. She glanced at the back of Cody's head. The man sitting beside him must be Boyd Ramsey.

"Those three were always together. Whenever you saw one of them, you saw the other two. It had been like that ever since they were boys. When they stayed together in Vietnam, we took it to be God's providence."

Pepper remembered Boyd's slight stutter and the not-quite-focused look in his eyes. Brain injury. Avivah had told her about the mortar attack.

"Six years ago, when they were sixteen, those boys didn't seek my counsel very often."

Pepper tried to imagine the three boys at sixteen. Hair slicked back with Brylcreem. White T-shirt, tight jeans, swaggering three-abreast down the sidewalk in Marshall on a Saturday afternoon. Dermid would have been the handsome one. She could tell that, having seen him only a few minutes, and then in death. Cody would have been the tall, gangling one. His face still had small memories of acne scars. Boyd? She hadn't paid enough attention to Boyd to form an opinion.

"So I was surprised when Dermid came to me one day and said, 'Mr. Pretcherd, Boyd, Cody, and I can't agree on something. Can you answer a question?'

"I said I'd try and Dermid began with, 'I know it says in the Bible to watch out, be on your guard against all kinds of greed; that a man's life does not consist in the abundance of possessions. But how do you know the difference between covetousness and needing something?'

"Now that was an interesting question, especially coming from a sixteen-year-old boy. I didn't have an answer. So the two of us, Dermid and I, we knelt down on my kitchen floor and prayed."

Don't these people ever pray in church, Pepper thought, and immediately rebuked herself. At least *they* prayed. She'd stopped a long time ago.

"After we asked for guidance, I turned to Joshua 7:21, where Acahan is speaking to Joshua." He opened his Bible and moved aside a bookmark. Several people turned the thin pages of the Bibles on their laps.

" 'When I saw in the plunder a beautiful robe from Babylon, two hundred shekels of silver, and a wedge of gold weighing fifty shekels, I coveted them and took them. They are hidden in the ground inside my tent, with the silver underneath.'

"We all know what happened to Acahan. Joshua sent soldiers to his tent to dig up the hidden treasure. Acahan was stoned to death. Only then did the Lord turn from His fierce anger."

Pepper had no idea what a shekel was worth. Perhaps Avivah knew. She hoped Avivah could find some clue in the story of Acahan and Joshua because she couldn't.

"Dermid studied on that passage a while. Finally he said, 'Boyd was right. I see my mistake now. I thought doing something for somebody else would entitle me to keep something that I wanted for myself. But it don't work that way, does it?' "

Reverend Pretcherd closed his Bible and laid it on the lectern in front of him. He took another drink of water, put the glass back, then held on to the lectern with both hands.

"Dermid wouldn't tell me what the boys had in mind. About a week later, he and his older brother pulled up in my driveway, towing the '32 Ford that Widow Teague had up on blocks in her barn ever since Sandy died."

No doubt, Sandy Teague had been related to Lilly Bell's egg-and-chicken man, Jimmy Teague. Pepper looked at the Hagan family pew. Tilda sat next to the end of the pew, then Dicey, then a pale, thin woman a few years younger than herself. Her large belly showed the last months of pregnancy. A small child napped with his head in her lap. Who was she? And why wasn't there an older brother in the pew?

" 'How'd you get that car?' I asked Dermid, cause I knew Dicey had said he wasn't going to put up the money for Dermid to buy any car.

"He said, 'Wachovia Bank bought it for me.' "

Several men tittered.

Reverend Pretcherd held up his hands. "I know, I know. Wachovia Bank isn't in the habit of buying cars.

"Dermid showed me a poster. The Junior Red Cross chapters of North Carolina were holding fund-raisers for the Red Cross, in memory of Fireball Roberts. NASCAR would match the highest amount raised, and the chapter that raised the most money would win a prize. Dermid, Cody, and Boyd talked Mr. O'Bryne—you recollect, he was the Junior Red Cross advisor then—into the chapter fixing up an old car, and selling it. Dermid and Mr. O'Bryne convinced Wachovia Bank to sponsor the project by buying the car."

Pepper guessed that Dermid did most of the talking. She liked Dermid's spunk and had a hard time accepting that the clever, handsome boy Reverend Pretcherd described, and the cold, dead deserter, lying on a bed in Normandy House, were the same person. Before and after, she thought. Before and after Vietnam.

Reverend Pretcherd undid the buttons of his suit coat. He slid the coat off, revealing a pure white shirt. Sweat stained the fabric under his arms. He laid the coat on a chair, then unbuttoned his sleeves and rolled them up, talking all the while.

"Dermid gave us no rest for the next few months. He bummed rides to every Ford dealer between Hickory and Knoxville, rummaging in their junk part bins. He sent Cody over to the café, looking for spare change, holding out his collection box, saying, 'There's crashes all the time. Takes a lot of blood to keep those drivers alive. That blood comes from the Red Cross.' He sent Boyd over to the movie house to talk them into showing a benefit movie on Saturday afternoon, with the money going toward the project. He talked his sister, Cathy, and her friends in the Home Economics class into making the seat covers. Ruined his mother's sewing machine, sewing the heavy leather. Isn't that right, Tilda?"

The woman to whom Colonel Tyler had given the flowers smiled and nodded.

"He hitchhiked to Asheville to talk the body shop there into a paint job in exchange for cleaning out the paint stalls. Then he talked the Junior Red Cross chapter into cleaning out those stalls."

So Dermid had a gift for talking people into doing things, even if it meant wrecking his mother's sewing machine, or co-opting his friends into a messy cleanup.

Reverend Pretcherd took a longer drink of water. "They finished that car about Thanksgiving. What a beauty! Two-tone blue paint job, black seat covers, chrome and lights polished so you could see your face in them. Remember the reaction when Dermid drove that car into the parking lot during our Thanksgiving celebration?"

Some of the congregation turned toward the side windows on the left side of the church, outside of which could be seen a simple tin-roofed shed covering long wooden tables. Pepper imagined white cloths and tables bent under the weight of food. Late November came cold to the mountains. The men and boys, gathered around the car, would have blown white breaths and stamped the ground every few minutes to keep the circulation going in their feet.

"The contest ended just after New Year's and, by December, Dermid's reluctance to sell the car worried Mr. O'Bryne. I tried to speak to Dermid, but he just waived my advice and said, 'I know what I'm doing, Reverend.' Then, two weeks before Christmas, Dermid and the car disappeared."

Pepper sat up straighter. So Dermid had a history of disappearing.

"Sheriff Ponder even came out himself to take the report on the disappearance. You'd think that a restored '32 Ford couldn't just vanish like that. Oh, there were sightings. Winston-Salem. Roanoke. Richmond. After that, nothing."

Disappeared off the edge of the Confederacy, Pepper thought. She tried to plot the road in her head. What lay beyond Richmond? Washington, D.C.? The steel towns of Pennsylvania? New York? Maybe even Canada, where Dermid had finally ended up years later.

"Tilda and Dicey were frantic. We organized a prayer circle for them, but it still grieves my heart to recollect how small it was. Dicey couldn't go to the café without hearing talk of Dermid being a thief. Tilda couldn't go to the grocery store without being snubbed. There was even mention of tar and feathers." He pointed his finger at the woman who chided Cody for using profanity. "Mrs. Davis, you remember how Tilda was snubbed?"

"I do remember."

Reverend Pretcherd pointed at a man on the other side of the church. "What about you, Neil Johnston? You remember that tar and feather talk?"

The man looked down at his shoes and shuffled uneasily in his seat. "I remember," he muttered.

"Come the Saturday after New Year's, down to the Motor Speedway in Charlotte, they had a platform and microphones set up. The Junior Red Cross chapters came up one-by-one to report on how much money they'd made. Most of 'em averaged three, four hundred dollars. They called Madison County three times before Boyd Ramsey stepped up to the microphone. 'Madison County Junior Red Cross donates three thousand and forty-eight dollars.'

"That crowd stood up and cheered. By the time Dermid walked into Marshall a few days later, hungry and half-froze, people thought him a hero. Those same people, who talked about tar and feathers, said how smart of him to take the car all the way to Pennsylvania and sell it to a man who owned a private car collection."

Reverend Pretcherd drained the water in the glass, picked up his coat, and slipped into it. People shuffled in their seats. One lady coughed. The preacher stepped off the platform, walked a few steps, and laid his hand on the casket. "We need to get on with our sad task of burying. You've been very patient, listening to that story. Did you wonder why I told it? Friends, I don't think Dermid would mind me telling you the part of the story you've never heard."

Pepper felt interest rising around her.

"When Dermid first came to me, he planned to raise as much money as he could by pretending he was restoring the car to sell it. Then he'd keep the car and give the Red Cross the money from the restoration fund instead. After we talked, he believed he'd be strong enough to sell the car he coveted so much, but he wasn't that strong.

"When the time came to sell that car, he couldn't let it go. Dermid *stole* that car. He had a vague idea of using what Red Cross money remained to go north, but no plan beyond keeping the car for himself. One night in Pennsylvania, with the remaining Red Cross money almost spent, that passage about Acahan and Joshua came to him. He told me, 'I realized that I'd behaved just like Acahan. The Lord knew exactly what I'd done.' He pulled over and knelt by the side of the road, asking the Lord what he should do.

"The Lord answered him. Dermid remembered a car magazine article about Silus Greenwald's private car collection and that Mr. Greenwald lived in Pennsylvania. The Lord guided him to Mr. Greenwald's house. The man's servant met him at the door and tried to turn him away."

He made it sound like a Bible parable, Pepper thought.

"Dermid would not be turned away. With the Lord's help, he prevailed, but by the time he convinced Mr. Greenwald to buy the car, Dermid couldn't reach Charlotte before the money had to be turned in. He wired every penny he had, including the money left from the Red Cross fund, to Boyd. Then Dermid hitchhiked home, going hungry, sleeping wherever he could."

Reverend Pretcherd's voice rose and fell, in a Southern singsong rhythm, as he paced up and down the center aisle of the small church. People turned their heads to follow him.

"Remember, brothers and sisters, that the Lord allowed

temptation to be put in Dermid's way and found him weak. But the Lord, in his goodness, gave Dermid a second chance, and Dermid came back to the right path.

"The Lord tried us and found us weak. We doubted that Dermid Hagan could be trusted. We called him a thief and worse. The Lord, in his infinite patience, waited six years to give us a second chance. Dicey Hagan recognized this when he met me, with 'I know in my heart that my son wasn't a coward.' Our place isn't to know the Lord's plan. Our place—no matter what outsiders say—is to trust that the Lord worked in Dermid's life."

Outsiders like me, Pepper thought.

"Our place is to pray. Pray for this fine family, bearing the burden of losing their son and brother for a second time. Pray for all of the young men who answered their country's call, the young men in Vietnam, those that are to go, and those who have come home. Pray for all soldiers who face temptations. Pray for Boyd Ramsey, who the Lord could have taken from us but who, in His mercy, He restored to his family. Pray for Cody Doan, that he finds the courage to bear his afflictions."

The back of Doan's neck turned red.

"Pray for that young man buried in our churchyard. We don't know him, don't even know if he was a Christian, but his body abided with us for a time. Pray that his family will receive his body and finally be at peace. I exhort you, brothers and sisters to remember Dermid's test of faith. Let us all pray that we find trust in the Lord the way he found trust. And now let us stand and sing a hymn of thanksgiving and joy, in the hope and belief that Dermid rests in the Lord."

As the congregation stood, Pepper glanced at the back of the church. Colonel Tyler's pew stood empty.

Chapter 18

Pepper sat in the shade, writing an account of the funeral for Avivah, while dark clouds built toward a thunderstorm. She was grateful the good weather held until after the burial.

The congregation had followed the hearse up the small hill behind the church for a simple graveside service. Reverend Pretcherd read Bible verses, workers from the funeral home lowered the coffin, and Dicey threw the first handful of dirt into the open hole. People drifted away, while the funeral home employees filled the grave.

"Yeah, no shit."

Laughter and Cody Doan's voice startled her as he and Boyd came down the path from the graveyard. Seated behind a large, leafy tree, Pepper could see them, but they couldn't see her. They disappeared along the far side of the church and reappeared at the front. Cody sat on the steps and rested his injured leg. Boyd leaned against the steps, idly tearing a long blade of grass into tiny strips. Their voices came to her, blown on the cooling wind that would soon bring rain.

Cody reached into his uniform pocket. "Got something for you." He handed it to Boyd, who looked inside, and handed it back.

"Don't need that."

"Everybody needs a little something to help them along now and then."

"My m-mother won't like it."

He closed his hand over Boyd's and pushed the envelope back toward him. "Your mother doesn't have to fucking know. This is just between you and me. For old times' sake. Go on, take it."

Boyd put the envelope in his pocket. "Thanks."

Cody stood up and balanced himself on his crutches. He looked around the parking lot. Pepper's car, the only one still there, was parked around the corner where he couldn't see it

"Looks like we're going to have to hump trail if we want to get to Dermid's folks. Won't be the first time, will it?"

"Won't be the first time."

Pepper watched them walk down the gravel driveway and turn left on the road. She waited a few minutes, then stuffed the notebook in her purse. They hadn't walked very far when she stopped beside them. "Give you a ride?"

Cody looked as if he wanted to tell her to "Fuck off," then he looked at Boyd. "Sure. Thanks."

He climbed in the front and Boyd in the back. "Boyd, this is Captain Pepperhawk, my head nurse at Fort Bragg. Captain, Boyd Ramsey."

Pepper twisted around and offered her hand. "How do you do?"

"P-Pleased to m-meet you."

"Where do you want to go?"

Cody pointed down the road. "Dermid's folks' place. You know where it is?"

"No."

"Turn right at the T-intersection."

She drove the mile and a half from the church in a couple of minutes, grateful she'd been able to spare Cody and Boyd the walk. She imagined they had made the trip on foot hundreds of time when they were younger. Before Vietnam.

Cars and trucks filled the yard in front of the Hagans' old, stone house. Elderly women rocked in three rockers set on the porch. A chicken coop, a small barn, and a pasture filled the farmyard. In the pasture, black-and-white cows chewed grass and looked at the crowd. Around the side of the house, Dicey and several men sat smoking and talking in a wooden gazebo.

Cody worked himself to a standing position. "You coming in?"

"Will I be in your way?"

"Nah, there's more than enough food." It was the first civil thing he'd ever said to her.

"Thank you." She hesitated. "About introducing me, could you not tell anyone I'm your head nurse?"

Cody looked hurt. "Suit yourself. Come on, Boyd, let's eat."

Pepper went in with them, nodding to the three older women on the porch. In the crowded living room, she sought out Tilda Hagan. "I'm Captain Pepperhawk from Fort Bragg. Colonel Tyler wanted me to ask if we could do anything further for you?"

"Thank you, no. We're all right. Is Colonel Tyler here?"

"He had to leave."

"He must be very busy. Please help yourself to food."

Pepper thanked her and went to the kitchen. Ham, chicken, macaroni casserole, potato salad, green salads, Jell-O, cut vegetables, biscuits, other homemade breads, and at least a dozen desserts filled the kitchen table and all of the counter space. Pepper fished a cold drink out of an iced tub beside the back door and made herself a couple of ham sandwiches on rolls. She nodded to the women washing dishes and moving platters around.

She didn't dare use the kitchen phone to call Avivah. Eating her sandwiches standing in a corner of the living room, she nodded and smiled at people. The pregnant woman she had seen in the Hagan pew came over to her.

"I'm Cathy Ramsey, Dermid's sister. My mother tells me you're from the Army."

Ramsey. Oh my God, she must be married to Boyd, Pepper thought. But why hadn't Boyd and Cathy sat together in church? Why hadn't she waited to give him a ride to the wake? Maybe they had divorced. Maybe Cathy couldn't live with Boyd's brain damage.

"I met a Boyd Ramsey this afternoon. Are you related?"

"By marriage. Boyd is my husband's second cousin on his father's side."

"Where is your husband?" Pepper blurted out, then wished she could take the question back. She knew from the woman's expression that she'd crossed the boundaries of polite conversation.

"He's at the roadblock. Wayne is a deputy."

At least he wasn't in Vietnam. "Oh, that's wonderful! . . . I'm sorry. It's been a long day, and I know an even longer one for your family. Could I ask a favor? Is there a phone I can use in private?"

"In the bedroom."

Cathy took Pepper to Dermid's parents' bedroom, then left her alone. As Cathy closed the bedroom door, Pepper realized she hadn't asked why Dermid's sister came over to talk to her.

White sheer curtains hung, unmoving, over the closed bedroom windows, filtering light and sound. The massive double bed and dark chest of drawers almost filled the bedroom, not furniture Pepper expected from the outside of the farmhouse. Then she remembered the furniture industry in western North Carolina. The bedroom set had probably been bought, as a discounted second, from one of the factory outlets in Hickory.

"MilitaryPoliceSpecialistRamerezMayIhelpyou?"

Pepper flashed back to July 4, standing in the lobby at Normandy House, looking at the neatly printed card.

"Ramerez, it's Captain Pepperhawk. Is Captain Rosen available?"

"She's right here. We've been waiting for your call."

So Avivah had told him what was going on. Ramerez probably spent the afternoon sitting close enough to the phone to hatch it.

Avivah contained her curiosity no better than he had. "Did you make it to the funeral?"

"Of course. Now I'm at the wake."

"Give already."

"What's Dermid Hagan's birthday?"

"Hold on, I'll get my notes . . . December 14, 1948."

Pepper made a quick calculation. Dermid turned seventeen on the road to Pennsylvania.

"See if you can find a man named Silus Greenwald, somewhere in Pennsylvania. He may be rich, but that's a relative term. I don't know how rich. Something to do with steel mills is a guess. He collects restored cars. Ask him about December 1965, about buying a restored '32 Ford, two-tone blue, with lots of chrome. Ask him if he knew the boy who sold it to him was seventeen."

"Why?"

"Because a seventeen-year-old boy is a minor and can't legally enter into a contract. I want to know how Dermid got around that."

"Why is it important?"

"I don't know. You said to find out about Dermid. I'm finding out about him."

"Anything else?

"Yeah, find out where Andrew Hagan is and why he isn't at his brother's funeral."

"Older or younger brother?"

"I don't know. Probably older. Andrew had a truck of his own; he and Dermid used it to tow the Ford when they took it to show to Reverend Pretcherd."

"Is this the same Ford that Mr. Greenwald bought?" Avivah sounded as if she had trouble keeping up with the conversation.

"I'll explain it all when I get back."

"Are you coming home tonight?"

"I should be back by midnight."

"I'll wait up. Okay, Mr. Greenwald and Andrew Hagan. Anything else?"

"Tell Private Osborne her flowers were lovely."

There was a knock on the door.

"I have to go. See you about midnight."

Pepper hung up and opened the door in time to hear Cathy Ramsey say to her mother, "You don't have to do this."

"Hush. I've made up my mind."

Mrs. Hagan looked tired. "Captain, could we talk to you after you're finished on the phone?"

"I'm finished. Thank you for letting me use the phone. I charged the long-distance call to my home."

Mrs. Hagan carried a package, about the size of a blouse box, done up in brown paper and string. Cathy closed the bedroom door and locked it, as her mother held the package out to Pepper. The package weighed more than Pepper expected.

"Dicey and I planned to ask Colonel Tyler for a favor. Seeing as how he had to leave, can I ask you?"

"Of course. I'll do whatever I can."

"This is the flag that covered the coffin, when we buried that man we thought was Dermid. Dicey and I want this flag to go to his family. It don't rightly belong to us, you see. Dermid didn't rightly earn it."

There were tears in her eyes. So much for Reverend Pretcherd's comforting sermon. Despite what Dicey said to the preacher, the Hagans knew their son had deserted.

Pepper pointed to the bed. "Could we sit and talk?"

The three women perched around the edge of the bed, on the shiny gold spread.

"I told you the truth when I said I was an officer from Fort Bragg. What I didn't tell you is I'm the person who discovered Dermid's body."

Cathy looked at her hands, moving over her pregnant belly. "Did he suffer?"

"I don't think so. He looked very peaceful in death."

Tilda Hagan nodded. "That's what Colonel Tyler said, but we thought he might be saying that to make us feel better. I'm grateful you said the same thing."

Cathy pulled back a little. "Why are you here?"

"I'm a Vietnam veteran." Pepper felt as if she was at confession. "Like your son. No, not like your son. I mean, I'm a nurse. I never saw combat." She stroked the top of the paper-covered box. "In Vietnam, I met a lot of guys like Dermid, guys from small towns, who found themselves in the middle of a war. What they wanted most was to survive so they could come home. Dermid spent over six months in Vietnam. He earned what this flag means. It should have been on his coffin today. When we find out who the other young man was, I'll make sure his family gets a flag, too.

201

You don't have to give up yours."

All three of the women began crying. They stood up and formed a circle, arms around one another. Cathy put her head on Pepper's shoulder. "I told my mother she didn't have to give it up."

Tilda rubbed the tears from her cheeks. "We wanted to make it right. We couldn't keep something that didn't belong to us."

Pepper squeezed her hand. "It *does* belong to you."

Cathy took a box of tissues from the top of the chest of drawers and handed them around. Pepper dried her face and tossed the tissue in the wastebasket beside the bed. "You've met Captain Delaney?"

Pepper could tell by their faces that they were *very* familiar with Captain Delaney. "I have a friend who is a military policewoman. She isn't sure Captain Delaney is doing the best things to find Dermid's killer. She wanted me to come to the funeral because learning more about Dermid may help find his killer."

"We never knew much about Dermid after he went to the Army. He wasn't one for letter writing. Now Boyd, he wrote his ma every week, afore he got hurt, that is, but getting a letter from Dermid was rare. I kept 'em all. Would you like to see them?"

"Please."

Tilda opened the top dresser drawer and took out a cigar box. Inside were pictures. Pictures of Dermid by himself, Dermid with Cody or Boyd. Pictures of the three of them in front of an orphanage. Pictures of them mugging for the camera. Pictures Pepper had seen many times, with many different faces. Pictures she herself sent home. She also recognized the stationery with a blue map of Vietnam down the left side of the page. Most of the letters were short and noncommittal. "I'm fine." "Thanks for the cookies." "This funny thing happened to Cody last week." Until she came to the last one. The letter covered two pages of the stationery the USO supplied free at their centers.

Saigon
19 January 1969

Dear Ma,

I went to see Boyd in the hospital this morning. They shaved all his hair off, but the nurses say it will grow back. He's got bandages around his head and two black eyes. They tell me he is in a coma, and they don't know when he will wake up. I talked to him for a long time about things back home, how we used to go fishing and work on cars and all, but I don't know if he knew I was there.

The doctor says if Boyd lives another week, the Army will fly him to Japan on a special hospital plane. There's a hospital in Japan for soldiers who are hurt real bad. The Army brings their families to see them. Tell Widow Ramsey to go to Japan just as soon as she hears Boyd is there. I figure if he hears his mama's voice, he might wake up. She won't have to worry about money for the trip, because the Army pays for everything.

If Boyd does live, tell Widow Ramsey to go to Lawyer Ferguson and do one of those papers, like we did on Uncle Cecil afore he died. The one that said we'd decide things for him. It's hard for me to write this, but I believe, even if Boyd does wake up, I don't think he's going to be in his right mind, at least for some time.

I know the church must have started a prayer circle for Boyd as soon as the Army told you he was hurt. Keep the circle strong and add prayers for Cody. You remember how I wrote you I was going on leave. That's how I came to Saigon, to catch the plane. Cody is alone in Long Bien right now. I wish to goodness I could have stayed and made sure he was all right, but I've got something important to do. Don't worry if you don't hear from me for a while. I'll be okay and I love all of you.

Dermid

Pepper folded the letter carefully and put it back in the box.

Tilda Hagan closed the box. "Do you know anything about insurance from the Army?"

"Not much. Why?"

The two women looked at one another. "You tell her, Cathy. Reckon it will have to come out anyway."

"About six weeks after we thought Dermid died, Widow Ramsey was called down to the Wachovia Bank. They had a check for ten thousand dollars in her name. A few days later, a letter came in the mail, saying how Boyd took out a special insurance policy, with extra money in it to pay for things if he got hurt. But the odd thing was, there weren't no papers to sign. That's the way the Army does things, isn't it? You got to sign papers?"

Oh, yes, Pepper thought, nothing happened in the Army without signing papers.

"Ma and I talked a lot about that check since we found out Dermid didn't die in Saigon. The more we talk on it, the more we think Dermid had something to do with that money, but how would Dermid have gotten ten thousand dollars?"

Chapter 19

Every contact Pepper tried to follow up with frustrated her. Wachovia Bank had closed for the weekend. Lawyer Ferguson left his office at noon every Friday to go fishing. Widow Ramsey was with her sister in Tennessee. The sister had no phone. She finally reached Avivah again. After Pepper calmed down, Avivah said, "On Monday, we'll follow up officially."

"I may be late. Don't wait up."

"What are you going to do?"

"I don't know yet. I have to do something."

"This is a police investigation. Don't screw this up for us."

Pepper hung up, angry that Avivah didn't trust her. She went to the kitchen and asked the woman washing dishes, "Have you seen Cody Doan or Boyd Ramsey?"

The woman put a glass to drain on the sideboard. "Cody's sister picked him up a few minutes ago. Boyd's collecting eggs for Tilda."

Through the kitchen window, Pepper saw Boyd come out of the chicken coop, carrying a large bowl. He'd changed from the suit he wore to the funeral into a pair of jeans and a blue and white T-shirt. To look at his solid body, his square face framed by tight, blond curls, no one would guess he had problems. Pepper met him at the bottom of the kitchen steps.

He held the half-full bowl of brown eggs out to Pepper. "How many?"

"Eight."

"That's w-what I thought," he said proudly.

Pepper searched for a scar, but his thick hair hid it. "Do you need a ride anywhere?"

"To Marshall, so I can c-catch the five-thirty bus."

"Where are you going on the bus?"

"Asheville."

"I can give you a ride to Asheville. It's on my way."

"I have to g-give Auntie Hagan these eggs and scatter some feed for the chickens."

"I'll wait for you at my car."

She longed to change out of her dress and stockings, but she didn't want to go into the house again. Almost everyone else had left; it was time for Tilda and Dicey to have time by themselves. Dicey, in overalls and a green work shirt, walked through the pasture, encouraging the cows toward the barn. Milking didn't stop because of funerals.

Boyd came out of the house ten minutes later, carrying a suitcase and a small Styrofoam cooler. He put them in the trunk beside Pepper's small suitcase. "Auntie Hagan made me take s-some of the leftover food. Can we g-get ice?"

"Sure."

They stopped in Marshall for gas and ice. In the service station bathroom, Pepper changed into shorts and a sleeveless blouse. When she came back to the car, Boyd handed her a cold drink and a package of cheese crackers.

"For the r-road."

Once they were on the road, she asked. "Going to Asheville for the weekend?"

"I live there."

"I thought you lived with your mom."

"Not for a w-while now. I have to be in Asheville s-so I can go to s-school."

"School?"

"At the Veterans' H-hospital. In Oteen. Three days a week. M-memory s-school." He looked embarrassed.

His memory must be Swiss cheese, Pepper thought.

"Is memory school hard?"

"Sometimes. But sometimes it's f-fun, too. It helps."

Pepper tried to think of a response, but none came to her. They rode together in silence.

"Cody said y-you were in Vietnam." He pronounced it to rhyme with jam, just the way Lilly Bell had.

"Sixty-seventh Evac Hospital in Qui Nhon."

"I was in Long Bien w-with an engineering company. Never w-went to Qui Nhon, not that I can remember," he finished with a grin.

He was less sensitive about his problems than she was, Pepper thought. She wondered if he remembered Long Bien and the engineering company or if someone had told him about them.

When they reached Asheville, Boyd asked, "You hungry?"

"I think I am."

"I know a g-good place near where I live in West Asheville."

"Can you direct me?" she asked, then was immediately embarrassed. Directions required memory.

Boyd took a small notebook out of his pocket. "I've got directions."

They drove through town and crossed over the French Broad River. Boyd directed her to the parking lot of a family restaurant. "I'll pay."

He reached in his back pocket, took out a worn brown wallet, and opened it. Pepper saw over a hundred dollars. She wondered if it was a good idea for Boyd to be carrying so much cash.

"I have enough," he said, but the tone in his voice and his puzzled face clearly said, *I think I have enough.* Pepper remembered the bowl of eggs, Boyd's proud look when she confirmed that there were eight eggs in the bowl. Boyd was relearning how to count.

"Do you want any help counting it?"

Hesitantly, he took the bills from his wallet, looked at the picture on each one, and separated them into piles. He picked up each pile as he counted it. "Maybe. . . . Three ones. A five. Four tens. We have enough for supper."

Pepper pointed to the twenties and the fifty he ignored. "What about those?"

Boyd curled his hand into a fist. "Those don't matter! I told you we have enough!"

They looked away from one another, then Boyd said hesitantly, hanging his head, "We haven't learned those in school yet."

"You want me to show you a trick some people use?" She almost said, "blind people use."

"Sure. Wait a minute." He turned to a clean page in his notebook and laboriously wrote at the top: *July 16, 1971.* "What do I call this?"

"How to recognize paper money."

He started to write, got as far as, "How to . . ." then handed the notebook and pen to her. "Write it down for me, will you?"

"You're doing fine. Write it down yourself."

"But I write real slow."

"Then this will be good practice for you."

"You sound just like my sister. Okay, spell *recognize* for me."

She did. "Do you always go to the same bank?"

"Yes. They have a l-letter from my mother telling them

h-how much money to give m-me every week."

"That's good. That means you can always deal with the same people. You know what one-dollar, five-dollar, and ten-dollar bills look like, so we can skip those. If the teller gives you twenties or fifties, have her fold the bills for you."

Pepper picked out the twenties and folded them in half crosswise, then the fifty and folded it in half lengthwise. Boyd drew pictures of the two shapes and Pepper helped him label them $20 and $50. She unfolded the money. "This is a twenty-dollar bill. How is it supposed to be folded?"

Boyd referred to his notebook and correctly folded the bill.

Pepper grinned at him. "Absolutely right. Now here's a fifty-dollar bill."

He folded that one correctly, too.

"Now how many bills do you have?"

"Three ones. A five. F-Four tens. Two twenties. A fifty."

They grinned at one another.

Several families, waiting for tables, crowded the small space by the cash register. The lady at the cash register recognized Boyd and told him the wait for a table would be about twenty minutes.

Boyd pointed to a small alcove where Pepper saw pinball machines. "Let's w-wait in there. You play?"

"I could learn."

Boyd took a handful of coins out of his jeans. "How much to play?

Pepper held up two fingers. "Two quarters. Fifty cents."

Apparently Boyd didn't have the same problem differentiating coins that he had with bills. He picked out all the quarters and lined them up on the windowsill. He put quarters in the slot and rammed it home, then pulled hard on the spring to put the first silver ball in play. "Got to k-keep the ball moving."

Pepper watched him handle the machine, his body hunched slightly over the glass, his middle fingers flicking the red buttons on either side of the machine, his eyes intent on following the ball. No words, no numbers, Pepper thought. Just light, sound, and fun.

He moved aside. "Your turn."

Her ball slid in a straight line down the machine and disappeared in the hole. Boyd laughed.

"No, like this." He moved behind her and wrapped his arms around her, putting his fingers over hers. Pepper suddenly found it hard to concentrate on the pinball machine. "D-don't wait for the ball. Keep the flippers moving. All th-the time."

Laughing, they played out the six quarters. As the hostess led them to their booth, Pepper said over her shoulder, "You play well."

Boyd slid into the red leatherette booth. "I got lots of p-practice in the hospital."

"Womack?"

"Walter Reed, in W-Washington, D.C. The brain-injured unit had pinball machines in therapy. I was lousy at first."

The waitress appeared at their table, carrying menus. "You want coffee?"

"Ch-Cherry Coke."

"Make that two."

Pepper watched Boyd look at his menu, looked around at what other people had ordered, and said to the waitress, "I'll have what he's having." If Pepper didn't know his history, she never would have known he couldn't read the menu.

"So you were never at Womack, that you remember?"

she asked, testing to see if other people could use the same line he used about himself.

"Not that I remember. S-Saigon, Japan, then Walter Reed. Other people had to t-tell me I was in S-Saigon. I didn't wake up until Japan."

"Do you remember being hurt?"

"No, p-praise God."

The waitress brought their drinks. Boyd's hand trembled as he took his glass.

Pepper was torn between getting information for Avivah and the dark look in Boyd's eyes. She took time to work up her courage, stirring the cherry flavoring into her Coke, taking a sip, and fishing the cherry out of the bottom of the glass with the straw. Now or never. Do it.

"What's the last thing you remember about Vietnam?"

"Thanksgiving. We had turkey dinner. Then we played b-basketball against the out-processing d-depot. Whipped 'em good. The s-score was ninety-eight to eighty, our favor." He pushed his drink away and played with the straw, tying it into small knots, not looking at Pepper. "How c-come I can remember one stupid basketball score and I can't r-recognize money?"

Pepper leaned closer to him and said very softly, "No one knows how memories are made, even less about how they are lost."

"Yeah, I know. T-Tissue damage. Swelling. The l-laying down of memory tracks. Y-You know what? I w-wish I remembered C-Christmas. I l-like C-Christmas."

Pepper thought about Christmas at the Sixty-seventh Evac. "I like Christmas, too. At the hospital all the tables were decorated. The hospital commander and the chief nurse came around and shook hands with everyone. We went caroling on the wards. Then we had a big turkey dinner. Just like you described for Thanksgiving."

"Cody says we s-stood down on Christmas. The general c-came to eat b-breakfast with us. Told us we w-were doing a real important job. Then w-we went and got the orphans. G-Gave them a big dinner and p-presents. G-Gave the nuns presents, too. At least, that's w-what Cody says happened."

Pepper remembered the pictures of the three young men outside an orphanage. "You cared a lot about the orphans, didn't you?"

He thought for a minute, then his face brightened. "I think I must have. We b-built beds for them. And we c-collected money for them, to b-buy food and all. We w-were going to collect more money for them after C-Christmas. I w-wonder if they e-ever got it?"

"I imagine they did." Pepper had a brief idea that instead of giving the money to the orphans, Dermid stole it and sent it to Boyd's mother. Then she discarded the idea. She seriously doubted the engineering company had raised ten thousand dollars in a few weeks. Or if they had, and that much money went missing, there would be a record of it. Easy enough to trace.

"Chow's up," she alerted Boyd to the waitress behind him with two full plates and a side order of biscuits.

When she felt hunger pressing less, Pepper laid her fork down on her plate and leaned forward.

"Boyd, I'm working with a military police officer at Fort Bragg. Captain Rosen is trying to find out who killed Dermid. I need to ask you a few questions. Do you want to wait until we're done here?"

"What k-kind of questions?"

"About Dermid. About if you knew he was still alive?"

"Naw, I n-never knew that."

"He never called you?"

"No."

"Nobody ever called your family asking for you?"

"Not that th-they told me."

Pepper hesitated. "I don't know how to ask something else without it sounding personal."

"Go ahead and ask. C-can't be any worse th-than some of the stupid questions p-people have asked."

I'll bet not, Pepper thought. She'd already heard visitors ask the patients on Ward Six-A some pretty stupid and personal questions.

"How do you handle . . . I mean, what do you do if you get mail?"

"I take mail to school with me. It's p-part of the class. They h-help us read the l-letters and answer them."

"How long have you been taking your letters to school?"

Boyd closed his eyes and thought for a minute. "S-Since last September."

"And before that, you lived with your mother. Did she help you with your mail?"

"Sh-She'd read it to me."

Avivah said Cody received letters beginning in April of this year, well after Boyd brought all of his mail to the people at the veterans' hospital. She was convinced that Dermid Hagan had never written to Boyd.

Boyd cleaned his plate with the last biscuit. He reached in his shirt pocket and took out a small calendar book. Pepper saw an entry for almost every day.

"You l-like bluegrass?"

"Yes."

Boyd turned the calendar around so she could see it. "Sh-Shindig on the Green is t-tomorrow night. Would you like to go?"

"What's Shindig on the Green?"

"They play m-music outside. By the c-courthouse. P-People bring food and a b-blanket and s-sit on the grass. S-Sometimes there's clogging."

Pepper looked at the clock on the wall behind Boyd. She had a five-hour drive ahead of her. In spite of telling Avivah not to wait up, Pepper knew she would be waiting.

"I'm sorry, I have to go back to Fayetteville tonight."

"Oh." He sounded genuinely disappointed.

Pepper looked at the calendar. "It looks like there's a Shindig on the Green every Saturday?"

Boyd thumbed through a couple of pages. "Every S-Saturday until September."

"What if I come back next weekend? Could we go then?"

"We sure could! You're sure y-you'll come?"

"I'll come."

"Then I'll w-write it down." He took his pen out and added a couple of words to July 24 so that it read *Shindig with Pepper*. Then, as an afterthought, under *1:00 Dermid's Funeral*, he added *Supper with Pepper*.

"Do you write everything down?"

"Only the things I want to remember."

"Can I see?"

Pepper flipped back to June, then to May, then to April. There was no note that mentioned Dermid. She looked at July 4. It said *Picnic*.

She pointed at the date. "Did anyone else go to this picnic with you?"

"My s-sister and her kids. We took food to the park. We stayed th-there all afternoon."

Pepper never considered Boyd for the murderer, but she knew Avivah would want to know where he was on the fourth.

"How do I get in touch with you next weekend?"

He turned to the front of the calendar and worked a business card from under the plastic cover. It said *Boyd Ramsey* and a telephone number. "That's my s-sister's house. She takes m-messages for me."

I wonder if she screens them, too, Pepper thought as she put the card in her purse. Like maybe messages from someone saying he was Dermid Hagan? Or someone whose voice sounded familiar but who refused to leave a name?

They finished their meal and Boyd paid the check. As they were leaving, Pepper bumped into a man coming in the restaurant door. Harlan Carter, dressed in civvies, looked tired, but as far as Pepper could tell, cold sober.

He looked embarrassed as he stood aside to let her and Boyd pass. "Captain Pepperhawk, what are you doing in Asheville?"

"Visiting a friend."

She took Boyd's hand and almost pulled him out of the restaurant. They sat in her car, watching through the restaurant window, as the hostess seated Carter in a booth at the back of the restaurant. "Friend of yours?"

"Someone from Fort Bragg."

Someone she never expected to see here. The first thing Cody Doan said to her in the church that afternoon came back to her. *Half the fucking hospital is here.* When and why had Cody seen Harlan Carter in Marshall today?

Chapter 20

At an early morning hour, Pepper put the key in her apartment door.

Avivah's door opened immediately. "What have you got?"

Pepper tried to mimic Avivah's New York accent. "Hello, Pepper. Did you have a good trip? Why yes, I did, thank you. You must be tired. Yes, I am. Would you like a chance to get inside your apartment before I bombard you with questions?"

Avivah picked up Pepper's suitcase. "Sorry."

While Pepper showered and changed into a nightgown and robe, Avivah sat on the couch, going through Pepper's notes. She wore a pair of white shorts and a white shirt, which made her black hair and dark tan more noticeable.

Pepper combed her wet hair. "How come guys aren't beating down your door?"

Avivah looked up from the notebook. "That's a weird question. What's gotten into you? You look like Benny when he comes back from Panama."

"Must be hanging around civilians. They make me edgy. You've got a wonderful face and black hair to die for and the body, the tan. Why aren't you dating anyone?"

Avivah had brought her own notebook, a twin of the one she had given Pepper. She compared notes between the two books and didn't look up. "I'm tall, I carry a gun, I have an attitude, and I work permanent evening shift. This does not lead to a healthy love life."

And you're obsessed with going to Vietnam, Pepper thought, hanging the wet towel over a chair and rummaging in the refrigerator for a cold drink. She remembered her own narrow focus in the three months between when she received orders for Vietnam, and when her plane landed there. A love life had been the furthest thing from her mind.

It came to her in an instant, standing with her damp head in the refrigerator, that she had survived Vietnam. It was over, behind her, like coming through a door in a dream. She knew if she looked behind her, the door wouldn't be there. There was no going back. Pepper felt an incredible weight lifted off her shoulders, a weight she hadn't even known existed. She felt like running or singing. Most of all, she felt like calling Benny. She wanted to say to him, "Benny, I survived Vietnam."

She imagined a few seconds of silence. Then he would chuckle and say something like, "Feels like coming up for air, doesn't it?" because that was exactly what it felt like. Just like when she swam the length of a pool underwater and came up gasping. For one moment, she fervently wished Avivah *could* go to Vietnam, if only for the pleasure of experiencing this moment when she came home.

Pepper closed the refrigerator door, handed a cold drink to Avivah and read over her shoulder. "I see you found the list I made."

Why did Mr. Greenwald buy a car from a seventeen-year-old boy?

Where is Andrew Hagan and why wasn't he at the funeral?

Did the engineering company in Long Bien play basketball with a team from the out-processing depot on Thanksgiving Day 1968, and what was the final score?

Did the engineering company give orphans from a Catholic orphanage dinner and presents Christmas Day, 1968? How much money did they give the orphanage?

Did they raise ten thousand dollars for orphans between Christmas 1968, and January 19, 1969, and did it go missing?

Who was buried in Dermid Hagan's grave?—Make sure his family gets a flag!

Where was Dermid going on leave? How long was he supposed to be gone? Did he ever arrive there?

Why was Harlan Carter in Asheville on Friday? When and why did he see Cody Doan in Marshall?

Did Dermid Hagan call Boyd Ramsey's sister?—I called her. She says not. Nice lady. I believe her.

Did Dermid Hagan know Boyd Ramsey was still alive? Did he know he can't read and that he took all his mail to the veterans' hospital for someone to help him read it?

Did Dermid Hagan know he was dead?

"That's some list."

"A five-hour drive in the middle of the night gave me a lot of time to think. Where do we start?"

Avivah looked at the questions again. "I can answer number two. Andrew Hagan works on an offshore oil rig near Venezuela. The helicopter that was supposed to bring him in from the rig to catch a plane couldn't get there for two days because of bad weather. They brought him to Caracas late Friday morning. He should be home by Sunday."

"How did Ramerez find that out so quickly?"

"Took one phone call. He thought he would start with the Madison County Sheriff's Office. He figured if Andrew Hagan wasn't at the funeral because he was, say, in jail or on the run from the cops, they would know about it. And it seems one of the sheriff's deputies is married to Andrew's sister."

"That would be Wayne Ramsey. He's married to Cathy Hagan and they're expecting their second child, around November, I would say, from the look of her belly. Wayne is Boyd Ramsey's second cousin, on his father's side."

Avivah gave Pepper one of *those* looks, then said, "My sister is wasting her time in university. She should just pay you for the privilege of following you around. And, for question number one, we found Mr. Silus Greenwald. Sixty-seven years old. Owner of not one, but two steel mills. At least he used to own them. He's retired now. We had to convince him we weren't trying to get him for an illegal car sale. And yes, he knew Dermid was underage."

"So why did he buy the car from him?"

"Dermid explained to him about the Red Cross fund-raising drive, and Mr. Greenwald checked and found it was legit. Dermid also had ownership papers for the car, registered in the name of the Marshall County Junior Red Cross and their advisor Mr. O'Bryne. He had a letter from Mr. O'Bryne saying he had permission to sell the car."

"But he was still seventeen and couldn't write a contract."

"Mr. Greenwald called Mr. O'Bryne, who verified that the ownership papers and the letter giving permission to sell the car were also legit."

Pepper threw herself on the couch. "Hold on, hold on. That doesn't fit with the story Reverend Pretcherd told. According to him, no one in town knew where Dermid was. His parents were worried sick. I can't believe somebody who knew where Dermid was would let them worry like that. And Dermid didn't even know he was going to sell the car until he got to Pennsylvania, so why was he carrying permission to sell it?"

"I have no idea. We're going to have to track down Mr. O'Bryne." She looked back at the list. "Did Dermid Hagan know *who* was dead?"

"Himself, that *he* was dead. What we know is that he left Long Bien, went to the Third Field to see Boyd, and went to the USO to write his mother a letter. His dog tags and ID were lost, stolen, or given to someone. We don't even know for certain if that happened in Saigon. Maybe he'd even lost them or left them at the Third Field by mistake when he was a patient."

"So maybe Harlan Carter had them all along? Planted them on the body, then pretended to identify it?"

"I hadn't thought of that. Think about this from Dermid's point of view. On the day he disappears in Saigon, a man is run over by a bus and Harlan Carter identifies him as Dermid Hagan. Dermid's death would have been reported in two places: the Marshall newspaper—it's a weekly, by the way—and *Stars and Stripes*, listed on the casualty page under *Died, not combat-related*. It's unlikely Dermid ever saw either of those papers. From his point of view, he'd deserted, not died. We should ask Cody if Dermid wrote anything specific in his letters about being dead, something like, 'I guess it's a shock for me to come back from the dead like this?' "

Avivah added the question to Pepper's list. "You actually want me to find out the score for a scrum basketball game two-and-a-half years ago?"

Pepper thought of her very proper Lieutenant Batta, the man with the high-octane liver damage. "Somewhere in the Army there is an anal-retentive company clerk or a second lieutenant who knows the answer to that question. Tell Ramerez to dig."

"How come it's important?"

"It's one of the few things Boyd Ramsey remembers, or says he remembers. People with brain injuries sometimes tell you the most gosh-awful stories that they think are the truth. It's called fabrication."

"You think Boyd Ramsey fabricates?"

"I want some concrete evidence that he doesn't." It would be nice to reassure Boyd. Pepper thought about telling Avivah she was going back to Asheville next weekend for a date with Boyd, but maybe that was her own business. She wondered if, on Sunday, he might like a trip out to look at Lilly Bell's flowers.

"What's this about a flag?"

"Something I promised Dermid's mother and sister I'd see about."

Avivah leaned back and closed her eyes for a couple of minutes. "Are you calm now? Gotten over your encounter with civilians?"

The wonderful revelation Pepper had experienced about surviving Vietnam faded to a steady rosy glow. "I guess so."

"Here's the big news from this end. We may know who was buried in Dermid Hagan's grave."

"How? Who?"

"They autopsied the body day before yesterday. Autopsied isn't exactly the right word. Not much left. The most interesting thing was what was left. A plastic heart valve."

"A what?"

"You heard right, a plastic heart valve. Apparently the person buried in Dermid Hagan's place had an artificial heart valve."

"He would have been unfit for military service if he had heart problems that bad."

"Yep."

"Oh great. Now we have to find a civilian who disappeared

221

from Saigon in January 1969. Let's see. Journalists. Free-booters. Bankers. Missionaries. Businessmen. Private contractors. Maybe just someone who married a Vietnamese woman and lived there. Maybe somebody who wasn't even supposed to be in the country. Maybe even a bloody tourist."

"How about Michael Fuller, an engineer for Pacific Architects and Engineers?"

"PA&E? The civilian contractors. A possibility. They were all over the place, even in Qui Nhon."

Avivah flipped the page in her notebook. "On February 1, 1969, the head of the PA&E office in Saigon filed a missing persons' report with the military police. One of his engineers, Michael Fuller of Chicago, Illinois, had gone missing in Bangkok. From the missing persons' report: 'Identifying scars or marks: several large scars, including open-heart surgery scar, center of chest.' We're trying to find out if Michael Fuller's surgery involved a valve replacement."

"But PA&E are civilians. Why file a report with military police in Saigon?"

"Maybe they were just covering all the bases. Maybe they figured the military police were better organized and more likely to stumble on something than the civilian police."

"*Did* they stumble onto anything?"

"Not really. It was just before Tet of '69. You remember Tet of '69?" Tet was the Chinese New Year. Every year, the Viet Cong and North Vietnamese made some of their most vicious and concentrated attacks throughout Vietnam.

"I saw it on television. It wasn't as bad as Tet of '68, but bad enough. During Tet, the military police would have had other things to do besides look for a missing civilian engineer."

"That's about it. What they did find out was that Michael Fuller took a plane to Bangkok on January twentieth."

"The day Dermid disappeared. Why was he going to Bangkok?"

"PA&E routinely had instruments that needed fixing or calibration that couldn't be done in Vietnam. Every three months they sent a shipment to Bangkok. One of their engineers always went with the shipment. It was a perk. Whoever went had to check it in at the repair company and describe what was wrong with it. Then he stayed in Bangkok until the equipment was fixed, tested it, and flew with it back to Saigon. In January, it was Michael Fuller's turn to go."

"He didn't come back?"

"Apparently not."

"If he wasn't reliable, why did they let him go to Bangkok?"

"A couple of months earlier, Fuller had almost been accidentally pounded by a B-52 raid on the Laotian border. His boss figured Fuller could use a vacation. When he didn't come back, the boss called the Bangkok hotel where PA&E people stayed. No Fuller. Never had been any Fuller. Someone who said he was Michael Fuller checked in the equipment at the repair company, explained what was wrong with it, walked out, and disappeared. Never checked into the hotel, never heard from again. We're still trying to find out if Michael Fuller ever worked as an engineer anywhere in the world after 1969."

"Bet you turn up empty," Pepper said, yawning. How was she going to convince the Army to give a flag to a civilian contractor's family?

Chapter 21

Pepper fought to extricate herself from a dream where she and Benny explained a smooth, black box to Dermid Hagan. Their safety depended on Dermid understanding how the box worked and, at the same time, they didn't understand what they had to explain.

The phone kept ringing. She tried to focus on the clock. Three a.m. Sunday morning. Suddenly afraid her father might have had an accident on the night shift at the rail yard, she grabbed the receiver.

"Hello."

"Elizabeth Pepperhawk?"

She shivered. The voice sounded official. Bad news.

"This is *Captain* Pepperhawk." As if rank offered protection.

"Officer Dillingham, Asheville City Police. Do you know a Boyd Ramsey?"

She sat up in bed, stomach churning, hoping for a simple problem, but she knew policemen didn't make phone calls at three a.m. for simple problems.

"I met Boyd Ramsey on Friday."

"How did your name and telephone number come to be in a notebook in Mr. Ramsey's possession?"

"I wrote it there in case Mr. Ramsey wanted to contact me." The two of them had sat in her car, talking, under the street lamp in front of Boyd's apartment, while she wrote it.

"What is your relationship with Mr. Ramsey?"

"Captain Avivah Rosen, from the military police brigade at Fort Bragg, and I are investigating a murder. Mr. Ramsey is a friend of the deceased. I collected background information relevant to the investigation." God, she sounded like Sergeant Joe Friday on a bad day.

"I regret to inform you that we found Mr. Ramsey dead this morning about one a.m. Indications are that he died of a drug overdose."

"No!" Pepper screamed silently, turning her face away from the telephone receiver. A whimper escaped.

"I'm sorry. I didn't get that?"

Pepper beat her fist into the pillow. Just like in the emergency room, she told herself, come apart later, but now things must be done. "I need details." Her voice sounded cold. All the better. She hoped Officer Dillingham would think her a cool, professional cop.

"I'm not allowed to discuss details."

"Officer Dillingham, you can talk to me now, or you can talk to Captain Rosen and Captain Delaney, the CID officer, Monday morning. Your choice. Captain Delaney will not be happy if we wait until Monday."

"I guess it's okay, you being brother officers—I mean, sister officers." Pepper guessed that the Asheville City Police wasn't co-ed.

"Shindig on the Green is a music and dancing event, every Saturday night, in the park in front of the courthouse. We put on extra foot patrols to do crowd control."

Pepper fought to sound calm. "I'm familiar with the concept." If she'd gone with Boyd to the Shindig, he would still be alive.

"A patrol made a swing through the area just before one a.m. They saw a man, lying on a bench. They looked a little closer and discovered he wasn't breathing. They started

CPR and radioed for an ambulance. He was DOA at the Mission."

Pepper guessed that *the Mission* was the local hospital.

"We found a syringe under the bench, and a small envelope in his pocket that contained a residue of white powder. Cocaine is my guess. Was Mr. Ramsey a habitual cocaine user?"

Pepper wanted to yell at him that Boyd didn't use drugs at all. But she didn't really know that. She tried to keep her voice from trembling. "I told you, I only met him Friday night. I saw no indication that he used drugs."

"We both know how guys can fool you. I wish I had a nickel for every time relatives insisted that their son or brother couldn't possibly be a drug user."

He believed she was a policewoman. "Captain Rosen will expect a courtesy copy of your report." She gave him Avivah's name and the address for the military police brigade.

As she dressed, Pepper called Ward Six-A. Lieutenant Forbes answered the phone.

"It's Captain Pepperhawk. Is Sergeant Doan back from pass?"

"He came back Friday night."

"How is he?"

"Not good. His doctor put him on strict bed rest, and he's thinking of taking him back to surgery next week."

"Who's the medical officer on duty?" All the services in the hospital took turns providing a doctor for night call. She prayed the doctor working tonight wouldn't be from orthopedics.

"Someone from internal medicine." Pepper relaxed.

"There's been a death in Doan's family. I'm on my way over."

"Did the chaplain call you?" Lieutenant Forbes sounded

confused. Usually the chaplain was the first to know about a death in a soldier's family.

"No, and don't wake Doan up. I want to be the one to tell him."

"Yes, ma'am."

Lieutenant Forbes accepted, without comment, her head nurse's arrival, dressed in rumpled jeans and a T-shirt, accompanied by a military police officer, also in civilian clothes. All she said was, "I made fresh coffee. I thought Doan might need some."

Pepper took several mints from a dish on the desk. "Thanks. Captain Rosen would probably like some, too."

Lumps of sleeping figures filled the beds in the dark, open ward bays. Pepper walked quietly past the first bay and into the second one, her way lit by small, yellow night lights near the floor. She had a great deal of practice moving quietly through a sleeping ward.

Pepper had learned a painful lesson in Kansas. Never stand within arm's reach when waking up a man who had been to Vietnam. She stood at the foot of Doan's bed and tossed a mint on his chest.

"Doan."

She threw another mint. "Doan," this time a little louder.

He came up swinging.

She lowered her voice to a whisper. "Be quiet and listen. Do you have any civilian clothes here?"

He pointed to the bedside stand. "In there."

"Put them on, then come to the nurses' station. Right now, as fast as you can."

He threw back the covers. "What the fuck is going on?"

Pepper jerked her head toward the nurses' station. "Not here. Out there."

Five minutes later, Doan, wearing blue hospital pajamas and carrying civilian clothes in his lap, rolled out of the ward. He wheeled himself to the bathroom and reappeared wearing the civilian clothes. He spotted Avivah. "What the fuck is she doing here?"

Pepper pointed down the hall. "Let's go find a private place."

Doan followed them to the uniform room next to the elevator. Pepper closed and locked the door.

She stood in front of Doan's wheelchair. "There is no easy way to do this. The Asheville City Police found Boyd Ramsey dead about one o'clock this morning. They think he took a cocaine overdose."

His face went white and Pepper put her hand on his shoulders, in case he fainted.

He pulled away and pounded his fist on the wheelchair. "No way! No fucking way! The three of us took the pledge in church: no drugs, no booze. Boyd kept that pledge; even in Vietnam, he never drank a beer or smoked a joint. He took a lot of hazing for it."

Pepper remembered that Boyd ordered a cherry Coke at the restaurant. "That's what I figured."

Avivah turned the bent metal chair around and sat on it backwards, facing Doan. "When the two of you came back from the graveside, what did you give Boyd? In the envelope. What his mother wouldn't like him having?"

For a second, Pepper thought Doan would come out of his wheelchair and attack her. "The branches of the big tree, at the end of the picnic shed, hid me. I saw you, but you didn't see me."

"It wasn't fucking cocaine."

"What was it?"

"Money. Widow Ramsey always worried about money,

even before Boyd got hurt. Can't say I blame her, the Ramseys never had much. Since he got hurt, she's kept him on a strict budget. I mean, a guy likes to have a little extra money, in case something comes up."

Like taking a woman out for pinball and a meal, Pepper thought. "What denominations?"

"A fifty, two twenties, and a ten. A hundred dollars in all."

"That's a lot of money."

"Boyd was saving up for a drum set. He wanted to take lessons. I wanted to help him out."

Pepper waited for Avivah to ask another question, then, when she didn't, asked, "In church, do you have—I don't know what you call it—but people get up and say things?"

"Anybody can say how the Lord has moved in their lives."

"Would you be willing to get up in church and say that Boyd never used drugs?"

"Why?"

Why, indeed? Because Pepper knew exactly what was happening in Madison County right now. Officer Dillingham would have also called the other number in Boyd's notebook, his sister. She called her cousin, the deputy sheriff, and news of Boyd's death now moved up and down the valley and into the coves. Telephones rang and lights snapped on in back bedrooms. People reached for their Bibles in—how had Lilly Bell put it—in their time of sorrow.

"Because I like and respect the people in your church. I liked Boyd and I don't want those people to think he broke his pledge. Boyd took me on a date and I owe him a favor."

Doan and Avivah asked in unison. "He took you on a date?"

"What's wrong with that? I'm datable."

"I can't recollect Boyd taking anyone on a date, not since he was hurt, I mean."

"Well he took me, and I am rightly pissed off at him getting himself killed. I want fucking answers and I want them right fucking now!"

Doan shifted in his chair. "How come you'd date a gimp, when you didn't want me to tell anyone you were my head nurse?" The guys referred to themselves as gimps, a private term for cripples that outsiders weren't allowed to use.

"I don't make a connection."

"When we arrived at Dermid's place, you asked me not to tell anybody you were my head nurse. I figured being seen with a couple of gimps embarrassed you."

Pepper leaned her head against the cold metal uniform rack and closed her eyes, remembered Cody's hurt expression. "I'm so sorry. I was at the funeral to collect information about Dermid, and I didn't want people to know too much about me. I'm so sorry I hurt your feelings."

"Okay, I might have misunderstood. I'm willing to go to church, but the doc put me on strict bed rest. How am I supposed to get there?"

Pepper unlocked the door. "Let me work on that."

After Pepper left, Avivah took out her notebook. "I know you've already given us a statement, but I need to ask you a few more questions."

Cody Doan slumped, the bravado he usually displayed gone. "All right."

"On Thanksgiving, 1968, did your company play basketball with a team from the out-processing depot in Long Bien?"

"What does that have to do with anything?"

"It's one of the things Boyd told Captain Pepperhawk. We need a baseline about what he could and couldn't remember."

"We played them."

"What was the score?"

"How the hell can I remember?"

"Did you win or lose?"

"We won. They supplied the beer."

"Did you invite orphans to your compound on Christmas Day, 1968?"

"Yes. A whole truckload of gook kids, and half a dozen nuns."

"How much money did the engineering company give the orphanage that day?"

He thought for a moment. "About two hundred cash and we opened a bank account for them in Long Bien. We put the equivalent of six hundred dollars, U.S., in it. In piastres, of course."

"Even in Vietnamese piastres, that's a lot of money."

"Dermid's tithe made the difference."

Avivah sat back. "What tithe?"

"After he had malaria, when he came back from the hospital in Saigon, he gave five hundred dollars to the chaplain. He said he'd won big in a poker game and wanted to tithe."

"When was this?"

Cody shrugged. "Somewhere around the beginning of November."

Avivah remembered Pepper's description of the collection and attendance board at the front of the church. "What's the usual tithe in your church?"

"Ten percent."

She wrote down figures. "That would mean Dermid won five thousand dollars in the poker game."

"It sounded ridiculous to me, too. That Junior Red Cross thing always bothered him, how people treated him like a hero. He told me, more than once, that if he ever did anything for anyone again, he'd keep it a secret. I figured the five hundred was everything he won, and he didn't want people making a fuss over him for giving it all away."

"Did your company raise ten thousand dollars for orphans between Christmas, 1968, and January 20, 1969?"

"Hell, no. The chaplain had to keep after us to get a couple of hundred a month from us."

"Where was Dermid going on leave?"

"Bangkok."

"How long was he supposed to be gone?"

"Ten days."

That, Avivah thought, would explain the letter to Dermid's mother, and why he told her that Cody would be alone for a while. At least when he wrote the letter, Dermid intended to return to Vietnam.

"Did Dermid know Boyd Ramsey survived his injury?"

"Yeah. After I believed the letters came from Dermid, I wrote him about Boyd."

"Did you tell him that Boyd couldn't read?"

"I told him about Boyd's special school, and that, if he wrote Boyd at his Asheville address, he'd take it to the hospital to have someone help him read it."

Not a thing Dermid would want. If Dermid made no attempt to contact Boyd Ramsey, why was Boyd dead?

"Did Dermid know he was dead?"

"Know *who* was dead?"

"That people thought *he*, Dermid, was dead. When he wrote to you, did he write anything like, 'I know my death upset all of you.' "

"Death was never mentioned."

"Did you ever meet a Michael Fuller in Vietnam?"

"Not that I remember."

"Did Dermid ever mention the name?"

"No."

"Did you ever work with Pacific Architects and Engineers?"

"That civilian group? They did their projects, we did ours. Never even saw one of them close enough to talk to him."

"Did Dermid ever talk to you about PA&E, about having any kind of contact with them?"

"Never."

Pepper came back and closed the door behind her. She nodded to Avivah.

"One last question. When and why did you see Wardmaster Harlan Carter on Friday?"

"The wardmaster from medical holding company?"

"Yes."

"I never saw him."

Pepper reminded him, "The first thing you said to me in church was, 'Half the fucking hospital is here.' "

"I was talking about the chief nurse and that sidekick of hers, the major that comes around in the evening."

Avivah looked very interested. "Major Buckner?"

"I think that's her name."

"Where did you see Colonel Norton and Major Buckner?"

"We took the same flight to Asheville."

"Did they see you?"

"They made a fuss about opening doors for me, like I can't manage a door after being on crutches for months. The colonel got all sympathetic when I said I was going to a funeral." He laughed. "I told them it was my uncle who ran moonshine, who'd wrapped himself around a tree."

Avivah could imagine him doing that just to see the women's expression.

"Some other nurses met them at the airport and they went off together."

"Military nurses?"

"Civilians."

"How did you know they were nurses?"

Doan gave her a look that said, *give me a break.*

"Tell me what you did on Friday?"

"My sister picked me up at the airport and drove me to the church. Captain Pepperhawk saw me there. Boyd and I stayed at the grave until they filled it, you know, talking about Dermid and how fucking strange the whole thing was. Captain Pepperhawk gave us a ride to the wake. We ate, talked to the men, then my sister took me back to the airport. I was back at the hospital by 1745 hours. My signature is in the pass book."

"You never saw Specialist Carter, at the airport maybe, or if your sister stopped for gas?"

"How many times do I have to tell you, I never saw the guy."

"Can you think of any reason someone would want Boyd dead?"

"Everyone liked Boyd. People trusted him. Even after being hurt, he still charmed people."

He appeared to have charmed Pepper. Avivah closed her notebook. "That's all the questions, Doan. Thank you."

He looked at Pepper. "What now?"

"I've wangled a pass out of the on-call doctor. The first plane to Asheville leaves at 0700, but I don't want you sitting for hours on a hard airport chair, so I booked you a motel room. When you get to the motel, lie down, put your

234

leg up. That's an order. After you go to church this morning, come straight back here on the first return flight. I'm laying myself on the line for this. Don't screw me around or you'll wish you hadn't."

Avivah and Pepper drove him to the motel. They watched him swing himself on crutches up to the registration desk. Pepper buried her face in Avivah's shoulder and cried.

Chapter 22

Avivah lay awake until dawn. She had told Pepper that the world would one day come as a great surprise to her. The memory of Pepper holding on to her, crying until she had no tears left, made her sorry that she'd been right.

Sunday was a disaster. It rained, stopped, became unbearably muggy, rained again, stopped again, and, finally settled into an ugly combination of grey sky and black clouds. Avivah did her laundry, started a letter to her parents, tried to read, all the time waiting for Pepper to knock on her door.

On his way to Mass, Benny stopped to invite her and Pepper to Lorraine's house for supper. She told him about Boyd's death and the two of them stood looking at Pepper's closed door. They didn't knock.

Early in the afternoon, the brigade duty sergeant called. Did Avivah want to talk to a Mr. O'Bryne from Atlanta? She did and he gave her the man's phone number.

"Mr. O'Bryne, I'm curious how you knew we wanted to talk to you."

"One of my former students from Madison County phoned me."

He sounded like a man in his forties, a clipped, precise voice. "I am devastated by this news about Dermid. This horrible Vietnam war. I don't know how you people cope. I want you to know I demonstrate against it, on your behalf, every chance I get."

236

He paused, as if waiting for Avivah to thank him. Pepper was right. Civilians made her nervous, too.

"I need information about the Red Cross drive, and the car sale in December, 1965."

Mr. O'Bryne hesitated. "All right."

"Why did Dermid Hagan have a letter with him authorizing him to sell the car?"

"Because he forged it." Despite his saying that the news about Dermid devastated him, his voice sounded angry.

"Dermid put you in a difficult position."

"Difficult. Young woman, I was fired because of that car fiasco."

"Let's back up. Dermid also had the car title with him. He couldn't have forged that."

"He had the title with him so he could legally drive the car around, show it off to raise interest in the auction we planned to hold before Christmas."

"Then he disappeared."

"Yes."

"When was the next time you heard about Dermid or the car?"

"When Silus Greenwald called me to verify that my letter was authentic. I had written no such letter."

"Why didn't you tell Mr. Greenwald that?"

"My job was already on the line, plus the bank hinted that, if that car wasn't sold for the Red Cross drive, I'd have to reimburse them for it. I wanted the car and Dermid Hagan out of my life."

"Even with your permission over the phone, a seventeen-year-old boy couldn't legally sign the bill of sale."

"The school's lawyer drew up the contract, which I signed, and sent special delivery to Mr. Greenwald. That was that, and good riddance."

Avivah consulted Pepper's notes. "Dermid's parents were terribly worried. You didn't tell them you knew where to find their son."

"I didn't want anything to do with the Hagans, ever again."

Avivah compressed her lips against her anger. "Where were you on July 4 of this year?"

"Touring New York City with the junior class and their chaperones from the private academy where I teach. You wouldn't have a picture of Dermid, would you?"

"Why?"

"I thought I might carry it the next time I protest. You know, make the protest more personal."

Avivah resisted the urge to slam the phone down in his ear.

About four, Pepper surfaced, haggard and dark-eyed. Avivah made her tea and toast.

"You sleep any?"

"Maybe a little."

"Benny stopped by on his way to Mass. He and Lorraine invited us for barbecued ribs. I told him I didn't know if you'd want to go."

Pepper took a deep breath. "Let's go."

"You're sure?"

"I can't curl up and stop functioning because Boyd died. Maybe being with Lorraine and Benny—and with you—will cheer me up, but don't expect scintillating conversation. I'll grunt once for more ribs and twice for more potato salad."

Lorraine and her boys lived as far from Fort Bragg as possible and still be in Fayetteville. Small houses lined one side of the road and there was an open field on the other side. Even this far from the post, the houses still showed a military influence. An Eighty-second Airborne flag hung

238

across one living room window and many of the cars carried Fort Bragg stickers on their bumpers. If Lorraine wanted to completely escape the military, she hadn't managed it.

Avivah drove past a round metal water tower in one corner of the field, idly looked at the tower, and made a sharp U-turn.

Pepper held on to the door handle. "What?"

"Three boys are climbing that water tower. Randy is one of them. I recognized his shirt."

She jerked the car to a stop on the soft shoulder and ran from the car. Two of the boys reached the top of the ladder and climbed onto the little metal platform surrounding the tank. Randy still clung to the ladder, about halfway up. A fourth boy, who looked about nine, stood on the ground, looking up at the tower.

Avivah put her hands on her hips. "Randy Fulford, come down from there this minute."

"I'm stuck." His voice sounded small and terrified.

One of the boys on the tower raised his arms in a flapping motion. "You're a coward just like your father. Chicken. Pluck, pluck, pluck."

Avivah climbed the ladder as fast as she could. Cold, wet wind whipped through her jeans and military police sweatshirt and her tennis shoes slid on each slippery rung. "I'm coming, Randy. Just hang on."

Below her she heard Pepper ask the fourth boy, "You know where Mrs. Fulford lives?"

"Yes."

"There's a man at her house named Sergeant Kirkpatrick. Bring him here. Right now!"

"Yes, ma'am." Avivah heard footsteps running through wet ground.

Rain broke from the black clouds, accompanied by a

blue-white lightning bolt and an immediate thunder clap.
Avivah smelled wet grass and the ozone of the nearby strike.
The two boys on the tower jostled each other to get on the
ladder so they could come down.

The metal rungs turned even more slippery under her
hands, and her wet shoes almost lost their purchase. "Stay
where you are."

Now just a rung or two below Randy, she looked up at
the grass stains on his tennis shoes. He looked down and
reached his hand out for her.

"No!"

Too late. Randy lost his grip on the ladder. Avivah
grabbed for him, got a partial hold, and tried to lift him to
her. He screamed, the high, hysterical screams of a terrified
child. Then he slipped out of her grasp and landed on the
ground with a wet splash. Another crack of lightning hit
somewhere nearby.

Pepper's voice came up to her. "Randy, stay still."

Avivah put both arms around the slippery ladder and
looked down. Pepper knelt beside the boy in the wet grass,
her hands on Randy's chest, trying to keep the struggling
child lying down. Blood covered his face. At least he was
alive.

Movement distracted Avivah and she looked at the road
where Benny, Lorraine, and several other people raced toward the field. Benny's shirt made a tangerine splash
against the grey wetness of the day. A siren wailed in the
distance.

Benny carried a large coil of rope over one shoulder.
Avivah didn't even ask herself why Benny arrived with rope.
It was just something he would do. He never broke stride,
racing across the field and up the ladder in one movement.
"Up," he yelled at her and she scrambled toward the plat-

form, Benny close on her heels.

The two boys shivered, holding on to the metal handles that led up over the rounded tower. Avivah pressed herself around them as if her body could protect them from lightning. One of the boys clung to her leg.

Benny stood behind her on the platform now, doing something with the rope. The space was too narrow for her to turn around to see what he did. She heard the swish of rope flying through they air. From the ground, a man's voice yelled, "On belay."

"Roger that."

Benny began to work rope around Avivah's waist and legs and hooked it into a large metal carabiner clip. "You ever rappelled?"

"I've seen it done."

"We'll send you down dead man's rappel. You don't have to do anything, they'll take care of you from the ground."

The sound of the siren, which had been getting closer, stopped. Avivah heard a radio squawk and flashing yellow lights reflected off the tower.

Benny squatted beside the boy who had his arms around Avivah's leg. He pried the boy's hands loose and held on to him. "Avivah, climb over the rail and hold on. I'm going to put this kid on your back."

Avivah got herself over the railing. Buffeted by the wind and rain, she fought to keep her wet shoes and cold hands on the metal. Someone pulled on the rope, tightening it around her body.

Benny said to the boy, "The lady is going to give you a piggyback ride. Close your eyes and don't open them until you get to the ground. Okay?"

The boy managed a weak "Okay" and scrunched his eyes

tight. Benny lifted him over Avivah's head and slung him across Avivah's back in a fireman's carry. Avivah used one hand to grasp his wrists and ankles.

Benny checked the rope. "Ready?"

"Ready."

He leaned over the railing. "On standby?"

"Standing by."

"Dead man's rappel. . . . On rappel." Benny shoved her, and Avivah swung into nothingness. She had a brief glimpse of the tops of houses and trees bending in the storm before the rope tightened and the ground slid toward her with dizzying speed. Hands caught her and prevented her from hitting the ground. Someone opened the clip and the rope fell away from her.

A man led her away from the rope and other people pried the boy from her back. A woman covered her with a coat.

She looked up to see Benny poised on the outside of the railing, the second boy across his shoulders. "Standby?"

The man on the ground, holding the end of the rope answered. "On standby."

"On rappel." He kicked off from the tower and Avivah watched him slide gracefully down the rope, as if he did this every day.

Lorraine and Pepper stood beside a civilian ambulance, parked beside the road. Blood covered their clothes. Avivah squelched through the wet ground. She pulled Pepper around the side of the ambulance. "How is Randy?"

"He's got a cut on his head and maybe a broken arm." She hugged Avivah. "Thank God you caught him. If you hadn't broken his fall, he could be dead."

The ambulance driver pushed past them. "His mother wants us to take him to Womack, not to Cape Fear. You coming?" Cape Fear was the local civilian hospital.

"Yeah."

"Climb in back."

Pepper paused on the step. "See you and Benny at the hospital."

Avivah watched the ambulance navigate slowly through the crowd, then speed down the rain-covered road. She found Benny at the foot of the tower, coiling rope over his arm.

"I'm going to kill that kid."

"What kid?"

Benny secured the end of the rope, slung the coil over his shoulder, and started across the field. "That kid I brought down. Some Army brats think they have to prove themselves every time their dad transfers to a new place. I know he's the one who dared Randy to climb the tower."

Avivah decided to not repeat the taunt she'd heard, about Randy's father being a coward. She took Benny's arm and forced him toward Lorraine's house. "Forget him. Where is Mark?"

"At a neighbor's."

They found Mark standing in the neighbor's yard, his thumb in his mouth, and his other arm curled around a chain link fence post, as if he needed to hang on to something solid. Benny scooped him up and hugged him.

It took them an hour to feed Mark, douse the fire in the barbecue pit, and refrigerate supper. Avivah offered to babysit, but Benny said they might as well all go to the hospital. They went in Benny's truck.

Pepper sat in a plastic chair in the emergency waiting room, her head back against a wall, her eyes closed. Remnants of blood still covered her damp clothes. Avivah sat down beside her, with Mark on her lap.

Benny sat on her other side. "Do they know anything yet?"

Pepper opened her eyes and sat upright. "His arm's only sprained, but he's got a cut over his right eyebrow. They're stitching him up. Lorraine is with him. You okay?"

"You mean outside of being madder than hell?"

"Yeah, outside of that."

"Outside of that, I'm fine."

"That was some show the two of you put on."

Avivah grinned at Benny. "I guess it was."

Lorraine came out of the treatment room area, leading Randy by the hand. He had a splint on his left arm and a thick bandage on his forehead. "Hi, Uncle Benny. I hardly cried at all. The doctor said I was brave."

"Good for you."

Lorraine turned to Pepper. "Would you take the boys to the lobby, buy them a cold drink, and phone a cab for us?"

Pepper looked at Lorraine, then at Benny. She got up and took a boy on each side. "Come on, guys, I know where the candy machines are."

Lorraine waited until the three of them disappeared through a door. "Randy told me how the fight started. One of the older boys taunted him about Randall being a coward, then he dared Randy to prove his bravery by climbing the water tower. I'm tired of him having to prove himself to every Army brat whose family gets transferred here."

"Taunting happens in civilian life, too. It's part of being seven years old."

"It's not a part I want for Randy or Mark. At least Randy fights back, but Mark is too shy. He isn't going to be able to stand the teasing when he gets older."

Benny started to say something, but Lorraine held up

her hand. "Let me finish, Ben. You're right. I can't live here and keep Randy and Mark from everything to do with the Army. So my choice is, I don't live here any more."

"You've said that before and changed your mind."

"You mean you changed it for me."

"That's not fair."

Lorraine looked at the floor. "No, it isn't. I'm sorry. This time, I'm not changing my mind. As soon as the doctor says it's okay for Randy to fly, I'm sending the boys to my parents."

"What about you?"

"I'll join them as soon as I can put the house up for sale."

Benny ran his hand over the back of his neck. "I have leave saved. I'll drive you to Oregon."

"No. Please just leave us alone. Go away."

"What are you going to tell the boys about moving?"

"I'll think of something."

Lorraine left. Benny seemed to have forgotten about Avivah. He dug his keys out of his pocket, and left the emergency room with his head bent. Avivah was glad she couldn't see his face.

Pepper came back a few minutes later. "What's going on? Lorraine looked absolutely white. How come Benny isn't taking them home?"

Avivah told her.

"What a rotten weekend all around."

"Let's go home and hope tomorrow will be better."

Pepper looked at her watch. "I want to go upstairs. Doan should be back by now. I want to know how things went at church."

The evening nurse, a red-haired civilian, looked up as Pepper came into the nurses' station. "What did you do to yourself, Captain?"

"A friend's child had an accident. He needed stitches."

"I was about to call you. I saw your note to expect Cody Doan back from pass by 1900 hours. He didn't come back. I called his next-of-kin, his sister, but she hasn't seen him since Friday and doesn't have a clue where he is."

Chapter 23

Before going to the brigade office, Avivah sent Pepper home with a military police driver. Pepper promised that she would eat, take a hot bath, and go to bed while Avivah made phone calls.

Cody Doan's sister had told him Friday afternoon that her children had been exposed to chicken pox. He had been so ill recently that she didn't want to risk exposing him, so she told him not to visit for two weeks. He never called her to say he was flying in Sunday morning. She hadn't been at church today and didn't know Doan was in Marshall.

Piedmont Airlines confirmed that Cody Doan took the Sunday morning flight to Asheville, but had not returned on any flight back to Fayetteville. Doan didn't answer a page at the Asheville airport. Calls to car rental agencies showed he hadn't rented a car.

Deputy Sheriff Wayne Ramsey said Cody attended church that morning. He delivered a moving testimony about Boyd. Cody hadn't spoken in church for years; some of the congregation wept. The last time Wayne saw Cody, he was talking to Reverend Pretcherd. He said he'd make some calls.

No one answered at Reverend Pretcherd's house.

Two hours later, Wayne Ramsey called back. No one in the congregation remembered seeing Cody after church. None of the hospitals, including the veterans' hospital at Oteen, had seen him in the emergency room or admitted him as a patient. Neither the Asheville City Police nor the Madison County Sheriff had any contact with him. Wayne planned to check the church grounds and the cemetery. Avivah remembered Pepper's description of the small, isolated church. She did not envy Deputy Ramsey exploring the deserted graveyard after dark, and she dreaded what he might find there.

Having exhausted the Marshall connection, Avivah tried closer to home. No one answered at Harlan Carter's number. She tried Jane Buckner's home.

"Colonel Norton speaking." At last, someone was home.

"This is Captain Rosen of the military police. May I speak to Major Buckner?"

"She is unavailable."

"Is she still in Asheville?"

"Is there a problem?"

"There has been another death, this one in Asheville."

"Not Jane." Colonel Norton sounded frightened, but fighting to sound calm, the kind of response relatives of policemen, firemen, and soldiers kept hidden, hoping they would never use.

"No, ma'am, not Major Buckner. A young man named Boyd Ramsey died."

"Oh, my God! His poor mother." This time the voice held genuine grief. How did Colonel Norton know Boyd Ramsey's mother?

"I know it's late, but I would appreciate it, Colonel, if we could talk."

"By all means come right over. I'm afraid I'm already in my dressing gown. Shall I dress?"

Avivah looked down at her jeans and sweatshirt. "That won't be necessary. I'm in civilian clothes myself."

Colonel Norton lived in one of the stuccoed, tiled-roofed

houses in the oldest part of the post. By the time Avivah arrived there, only a few houses still showed lights behind lace curtains or through open windows. Avivah looked down the tree-lined street and realized that Colonel Norton's back yard opened on the alley that led to Normandy House. It would have been a couple of minutes' work to slip out of Normandy House, go down the alley, and into her back yard. Avivah stared at the house for a minute, worrying her lip, considering the pros and cons of making this visit alone and out of uniform.

A man with short-cropped grey hair jogged by with his golden retriever. He stopped at the corner and pretended to fiddle with his shoelace. Avivah knew he was watching her. She locked her car door and walked up to the tiny covered porch. The man resumed jogging.

Colonel Norton answered the door, wearing a pair of silk pants and a Japanese silk jacket, embroidered with chrysanthemums. Two crossed bobby pins held each tight curl against her head. Avivah hadn't seen anyone use bobby pins to set her hair since her Aunt Harriet died. The colonel showed Avivah into her living room and indicated that Avivah should sit on the delicate blue and green sofa. "I've made coffee."

Avivah accepted a cup. The colonel poured from a real English coffee set: a red and white chintz pattern. The spoons and sugar tongs felt like solid silver.

The reflected glow from the light in the china cabinet, and two small table lamps dimly lit the room. Lace curtains hung at the open windows. A cooling breeze, bringing with it the summer night smell of damp grass, blew across the small Federal sofa, chairs, and tables.

Souvenirs from all over the world filled the room. A huge lit, glass-front china cabinet dominated one wall. Porcelain, mostly bowls tilted on a holder to show inside and outside detail, filled the cabinet. Avivah knew that the one Dresden bowl, on the top shelf, cost more than all the souvenirs she'd sent home during her tour in Germany.

A hand-embroidered silk panel, lettered in Korean, hung on the wall over the sofa. A Japanese doll, in a glass case, stood in the middle of the mantel, flanked on either side by tall pewter candle holders.

Avivah rested her cup and saucer gently on a fragile-looking end table. "Colonel, I appreciate you seeing me this late."

"I would be glad to help Mrs. Ramsey any way I can."

Colonel Norton took a photograph from her jacket pocket and handed it to Avivah. The young man in the picture matched the description Pepper gave her of Boyd. He stood next to a woman in her sixties. Avivah turned the picture over. The greeting, written in an old-fashioned, spidery hand, said, *From Greta and Boyd Ramsey with many thanks and a wish of God's blessings in the New Year. Christmas, 1970.*

"Is that the young man who died?"

Avivah's hand brushed against the colonel's cold fingers as she handed back the picture. "I believe it is. Tell me about the Ramseys?"

Colonel Norton got up, replaced the picture in a drawer in one of the tiny end tables, and crossed the room to turn off the light in the china cabinet. Avivah's eyes took a minute to adjust to the remaining dim lamp light.

"Has the Army been good to you, Captain?"

Startled by the question, Avivah fumbled an answer. "I believe so."

"Has there been anything you wanted from the Army that you didn't get?"

Avivah thought about orders for Vietnam.

The colonel continued, "You don't have to answer that. I can see from the look on your face that the answer is yes." She sat down again, picked up her delicate coffee cup, and took a reflective sip.

"Women in my family did not work. My parents thought my going to nursing school a whim. I'm afraid they did not understand how much I wanted to be of service."

Old money, antiques, old ideas about what a daughter should do.

"Are you familiar with the words Abraham Lincoln used when he founded the Veterans' Administration?"

"I'm afraid not."

" 'To care for him who shall have borne the battle.' That sentiment moved me deeply the first time I read it. I enlisted in the Army before the Japanese attack on Pearl Harbor. After that attack, all of us nurses thought we'd be sent overseas immediately. For most of my friends, that's what happened."

"Not you?"

The colonel put her cup back on the tray. "Not me. I had pediatric and obstetrical experience. The women and children who followed their husbands from one Army camp to another needed someone with my background. I did military public health all over the United States, but never overseas."

Her voice still reflected the pain. Avivah realized this could be her in thirty years, recounting to a niece or nephew how she never had a chance to go to Vietnam.

"I left the Army in 1946, but remained active in a reserve unit. I even took a course in surgical nursing. I thought—if there were another war—a background in surgery would guarantee that I'd be sent to the battlefield.

251

When Korea started, I went back on active duty. It was terrible, wasn't it, to be excited about personal gain from war?"

Avivah thought of how many places she had already been stationed. "We all get personal gains from the Army."

The colonel pointed to the embroidered scroll. "President Syngman Rhee presented that to me himself, for helping establish the Korean Army Nurse Corps. I spent the entire war at Korean Army Headquarters in Seoul. I never saw a field hospital, other than as a touring dignitary."

"Is that where you met Colonel Euston?"

"Frances Euston was my roommate in Seoul."

"After Korea, you stayed in the Army?"

"I stayed." She waved at the collection of bowls, the scroll, the Japanese doll. "I've had some marvelous assignments, met lovely people, traveled, advanced further in my nursing career than I even imagined possible."

"Vietnam?" Avivah asked tentatively, poking at the question like one might poke at a sore tooth, just to see if it were still sore.

"No. Perhaps I got lost in the mass of military detail, perhaps the Army thought I had talents that were better used elsewhere. Perhaps," she said with a trace of bitterness, "they thought I was too old for a combat hospital. They assigned me to Japan as the supervisor of the special needs unit."

Pepper had explained about the special ward in Japan to which critically ill soldiers were evacuated. "That assignment must have been hard."

"It was. I know I've taken a long time to get to your question about Boyd Ramsey, and I appreciate you letting me wander. I knew Japan would be my last overseas assignment before I retired, and I wanted to reassure myself that what I'd done there meant something. As I got close to the end of my tour, I spent a lot of extra time talking to families."

"This is where you met Boyd."

"I met Mrs. Ramsey. Boyd was only beginning to regain consciousness. We had no idea how much brain damage he had. I spent hours talking to his mother or, rather, letting her talk to me. The poor woman needed someone to listen."

"What did you talk about?"

"Mostly about her son. What he had been like as a boy, how proud she was of him, how she didn't know how she was going to manage without him."

"During your conversations, did she ever mention a man named Dermid Hagan?"

"She said that one of her son's friends was named Dermid. She said he died in Vietnam. I remember it because it was such an uncommon name. I don't think she ever mentioned a last name."

"Did you keep in touch with Mrs. Ramsey?"

The colonel ran her hand wearily over her forehead. "I regret to say that I did."

"Why do you regret it?"

"I permitted a very unprofessional thing. I traded on my position to encourage Mrs. Ramsey to think of me as a friend. I gave her my name and home address and asked her to write."

"Did she?"

"We exchanged letters and Christmas cards."

"Did you ever visit her?"

"No."

"Did you know Boyd had moved to Asheville?"

"Yes. His mother wrote me when the brain-injury re-training program accepted him."

"Did you ever write to Boyd?"

"I sent him several cards of encouragement."

"Did you ever visit him?"

"No."

Avivah glanced at her watch. It was very late. "I'm sorry to keep you up, Colonel. Just a few more questions."

"It's all right."

"Did you meet anyone from the hospital on the plane on Friday?"

"Yes, a young man on crutches, going to his uncle's funeral."

"Do you know his name?"

"I'm afraid not. Since he used crutches and was in uniform, I concluded he was from one of the orthopedic wards, either Six-A or Six-B. I'm afraid Major Buckner knows the individual patients better than I do."

"Why were you and Major Buckner in Asheville?"

"To look at a hotel for a nursing conference next year. We're on the planning committee."

"May I have the names of the people who met you at the airport?"

"If that becomes necessary."

"What did you do on Friday afternoon?"

"We had lunch and a planning session. At 1700 hours, we drove Jane to register at a motel, and pick up a rental car."

"Why didn't you stay together?"

"Captain Rosen, I don't own my officers. Jane never visited western North Carolina before and wanted to do some sightseeing."

"What did you do over the weekend?"

"I stayed with the woman who is head of the banquet committee. Saturday morning, I slept in until after 0900 hours. We ate brunch and spent the afternoon going through the Biltmore House. Saturday evening we went to Shindig on the Green."

Avivah tried not to appear too interested. "When were you there?"

"About 2100 hours. A clogging team, who performed that night, will be part of the entertainment at our banquet. I wanted to see the quality of their performance."

"How long did you stay?"

"About half an hour. I must admit that while I think people at the banquet will enjoy them, bluegrass music and clogging give me a headache."

"Did you see Boyd Ramsey in the crowd?"

"Not that I know. I'm not sure I would have recognized him."

"Did you see anyone else there that you knew?"

"Jane Buckner."

"What was she doing?"

"Walking around, enjoying the music, eating an ice cream cone."

"Was she alone?"

"She seemed to be."

"Did you speak to her?"

"Yes, we asked her how her sightseeing had gone. She said she drove up to Boone and Grandfather Mountain. She thanked my hostess for recommending the Scottish shop in Linville and showed us a lovely brooch she bought there."

"Did you see anyone else you recognized?"

"No."

"Did you see Specialist Carter, the wardmaster from medical holding company?"

"I did not."

"What did you do after the Shindig?"

"We came home and went to bed. I went with my hostess to church on Sunday morning, we had lunch at the Grove Park Inn, and I flew home this afternoon."

"Major Buckner is still in Asheville?"

"As far as I know."

"How long will she be there?"

"I expect her back tomorrow by the time her shift begins at 1445 hours."

Avivah sat back against the thin chair frame. "Colonel, may I ask you a personal question?"

"I reserve the right not to answer it, if I consider it too personal."

"How long have you and Major Buckner shared this house?"

"Since she was posted here in January of 1970."

"It's a bit unusual, isn't it, for a chief nurse to share her quarters with one of her officers?"

"Some people might think so, but I don't. I'm retiring next month and I'm afraid I have a bit of short-timers' attitude."

Avivah chuckled.

"I see you have heard of short-timers' attitude."

"It's where you figure you can get away with things you wouldn't ordinarily do, because what are they going to do to you? I didn't know colonels succumbed to it."

The colonel chuckled also. "Colonels succumb to all sorts of things. Now about Jane. I've thought, for a long time, about what legacy I might leave the corps. General Hayes broke the taboo against a woman being promoted to general. I believe Jane has the career officer qualities to eventually outrank even General Hayes. An outstanding record isn't enough to cross that hard line from colonel to general. She will need social graces, contacts, a sponsor. I'm pleased to offer her that, to give her the benefit of thirty years in the service, to introduce her to people she needs to know."

"Are you lovers?"

"No. And to preempt your next question, neither of us has inclinations in that direction."

Avivah stood. "Thank you for seeing me so late in the evening. May I help you take anything to the kitchen?"

Colonel Norton also stood. "Don't bother. My girl will take care of everything in the morning."

As Avivah unlocked her car door, she thought, That's one frustrated lady. Colonel Norton had been in the *60 Minutes* segment. Avivah tried to remember whether she had been identified by name. She would check the tape again tomorrow—later today, Avivah corrected herself, as she looked at the dash clock—but she knew a letter addressed to the Chief Nurse, Womack Army Hospital, would have reached Colonel Norton.

Had Dermid Hagan, a deserter, written to her? Had he wanted help, the use of her influence in helping him come back to the States? Had he picked wrong, written to a person likely to be enraged by a young man who deserted in Vietnam? Rage resulted in murder; so did love. What if Colonel Norton took revenge on one deserter for all the young men she had never been permitted to nurse? What if Jane Buckner received a letter and Dermid knew something that could threaten all the plans Colonel Norton had for her protégée?

The colonel could have easily stolen Colonel Euston's room key, but why not meet Dermid in the security of her own home, a place more private than Normandy House? Because she had a housemate and she didn't want Jane Buckner anywhere near Dermid Hagan? Because murder was messy and Colonel Norton tolerated no mess?

Avivah thought about how neat the crime scene had been. Dermid, shot once through the heart, all the blood seeping invisibly into the mattress below the body. The room had been very cold. Colonel Norton's surgical training would have taught her exactly where to place the gun so that one shot would kill instantly. She might know that a very cold room made it harder to determine the exact time of death. And she was a hefty woman, sturdy enough to have delivered the blow that rendered Dermid Hagan unconscious.

She might have lied about Boyd as well. It would have been easy to sneak away from her companion at the Shindig, pretend to go to the bathroom, for example, and make an appointment to meet Boyd later.

Rage killing, love killing, and mercy killing. Avivah added Colonel Norton's name to her list of suspects. Deep in thought, she got out of her car at her apartment, locked her car door, and failed to notice that Benny's parking spot stood empty.

Chapter 24

The next morning, Avivah sat on the side of her bed, polishing her shoes, with the phone jammed between her ear and shoulder, talking to Pepper. "How are you?"

"Rotten."

"You sleep any last night?"

"More than I thought I would. I dreamed about Vietnam. I guess it was the excitement and the blood all over Randy's face."

Benny would know what to say. All Avivah could think of was, "I'm sorry."

"That which does not kill you makes you strong. . . . It's a joke, Avivah. Laugh."

"Doan still missing?"

"Afraid so. His doctor makes rounds in a few minutes and he is going to be *so* pissed off at me. If I'm not home when you get off work, try the Aleutians."

Avivah put one shoe down, picked up its mate, and polished to the toe.

"You going to report Doan absent without leave?"

"I hope not, but it depends on his doctor. He can extend Doan's pass, in which case he's not AWOL."

"I need to know something about hospital procedure. Is there any cocaine in the hospital?"

"I have some in my narcotics cabinet."

Avivah lost interest in shoe polish. "How is it packaged: in a syringe or a glass bottle?"

"It's in a brown, glass atomizer, like the kind opera stars spray their throats with in old movies. There's a seal around the top. When you use it, you break the seal, add sterile water, and mix the powder."

Avivah looked at the clock. She had an appointment with Delaney in thirty minutes. She gave the shoe a hurried brush and hopped on one foot, then the other, putting on her shoes.

"So you can't see if the cocaine is really inside?"

"No. When we do the change of shift count, if the atomizer feels heavy and the seal is unbroken, we assume cocaine is inside."

"What if you use it? How do you get more?"

"Fill out a narcotics request sheet, and pick it up when the pharmacy calls to say the order is ready."

Avivah switched the phone to the other ear and brushed her hair. "Does it have to be a nurse who picks it up at the pharmacy?"

"For narcotics, it has to be a nurse or a wardmaster."

She considered the lipsticks in her top dresser drawer and rejected all of them. Her meeting with Delaney was business, not a date. She slammed the drawer shut. "What if you need cocaine and the pharmacy is closed?"

"Narcotics must be dispensed on day shift. If you need narcotics after 1500 hours, the evening or night supervisor borrows from another ward. If there is none on any ward, we call the on-call pharmacist, but I've never seen that happen. Supervisors scrounge well."

"What if someone told you another ward needed to borrow cocaine? Would you give it to them?"

"I would if the person who came to me was another nurse or a wardmaster. They would have to sign it out in my book."

"What about the chief nurse? Would you give it to her?"

"Sure."

Avivah took one final swallow of cool coffee from the mug on her dresser, put her wristwatch on her arm, and picked up her hat and purse. "Got to go. Take care of yourself."

Thirty minutes later she sat in Captain Delaney's office. Avivah noticed he had a deeper tan than before he went to Marshall. She suspected he hadn't spent all of his time there digging up bodies and questioning people. She realized that although she had known Delaney as long as she had been at Fort Bragg, she had no idea what he did for recreation.

"I want in."

He didn't even give her the courtesy of looking up from his paperwork. He closed one folder and put it in his out-basket. "Why?"

She wasn't about to tell him about Pepper sobbing on her shoulder.

"I'm a trained policewoman with two successful murder investigations under my belt." She didn't mention they had been straightforward cases, with lots of witnesses. "This is the hottest thing to hit Fort Bragg since the MacDonald murders, and solving hot things looks good on performance evaluations."

The look on Delaney's face said he understood performance evaluations.

"Besides, a hell of a lot happened this weekend and you have a choice. I can share what I know right now, in person, or you can wait until you get my written report. Written reports can be so sketchy, don't you think? Sometimes it takes days, circulating them back and forth, asking for clarifications, to get all the details."

Delaney considered for a minute, tossed the folder he

was reading on his desk, and said, "You had no business investigating on your own."

"So? Send me to Vietnam."

"You aren't even CID."

"Get me a temporary-duty assignment for a month. I'll
work double-shifts if I have to."

"I'll think about it. Now tell me what happened this
weekend."

Once she told him, Avivah knew Delaney might not
honor his part of the bargain, but she didn't have much
choice. Bringing him up to date took most of the morning.

"All right, you're in," Delaney said, grudgingly, when it
was almost noon. With a smirk he asked, "I suppose you
have an idea what we should do next?"

"I want to interview Jane Buckner this afternoon. I
thought the interview might go better, you know, woman-
to-woman. And I want to follow up on a lead about cocaine
at the hospital. I thought you might want to interview
Harlan Carter again. I checked. He's at work today in the
medical holding company; his shift ends at 1515 hours."

Delaney laughed, a small, sarcastic laugh that Avivah
would prefer not to hear again. "You've been a busy little
lady. Isn't it good that, for once, we both think the same
thing?"

Avivah took Gilbert Plauche to lunch at the officers'
club, and brought him up to date. His only comment was,
"Be very careful, *ti chou*." She wondered if he meant because of the murders or because of Delaney.

They returned to the office to find Lorraine Fulford
talking to the duty clerk. She wore thong sandals, an old pair
of cut-off fatigue pants, and a faded, dirt-streaked T-shirt
that said *Fulford Orchards, The Best in the West*.

Avivah had never seen Lorraine in dirty or rumpled

clothes before. "Hi, what's going on?"

"Randy and Mark have disappeared."

Avivah opened the door in the counter. "Come on, you look like you need to sit down."

Gilbert Plauche brought the two women into his office.

Avivah handed Lorraine a cold drink. "Start at the beginning."

"I fixed the boys a late breakfast and explained that, in a few days, they were going to live with Grandma and Grandpa Fulford. Randy asked if Ben would live there, too. I tried to explain that Ben and I had broken up. Randy became hysterical."

Poor kid, Avivah thought. The past two days had been horrible for him.

"I gave him Tylenol and took him to my room to lie down, then went outside to weed the back flower beds to calm down. About an hour later, I went in to check on him. The boys were gone."

Gilbert Plauche asked, "Did they take anything with them?"

"Mark's red wagon is missing. So is some food, and I think some of their toys."

"Is any money missing?"

She reached for her purse. "I never thought of that. . . . No, all of my money is here."

"Did either of the boys have money?"

"They both get allowances and they have piggy banks. Ben slips them money once in a while. I've asked him not to do that."

Avivah remembered Benny giving the boys money several times. "What have you done to look for them?"

"I went to all the neighbors. I went to the park. I even went to the water tower. I tried to call Ben at work, but they said he'd taken emergency leave this morning. I went to his apartment, but no one was there. I have a key," she finished, blushing.

Deep down Lorraine and Benny, whatever else they might be, were a couple of Catholic farm kids embarrassed about anyone knowing they had keys to each other's houses.

"I don't think Ben came home last night. His apartment looked just the same as it did when we stopped by after Mass."

Avivah pictured the apartment parking lot. Benny parked directly across from her. She always walked beside his truck to get to the sidewalk. Last night she'd walked straight through his parking spot. Lorraine could be right about Benny not coming home.

Major Plauche said, in a reassuring voice, "All right, Mrs. Fulford, I want you to wait out in the main office. Try to relax. We find lost children all the time."

Once Lorraine left, Gil and Avivah conferred. "Call the taxi companies, the bus company, get the word out to the Fayetteville police and the Cumberland County sheriff. I'll get a couple of policemen to make a swing through the post. Two little boys pulling a wagon shouldn't be hard to spot."

Avivah looked through the glass at Lorraine. "It's odd."

"What is?"

"She says she wants nothing to do with the military, yet she wears her husband's old fatigues, she takes her son to Womack instead of a civilian hospital, and when she needs a policeman, she comes here, not to the Fayetteville police."

"Army life sinks in deep."

What was it Benny said when he talked about the Mac-Donald murders? The Army family. Well, Benjamin Kirkpatrick's family needed him now and Avivah wished to hell she knew where to find him.

It took the Army family twenty minutes to find two of their own. Randy, Mark, and their wagon were on a cross-town bus on its way to Fort Bragg. Avivah and Lorraine met them at the first bus stop on the post.

A neatly-tied blanket covered their full little wagon. Avivah asked Randy if she could look inside. Randy had collected Mark's favorite toy cars, bread, peanut butter, bananas, cereal, two toy mess kits, a plastic canteen of water, two pillows, a change of clothing for each boy, Randy's Cub Scout manual, a first aid kit, and a flashlight. In the hour between when his mother put him to bed and when she came back to check on him, he arranged everything neatly in the wagon, covered it with a blanket, tied the blanket down with rope, and got himself and his brother on the road. Both boys wore hats and sunglasses. Randy also wore an old Army belt pouch with a map of Fayetteville and twenty-six dollars, most of it in coins and one-dollar bills, in it. Randy had not so much run away as gone on maneuvers.

Avivah asked him, "What about milk for the cereal?"

"Milk has to stay cold. If Uncle Benny didn't have any, we were going to buy some tomorrow morning before breakfast."

"Where were you going to sleep?"

"We were going to the JFK Center to ask Uncle Benny if we could sleep at his apartment." Randy folded his arms across his chest. "I have to talk to him and I'm not going to Oregon until I do."

Mark imitated his brother's position. "Me, too."

"All right, we'll talk to Ben, but I think he's away for a few days. We have to be patient until he comes back. Sometimes civilians can't go where soldiers go."

Avivah looked at the two boys standing beside them.

"Where is he?" she mouthed, trying to be circumspect. She didn't want Randy off again to find Benny, especially not in a restricted area.

"Maybe where Randall went when we fought. They thought I didn't know about it."

Avivah took her notebook out of her uniform pocket, wrote *Write it down,* and handed it to Lorraine. When she got the notebook back, Lorraine had written *Vietnamese village.*

Chapter 25

Shortly before 1500 hours, Captain Delaney walked past her desk, whistling. "Captain Rosen, you are a credit to your profession and to the Army. I consider myself privileged to work with you."

Having delivered this opinion, he put his cap on his head and left, going, Avivah assumed, to see Harlan Carter. Avivah stared after Delaney. "Ramerez!"

He came out of the teletype room, casually thumbing through a pile of folders.

"We have to file a missing persons' report. Aliens kidnapped Captain Delaney and replaced him with a human being. Come to think of it, hold that report. The aliens can keep him."

"He just got news from Langley that made him very happy, but *you* won't like it at all."

"Ramerez, please, please, please do not tell me that the CIA is involved in Dermid Hagan's murder?"

He stood silent, shifting from foot to foot, looking around at nothing.

Avivah banged her head against her desk. "Oy! All right, tell all."

Ramerez pulled up a chair from another desk, and turned it around so he could sit backwards on the chair. "The story goes back to November, 1968. The CIA wanted to buy Laotian support and arranged a meeting on the Vietnamese side of the Laotian border. They brought with them a hundred thousand dollars, cash, in U.S. greenbacks.

"They make a deal, the Laotians walk away with a bag full of money, and the CIA spooks go back to wherever CIA spooks go. Only, on the way back to Laos, the Laotians ended up too close to a B-52 strike. Imagine lots of noise, bodies flying through the air, terrified people running into the jungle, fire, and confusion. Half the vehicles, including the one with the money in it, burned."

Avivah shook as she tried to imagine being on the receiving end of a B-52 strike. "The money?"

Ramerez opened his hands in a "who knows" gesture. "The Laotian contact came back to the CIA saying, 'We lost your money and, please, sir, could we have some more.' They sent some poor schmuck out to the middle of the jungle to do an accident investigation. He came back, and yes, the money was really gone. The CIA came up with another hundred thousand dollars and gave it to the Laotians."

"The first hundred thousand?"

"Nada. Of course, in the Asian banking system that much was pocket change. No one would have noticed if the money went in a bank in Hong Kong, and came out of a bank in Singapore."

Avivah wrote *$100,000* on her legal pad, circled it, and then wrote the word *Tithe* and drew an arrow connecting the two. Ten thousand dollars to Boyd Ramsey's mother would have been ten percent, the usual amount for a tithe. She wrote the names *Michael Fuller* and *Dermid Hagan*, circled both, drew a double-headed arrow from *Michael* to *Dermid*, and put a large question mark over the arrow. Something in Michael Fuller's missing persons' report mentioned the Laotian border. "Was Michael Fuller there when the money changed hands?"

"No mention of him or Dermid Hagan either."

She wrote a few more questions, then looked at the clock. "Come on, we have an appointment to interview Jane Buckner."

Major Buckner showed them into a small conference room next to the chief nurse's office. Her perfectly-tailored white duty uniform impressed Avivah the most. Avivah had seen many Army nurses, usually on the other side of an emergency room gurney, as she and a nurse wrestled a patient into submission. None of them had looked as striking as Major Buckner.

A stylish fringe of light brown hair framed her thin, tanned face. At first, Avivah thought she wasn't wearing any makeup, then realized skin couldn't look that perfect unassisted. The major would make a wonderful recruiting poster. What did the recruitment ads say now? "The most beautiful woman in the world is an Army nurse." Looking at Jane Buckner, seated with a poised and professional attitude, Avivah believed the ad copy.

They completed the preliminaries, with Ramerez taking notes.

"Can you describe your trip to Asheville this past weekend, beginning with when you picked up the rental car on Friday night?"

"I went to supper at the Mountaineer Inn Restaurant on Tunnel Road, went to my motel, and watched television until bedtime."

"Were you alone?"

"I was."

"Describe Saturday, July 17."

"I arose at 0500 hours, had breakfast at an IHOP, drove to Boone, came back by Grandfather Mountain and Linville, stopping at the Scottish shop in Linville. I also stopped to see the falls at the gorge. Once I returned to

Asheville, I ate supper at a downtown restaurant—I'm sorry, I don't remember the name. There I saw a poster advertising Shindig on the Green. I visited the Shindig, and then back to the motel."

Too pat. Too cool. Major Buckner had obviously rehearsed.

"Five a.m. is very early."

"Boone was a three-hour drive."

"What time were you at the Shindig?"

"About 2000 to 2100 hours."

"Did you see anyone you knew there?"

"Colonel Norton and the woman she was staying with."

"Anyone else?"

"No."

"You're sure?"

"Absolutely."

"What did you do on Sunday, July 18?"

"Ate breakfast in the motel dining room. Went to the Great Smokies National Park. Came back to the motel after supper and went to bed early. This morning I had breakfast, returned the rental car, and caught a flight back to Fayetteville at 1000 hours."

"Did you ever meet Boyd Ramsey?"

"The name is not familiar to me."

Avivah described Boyd.

"No, I never met anyone like that that I remember."

Avivah got up and slowly paced the length of the room, pausing for a moment to look out the window at the half-empty parking lot beside the hospital.

"Major, are you a good nurse?"

"I am an excellent nurse."

"Then you're familiar with how a small detail can signal a change in a patient's condition?"

"Yes."

"If a nurse brought one of those tiny details to your attention, would you consider acting upon it?"

"Yes, nurses often have a sixth sense."

So did policemen. Avivah had no way to prove Jane Buckner had lied, but she knew she had.

"Specialist Ramerez, would you read back the major's statement concerning Friday night?"

He flipped back a page. "Captain Rosen: 'Can you describe your trip to Asheville this past weekend, beginning with when you picked up the rental car on Friday night?'

"Major Buckner: 'Certainly. I went to supper at the Mountaineer Inn Restaurant on Tunnel Road, went to my motel, and watched television until bedtime.'

"Captain Rosen: . . .'"

She took a notebook out of her pocket and pretended to consult it. "That's enough. If you watched television in your motel room Friday night, how did an Asheville City Police officer spot your rental car in the parking lot of the Sit-a-Spell restaurant in West Asheville?"

The coolness turned brittle. "I'm sure I don't know."

"You're sure you don't want to change your story. Say you had a sudden craving for a malt or French fries and that you were gone from your motel only a few minutes."

Major Buckner sat rigid, her hands in her lap. "I don't want to say anything of the kind."

A lie for a lie, Avivah figured. "The police had instructions to take special note of all rental cars that evening because thieves targeted rental cars during the past week. An officer will testify to your car's location. You are a strikingly beautiful lady. He will have no trouble remembering that he saw you in the restaurant, too."

Avivah admired the way that Jane Buckner didn't flinch.

271

"I see." Her voice cracked like ice splitting when hot water poured over it. "Who sees this transcript?"

"Myself, Specialist Ramerez, Captain Delaney of the CID."

"No one else?"

"Not unless it is needed as evidence in a murder trial."

"I was at the restaurant."

"Were you alone?"

"No, I met Harlan Carter there."

Avivah's heart sang. "For the record, would you identify Harlan Carter?"

"Specialist E-7 Harlan William Carter, Wardmaster of the Medical Holding Company at Fort Bragg."

"When did you meet Specialist Carter?"

"About 2100 hours on Friday night."

"Why did you meet him?"

"Several months ago—when I learned about the Asheville trip—Specialist Carter and I planned to spend the weekend together." The cracked ice began to drip. For the first time Major Buckner slumped slightly in her chair and a tiny wrinkle appeared in her uniform.

"Are you and Specialist Carter a couple?"

"Not any more."

"When did you stop being a couple?"

"Friday night."

Avivah came back from the window and sat down. "When did you start being a couple?"

"At the Third Field Hospital in Saigon. Harlan was so unhappy there."

"Why did you think him unhappy?"

"He often came to work drunk. Sometimes we'd have lunch together and he'd confide in me."

"Did you report his alcohol use?"

"No. I thought I could help him better than the Army could."

"Were you successful?"

"Yes. He stopped drinking for the rest of his tour."

"Your relationship developed?"

"We spent a lot of time together. One thing led to another."

"You're familiar with the Army's 'no fraternization' policy?"

Jane Buckner looked Avivah squarely in the face with no trace of embarrassment, a look that said they both knew the real world. "And *you're* familiar with how often that policy is ignored. We kept our relationship quiet."

"On a hospital compound that couldn't have been easy."

"Harlan rented a small apartment in Saigon."

The look on her face sagged just enough that Avivah knew she recognized just how many rules that arrangement broke. "How does Dermid Hagan fit into this?"

More wrinkles showed. "Harlan lost five thousand dollars to him in a poker game."

"The game at the hospital?"

She clenched her hands into fists. "You see, I knew about the game; I'd even played. I thought it was penny-ante, but I should have suspected something when some patients asked me if the game was on the up-and-up. I encouraged them to play. I thought it was just good recreation for them."

"Was it rigged?"

"No, Harlan played well enough that he didn't have to rig anything. He was very clever. For people like me, the bets really were nickels and dimes. For other people, like Dermid Hagan, they agreed on a code beforehand. A penny meant a dollar bet, five cents meant five dollars, ten cents

meant ten dollars, and so on. That way Harlan had witnesses who would say that Dermid won only fifty dollars."

"In reality he won five thousand dollars?"

"Yes."

Avivah ticked off the offenses in her head: sleeping with
an enlisted man, who was her wardmaster to boot; lying
about his fitness for duty; being away from a military compound, in a war zone, overnight; being in downtown Saigon
overnight; shilling for a high stakes poker game. If this came
out, Jane Buckner faced court-martial and imprisonment.
At best, she would be forced to resign her commission
without a trial.

"What happened after Dermid Hagan won the money?"

"Harlan came to me and confessed. He couldn't pay."

"You lent him the money?"

"I didn't have that kind of money, either. I took out a
loan." She sounded like she wanted Avivah to commend
her for her generosity.

"Did he pay you back?"

"It was a gift, but, when I gave it to him, I told him that
he had to close the game down."

Generosity with strings attached. "Did he do it?"

"Yes."

"You continued to see one another?"

"Yes."

An addiction, Avivah thought. She didn't know who had
the worst deal, a country boy being seduced by a beautiful
woman, or the woman buying a relationship.

"Did Dermid know about your relationship and the
apartment?"

"I wish I knew. Harlan wasn't in a shop buying a vase
before the accident; we were in our apartment. Standing at
the window, I saw an American running down our street."

"How did you know he was an American?"

"The clothes, the height, the way he ran."

"Could you see who it was?"

"He had his back to me. He ran very hard, as if someone chased him."

"Did you see who?"

"No. The bus distracted me. The Vietnamese drove like maniacs. I knew the bus couldn't stop before it hit him, but I hoped he'd jump out of the way. It was odd. He fell down an instant before the bus hit him, gripped his chest, and fell over, right in the path of the bus. It was horrible."

Michael Fuller's heart gave out before the bus hit him. She wished the major had seen, even for an instant, the person who chased Michael Fuller.

"I yelled at Harlan that an American had been run over by a bus. He went to see if he could help. He was a combat medic, you know. He won a Silver Star for rescuing wounded men under fire."

"Yes, I know."

"He came back shaking. He said the man was Dermid Hagan. Hearing his name was almost worse than seeing him run over."

Depends on your priorities, Avivah thought. "Did you think Dermid was coming to see you, that he somehow found out about the apartment?"

Major Buckner closed her eyes. "Yes. We thought, somehow, he'd learned about us and planned to blackmail us. I actually thanked God that he had been killed."

One more of those personal gains from war that Colonel Norton hated so much. "Did you or Harlan ever hear from Dermid Hagan after that day? Receive any letters or phone calls?"

"Of course not. We thought he was dead."

"Did you continue your relationship with Specialist Carter in Vietnam?"

"Not after the day of the accident. It seemed too dangerous."

"When did you see Harlan Carter for the first time after Vietnam?"

"About two weeks after I arrived. We passed each other in the hospital corridor."

"Did you think about restarting the relationship?"

"Absolutely not. I'd gotten him out of my system."

"What changed that?"

"The MacDonald murders. The evening after the murders, he was waiting by my car when I came off duty. I'd had an emotionally draining shift, supporting the patients and the staff. It was like Vietnam all over again. The whole post was in shock. I guess you could say we literally fell into each other's arms."

Avivah thought about how her work schedule played havoc with her own social life. "Wasn't it difficult to keep up the relationship with him working days and you working evenings? And with you living in Colonel Norton's house?"

"Mary always went to work by 0600. Harlan waited around the corner until she left, then came for breakfast. Sometimes we'd take a ride for an hour or so after I finished my shift. We worked it out."

Avivah almost felt sorry for the woman. "I gather it didn't work well."

"Harlan began drinking again. He was terrified his wife would find out about us. When she left him, Harlan decided he'd give her a divorce, if she asked for one. He asked me to marry him Friday night."

"In the restaurant?"

"No, sitting outside the restaurant in his car."

"You turned him down?"

"My plans, at this point, do not include marriage to Harlan Carter."

Icy bitch.

"What happened when you said no?"

"We fought. I went back to my motel, but I couldn't sleep. About five a.m., I decided to get up and go to Boone."

"The rest of your statement about how you spent the weekend is the truth?"

Avivah had never seen dark circles form so quickly under someone's eyes. "The absolute truth. I swear it."

Avivah believed her. "Did you ever know a Michael Fuller in Saigon?"

"What has Michael got to do with this?"

"We think he might have been involved with Dermid Hagan."

"It can't be the same one."

"Was he a member of the poker game?"

"A hospital poker game wasn't Michael's style."

"How did you meet?"

"At the Continental Shelf."

"The what?"

"The Hotel Continental in Saigon had a bar, at the back, on the first floor, called the Continental Shelf. It was an open courtyard with tables under thatched roofs. Going there was almost like being away from the war. Even the journalists and the five o'clock follies were more like a comic opera than a war."

"Five o'clock follies, is that like happy hour?"

"Far from it. A lot of journalists stayed at the Continental and, at five o'clock every day, they did their daily press briefings about the war. Michael and I loved to giggle at them. Some of the reporters never left the hotel; they made up their stories from what people told them in the bar. Michael called it *Reporting from Mahogany Ridge* because the bar was made of mahogany. He had a very sharp sense of irony."

He was killed outside her apartment, with her watching, and misidentified as Dermid Hagan. Very ironic. "Was Dermid Hagan ever at the follies?"

"Enlisted men didn't go to the Continental Shelf."

"So, as far as you know, Dermid Hagan did not know Michael Fuller?"

"I never saw them together or heard anyone else say that they knew one another."

"Did Harlan Carter know Michael Fuller?"

"Harlan and Michael did not move in the same circles."

"The two of you never talked about Michael Fuller?"
"Never."

"What happened to Michael?"

"He ran out on his PA&E contract, went to Bangkok, and never came back. His boss was furious. He thought Michael had more honor than that. So did I, but I guess you're always wrong about some people."

"Did Michael ever tell you about being in a B-52 raid on the Laotian border in November, 1968?"

"Constantly. His story became tiresome. He worked in Laos before he came to Vietnam, learned to speak Laotian, and had friends there. He went to visit some of them, and got too close to the strike on the way back. He was a basket case for a few months after it happened. Looking back, I guess we shouldn't have been surprised when he ran out on his contract."

"Did Michael know about the apartment you and Harlan shared?"

"No."

"Did you sleep with him?"

"How dare you! I did not sleep with Michael Fuller or anyone else, except Harlan."

At last, genuine emotion. Avivah guessed that Major Buckner thought about sleeping with Michael. She wondered if it had been a fantasy, or if she'd offered and been turned down.

"Is there anything else you can tell me about Dermid or Michael?"

"I've told you quite enough."

"Where were you on July 4 of this year?"

"What time?"

"Between 0800 and 1300 hours."

"I was at home."

"Was Colonel Norton with you?"

"No, she left about 0730 for a breakfast at the officers' club. She came home about 1400 hours."

"Was anyone else with you?"

"I was alone."

"We'll have your statement typed and ask you to come down to the military police office to sign it when it's ready."

Jane Buckner stood.

"There's one more thing. I understand that as the evening supervisor, you can call a pharmacist back if needed?"

"That's correct."

"I am asking you to do that, right now."

"Why?"

"I need to collect all of the cocaine atomizers currently on the wards, so that the contents can be analyzed. I imagine the pharmacist will need to assist with that."

"Why are you doing this?"

"I have reason to suspect that cocaine from this hospital is related to a suspicious death."

"I'll have to call Colonel Norton to authorize this."

A little parade—Colonel Norton, Major Buckner, the on-call pharmacist, Avivah, and Ramerez—went from unit to unit to collect and label all of the atomizers in the hospital. They visited the emergency room last. Ramerez placed the final atomizer in the evidence box, locked it, and gave Avivah the chain-of-custody slip to sign. A group of doctors, nurses, and corpsmen hurried by, pushing a stretcher into a trauma room. An ill-looking man on the stretcher had an IV running. Avivah caught only a glimpse of his face, but a glimpse was all she needed. The man was Cody Doan.

Chapter 26

Avivah ordered Ramerez to watch the evidence box. No one stopped her as she followed the stretcher into the trauma room and stood against the far wall. Military police were a familiar emergency room sight.

One of the corpsmen handed the doctor a field chart. "They called for an Army ambulance at the Fayetteville airport. He collapsed on the plane from Atlanta."

Why had Cody been on a plane from Atlanta?

Cody grimaced and ran his hand up and down his leg. "I got up to go to the bathroom on the plane. I only put my foot down once. I swear only once."

The emergency room doctor placed a hand on Cody's shoulder and looked at one of the nurses. "Get me his orthopedic surgeon on the phone."

She left. The doctor ordered pain medication, lab tests, and x-rays, and asked for Doan's chart from Six-A. In a few minutes the doctors and nurses dispersed, leaving Doan with Avivah. She walked over to the stretcher. Doan's grey face looked much sicker than he had Sunday morning.

"You're the woman who drove me to the motel."

"Yes."

"Tell Captain Pepperhawk I really tried to get back yesterday."

Avivah sat on a stool next to the gurney. "Tell me your story. Make it quick before somebody interrupts us."

"Boyd's sister asked Reverend Pretcherd and me to tell

281

Boyd's mother he was dead. We made a pact—Dermid, Boyd and me—that if anything happened to one of us, the ones who were left would look after each other's parents. I had to go."

Avivah remembered her conversation with Pepper on Friday. "She was still visiting her sister?"

"Yeah, in Tennessee. It should have taken only a couple of hours for Reverend Pretcherd to drive us there and back. I would have had plenty of time to catch the afternoon plane, but, once we got there, the fog closed in. Fog comes up quick, like that, in the mountains. We couldn't get back to the airport Sunday night, and Widow Ramsey's sister, she didn't have a telephone."

"How did you get to Atlanta?"

"Reverend Pretcherd took me to Johnson City. I figured I could catch a flight back to Fayetteville from there, only you have to go through Atlanta and change planes."

"Why didn't you call from Johnson City or Atlanta?"

"Didn't have time. I'd have missed my plane. Tell Captain Pepperhawk I'm really sorry."

"I think she'll just be glad you're back."

Avivah stayed with Doan until an x-ray tech arrived. He seemed grateful for the company and once reached out to take her hand. She felt an unaccustomed lump in her throat.

She and Ramerez grabbed take-out food on the way back to the office. She'd already worked a shift and a half and didn't look forward to the next four, muggy hours.

Lieutenant Colonel Tyler, dressed in slacks and a golf shirt, met her at the brigade office door. He followed her to her desk. "I've been waiting for you for an hour and a half."

Avivah wanted to eat supper. Even more, she wanted to phone Pepper. "I didn't call you."

"The editor of the Fayetteville *Observer* called me. I understand you had two lost boys this afternoon, dad is a green beret, missing in action, older boy being the man of the house, lots of human interest. They want a picture of the kids, their wagon, and the bus driver who took care of them."

Avivah didn't dare ask him if he heard about the water tower rescue, too. That would only add to the human interest. "Deflect this one, will you?"

"Why?"

"Their mother has had a rotten week. Personal problems. She's ambivalent about the military at the best of times and she doesn't have the stamina to cope with publicity right now."

"The *Observer* will scream. And it's nice to have a good story once in a while."

Avivah set the take-out food on her desk, took out the food, and waved for Colonel Tyler to help himself to fries. "Give them a story about military and civilians working together—found the kids in twenty minutes—make it sound like we're all there for parents. Just keep the kids' names out of it. Have special forces do something nice for the bus driver: give him a certificate or take him for a helicopter ride." Give him an autographed copy of *The Ballad of the Green Berets*, she wanted to add, but she wasn't sure Colonel Tyler would get the joke like Benny would. Oh, God, Benny. Was he still missing? Did she still have to deal with that problem?

Tyler munched on her fries. "It doesn't have the same human interest appeal, but they like stories about the post and the city being good neighbors. I'll try it, but that's three favors you owe me."

"Three?" Avivah asked around a mouthful of food.

"The kids, the murder on July 4, and convincing the editor of the Marshall weekly that the death in Asheville had nothing to do with the murder here. I had to fly that one cold."

It hadn't occurred to Avivah that the press would connect the two deaths. "How did he put them together?"

"Two best friends from the same town, both veterans, die within two weeks of one other. Even a small town editor can smell something. So please tell me that the two deaths aren't related. Otherwise, I have to call him back and retract my original story. I do not like having egg on my face."

Avivah tossed the rest of her sandwich on the paper bag. "They are related."

Colonel Tyler looked stunned, his mouth open, a French fry dangling in his hand.

"It's a long story, Colonel."

Chapter 27

At one in the morning, Pepper's apartment door stood open. Avivah knocked on the screen, opened it, and poked her head inside. One small bayberry candle burned in the dark room, giving enough light to see a pile of empty beer bottles on the carpet. A dark figure on the couch waved a beer in Avivah's direction, and said in a slurred voice, "Tried to wait for you outside, but there were too many mosquitoes."

Avivah tossed her purse and cap on a table. "What's going on?"

Pepper struggled to rise. "They cut his leg off. They cut his fucking leg off."

Avivah knelt beside the couch and put her hands on either side of Pepper's face. "I am so sorry. I was there when they brought him into the emergency room. I meant to call you, but it was a crazy shift. I am so sorry."

Pepper shook her empty bottle. She wiggled out of Avivah's hands and made her way unsteadily towards the kitchen. "My fault. My fucking fault."

"No, it wasn't. Doan wanted me to tell you this wasn't your fault." Avivah recounted the story of Doan's peripatetic trip back from Marshall. "You said yourself that he might eventually lose his leg, and that it was the best thing."

"I lied. I wanted him to keep his leg. I wanted a miracle."

"The miracle is that he's still alive."

Pepper opened two bottles of beer, letting the caps join others on the floor. She handed one to Avivah. "It's only below the knee. God, I hope they went high enough."

Avivah sat on one of the counter stools. "I have no clue what you're talking about."

"Doan's bone dissolved from the chronic infection. He had only mush left in his ankle, so they amputated below the knee. If they didn't go high enough to get good, healthy bone, they'll just keep whittling at the leg, over and over, until they reach good bone or until he's dead. Maybe they should have gone above the knee to start out. Oh, God, I don't know. I got to call in."

She slammed her bottle on the counter. Beer foamed up. Avivah mopped it up before it dripped to the floor.

Pepper dialed a number and took a couple of slow breaths. "Lieutenant Forbes, it's Captain Pepperhawk again. How's Doan doing?"

Avivah closed her eyes and listened to Pepper's voice, trying to decide if Lieutenant Forbes could tell, over the phone, that Pepper was drunk. Probably not. Pepper's voice sounded calm and steady.

"Okay, I'm going to call his doctor. Thanks."

She dialed another number. "Captain Pepperhawk, sir. Sorry to bother you so late at night, but Cody Doan is still vomiting. . . . Yes, sir, even with the anti-nausea medication. . . . I read an article in a nursing journal about small dosing of IV morphine for postoperative pain control. Demerol and morphine are both narcotics. If we're going to give him a narcotic anyway, why not use the one that works?"

Fascinated, Avivah watched the conversation. If she looked at Pepper, she saw a woman barely able to stand; in fact, Pepper had her back against the kitchen wall, slowly sliding down it. If she closed her eyes, Pepper sounded calm and professional.

"For a person of Doan's weight, the article recommended two to four milligrams of morphine IV every hour. . . . No, sir, not as needed, every hour, on the hour, for twelve hours post-op. . . . Yes, sir, it does sound like a big dose, but it works out to only eight to sixteen milligrams in four hours, and we give up to fifteen milligrams every four hours as a single dose. The article said it worked better intravenously, in small doses instead of as one big dose. . . . Yes, sir, thank you, sir, I'm sure Lieutenant Forbes would appreciate you calling in that order. Good-bye, sir."

She hung up the phone before she slid to the floor. "I hate that shit."

"What shit?"

"It's a game. He knows everything because he's a doctor, and I'm a nurse, and I don't know anything. So I have to make it seem like it's his idea before he'll order what I damn well know is right. Doan throws up because we're under-medicating him; we've probably under-medicated him all along. He's had to suffer because we haven't done our jobs right."

Avivah looked at the clock. One-fifteen. "You ever pull an all-nighter in college?"

"Lots of times."

"Feel like pulling one tonight?"

"I thought that was what I was doing. What you got in mind?"

Avivah opened the refrigerator. "With the beer you've got in here and what I've got in my fridge, we have enough. I'm going to get my cooler, then we are going to make Sergeant Benjamin Kirkpatrick come to his senses."

287

★ ★ ★ ★ ★

Forty-five minutes later, Avivah parked her car on a graveled area near a cattle guard and gate. Pepper squinted at the painted white sign, just visible in the moonlight. *John F. Kennedy Special Warfare Center Vietnamese Village. Danger. No trespassing.* Pepper tried to remember what they were doing here. Making Benny come to his senses. They wrestled the cooler from the trunk.

Avivah rattled the metal gate. "Don't shoot, Benny. It's us, Avivah and Pepper."

In a moment, a figure in combat fatigues and a beret stepped out of the shadows. "The two of you make more noise than an NVA regiment." He took a key out of his pocket and leaned over the gate, unfastening the padlock. "What are you doing here?" The gate swung open silently on oiled hinges.

"Lorraine told us you might be here."

Benny fastened the gate behind them. "How is she?"

"Scared and worried, just like the boys. Incidentally, the boys ran away from home this afternoon so they could talk to you. They say they won't go to Oregon until they see you."

"Are they all right?"

"No thanks to you. And Lorraine called your mother after we found them, so Ma Kirkpatrick's not having a good night either."

Benny said nothing.

"Don't just stand there. Give us a hand."

Benny hoisted the cooler over one shoulder without effort. He led them along a small trail through the pine trees, barely visible in the moonlight. Pepper held back. "What about punji stakes?"

"I've disengaged the trip wires. They aren't real punji stakes, just tennis balls on the end of sticks. They bruise you and scare the piss out of you. Makes you more careful next time. Is either one of you sober?"

"Pepper isn't. There's been another murder."

"On post?"

Pepper caught herself before she tripped over a root. "In Asheville, a friend of the man who was murdered here, a friend of mine, too. It's my fault."

Avivah protested. "I was the one who talked you into going there."

The trail opened up into a small clearing, surrounded by half a dozen straw huts.

Benny walked toward one of the huts. "Look familiar?"

Pepper squinted at the small buildings. "Looks like the Vietnamese village at Fort Sam Houston. Qui Nhon was a city. I never saw a real Vietnamese village."

Benny pushed aside a black cloth curtain that covered a hootch door. He put the cooler on the floor and lit a candle. A straw mat covered the dirt floor and an air mattress and sleeping bag lay along one wall. A cooler and a pile of empty beer bottles filled one corner. The two women sat on the air mattress, while Benny paced.

Avivah asked, "You want to talk?"

"No."

"So it's better maybe that you should sulk?"

"Lay off, Avivah!"

Pepper had never heard Benny yell before. She didn't want to hear it again.

Benny opened three bottles of beer and handed them around. "Tell me about the second murder."

They told him about Pepper's trip to Asheville, the funeral, Boyd Ramsey's death, and Cody Doan's surgery. Pepper finished with, "I screwed up. I should have gotten Boyd police protection or something."

"There wasn't any way to see this second murder coming."

"We know a lot more about Dermid Hagan than we did four days ago," Avivah contributed, as if that somehow balanced the scales.

Pepper thought about the little church and about Reverend Pretcherd. "We know a lot more about Boyd Ramsey, including that he's dead. I guess there'll be another funeral now."

Avivah took a long swig of beer. "I expect so."

"You want me to go to this one, too?"

"No."

Benny looked in Avivah's cooler. "We need a wake. Or that thing that you Jews do, where everyone goes to visit the family."

"You mean sitting shiva?"

"Yeah."

"You only sit shiva for a member of your family or your community."

Pepper thought back to Dermid Hagan's body lying on the bed in Normandy House. "Dermid and Boyd were both soldiers, who had been to Vietnam. That makes us part of the same community."

"Not my community."

Benny flopped on the air mattress between the two women. "Get off it, Avivah. So you may not get your fucking chance to go to Vietnam. So what?"

Pepper raised her bottle in a salute. "We're still all soldiers. That's community. To Boyd Ramsey."

Avivah raised hers. "Dermid Hagan."

"Randall Fulford. Before we went to Vietnam, we came out here to talk to the ghosts of berets we knew. God, I fucking miss him."

The three of them drank and grieved in silence. Several beers later, Pepper waved her bottle at him. "On the way here we talked war. From a feminist perspective, of course."

"Did you come to any conclusions about war? From a feminist perspective, I mean."

"Yeah. Avivah's not a lesbian. Did you know that? I wasn't sure until tonight. Neither are you. Gay, I mean. But you could be. I mean, just because you're in special forces doesn't *a priori*—that's the word isn't it, Avivah—*a priori* mean you're not gay. Right, Avivah?"

"Right."

"But you love Lorraine, so even if you were gay, you'd have to be, what is it, Avivah? Mixed?"

"Bisexual."

"Oh yeah bisexual," Pepper rolled the word around in her mouth like it was a new taste. "You're not bisexual, are you, Benny?"

"Not the last time I checked."

"And we've decided that if Avivah wants to go to war, she should. Right, Avivah?"

"Right."

Benny fished in the ice standing in the cooler and picked out the last beers. He opened them and handed them around. "A sentiment I don't share."

Avivah set her beer on the dirt floor with a solid thunk. "You know what else we figured out, Benny? Besides you not being *a priori* gay, I mean. We figured you and Lorraine should get married. We figured out that Pepper cares about her patients, and that I believe in social justice, and that the Army stinks. You know what we couldn't figure out, Benny? We couldn't figure out combat. Tell us about combat, Benny. Tell us war stories."

Pepper ran her hands over the goose bumps on her arms. "Don't, Avivah."

"Why not? What makes it so fucking sacred? War stories come with the territory."

Benny said quietly, "Not my territory, they don't."

"You mean not with women. You'd tell them fast enough if guys were here, if Randall was here."

Benny put his half-empty beer bottle on the ground. "What do you want, war stories or the truth?"

"Truth and honesty. Pepper and I decided truth and honesty was the price of admission tonight."

Benny sat, silent, his eyes closed, his body swaying. "Combat isn't just one thing. For me, going into a hot landing zone is the greatest adrenaline rush I've ever felt. My heart starts racing as soon as I climb on the chopper. By the time we land I feel like I'm flying. I could be in a foot of mud and it feels like I'm flying over the ground."

Pepper wanted to be able to not pay attention. She'd heard similar stories before, from people she didn't know very well. This was Benny. She couldn't afford to let his stories too far inside her, not if she still wanted to be his friend, because the stories of what he'd done and where he'd been hurt too much. To dampen the sound of his voice, she leaned over and collected empty bottles.

"It's worse when we did a quiet insertion. Waiting is the hard part. Just thinking any minute now something will happen. Every sound is magnified, every color is so bright it burns your eyes. When something finally happens, it's like I'm not on this planet any more. Time stops. Place stops. It's like whatever I do there isn't really me."

Pepper lined the bottles up in columns. The British called empty bottles *dead soldiers*. There was one left over. She put the bottle at the front, the leader. She couldn't decide if she wanted it to be a man or a woman.

Avivah said, "You haven't told me a thing a woman couldn't survive."

"I'm not finished. When you come out, you stink. It isn't just the explosives and the jungle, it's what boils up from inside you. I've been too tired to sleep for three days. I've been starving and knew if I ate I'd puke. And the reflexes don't go away. Randall and I were in a Mike Force bar one night. He said something I didn't like, and I would have put a knife into him, if people hadn't pulled us apart. One of the things I miss most is that he died before I could apologize for that night. That's the kind of thing I don't want for you. Women don't belong in combat."

"But they will be there, Benny; one day, very soon, when you take a team to Panama, there will be a woman on it."

"That's the day I turn in my beret and walk away."

"No, you won't." Pepper interrupted, with more conviction than she felt.

"What makes you so smart?"

"Truth and honesty time. Why do you do what you do?"

"Pepper, with all due respects to the work you do, I don't want my guys ending up on a Dustoff chopper or in a body bag. Being wounded sucks. The idea of being dead sucks even more. I'm a survival instructor. My guys think I'm teaching them to survive in the jungle. What I'm really teaching them is how to survive after you come out of the jungle."

"That's why you won't walk away. Women need to know how to survive, too."

Benny made a noncommittal gesture of not wanting to argue rather than having been convinced.

Pepper pushed herself to her feet. "Come on, Avivah. I got to be at work in a few hours."

Avivah fell over and crawled to the far edge of the air mattress, curling into a tight ball. "Over the limit. Very, very bad on my record to drive impaired."

Benny blew out the candle. He picked up a camouflaged sleeping bag and threw it over Avivah. "At least if you are going to crash here, stay warm. Pepper, I'll take you back to town early enough so you can get to work."

"I've got to take a leak."

"I'll show you where."

Benny took her elbow and guided her through the cloth doorway and across the clearing to a clump of bushes. Pepper relieved herself, then joined him in the clearing. Her eyes had adjusted enough to the moonlight to see his face. The look in his eyes frightened her. She reached over and laid the back of her hand against his cheek.

"Where are you?"

"Away." He held her hand to keep her from stroking his cheek. "Do you still feel guilty about Boyd and Cody?"

"I do."

"Ever heard of the Son Tay raid?"

"No."

"November 21, 1970."

"I was in Qui Nhon and I wasn't interested in much outside news."

"Happened right down the road from you, well, figuratively. Colonel Bull Simons took in about sixty green berets and commandos to free prisoners from the camp in Son Tay, a few miles away from Hanoi. Only there weren't any prisoners there. There are different stories about when they had been moved and why, but the bottom line is our guys spent forty minutes on the ground for nothing."

Tears rolled down Benny's cheeks. "Our guys brought acetylene torches, chain saws, bolt cutters, things they would need to cut the door and shackles. One of the berets with a pair of bolt cutters went down the row of cells, snapping locks, saying, 'No one in here.' Just that, over and over again. Snap. 'No one in here.' Snap. 'No one in here,' down the whole length of cells."

"Were you there?"

He shook his head. "Thank God, no. Bad enough to listen to the story. But that doesn't mean I don't feel guilty about it. I told you before, Pepper, berets are family. You and I can't afford guilt. If you think you contributed to Boyd's death or Cody losing his leg, then do something about it. Find the killer. Take care of Cody. Don't wade in guilt. You'll drown before you know it."

"You drowning?"

"Let's just say, tonight, I'm treading water. Hell, I'm a survivor, and so are you, and so is Avivah, even if I do have a hard time telling her that. Now go back with her and get some sleep."

"You going to sleep tonight?"

He sounded absolutely alone. "Probably not. It comes with the territory."

"Want me to stay up with you?"

"No."

"I don't want you to be alone. Not ever."

He kissed her on the palm. "I'll call you if I need you, pretty lady."

"Promise?"

"Promise. Always."

Pepper went inside the hut, pulling the cloth across the door. In a minute, she heard the muffled sound of a bamboo door close on another hut. That sound shut out the world.

Chapter 28

Pepper awoke, aware of someone beside her. Before she could sit up, the figure shoved a field dressing into her mouth. She choked on the cottony, slightly medicinal taste.

The figure squatting beside her wore a black jumpsuit, black gloves, black boots, and night goggles over the eyes. Was it a man or a woman? The figure pointed a gun at Avivah's sleeping form, and motioned with a gloved finger for her to be quiet. Be quiet or I hurt your friend. Pepper nodded. The figure motioned for her to stand and she wiggled out from under the camouflage blanket and put on her shoes.

In a minute, outside the hut, the dark, hot night enveloped them. Pepper knew she couldn't have slept more than an hour. Was Benny still awake?

Oh, God, don't let Benny be wandering around the compound. She scanned the small village, but saw no one. Suppose whoever this was had already found Benny and tied him up or worse. She wanted to believe that Benny wouldn't let himself be surprised.

The figure motioned for her to walk down the trail. Had Benny reset the trip wires for the rubber punji stakes? If they went off, would that be enough of a diversion for her to escape? Could she run after being stunned by a tennis ball hitting her at full force? Where would she run? She knew no more of the village than the trail and the small circle of huts.

At least they were moving away from Benny and Avivah. Unless, Pepper thought suddenly, this figure was Benny. A man who almost knifed his best friend and who talked to ghosts couldn't be all that sane. They had only his word that he was in Panama on July 4. Avivah would never think to check. Pepper listened to the footsteps behind her, trying to hear if anything reminded her of Benny, but the steps were too muffled.

They came to the gated cattle guard. Relief flooded her when she realized the figure indicated they had to climb over the gate. It couldn't be Benny; he had a key.

They couldn't go over it together, and that meant one of them would be on one side of the gate and one on the other. She resolved to make a run then, though the thought of being shot nauseated her.

The figure removed a pair of handcuffs from a leg pocket in the pants and motioned for her to put her hands on either side of a bar in the gate. Pepper extended her hands and watched the cuffs snap around each wrist. She no longer had to decide if she had the courage to run.

Her captor climbed over the gate, unhooked one of the cuffs, refastened it to his/her wrist, and motioned for Pepper to climb the locked gate. When she cleared the gate, the figure unlocked one cuff and fastened both of Pepper's hands behind her.

She saw only Benny's truck and Avivah's car. Whoever this was had walked to the compound. The figure motioned for her to walk down the dirt road. The question wasn't why her; she knew why, she'd been asking too many questions. But why *tonight?* Why *here?* How had this person known she was here? Her, not Avivah. She had something the killer wanted, something Avivah didn't have, and she had no idea what. That she had something bought her time and, as long as she was alive and thinking, she had a chance.

Basic training hadn't taught her useful combat skills, only how to salute, read an organizational chart, and what to do in case of chemical, biological, or nuclear attack. She spent a brief moment trying to think of a way to use an atropine injector—nerve gas antidote—as a weapon. Even if she came up with a way, she didn't have an injector.

In the recesses of her memory, she found Darby Baxter's class on self-defense. He said, "You're stronger than you think. Stay calm. Pretend to go along with what's happening. Look for anything that can be used as a weapon." *You're stronger than you think. Stay calm. Pretend to go along with what's happening. Look for anything that can be used as a weapon.* She repeated the four phrases over and over like a mantra.

They walked for a long time. If her luck held, if Avivah didn't wake up and notice she was gone, or if Benny didn't come to check on the sleeping women, every step moved them farther away from her friends.

She saw a rental car parked under dark shadows in the dense pine woods. The figure unlocked the passenger door, unlocked one of her handcuffs, and motioned for her to climb into the back seat. The inside of the car remained dark, even with the door open. This person had unscrewed the dome light.

A black, gloved hand fastened the handcuff to the clothing hanger beside the back seat, then removed the gag from her mouth. For that small relief, she was grateful. She added a fifth element to her plan. *You're stronger than you think. Stay calm. Pretend to go along with what's happening. Look for anything that can be used as a weapon. Get the person talking and keep him talking, because the more talk, the more distraction.*

The figure opened the driver's door and removed a plastic garbage bag covering the seat. Pepper heard the trunk open and the rustle of the plastic bag being turned inside out. Fibers, she thought. In television mystery shows, the police always vacuumed the suspect's car. This person had put the plastic bag over the seat to drive out here and was now turning the bag inside out to catch any fibers that had been deposited on the bag. There were some small cloth sounds and Pepper decided the person was taking off the night gear and putting it all in the plastic bag. Wherever they were going, Pepper bet a person in a set of black coveralls and night goggles would be noticed.

Darby Baxter taught her one other useful thing in basic. She pictured him standing in front of her class at the edge of the compass and map course. He drilled into them, "The first rule in finding your way is to know your terrain, know your position." Pepper closed her eyes and visualized the map of the post she looked at so many times during the past month, wondering what her new assignment would be like. The only road through the back of the post ended in a T-intersection. A right turn went toward Spring Lake and, from there, down Bragg Boulevard to the post. A left turn wound through rural country, eventually to the golf resort, Southern Pines. She'd form a plan after she knew if they turned right or left. At least now she felt like she had options. Bless you, Darby Baxter. If she ever got out of this . . . when she got out of this, that's the way Baxter would want her to think . . . when she got out of this, she intended to thank him.

The trunk slammed shut and a man, dressed in civilian shirt and pants, opened the door, got in, and started the car. They drove off without headlights. Pepper sank back against the seat cushions trying to make sense of the face.

Finally she said, "You're pretty good at clandestine operations for a public information officer. Or is being a PIO just a cover?"

"Not in the least," Colonel Tyler replied, "I'm an excellent public information officer, but I started my Army career as an infantry officer. Old habits die hard."

"Why didn't you just kill me back there? Me and Avivah both?"

The car stopped at the T-intersection. "I need you to do something for me."

Turn right, turn right, Pepper willed, as if she could force the car to the right. A right turn almost certainly meant they were going to Fort Bragg or Fayetteville; a left turn meant a huge pine woods where Colonel Tyler could easily hide her body. He switched on the headlights and turned right onto the secondary paved road. Pepper almost laughed. Okay, they were going to either Fort Bragg or to Fayetteville. Civilization almost, even at 0300 hours. Police cars. Traffic lights. Lots of opportunities to attract attention. She was so busy trying to think of how she could escape that she almost missed what Colonel Tyler said next.

"You're going to get me in to see Sergeant Cody Doan."

"Doan doesn't know anything."

"You'd be surprised what Doan knows. He has something that belongs to me and I want it back."

Rule number five: keep him talking. "What do you think Doan has?"

The colonel didn't reply. Okay, so Doan wasn't a topic that would keep Tyler talking. "What makes you think I'll help you?"

"You have two choices: walk quietly into Womack with me and get me into Doan's room or I shoot you in the hospital. There are almost certain to be bystanders, even at this time of the morning."

Pepper knew he had guessed right. She would cooperate rather than risk a shooting in the hospital. "We're just details to you, aren't we?"

"Details are very important."

Keep the conversation going. "You're right about details. You were very clever with the plastic bag, but they'll still be able to find evidence that I was in this car. You should have put plastic over this seat, too."

"Oh, lovely lady, of course you were in this car. When you called earlier this evening you were hysterical and drunk. Gave me some garbled story about how guilty you felt because someone named Boyd Ramsey died."

At Boyd's name, tears came unbidden to Pepper's eyes. She blinked them away. Darby would be disappointed in her if she cried. Tears weren't helpful in staying alert.

"Why did you have to kill Boyd? He wasn't any threat to you."

Again silence. All right, he wasn't willing to talk about Cody or Boyd, but he did seem willing to talk about his own cleverness. "Just when am I supposed to have phoned you?"

"Some time after Captain Rosen came home, and found you drinking alone by candlelight."

Even in Vietnam she had never felt so vulnerable. "You've been watching my apartment."

"I've watched you quite closely. The day I met you, I realized how sharp you were. You're so innocent and trusting that keeping an eye on you was almost easy."

"Almost?"

"I was careless to not realize curiosity would drive you to attend the funeral."

She heard contempt in his voice. So Tyler hated any kind of carelessness. *Look for a weapon,* Baxter said. Maybe she could use carelessness as a weapon. "You've missed another important detail. You said I called you. When they check my telephone records, Southern Bell won't have any record of a phone call to you."

"You really should have a better lock on your door. While the two of you were struggling to put the cooler into Captain Rosen's car, I let myself into your apartment and made a telephone call. I also left you a little present. I think you'd find it amusing, assuming, of course, you get to see it. By the way, you should not sit alone at a picnic table in the middle of the night. Fayetteville's not that safe."

"How long were you watching me?"

"Long enough. It's been a very frustrating evening. I was about to approach you when you went inside, and I was about to knock on your door when Captain Rosen arrived. Your voices carried clearly through your screen door."

They passed through Spring Lake, a tiny community on the edge of the military reserve. As they drove down the main street, Pepper looked for a police car, for *any* car, but the street was deserted and the community quiet.

"Yeah, well Avivah will know that I never called you."

"You called when she wasn't with you. She left for a few minutes just before you started on your so-called road trip."

When Avivah went to the storage room to get her cooler. Pepper had been alone for ten or fifteen minutes. The story would work, Tyler was slick enough to make it work.

"What did I say to you on this mythical phone call?"

"That you had been depressed ever since you came back from Vietnam and, that after two deaths in two weeks, you were going to kill yourself. Then you became quite incoherent and hung up on me. Of course, I tried to call you back, but got no answer. I decided to go to your apartment and reached there just in time to see you drive away with Captain Rosen. Driving in a most erratic manner, I might add. I followed at a discreet distance, and parked down the road, trying to decide what to do. Fortunately, you came stumbling down the road, still drunk, still hysterical. You pleaded with me to take you to Cody Doan, so you could apologize because it was your fault he lost his leg. I thought the best way to calm you down was to honor your wish."

He was turning the conversation he overheard against her and, even to her, it sounded plausible.

"What are you going to do with me after we see Doan?"

"An Army nurse just back from Vietnam, sickened by all of the horrors she witnessed, unhinged by one more soldier crippled in her care, one she feels responsible for, is an ideal profile of a cocaine user. Perhaps you were already hooked on cocaine, using it to get you through your tour of duty. I imagine cocaine was easily available in Qui Nhon."

Too easily available. At least one soldier died from a drug overdose every week. She could have gotten cocaine easily, if she hadn't preferred to stick to booze.

"Free-basing cocaine can be so dangerous. A remote, hidden spot. A moment's inattention. A fireball. Another tragic victim of Vietnam, and the drug problem rampant in the military. Being a woman and an officer, it will be easy for me to get you good play in the press. You might even make the cover of *Time* magazine."

Pepper thought of Benny's burns. She fought down her rising hysteria with the mantra. *You're smarter than you think. Stay calm. Pretend to go along with him. Look for a weapon. Keep him talking.*

Colonel Tyler drove through the almost-deserted hospital parking lot, and along the service road around to the back of the hospital. He parked in shadows next to the building, got out, and came around to Pepper's side of the car. After he removed her handcuffs, Pepper rubbed her wrists. When she climbed out of the car, Tyler took her elbow and pushed the gun into her side. "Walk quietly with me through the hospital and up to Cody Doan's room."

"There's an admissions clerk on duty in the lobby. He'll remember seeing us together."

He motioned for her to walk to a secluded back door and used a small key to open it. "We aren't going through the lobby."

Even in the dim light, Pepper realized they were in the Red Cross Recreation Room. "Do you have keys to the entire post?"

"You'd be surprised how careless people are about keys."

Carefully, he opened the door into the hospital corridor, then motioned with the gun. "You go first."

Chapter 29

A clock at the end of the deserted hall said 0350 hours. As they climbed the stairs, Pepper tried to remember who had night duty this week. Lieutenant Forbes and Corpsman Pinna. It was the corpsman's last week of shifts before he left the Army. They stepped from the stairwell into the silent sixth floor. The hall leading to the wards was deserted, the doors to both wards Six-A and Six-B shut.

Pepper whispered, wetting her dry lips. "I have to talk to the duty nurse. Wait in the stretcher alcove in the hall. It's dark there. No one will see you."

"Stay where I can see you. If you go into the nurses' station, give any signal, write any notes, I'll kill her, too."

Trying to keep her shoes from squeaking on the linoleum floor, Pepper opened the unit door and walked toward the brightly-lit nurses' station. Lieutenant Aileen Forbes came out of the nurses' station and looked down the corridor. Pepper quickened her pace so they would meet closer to the nurses' station. She wanted to yell at Aileen to leave, go down the far stairs, get out of danger. She thought about the hand signals used to give silent commands in the field. There was no hand signal for *there's a murderer, with a gun, hidden in the stretcher alcove.*

"Captain Pepperhawk, what are you doing here?"

"Where's Corpsman Pinna?"

Lieutenant Forbes glanced uneasily towards the ward. "Um . . . he's um . . . I'll get him for you."

Corpsmen sometimes slept in the middle of night shift. She'd covered for her own corpsmen in Qui Nhon, though doing so always made her uneasy. She thought if you were on duty, you should stay awake. Now she was grateful for the tradition. Pinna asleep on an empty bed in the ward was safer than Pinna roaming the halls.

The two women walked down the hall, falling into the same strolling rhythm. "That's okay. I couldn't sleep, thinking about Sergeant Doan, so I came to check on him."

"He's better. We're holding him with just two milligrams of morphine an hour. He stopped vomiting, and he's sleeping."

They stopped across from the nurses' station. Pepper gauged the possibility of grabbing Aileen's arm, running into the station, slamming the door, and dialing the military police. There would be casualties. Maybe her and Lieutenant Forbes, maybe Pinna, maybe the patients. Pepper couldn't take the risk.

During night shift the nurse parked the clean linen cart, a dirty linen bag, and the dressing cart in the hall. Pepper ran her hand over the smooth frame of the clean linen cart and wished she could write a message on the sheets, in invisible ink that would show up after she and Tyler were in Doan's room.

Don't get fanciful, she chided herself. *You're smarter than you think. Stay alert. Look for a weapon.* Could you make a weapon out of linen? Pepper began to toy idly with the row of bottles lined up at the back of the dressing cart. "I'm feeling pretty bad about Doan. I mean, if I hadn't gotten him that emergency pass, he might have kept his leg."

Damn, she was playing right into Tyler's hands. When she turned up dead, Aileen Forbes would make a credible witness about her distressed state of mind.

"Oh, Captain, it's not your fault. His doctor said he would have lost his leg anyway; it was just a matter of time."

Pepper managed a wan smile, as if grateful for attempted reassurances. She intentionally didn't look at what her hands were doing. She didn't want Aileen to look at her hands either.

"I want to spend an hour or so with Doan, have some time to talk privately to him. I don't want anybody to interrupt us. Can you see to that?"

"I suppose so. Is there anything I can help you with?"

"No, that's exactly what I don't want you to do! Just leave us alone! That's an order, all right?" Pepper unscrewed the black plastic cap on a final bottle, sniffed it, put the cap back on, tried to appear distracted.

"I was just about to hang his four o'clock antibiotic. You want to do that?"

Pepper picked up another bottle, took the cap off, toyed with it. "Yes. I'll be with him between now and six." By 0600, Doan could be dead. She could be, too. "I don't want anyone to bother us. Got that. No one. Make me a sign for his door. 'Do not disturb by order of Captain Pepperhawk.' "

Lieutenant Forbes disappeared into the nurses' station and Pepper busied herself with the linen and dressings. She gathered up dressing material and linen, folded a sheet neatly in quarters, and laid it across the top of the wheeled soiled linen bag. Corpsman Pinna's cigarettes, lighter, and ashtray lay on the counter outside the nurses' station. She took a cigarette out of the pack and lit it, tried to imagine herself as Lauren Bacall, and desperately hoped she wouldn't cough. She moved her hand down the side of her body away from Colonel Tyler and slid the lighter into her pants pocket, all the time feeling the gun pointed at her back. There was an exquisite moment of silence after the lighter slipped into her pocket. No gunfire, no pain. Hurry, she willed at Lieutenant Forbes. Colonel Tyler wasn't going to wait much longer.

When the other nurse reappeared, Pepper snubbed out the cigarette. Aileen gave her a large metal medicine tray containing a bottle of IV fluid, a smaller bottle of IV antibiotics, tubing, medicines, and syringes. A sign written on lined notebook paper with a heavy black marker. A piece of Scotch tape hung on the rim of the tray. "Here's his four o'clock antibiotic, his next bottle of IV fluids, and his six o'clock medications. Oh, and I signed out two ampules of morphine for you."

"Thanks. Okay if I take the soiled linen cart with me?"

"Sure. I'll get another one for out here."

Pepper threw the linen carelessly over her arm, took the tray in one hand, and pushed the dirty linen bag with her other hand. "You'd better get on with your rounds."

She walked down the corridor to Doan's room. She watched Lieutenant Forbes take a flashlight from the counter and go in the opposite direction down the hall. As soon as she was safely in the darkened ward, Pepper used the linen cart to push open the door to Doan's room. Tyler followed her into the room. Her heart thundered, waiting for him to reach in her pocket and remove the lighter. He didn't do that. She'd found a weapon. Fire.

Pepper dropped the linens on the chair beside the door and put the metal medicine tray on the over-bed table. Tyler read the note over her shoulder. He nodded approval. She taped the sign on the outside of the door. For once she wished hospital doors had locks on them. She didn't trust that, despite the sign, Corpsman Pinna or David Willett, who always arrived early, wouldn't look in to see if they could help. She had to get this over as fast as possible.

Only the small, square night light lit the room. Doan slept, his blue pajama-clad chest rising and falling. The foot of the bed looked like a small white tent, keeping pressure off his fresh stump.

Tyler whispered in her ear. "Wake him up."

"I have things to do first. You want him to be able to talk, don't you?" What she was doing wouldn't make Doan any more or less able to talk, but it bought a little time.

Tyler walked across the room and positioned himself with his back in a corner. Pepper remembered guys in 'Nam doing that. Always protect your back. Maybe Tyler really had been an infantry officer.

Tonight Doan looked almost peaceful. Was it the morphine or was he relieved that his struggle to keep his leg was finally over?

Only a tiny triangle of fluid remained in the neck of the IV bottle. She'd speak to Aileen about cutting the time too close before changing the bottle. She almost laughed. Both she and Doan were going to die and she worried about his IV running dry. Pepper peeled back the aluminum cap on the IV fluid and scrubbed the seal with alcohol-soaked gauze. She dropped the alcohol-laden gauze into the wastebasket, grateful as the medicinal odor filled the room.

She changed IVs and hung the smaller antibiotic bottle, then drew morphine into the syringe, rubbed the tubing port with more alcohol-soaked gauze, and injected two milligrams. She backed away from the bed. "Doan . . . Doan, wake up."

Groggy from sleep and morphine, Doan didn't come up swinging. He peered at her as if trying to focus. "Captain Pepperhawk, is it morning already?"

"It's a few minutes after four."

"What are you doing here?"

Pepper made her voice sharp and crisp. "Sergeant Doan, I need you to wake up and pay attention. Right now. You and I are in a shitload of trouble." She pointed to Colonel Tyler.

Doan took a minute to register the gun in Tyler's hand, then sank back against the pillows. "I was fucking afraid this would happen. You asked too many questions."

Tyler moved closer to the bed. "Where's the letter?"

Pepper was completely confused. What letter?

"What's it worth to you?"

Pepper felt an incredible sadness spread through her. She had been so convinced Doan wasn't involved.

"Maybe your life."

Doan looked down at the tent-like covers at the foot of the bed. "I figure that's pretty well shot anyway." He hiked his head in Pepper's direction. "How about her life?"

"Captain Pepperhawk's life is not up for discussion."

Doan shrugged. "No skin off my nose. The letter is in my locker at the medical holding company. You didn't think I'd carry it around with me, did you?"

"Did you read it?"

"Of course I fucking read it."

"Then why didn't you get in touch with me?"

He waved his hand at the bedclothes. "I've been a little busy the past couple of weeks. Besides, like Dermid said, blackmail can always wait. The longer you prolong the suspense, the better the final payoff."

Small tears ran down Pepper's cheeks. She'd held out a shred of hope that Cody Doan wasn't involved.

"How do I get it out of your locker?"

He leaned over the bed as if to open the door at the

bottom of the bedside stand. "Keys are in my pants."

Tyler moved to where he could see that side of the bed. "Stay where you are. Captain Pepperhawk, you get it."

She took a blue plastic hospital bag out of the bedside stand, and handed it to Doan.

"Dump it on the bed," Tyler ordered.

Doan turned the bag over and shook out the contents. There were the shirt and pants he'd worn when Pepper and Avivah dropped him at the motel. Tyler looked at the clothes, and, satisfied there was no danger there, told Doan to hand the key to Captain Pepperhawk. He did.

"Room fifteen, Locker A. Wait until after seven o'clock to take her over there. She can tell the wardmaster I want some things from my locker. Carter never asks questions, but the guy on night duty is a real busybody. You go before seven, he'll ask questions."

Three more hours. Doan had given her three more hours to live and, at the same time, he had made the situation more complicated than he could imagine. What were they going to do for three hours?

Tyler picked up the second morphine ampule from the tray and held it out to Pepper. "Put all of it in the syringe."

Pepper opened the ampule and drew up the medication.

"It was very kind of Captain Pepperhawk to provide the means for your demise. A large dose of morphine IV will do nicely. It will be painless, I assure you, just drifting off to sleep. Of course, there may be some questions later about Captain Pepperhawk's decision to give you so much."

A mercy killing would fit in nicely with Tyler's plans. She expected Doan to look afraid, but he didn't change expression. "I got to piss first!"

"That won't matter in a few minutes."

Doan threw back the covers, sat up, and reached for his

crutches hooked on the head of the bed. "I got this thing about wetting the sheets, okay? My dad used to beat the tar out of me when I did that. I don't want to piss myself, okay?"

Pepper had lost track of how many young men she had seen who were missing body parts. Seeing Doan's empty pajama leg broke her heart. Deep inside, a small part of her frightened brain was astonished at the resilience of the men she cared for. Doan already stood beside the bed, balanced on his crutches. She stepped forward to help him, but he pushed her away.

He nodded at the IV pole. "You take care of that."

They walked slowly across the room. The tiny bathroom was hardly bigger than a closet, a windowless, green-tiled cubicle with a commode and a sink. There was barely room for the two of them, Doan's crutches, and the IV pole.

Doan faltered as he tried to undo the tie cord that held his pants. Pepper put her hands under his armpits and kept him from falling. Maybe he wasn't as resilient as he pretended. She lowered him to the toilet.

"Give me his crutches."

Doan handed them out, one at a time. He leaned his head on Pepper's shoulder and turned his mouth to her ear.

"When I say I'm ready, make sure you're next to the door. I'll make a diversion. You get out." The words were wisps of sound in her ear.

Then Doan seemed to recover from his dizzy spell and sat upright.

Conscious that her back was toward Tyler and that he could not see her face, Pepper mouthed. "Won't leave you."

Concealed by her body, Doan's hand signed *follow my lead.* Pepper realized that whatever Doan had in mind, whispered conferences and hand signals wouldn't talk him out of it. She just wished she had a way to tell him she had a diversion of her own planned. She backed out of the bathroom and started to shut the door.

"Leave the door open."

Doan looked around at the windowless room. "Where do you think I'm going? I can't piss with you watching. That gun makes me too nervous."

"All right, close the door."

Pepper closed the door and tried to look casual as she positioned herself between the door to the hall and the covered linen bag. She stuffed her hand in her pocket and fingered the heavy lighter. Pinna boasted that it never failed to light. She prayed it wasn't just a boast.

Stay calm. Get ready to move. One chance. If she could get out of the room, there was a fire extinguisher beside the ward door. She could use that as a weapon: spray the foam in Tyler's eyes. Or hit him over the head if it came to that.

Tyler stood with his head inclined toward the door. "I don't hear anything in there."

"I'm having trouble getting started."

"It's the medicines," Pepper contributed, loud enough for Doan to hear through the closed door. "They make it hard to piss. Try running some water."

She heard running water and, after a few minutes, sounds of urination and, then, a toilet flushing.

"Ready, Captain."

Tyler reached for the doorknob. Pepper pulled the lighter out of her pocket, flicked the ignition wheel, raised the sheet covering the laundry bag, and tossed the lighter in. The laundry bag exploded in a fireball. Pepper was out the door. She heard two shots, the crash of glass, the sound of flesh connecting with flesh. Then she was down the hall and through the double doors heading for the fire extinguisher. She ran right into the arms of a military policeman, wearing body armor and a helmet. More military police flowed around her like she was a rock in a stream.

As she raced past her, Avivah yelled. "Get down. Stay here."

Pepper turned and followed on Avivah's heels. She threw on the room lights. Dense, acrid smoke filled the room—benzene-and-alcohol soaked linen burned dirty. Broken glass, water, burning linen, two bodies, and six military policemen covered the blood-streaked floor.

Two policemen peeled Tyler off Doan and shoved him face down on the bed. Pepper crawled through a forest of legs to reach Cody. Behind her she heard the sound of a fire extinguisher being used on the burning linen bag and felt a residue of cold spray on her back. She looked Doan over frantically for the source of the blood. "Where are you hit?"

He ran his hands over his pajamas. "I'm not hit. At least, I don't think I am."

"Where is the blood coming from?"

He held up his right hand. Blood dripped from the IV site. "I didn't have time to put pressure on it when I pulled the IV out." He looked at the handcuffed figure on the bed. "Who the fuck is that and what letter is he talking about?"

Chapter 30

Avivah jabbed the pause button. The wavering screen showed a credit line at the end of the *60 Minutes* program. "There it is."

Eighty-second Airborne Segment
Special thanks to Lieutenant-Colonel Gardner Tyler
Public Information Office, Fort Bragg, North Carolina

She switched off the video player and opened the curtains. Early morning light flooded the room. "We never looked at the final credits."

Avivah joined Pepper and Benny at the small table. She wore fatigues and her hair had a ridge in it from her helmet. Benny also wore fatigues; the tip of his rolled beret protruded from a leg pocket. Pepper, dressed in jeans and a T-shirt, felt almost naked. Her and Avivah's clothes still smelled like smoke and benzene.

By the time the military police took Tyler away and Pepper settled Doan back in a newly-made bed, Colonel Norton and Colonel Granger arrived on Ward Six-A. Colonel Norton ordered Pepper to go home. Instead, she followed Benny and Avivah to the military police brigade office.

Benny picked up a Styrofoam cup, swirled the last bit of coffee in the bottom, and took a swallow, then made a face and put the cup down. "Okay, so you can prove Dermid

315

Hagan knew where to find Tyler. Would Tyler's secretary remember if he received a letter, several months ago, with Canadian stamps?"

Avivah pushed a bit of congealed grits around with a plastic fork. "Doubtful, and not conclusive, unless she could testify that Dermid's name and address were on the envelope."

"What about a ballistics match on his gun and the bullet from Dermid's body?"

"Completely different gun, different caliber. He probably ditched the murder weapon and I doubt we'll ever find it. Think Pepper, did he say anything that would connect him to Dermid or Boyd Ramsey?"

Pepper ran her hand through her hair. It came away sooty and she wiped it on her jeans. "He never responded to anything about Dermid or Boyd. At the hospital, all he did was ask Cody where the letter was."

"Did he say Dermid's letter?"

"No, just *the* letter." Pepper kept replaying the abduction, the drive to the hospital, the half hour in Cody's room, as if her mind stuck on one film loop. She was certain Tyler said nothing that linked him to either of the two murders.

"Sergeant Doan had no idea who he was?"

"He said he never saw him before. He played for time, saying the letter was in his locker. I suppose the policeman you sent over to medical holding company didn't find a letter?"

"No letter."

Benny picked up a plastic knife from the takeaway container and turned it end-over-end on the table. "You've got him for abduction. I saw him handcuff Pepper and take her away at gunpoint."

"How did you know I was being kidnapped?"

"I heard the two of you go over the gate. I was on you about thirty seconds later."

"We weren't that noisy."

"You weren't that quiet."

"Did you have a weapon?"

"No."

"If you'd had one, would you have used it?"

Benny waved the question away. Pepper wasn't sure she wanted to know the answer. She laid her head on the desk. "But you had a radio."

"I'm cross-trained in communications. I always have a field radio with me. Thank God I did."

Avivah reached over and patted him on the arm. "Amen to that, as you Catholics say. Benny called the special forces duty sergeant and we got a patch through to the military police. We had you covered by the time you reached Spring Lake."

Pepper remembered the deserted street. "I didn't see anyone in Spring Lake."

"There was a police cruiser parked between the laundromat and the grocery store, back in the shadows, in the alley."

"How did you know we were going to Spring Lake? I didn't even know that myself at first."

"We didn't, but we could cover Spring Lake quicker than we could cover Southern Pines. If he had turned toward The Pines, we might have lost you. There're a lot of back roads between the post and the secondary highway."

"How did you know we were going to the hospital?"

"We were coming hell-bent for leather back into town in Benny's truck and the dispatcher kept radioing reports to us. After a couple of turns it became pretty obvious that was the only place you could go. We were as confused as hell when you disappeared around the back of the hospital and didn't come out again."

Pepper had never heard Avivah curse before. In the space of the last fifteen minutes, she had said *damn* once and *hell* twice.

A whole flood of memories decanted through Pepper's head. "This is it."

Avivah looked confused. "This is what?"

"You asked me what Vietnam was like. This is it. Right now, I feel just like the night we lost three patients in a row in the emergency room. None of us could sleep, so we walked over to the airport and had breakfast. Fried eggs, ham, hash browns, toast swimming in butter, and a chocolate milkshake. Vietnam was that been-up-all-night, drank-too-much, used-too-much-adrenaline feeling." Pepper pointed out the window. "Look at that guy."

A soldier walked along the sidewalk in front of the military police headquarters, carrying several folders under his arm. An officer passed him and the soldier rendered a crisp salute, which the officer returned. "He slept last night. He might have heard about what happened at the hospital on the radio this morning, but he wasn't part of it. It's like we know something he doesn't, something we couldn't explain to him. We're different from him because of last night. That's what Vietnam does, it sets you apart. Right, Benny?"

"I suppose it does." Pepper knew it rankled him that Avivah ordered him to stay with the back-up unit across the street from the hospital while she, Captain Delaney, and the squad of military police went into the hospital. It was probably the first time anyone had told Benjamin Kirkpatrick he was under-qualified for a mission.

"That reminds me, can you find Darby Baxter?"

Benny looked perplexed. "I suppose so. Special forces is a small family."

"Find him. Tell him there is a *pretty lady* at Fort Bragg who wants to buy him a steak. I did exactly what he taught us. 'You're smarter than you think you are. Keep calm. Pretend to go along with them. Know the terrain. Know your coordinates. Find something you can use as a weapon.' Tell him it worked."

She turned back to Avivah. "How did Lieutenant Forbes know what was going on?"

"We called her as soon as we knew you were on the hospital grounds. Told her there was a man, probably with a gun, on the way to her ward with you as a hostage. We told her to get herself and the corpsmen out, but she wouldn't go."

Benny contributed. "She told the dispatcher that she wouldn't leave her patients. In the end, you showed up within five minutes of the call. They wouldn't have had time to evacuate the patients even if they tried, so they did the best they could."

Corpsman Pinna had not been sleeping in the ward. He had been moving beds, with patients in traction in them, into the ward's back bay. The patients who could walk or use a wheelchair filled the spaces on the floor under and around the beds. When Lieutenant Forbes went to the ward, flashlight in hand, ostensibly to make rounds, she and Pinna rigged what they hoped would be a bulletproof covering over the ward door, three mattresses pushed against the door and held in place with an assortment of furniture.

"They deserve a medal. Do you think I can get them a medal, Benny?" Corpsman Pinna wouldn't be happy if he had to stay in the Army just to be awarded a medal.

"Probably not, but you might get them a citation. I'll show you how to write one up."

Pepper sat back in her chair, spent, while the last threads of Vietnam memories dissipated from her mind. "We can also get Tyler on breaking and entering," she said in a half-distracted voice. "He said he went into my apartment and used the phone. He said he left something in my apartment."

Avivah collected up the three breakfast containers and wedged them in the trash can. "Problem is we can't prove that either. Tyler is too cagey to leave fingerprints. He'll contend he was never in the apartment. My guess is he'll plead guilty to kidnapping because he can plead a delayed stress reaction to having served in Vietnam."

"From being a general's aide in Saigon?" Benny scoffed.

Pepper replayed their conversation in the car once again. "Hold on, he said something about starting out as an infantry officer. I bet if you check back, you'll find that Saigon was his second tour of duty and that he did his first one in the field."

It would fit too well, she thought. Plead guilty to kidnapping, claim it was stress-related, spend a few weeks on a psych ward, and walk away from a double murder charge.

"We have to find that letter."

"We don't even know who wrote the letter, or if it still exists."

Avivah tapped her fingernail on the desk. "Assume it exists. Assume Dermid had it, and it implicates Tyler in whatever happened in Vietnam. Think. Where is it?"

The door opened. Captain Delaney had gone home, showered, shaved, and dressed in a neatly-pressed uniform. His hair was combed, his shoes shined, and his polished captain's bars gleamed in the fluorescent light.

Benny looked back and forth from Avivah to Captain Delaney, then stood up.

Captain Delaney looked at him. "You were with the back-up unit. You are?"

Benny took his beret out of his pocket and smoothed it over his head. "I'm just leaving. I'm the guy who delivered breakfast. Avivah, you and Pepper eat whatever is in the fridge. I've still got the rest of the week on leave. I'm going to try to convince Lorraine to go away with me, without the boys. We have to talk."

Avivah looked at his fatigues. "You going to see her dressed like that?"

Benny dug truck keys out of one of his deep pockets. "Hell, you know better than that. I'm going home, run a few miles, take a shower, put on civvy clothes, and show up all neat and proper."

Pepper recognized the pattern. "That's what you do when you come back from Panama, isn't it? You work all traces of being a soldier out of your system before you see Lorraine."

"Yeah," Benny said, jingling the keys and looking at the floor.

"You're doing it wrong. Go over there right now, just like you are, in your fatigues and beret. No shower. Ask her to cook you breakfast."

Benny looked at the breakfast containers in the trash. "I'm not hungry."

Pepper and Avivah said in unison, "Ask her to cook you breakfast."

"It's one of those women things isn't it?" He winked at them and left, closing the door behind him.

"Ladies," Delaney said, "we have lots to do."

Avivah put her chin on her hand and leaned across the table. "Captain Delaney, with all due respect to a fellow officer, fuck off. I'm going home, shower, and fall into bed. In a few hours, I will report to you."

Delaney pulled the chair out for her as she stood up. "No, you won't. The three of us are due in the post commander's office in thirty minutes. He specifically asked for the three of us, so get yourself cleaned up, ladies. Off we go."

Pepper ran both hands through her hair and wearily stood. For the first time, she truly understood the motivation behind fragging an officer.

Chapter 31

On Thursday the tabloids went berserk. One front page read, *Crazed Vietnam Veteran Sets Fire to Army Hospital*; a second one, *Ghost of Omaha Beach Soldier Saves Army Nurse's Life*.

Southern Bell disconnected Pepper's phone, at her request, about the time Doctor Singleton Tyler, his personal assistant, a lawyer, and a consulting psychiatrist arrived by private jet.

Doctor Tyler proved to be a round, pink man, with a round, pink head. He wore wire-frame spectacles and English-cut suits and insisted on what he called "a strategy session" every morning. The post commander ordered Captain Delaney to extend every courtesy to Doctor Tyler. Captain Delaney insisted Avivah share the pleasure.

The ward staff on the locked psychiatric ward found Colonel Tyler helpful and cooperative. He assembled blank patient charts, served coffee, sorted and folded linen, and distributed trays when the food cart arrived. In exchange, he expected his brother to be allowed to visit at any time, and himself to be allowed to shower and change clothes several times each day.

Tyler alleged that Captain Pepperhawk flirted with him the night of the murder and that, subsequently, her constant, unwanted attentions caused him to have flashbacks of his first tour in Vietnam. He believed she had a serious emotional problem and was trying to help her, no matter the cost to himself.

Everywhere she looked, Avivah found evidence to support Tyler's. He'd mentioned to Colonel Granger—without naming names—that he had problems with a nurse. He consulted a chaplain, asking about resources for officers with emotional problems. He mentioned to people in his office that a female officer was pursuing him.

Avivah even admired the chutzpah of the present he left in Pepper's apartment, a packet of letters, supposedly his responses to notes she wrote him. Read as one side of an imaginary correspondence, the letters showed Tyler trying to extricate himself from an undesired relationship. Of course, being a gentleman, he had destroyed Pepper's letters to save her embarrassment.

A background check on Tyler showed he left William and Mary University in his senior year, not, as he told Pepper, because of financial difficulties, but because of a scandal the university would not discuss. Delaney's application for a court order to open his sealed university record was still pending.

He'd told the truth about one thing. His first tour of duty in Vietnam had been spent as an infantry lieutenant.

Nine days after arresting Colonel Tyler, the Tyler contingent, Captain Delaney, and Avivah settled themselves for another early-morning session. Today Dr. Tyler wore a grey and pink tweed. His starched white shirt and pink-and-grey bow tie made him look like a combination of an English country gentleman and the ice cream man.

His personal assistant, lawyer, and consulting psychiatrist wore charcoal grey suits, off-white shirts, and dark grey ties. Avivah had trouble telling them apart.

As always, Doctor Tyler spoke first. "Now that my team has finished their preliminary investigation from both legal and psychiatric standpoints, I have an offer about my brother's care."

The personal assistant handed a letter to Captain Delaney, who read it and passed it to Avivah.

He gave them a letter every morning, always on thick cream stationery with *Dr. Singleton Tyler, MD, FACOS, FRCOS*, an Atlanta address, and *Practice limited to orthopedic athletic injuries* engraved at the top. Pepper said the letters after his name meant that he was a physician, and had qualified as a board-certified orthopedic surgeon in both the United States and Great Britain.

The engraved lines at the bottom of the letter read like a *curriculum vitae*:

> *Consultant, Orthopedic Residency Program, Grady Memorial Hospital, Atlanta*
> *Guest Lecturer, Guy's Hospital, London, England*
> *Past Recording Secretary, Georgia Medical Association*
> *Chair, Georgia Council on Athletic Safety in Secondary Schools*
> *Training Consultant, Georgia Tech Department of Athletics*

Avivah marveled that he found time to see patients. She read the letter, folded it, tucked it under her stenographer's pad, and paid attention to what Doctor Tyler was saying.

". . . seventeen years in the service of his country. Two tours of duty in Vietnam. Highly decorated."

A Bronze Star, not even for valor. Pepper said they were as common as dishwater.

"I am sure you will agree, Captain, that no one knows the long-lasting effect this horrible war will have on our young men." He nodded toward the psychiatrist. "My psychiatrist is doing seminal research on the lasting effects of war stress. He presented a fascinating paper at the last convention of the Georgia Medical Association. I can get you a copy, if you would like."

Delaney fingered the pen in front of him. "Doctor, we have an excellent case against your brother for kidnapping, unlawful confinement, attempted assault with a deadly weapon, and endangering the lives of fellow military personnel."

They *didn't* have him on two counts of murder. Avivah ran her thumb along the folded letter edge, thinking of the other letter, the one no one could find.

Doctor Tyler opened his hands in a placating gesture. "Of course you do, of course you do. I don't deny that Gardner did those things, but we must have compassion and understanding about horrible events—events experienced in the service of his country—that drove him to these desperate acts."

Delaney leaned back in his chair. "Your letter proposes that we release your brother in your care, until such time that we are ready to proceed to trial."

"Ravenglen is an outstanding private psychiatric hospital. We can even confine him, temporarily, to a locked ward, if you prefer, though I can't see why that would be necessary."

Avivah speculated whether the golf course at Ravenglen was nine or eighteen holes.

"I'm not even sure there will be a trial. The young lady involved is herself a Vietnam veteran, just returned from overseas. She is hardly a reliable witness."

The veins stood out on both sides of Thomas Delaney's neck. "What makes her unreliable?"

"No doubt a fine woman, who did excellent work with our boys, but you must be aware of the reputation Army nurses have. A woman like that could easily make unrealistic sexual demands on my brother."

Avivah wondered, if Pepper were here, how much of her Qui Nhon vocabulary she could string together into coherent sentences.

Delaney laid down his pen and rested his clasped hands on the table. "Your brother is a lieutenant colonel in the United States Army. He is subject to the Military Code of Conduct and he will stand court-martial under that code. He will remain either on the psychiatric ward of Womack Army Hospital or in the post brig until that court-martial takes place. It will be an *Army* psychiatrist who advises me on his safe confinement, and an *Army* lawyer who advises me on appropriate charges. Is that clear, or should I try words of fewer syllables? How about, 'No, Doctor Tyler, request denied.' "

The Army takes care of its own, Avivah thought, even if its own was a sociopath and a murderer.

A red flush rose from Dr. Tyler's stiffly starched collar, up his neck, to the top of his bald, pink head. His administrative assistant coughed slightly into a white, folded handkerchief. The psychiatrist pressed his lips together as if holding back a smile.

Doctor Tyler rose. "Very well, Captain Delaney, we will meet again for another strategy session on Monday morning at seven a.m.'"

"No, Doctor Tyler, we will not meet on Monday morning, or on any other day in the foreseeable future. Captain Rosen and I are going out of town."

"Is this concerning my brother's case?" Tyler asked in his fussy, precise voice. "Perhaps I should accompany you."

"Captain Rosen and I are going on maneuvers. It's something soldiers do. Army stuff. Marching fifty miles a day, sleeping on the ground, eating snakes for supper. You're welcome to accompany us if you wish."

Avivah could tell by the look on Doctor Tyler's face that Delaney would pay for his flippancy and she almost felt sorry for him. He stood up to indicate that the interview was over. Avivah found her self surprised that the prospect of a road trip with Thomas Delaney overjoyed her.

Monday, at Wadesboro, Delaney stopped at the motel where Dermid stole Curtis Butterfield's uniform. They spent an hour doing what Delaney called "walking the ground" without discovering anything more than they had from Curtis Butterfield's statement.

About the time the top of her head became sunburned, they went inside to interview the waitresses and the desk clerk. The clerk remembered Mister Butterfield because she called the sheriff for him. No one remembered Dermid Hagan.

Waiting for Delaney to pay for their lunch, Avivah stood in the space between the lobby and the outside door. A narrow, glass-fronted cabinet covered the wall. It contained two champagne glasses stuffed with napkins, plastic green grapes, and a poster describing the motel's wedding reception package.

Another poster, curling at the edges, promoting the Eighty-second Airborne's Fourth of July reunion. Hundreds of these posters had been distributed on the post and in Fayetteville. She never thought that they might have been distributed as far as Wadesboro.

"Mint?" Delaney said in her ear, making her jump. He held out a green and white candy.

"Thanks."

Delaney turned the car air-conditioner to its highest setting, blasting Avivah first with hot, dusty air, followed by rapid chilling. She turned the vent away from her face, leaned back against the seat, and closed her eyes.

After fifteen minutes of silence, Delaney asked, "What do you think?"

"About what?"

"About the poster. You looked at it a long time."

She hesitated, not wanting to put up with one of Delaney's sneers, then took a chance. "I think the World War II uniform wasn't part of the plan. I think Dermid saw that poster, or one like it, heard Curtis bragging to his brother-in-law about the uniform in his truck, and improvised."

Delaney sped up to pass a semi. "I agree."

They agreed. Avivah felt the ground open in front of her. She had just fallen off the map of their relationship.

She ventured, "Whose plan?"

"You want to be a detective, you figure it out."

Relieved, she climbed back on the edge of the map, and thought about his question for another few miles.

"Colonel Tyler almost certainly knew more about the reunion than Dermid did. He might have even known about the shuttle buses and parking at Kmart."

"He was on the committee that planned shuttles and parking. I checked." Delaney said it defensively, as if Avivah might attack him for doing his job.

"So you think Dermid wrote to Tyler and Tyler came up with a plan to kill him?"

"Don't know," Delaney said absently, as the semi they had just passed started to pass them. He tried to match speeds for a few seconds, then grudgingly slowed down and let the truck pass. "Too early to tell."

"But you do think Tyler planned something."

"You ever see Tyler with a hair out of place? Or a spot on his uniform? Or looking like he needed a shave?"

"No."

"Even in the hospital, he insists on showering and changing clothes several times a day. The guy's about as anal-retentive as they come. He's compulsive and obsessed with details. He probably sent Dermid a plan containing step-by-step instructions."

"He must have been surprised to see Dermid get off the shuttle in a World War II uniform. Dermid messed with his perfect plan. Way to go, Dermid." She raised her hand in a mock salute. "Do you think that angered Tyler enough to kill him?"

Delaney shrugged. "Possibly."

"What do you think is in the letter?"

"What makes you think there is a letter?"

"You think Tyler imagined it?"

"Maybe. Maybe not."

Avivah clenched her fists and groaned. She wasn't looking forward to this trip with joyful anticipation any more.

Delaney glanced at her. "All right, I think the letter exists."

"Maybe Dermid left the letter in Montreal."

"He paid extra to leave the car in North Carolina. He wasn't going back."

"Maybe he left it in the rental car. Tyler probably told Dermid exactly where to park his car. We didn't find it for two days; he had lots of time to search it."

"If he'd found it, he would have stopped looking. We took that car apart before we returned it to the rental company. There was nothing hidden in it."

"You know where the letter is, don't you?"

"No, but I know what has to be with the letter."

"What?"

Delaney reached over and turned the air-conditioner

down. "Want to hear about my fishing trip to Canada? Lovely place called Tamarac Lodge."

Delaney wouldn't talk until he was ready. "Sure."

Later that evening, they went to supper with Wayne Ramsey. After they placed their orders, Wayne took a small Christmas tin out of a paper bag. "I looked through Boyd's things just like you asked. There wasn't a letter, but I found this." Wayne opened the tin and dumped money on the table. "He was saving for a drum set."

A fifty, four twenties, three tens, and three fives littered the table. All of the twenties were folded in half crosswise and the fifty was folded in half lengthwise.

The wallet found on Boyd's body contained less than ten dollars. When Avivah told the Asheville City Police about the money Cody gave Boyd Friday afternoon, the police thought he'd used it to buy cocaine. He hadn't.

Wayne put the money back in the box. "Whoever did this, I want him real bad."

Delaney nodded. "Who would Dermid have trusted enough to safeguard an important letter for him?"

"Boyd or Cody."

"Sergeant Doan insists he has no idea about the letter, and you didn't find it in Boyd's things. What about parents or other relatives?"

"Nobody here knew Dermid wasn't dead until his parents got the call from Fort Bragg. I can swear to that."

Delaney leaned back against the booth. "Who does everyone in Madison County trust? Who do you go to if you've got a problem?"

Without hesitation, Wayne said, "Sheriff Ponder."

"They'd go to the sheriff?"

"Madison County politics are a little complicated."

"Can you ask the sheriff about the letter?"

"Yeah, but I'd rather succor tobacco in July heat than ask Eli Ponder if he's withholding evidence. Never mind, I'll do it."

"Who else?"

"Doctor Treadway. He doctors most everyone around Marshall. He's no Dr. Sams, but lots of people trust him."

Avivah resisted asking who Dr. Sams was. Delaney took a notebook out of his pocket and she watched him write down the two names. She stifled a yawn.

"Is there anyone else Dermid might trust?"

"Becky Ramsey. Dermid was sweet on her in high school."

"Relative of yours?"

Wayne waived his hand. "Not close enough to count. She's blood kin once and married-in kin twice, part of the religious Ramseys."

Avivah's head spun with how long it would take to dissect the Ramsey family tree.

"Where is Becky?"

"She's in the missions. Peru, I think. The Baptist Mission Society probably knows how to reach her."

Avivah hoped Dermid had not sent the letter to Becky Ramsey in Peru. She could not, in her worst nightmares, imagine traveling to Peru with Thomas Delaney. She was certain that only one of them would return.

"Reverend Pretcherd, but I'm sure if he knew Dermid was alive, he wouldn't have kept it a secret."

Delaney wrote his name down anyway.

"I guess you'd better put Miz Davis on that list. She was Dermid's homeroom teacher in high school. He liked her a lot."

Dr. Treadway could probably be found either at the Haywood County Hospital or in his office. Reverend

332

Pretcherd lived "not a fur piece" from the church. Wayne drew them a map. Mrs. Davis lived in Marshall, but there was no sense trying to see her first thing in the morning. He knew she was going to be away until evening.

Late that night, as Avivah snuggled into her motel bed, Delaney's list ran behind her eyelids.

Sheriff Ponder
Dr. Treadway
Reverend Pretcherd
Becky Ramsey—mission in Peru
Mrs. Davis

She fell asleep wondering what Delaney meant when he said, "I know what has to be with the letter."

Chapter 32

The next morning, Avivah and Captain Delaney found Doctor Treadway at the Haywood County Hospital. An affable man in his forties, his last contact with Dermid Hagan had been years ago, when he sewed up a cut on Dermid's hand. He knew nothing about a letter.

Following the hand-drawn map Wayne Ramsey gave them, it took them about an hour to locate Reverend Pretcherd's house.

"We've come about the letter with the money," Delaney said, as Reverend Pretcherd opened his screen door.

Reverend Pretcherd looked surprised, which matched the way Avivah felt. "I didn't figure it had anything to do with Dermid's troubles."

"Do you still have it?"

"It's around here somewhere. Shall I look for it?"

Avivah wiped her sweating hands on her pants. "Yes, please."

Reverend Pretcherd finally produced a card in a thin pink envelope. "Handle it careful now, it's delicate."

Delaney took the envelope. No usable fingerprints by now, Avivah thought.

The front of the Vietnamese Christmas card had an oval insert. The painted silk showed Vietnamese houses, a man plowing with a water buffalo, and a streaked sky with birds flying across it. Straw had been glued to the card to spell *Merry Christmas*.

10 December 1968
Long Bien, RVN

Dear Reverend,

I thought you might like this card from Vietnam. There are many Christians here and you should pray for them because they are going through a terrible war.

Boyd Ramsey, Cody Doan, and I are all right so far. I will leave Vietnam in 151 days and should be home towards the end of June.

Here is a bit of money for the Christmas hampers. I'd appreciate it if you would not tell anyone it was from me. Just put it in an envelope from "a friend."

Merry Christmas to you and yours,

Dermid Hagan

"How much money was with it?"

"A hundred-dollar bank check, made out to the church's Christmas hamper fund. Is that what you're looking for?"

Delaney put the card back in the envelope. "I'm afraid not."

As they drove back to Marshall, Avivah said, "You think there will be money with the letter."

"Stands to reason. Dermid got into some heavy money. He probably realized he'd need more proof than a letter. Serial numbers on bills can be traced."

"Where does that Davis woman live?" Delaney asked, as they reached Marshall.

Avivah consulted Wayne's handwritten directions. "First left turn past the courthouse, up the hill, a big grey house with a red roof."

They parked in front of a late-Victorian house that looked in better repair than many of the places around it. A young man of about thirty-five, dressed in a suit, tie, and a white shirt, was unloading a suitcase from a car in the driveway. As Avivah and Delaney walked up the sidewalk between rows of marigolds, he asked, "Can I help you?"

"We're looking for Mrs. Rebecca Davis. Are you Mr. Davis?"

"Mr. Ferguson, actually. Mr. Davis died several years ago. Rebecca is my sister, but I don't think she is home right now." He looked at the empty spot in the driveway as if his sister's car might magically appear.

Avivah looked at the brass plaque beside the door. "Are you Lawyer Ferguson?"

The man smiled. "Some folks around here call me that."

When they introduced themselves, the man looked embarrassed. "I'm sorry. My secretary left a message that you called a week ago Friday. I meant to phone you, but I was called to Raleigh unexpectedly. I hope you haven't made the trip out here just because I didn't return your telephone call."

"No," Delaney said with surprising politeness, "but we would appreciate talking to you."

"Come on in. It'll just take me a minute to put my things away."

He led them to a screened porch, disappeared through the back door, and returned a few minutes later with tall glasses of iced tea.

"So sad about Dermid," he said, taking his own glass of tea from the tray and sitting in a wicker chair. "So sad, and so strange."

"And about Boyd Ramsey?"

"We must not give up hope there. Widow Ramsey told me he's making some progress in that special program."

Delaney pursed his lips. "Apparently you haven't heard that Boyd Ramsey died last Saturday night in Asheville."

White-faced, Lawyer Ferguson put his glass on the porch between his feet. "Poor Widow Ramsey. She had her share of troubles. An accident?"

"Murder."

"Is it related to Dermid's death?"

"We think so."

"I never knew either of those boys very well. My family didn't grow up here. My sister knew them better, of course. She taught them in high school and goes to their church."

"Did you ever do any legal work for Dermid Hagan?"

"Not for him specifically, but I've done a few routine legal tasks for his parents."

"When was the last time you saw Dermid?"

The lawyer turned his eyes toward the porch roof and tapped his chin with the side of his index finger. "Let me think now. It would have been the fall of 1967, probably September. I can look it up for you, if you want."

"Why did you see him?"

"I was doing business for his mother. Tilda doesn't drive, so Dermid drove her to my office, and waited to drive her back."

"That's the last time you saw him?"

"Oh, passing on the street, in the check-out line at the grocery store. You know how it is in a small town. I believe he went away to the Army a couple of months later."

"What about legal business for Boyd Ramsey? Did you handle a guardianship order for his mother?"

"I did."

"Did you know about her getting ten thousand dollars, supposedly from an Army insurance policy?"

"Yes, but I thought all along that money came from her husband, not the Army."

"You call her *Widow* Ramsey?"

"A courtesy title. That woman does deserve what respect she can muster." He waved his hand again and Avivah realized what bothered her about him. His mannerisms reminded her of Gardner Tyler; he had the same polished, educated, slightly disdainful Southern attitude that Tyler showed.

Delaney looked annoyed. "Either the woman is a widow or she isn't."

John Ferguson rested his chin on one hand, his finger up against his cheek. "I'm not supposed to talk about my clients—professional ethics, you know—but you could find this out down at the café, so I believe it's all right to speak of it. Glenn Roy Ramsey was, as they describe it around here, 'born with a wandering streak in his hair.' He left Miz Ramsey about ten years ago, supposedly to look for work in the oil fields. But there was a rumor that he ran off with a woman from Asheville. About six months after he left, Miz Ramsey said she got a telegram about how he'd died in a rig fire out in Oklahoma."

"You didn't believe he died?"

Ferguson smiled. "Hard to tell. The body was supposedly destroyed in the fire, so there was no funeral."

"What about an investigation, insurance, something from the company he worked for?"

"It was one of those tiny wildcat companies, not more than two or three wells. No insurance. She never consulted me about any legal matters related to it, so I figured it was none of my business."

No way to make a profit from it, Avivah thought.

"Of course in a small town you hear things. Speculation. Gossip."

"What sort of speculation?"

"For one thing, no one ever saw the telegram. For an-

338

other, she just wouldn't discuss how he died. If anyone asked her for details, she said she didn't care to speak of it. Around here, telling death stories, especially unexpected and tragic death stories, is an art. She put a stone in the churchyard for him. It's a sight easier to be known as Widow Ramsey than as Mrs.-Ramsey-what-got-deserted-for-another-woman.

"When she got that money for Boyd, I wondered if his dad wasn't still alive and hadn't kept track of him somehow, knew what happened to him in Vietnam."

"From the way you describe him, I can't imagine Glenn Roy Ramsey having ten thousand dollars."

"He gambled. I figured if he struck it lucky, he might want to square things with the son he'd deserted."

Delaney took a small notebook from his shirt pocket. "Tell us about the money."

Ferguson made a tent with his fingers and rested them on his chin, looking at the white porch ceiling as if in prayer. "Let's see, it was about Valentine's Day in 1969. My secretary gave me a phone message to call a bank in Washington State—Bellingham I think. I can look it up. Anyway, I called the bank and they asked me if I knew a Boyd Ramsey. I said I knew of him and they said someone had put a little over ten thousand dollars in an envelope in their night deposit slot."

"In cash?"

"In cash. With a note that had my name and telephone number on it and said that I was to be sent the ten thousand dollars to open an account for Boyd Ramsey and that the rest of the money was to pay taxes and take care of my fees."

"That was all?"

"Yes."

"What about the note?"

"It was typed. No address, no name other than *A friend of Boyd Ramsey.*"

"What did you do?"

"Exactly what the note asked me to do. I made arrangements for the money to be transferred to the Wachovia Bank, figured out how much taxes were likely to be owed on it, and paid them."

"Did you contact Mrs. Ramsey?"

"No. The note said specifically to not contact her, that the person who wrote the letter would see that was done."

The letter of the law, Avivah thought. She remembered again why, even though she loved her father dearly and was proud of the work he did, she didn't want to be a lawyer.

"How did Mrs. Ramsey find out about the money?"

"She received a letter that said the money had come from an Army insurance policy her son held. Naturally, she brought the letter to me."

Naturally, Avivah thought.

"Did you tell her the truth?"

"Of course not. This woman had already lost her husband. Her son was in the Veterans' Hospital at Oteen and no one knew how much brain damage he had. She was so thankful and relieved, I didn't see any reason to dampen her joy. I simply told her that I was glad her son had the foresight to take out such a policy. And I put her in touch with a good money manager."

Delaney sat back in his chair and blew out a sigh. Ferguson looked at his watch. "I apologize for Rebecca not being back yet. I have no idea where she's gone. Do you still need to see her?"

"I'm afraid we do," Delaney said. "We can come back later."

Avivah explained about the missing letter. "Do you think Dermid could have sent it to your sister?"

"He might have. I think she was his favorite Sunday school teacher."

"Would your sister have showed it to you?"

He smiled a little Gardner Tyler smile that Avivah didn't like. "Not necessarily. Contrary to the images novelists and movies have about Southern brothers and sisters who share a house, Rebecca and I do not live in each other's hip pockets. She has her life, I have mine, and we occasionally meet out here on the porch at the end of the day for drinks and conversation. A letter from Dermid Hagan never came up in conversation."

"Do you have the note from the Bellingham bank about Boyd's money?"

"Yes."

"Can we see it?"

"I should require a warrant, but you'll be able to get that easily and the boy is dead, so why put us both to that trouble? My office is just inside." John Ferguson got up and opened the screen door.

The lawyer led them down the cool, dark hall. His office, covering the left side of the house, looked out on a pleasant side garden, bright with summer flowers. Ferguson's oak roll-top desk looked about a hundred years old. So did the rest of the furniture. A black leather couch filled one wall; many framed photographs of musicians hung over the couch. A small stereo and two shelves of records sat beside it. Mounted fish and shadow boxes of tied flies covered the other three walls. Delaney looked like a child in a toy shop. He murmured, "Oh, my."

Ferguson looked at him eagerly. "You fish?" he asked in a voice Avivah previously thought reserved for intimate encounters between consenting adults.

"Yeah."

Like sharing a secret piscine handshake, the two men dissolved into a technical conversation about river trout versus mountain trout. They bent over a scrapbook of Ferguson's fishing trips, leaving Avivah to wander around the office. She looked at the records. Clogging tunes, mountain fiddlers, banjo players, ballad singers, a wide selection from a company called Folkways that seemed to specialize in the old, the hard to find, and the just plain weird.

Tired of looking at long-playing album jackets and equally disinterested in the background conversation about which color flies attracted more trout, she looked at the musicians. A few names were familiar: Mother Maybell Carter, Lester Flatt, and Earl Scruggs. She had no idea about Bascom Lamar Lundsford or Doc Watson. Each photograph had a personal greeting to John Ferguson.

Her glance wandered down to the last row of photographs, to a Louisiana fiddle player named T. Will Knight. Four men holding musical instruments surrounded T. Will. Dewey and Will Balfa. Sonny Herbert. Doucet Sonnier. Doucet had written a short lesson in how to pronounce his name for those unfamiliar with Cajun French. "You say, dou-say."

Dermid Hagan, bored with his mother and Lawyer Ferguson completing their business, might have stared at these pictures a long time. Years later, in Montreal, when he desperately needed an alias, the names on the pictures came back to him.

"Mr. Ferguson," Avivah said forcefully enough to break into the men's conversation, "when was the last time you heard from Doucet Herbert?"

After that, it was easy.

Chapter 33

Doucet Herbert first wrote to John Ferguson in May of that year. He described himself as a Montreal fiddle player, who planned to play at American folk festivals over the summer. Several of his fellow performers spoke highly of Mr. Ferguson. Would he be so kind as to do him a favor? He sent two hundred dollars, asking that a bank account be opened for him, so he could have American cash available during his tour. Ferguson opened the account and sent him a bankbook.

In June, Doucet sent Ferguson a registered letter, saying the enclosed sealed envelope contained papers he would need to sell a fiddle he planned to bring with him. He asked that the envelope be put in a safety deposit box, in the same bank as his money. Ferguson did this, too.

Ferguson knew judges. Even though it was late in the afternoon, and the bank closed for the day, within an hour, Captain Delaney had a court order to open the safe deposit box. The bank manager himself opened the box for them.

In the sealed manila envelope were two one-hundred-dollar bills, a letter, and a note from Dermid Hagan.

June 20, 1971
Montreal, Quebec

To whom it may concern:
Boyd Ramsey wrote this letter a few days before he was hurt. He left it with our chaplain and, after he got hurt,

the chaplain asked me what he should do with it, so I told him to give it to me and I'd see it got to the right person. You could have knocked me over with a feather when I opened it and read it, but I guess it fits. Boyd worried all the time about those orphans and he'd have done anything for them.

After I saw how bad Boyd was hurt, I figured his ma would need a lot of money to take care of him. I contacted Colonel Tyler and persuaded him and a man named Michael Fuller to let me take Boyd's place. Michael and I traded identification. They promised me ten thousand dollars if I delivered the money safely.

On the plane to Bangkok I got to thinking about what a crock of shit the colonel's story was, and I knew he wouldn't want me to leave Bangkok alive. So I took the money to another bank—not the one I was supposed to use—and deposited all but ten thousand dollars of it. I figured I'd earned that. These two bills are from the money I kept. Then I sent the bankbook to Colonel Tyler, and disappeared into Bangkok.

I made arrangements for the ten thousand dollars to go to Boyd's ma, so she can take care of him. I reckon it won't cover everything he needs, but at least it's something.

Tell my folks I'm sorry. I know I'm a deserter, but I had to help Boyd. Some things are more important than the Army.

Dermid Hagan

Boyd's letter was on blue-bordered stationery with a map of Vietnam running down one side, like an arthritic finger.

Some Welcome Home

Long Bien
3 January 1969

Dear Reverend Pretcherd,

I hope you and yours had a good Christmas and New Year's. You should have seen how happy the orphans were when we gave them a turkey dinner, and the gifts the people sent from church. We took lots of pictures. If they turn out, I'll send you some.

You remember how I wrote you about how I was praying for Cody and Dermid because of all the temptations of drugs around here. Like you say, God works in mysterious ways.

Christmas Day our general came to eat breakfast with us. His aide is a man named Lieutenant Colonel Tyler. He talked to me after breakfast and asked me what I thought about our troops using drugs. He told me the general had heard how I was against drugs and alcohol and wanted to know if that were true. I told him using drugs was a sin and about the pledge I'd taken in church.

There's a civilian company here called Pacific Architects and Engineers (we call them PA&E) and Colonel Tyler says they are the ones who sell drugs to soldiers. They have a very clever way of buying drugs. Colonel Tyler says that PA&E sends equipment out to Bangkok to be fixed. They put the money they have made from selling drugs in the equipment. No one checks because everybody knows PA&E sends stuff out all the time.

In Bangkok, they exchange the money for more drugs, which they load in the equipment to come back to Vietnam.

Later this month, the general is going to arrange leave for me. He wants me to pretend to work for PA&E and go to Bangkok. I'm supposed to take notes about everything,

*like the names of the people at the airport who okay the
shipment without inspecting it. I put the money in a bank,
and call a number that Colonel Tyler will give me. The
military police pick me up and I give them my notes. The
general has promised a thousand dollars for the orphans if
I help him.*

*Colonel Tyler made me promise not to tell anyone
about this. He says it's "Top Secret." But I figured, since
you're a preacher, it would be all right to tell you. I'm
leaving this letter with our chaplain and I'll ask him to
mail it to you while I'm on leave. By the time you get this,
the orphans will be a thousand dollars richer and the drug
sellers will have been caught.*

*Remember me in your prayers. Looking forward to
being home in six months.*

Boyd Ramsey

As Captain Delaney folded the letter carefully and
placed it in an evidence bag, someone knocked on the bank
window. The manager pointed to the *Closed* sign but the
rapping became more insistent. Avivah recognized Deputy
Sheriff Wayne Ramsey. The manager unlocked the door.

"Captain Delaney, good thing I spotted your car. I've
been looking for you for an hour."

"What's the problem?"

"We got a call from Fort Bragg. Your suspect escaped
from the psych ward and took hostages. A Private Osborne
said to tell you that Specialist Ramerez has been shot."

Chapter 34

Pepper learned of Colonel Tyler's escape when two military policemen came to Ward Six-A to take her into protective custody. As she handed her keys to Dave Willett, she wondered what it would be like, just once, to work an entire week without military police interference.

She spent the afternoon in a windowless conference room at brigade headquarters. About 1600 hours, Private Osborne, dressed in fatigues and a helmet, came into the room. The young woman's face looked pale against the camouflaged clothing. "Tyler shot Specialist Ramerez!"

Pepper pulled out a chair for her and forced her to sit. "When? How?"

"About forty-five minutes ago. Ramerez was doing a house-to-house search."

"How is he?"

"I don't know. He was shot in the chest. He's in the emergency room."

Pepper thought of calling the emergency room, but knew what kind of chaos they would be in right now. It wasn't fair to Specialist Ramerez to pull people away from his care to answer her questions. She started to put her arm around the young woman's shoulder, then quickly stopped when she remembered an officer must ask permission to touch a subordinate. "In combat, ninety-nine out of a hundred soldiers who reach the hospital alive, survive. Those are pretty good odds."

Specialist Osborne didn't looked convinced. "Yes, ma'am, I suppose they are. Major Plauche asked me to bring you to him."

A few minutes later, Osborne stopped her jeep at a checkpoint in front of Normandy House. It was raining heavily. We've come full circle, Pepper thought, looking down the street, into senior officer territory, to a police cordon. A sandbagged wall blocked a corner of the small park. Two men in fatigues, helmets, and ponchos strung electric wires toward a command trailer. Armored vehicles closed the streets by parking at right angles across them. A deuce-and-a-half truck crossed the street in front of her and parked in the officers' club parking lot. Men unloaded a field kitchen. Good idea. She could use a cup of coffee.

Pepper followed Private Osborne up the metal stairs of the command trailer. Inside, Osborne knocked on a door.

"Come."

Pepper entered the room and saluted. Three combat-fatigue-clad officers Pepper didn't know sat around a metal table, which occupied most of the small room. The officer with military police insignia returned her salute. "I'm Major Plauche. Thank you for coming. Please sit down." The other two officers half rose as she sat.

"Do you know Major Beaton?" Major Beaton wore medical corps insignia.

"I don't believe so."

He shook her hand. "Psychiatry."

"Captain Ortago." Captain Ortago looked about thirty-five, a chunky man, who in some ways resembled an older Ramerez. He wore fatigues, but no insignia. Pepper knew better than to ask a man in combat fatigues why he wore no insignia. He wouldn't tell her anyway. He had a reason for being here and that was all she needed to know.

"Have you heard anything about Specialist Ramerez's condition?"

"He's in surgery. The doctor thinks he will be fine."

"Thank God. Is this Colonel Tyler's house?"

"Colonel Norton's house."

Pepper shivered. "My chief nurse?"

"Yes."

She sank back against the chair. "What is going on here?"

"Tyler apparently went to his apartment after he left the hospital, showered, changed clothes, and drove here. We found his car in the officers' club parking lot. Military police teams cordoned off the senior quarters and instituted a house-to-house search. When Specialist Ramerez approached Colonel Norton's house, Tyler shot him."

"How did Tyler get inside the colonel's house?"

"We believe Major Buckner let him in. She never reported for her shift. Colonel Norton became concerned about her, left work early, and was also taken hostage."

Pepper sank in the chair. "You're telling me that Tyler has my chief nurse and my basic class advisor as hostages."

"We hope so."

She considered the alternative and hoped so, too.

Plauche turned to a reel-to-reel recorder on the table behind him. "We managed one phone contact."

He pushed the on button. Four rings, then "Colonel Norton."

"This is Gilbert Plauche, Military Police. Are you all right, ma'am?"

"Yes. Colonel Tyler wants me to ask about the young man who came to the door."

"He's in the emergency room."

"Colonel Tyler apologizes for the incident, but he finds

it intolerable that you confine him to a psychiatric ward. You have his personal guarantee that, if you release him, he will be available as needed."

"May I speak to Colonel Tyler?"

"He doesn't wish to speak to you."

The line went dead. Gil Plauche switched off the tape recorder. "He's answered a couple of times since, but never says anything. Just waits a few seconds, then hangs up. Doctor Beaton, tell Captain Pepperhawk what you told us earlier."

"It's obvious that Colonel Norton repeated what Tyler instructed her to say. Aligning himself with powerful people allows Tyler to feel in control. He expects people to do him favors as a matter of course."

"He's killed two people, kidnapped me, threatened Cody Doan, shot a military policeman, and taken hostages! He expects favors?"

Dr. Beaton shrugged as if murder and kidnapping were of no consequence. "He believes he does what others force him to do. In his mind, he has no other course of action and, therefore, shouldn't suffer consequences. He sees this entire situation, not in terms of right and wrong, but as an inconvenience to himself. It's classic sociopath behavior."

"Why is he answering the phone but not saying anything?"

"It keeps him in control. He decides whether to answer, he decides when to hang up. He's waiting for us to do him a favor, to let him come and go as he pleases."

Captain Ortago cleared his throat. "We want to open negotiations with him. Major Beaton believes you're our best choice for a negotiator."

Pepper laughed. "Dr. Beaton, with all due respect, I am

the last person Colonel Tyler would negotiate with. He hates me."

Dr. Beaton continued in a soothing psychiatrist's voice. "Quite the contrary. You're a known quantity to him and he took great pains to set up an elaborate scheme to give him—in his own mind—power over you. Part of his delusion is to expect you to care about his welfare. He would love an opportunity to brag to you, to show you how clever he is."

"If he's not talking to anyone on the phone, how do I negotiate with him?"

The other two men turned toward Captain Ortago. "We start by offering food. It's a standard negotiating ploy and it fits Colonel Tyler's psychology. He expects others to anticipate his needs."

"Are you going to put something in the food that would render him unconscious?"

"We have nothing that would take effect immediately. If Tyler feels sleepy, he might shoot the hostages."

"He'd shoot them because he needed to sleep?"

Dr. Beaton contributed, "People are obstacles. He was last medicated at 0730 this morning and has already missed one dose. The longer this goes on, the more unstable he becomes."

"Who takes food to him?"

The three men looked at her. She remembered an Army expression: this was where the rubber hit the road. As an officer, she had a duty to her fellow officers. "What do I do?"

"Talk to Tyler on a bullhorn. Tell him you are concerned about him and that you're bringing some food to the door. Carry the food across the street and put it between the screen and the front door. Come back as fast as you can. We wait fifteen minutes, then you phone him."

Pepper sat back in her chair and looked hard at Captain Ortago. He reminded her of Darby Baxter, of the way Baxter looked while convincing the nurses that they were going to *enjoy* being dropped off alone, with only a compass and a map, in a remote, hot, snake-infested part of Camp Bullis, Texas. Why the hell was a special forces officer involved in a hostage situation?

She cocked her head to one side. "How many snipers do you have trained on the front door?"

Captain Ortago looked her in the eye. "Three."

"Do they have orders to shoot him when he opens the door to pick up the food?"

"No. We truly want to negotiate with him."

For a long minute rain pelted the metal trailer roof. "Let's rock and roll, Captain Ortago."

"We'll send someone to your apartment to get you different clothes. A dress, something that makes you look . . ." He hesitated.

"Small. Female. Vulnerable."

He nodded.

An hour later, with a fatigue jacket several sizes too big draped over her rose-print sundress, Pepper stood behind the wall of wet sandbags, clutching a green canvas haversack. The twin thermoses inside—one soup, one coffee—made two warm spots against her body. She wished Avivah was here.

Major Plauche walked up to a military policeman, who scanned the house with binoculars.

"Not much going on, sir. Someone turned on a small light, not enough to let us see shadows moving behind the drapes."

The major nodded and turned to Pepper. "Any questions?"

"No, sir. I'm to talk to him, walk up to the porch, put the food behind the screen door, then beat it back here."

"If anything happens, fall flat on the ground. Got that?"

"Yes, sir."

He handed her a bullhorn and took the fatigue jacket from her shoulders. "Tell him who you are and what you plan to do. Go slowly."

The rain gently soaked Pepper's hair and bare arms. Looping the haversack straps over her right hand and taking the bullhorn in her left, Pepper looked around at the big trees and dark houses. She saw no snipers. She hadn't expected to see them.

"Colonel Tyler!" The bullhorn squealed. Pepper cleared her throat and spoke again, this time in a normal voice, "Colonel Tyler, it's Elizabeth Pepperhawk."

No response from the dimly-lit house. She started to ask Major Plauche if Tyler could hear her. Anyone for blocks around could hear her. Knowing that strangers listened made her feel more vulnerable and exposed. That was good. Tyler liked his people vulnerable. She stepped away from the protection of the sandbagged wall.

"Gardner, I'm worried about you. I brought some food for you and the women with you." Dr. Beaton cautioned her not to use the word *hostages*. She held up the haversack.

"It's good: hot soup, coffee, sandwiches. You must be hungry, especially since it's such a cold and wet day."

She walked through water near the street curb, thoroughly soaking her tennis shoes. Keep moving. Slow. Steady. Don't stop. What was it helicopter pilots called a mission that wasn't hard? *A walk in the park.* This was a walk in the park, just another compass-and-map course.

"I'm going to leave the food at the front door. It's up to

you if you want it, but I hope you'll take it. I don't like to think that you're hungry."

She stood on the edge of the small front yard, so close to the house now that using the bullhorn seemed unnecessary. Pepper put it down on the wet grass. She heard the front door lock turn.

"You must have had a rough day, Gardner. I know the rest of us have."

She walked up the three steps, opened the screen door, and bent down to place the haversack against the wooden door. Suddenly the door opened; a hand grabbed her wrist and pulled her inside.

Tyler pushed the door shut, scraping her leg on the edge of the door. He locked the door behind him. The snipers had to know approximately where he stood. They could fire through a closed door. Her heart pounding, Pepper waited for gunfire. After several seconds, she realized there would be none.

She looked into the dimly-lit living room. Besides herself, Tyler had three other hostages, not two as everyone thought, and, from the looks of them, none of them were in any shape to leave. Captain Ortago expected her to negotiate. She held up the haversack, not knowing what else to do.

"Food?"

Chapter 35

It always came back to gender, Avivah thought, standing in the dark, rain-slicked shadow of the sandbagged wall. If she were a man, Gilbert Plauche would never have said, "You've been inside Colonel Norton's house. I need you to explain to Captain Ortago's men how the furniture in the living room is arranged. You know, the details a woman notices in another woman's house."

She stared at the house, willing Pepper to be all right. A jeep with a three-star flag pulled up on the far side of the park. Three women officers taken hostage brought out even the post commander. Never mind that Pepper volunteered. The public didn't like women in danger. If anything happened to any of the hostages, Gil would be lucky to have a commission left to resign.

An older man, a colonel she guessed, got out of the jeep first. She expected the post commander next, but instead got Doctor Tyler, dressed in a mackintosh and hunting hat. He opened a large umbrella. Avivah suppressed a giggle. Doctor Tyler was the kind of person who would bring an umbrella to a hostage-taking.

She definitely did not want him to see her, so she pulled herself into the sandbagged shadows. The metal steps rattled as the doctor climbed them, puffing.

In twenty minutes, Captain Ortago came down the steps from the command trailer. He looked unhappy and, as he reached in his fatigue pocket for what wasn't there, he confirmed what Avivah already suspected. Gil had introduced Captain Ortago as a military police hostage rescue specialist from Fort Gordon. Like hell, he was either military police or from Fort Gordon. Avivah would have to ask Benny how green berets could wear the same uniform as everyone else and still look like special forces.

The rain pelted harder. Pools of rain water reflected the strings of lights, making the area around the command trailer look like a cheap amusement park. Avivah and Captain Ortago walked to a jeep parked in the officers' club parking lot. He climbed in the back seat. She climbed in the front.

The driver glanced over and saw Avivah. "Shit! You're supposed to be out of town."

"I'm back."

"I see that. Now, Avivah."

"Don't 'now Avivah' me; you are not a hostage-rescue specialist, whatever the hell that is!"

"Yes, I am."

"You lied to me."

"I just didn't tell you the whole truth."

"Kirkpatrick, take it somewhere less public." Benny drove a couple of blocks and bounced the jeep to a stop. With the golf course on the right and a row of dark houses on the left this was as private a spot as they were likely to find, but even here, voices carried. Avivah had enough sense to keep her voice low. Low and furious. "What the hell is all the secrecy about, Benny?"

He turned around. "Captain?"

The officer sighed. "What is your security clearance, Captain Rosen?"

Before she could answer, Benny answered for her.

She turned on him. "How do you know my security clearance?"

"I make it a point to know the clearance on all my friends."

"You rat."

Benny shrugged. "Comes with the territory. Let me introduce you to Captain Jorges Ortago, Team Leader for the Green Berets' Central American Hostage Negotiation and Rescue Team. I haven't exactly been out in the jungle all the times I've gone to Panama, just enough to establish jungle survival instructor as a cover story."

Avivah's mind buzzed between two alternatives: gratitude that at least there was somebody trained to handle this situation and fury at the game they were playing. "Have you ever rescued hostages for real?"

"Yes."

"Successfully?"

Benny said quietly. "Not when I came home with a red tropical shirt."

Avivah remembered two red shirts. Benny never wore them again after the day he arrived home.

She waved in the direction of Colonel Norton's house. "That's Pepper in there."

"You think I don't know that."

Captain Ortago said, "Some of the things our team does would, in some quarters, be called into question. According to the Army, we don't exist. We'd like to keep it that way."

"Then you should work on your body language."

"Our what?"

"The way you stand makes you look like a green beret. When you came out of the command trailer, you automatically reached in your pocket for your beret."

Captain Ortago smiled. "Thank you. . . . I think. Make a note, Sergeant Kirkpatrick. We're going to look at everyone's body language. All right, Captain Rosen, what's it going to be? In or out?"

In other words, would she blow their cover? She hated dishonesty and games, but, like it or not, these guys were Pepper's best chance of survival. "How was the weather when you left Fort Gordon? I remember it got pretty hot there in the summer."

Both men relaxed. Captain Ortago said, "The weather at Fort Gordon was fine, just fine. Drive on, Kirkpatrick."

He drove a few blocks to a house just like Colonel Norton's. Like the rest of the houses, no lights showed. The area for several blocks had been evacuated, all the residents, including wives, children, and pets, moved to an evacuation area in the post high school. The military had a plan for everything, even relocating senior officers' pets on a moment's notice.

The house's front door stood open. The three of them went inside, and added their combat boots to the two precise rows of boots lined up on a towel. Avivah counted. A special forces team had twelve members. With hers, there should have been thirteen pairs of boots. There were only seven. "Where are the other six members of your team?"

Benny replied as if it were no big deal. "Three snipers covering the front of Colonel Norton's house, three covering the back."

Unlike Colonel Norton's living room, this one looked cozy, with brown and red furniture and a Mexican rug. Men sat in the dark on the couch, chairs, and the floor. They hadn't turned on the lights because they wanted to preserve their night vision. One of the men got up so Avivah could sit on the sofa, but she waved the offer aside and took a place on the floor, next to a man who looked as young as Specialist Osborne.

Captain Ortago stood in front of the group. "Gen-tlemen."

At least he didn't say, "Gentlemen and Captain Rosen."

"The situation is essentially unchanged. It is unlikely we will establish further telephone contact with Colonel Tyler. We have two confirmed hostages and one possible. The shrink says that Tyler will likely become more paranoid as the night progresses. We insert as soon as possible."

Benny asked, "Degree of force?"

It took Avivah a second to realize he was asking if they could kill Colonel Tyler. Captain Ortago hesitated. "We have encountered unforeseen political implications. Colonel Tyler's brother has influence in Washington. The order from the general is minimal force. You will not harm Col-onel Tyler, in any way, unless absolutely necessary to pro-tect yourselves or the hostages."

Body language changed around her. They weren't happy with the restrictions. The very young soldier raised his hand.

"Sergeant Breszowski."

"Our general or their general, sir?"

Muffled laughter. Just like brigade, Avivah thought. They used their newest member to take the flak.

"You can assume *our* general would agree with *their* gen-eral."

From the faces around her, Avivah wasn't so sure.

"Incidentally, gentlemen, Captain Rosen penetrated our cover."

Sergeant Breszowski's hand went up again. "How?"

Captain Ortago turned to Avivah with an amused smile. "Captain?"

"You stand and move like you own Smoke Bomb Hill."

Fort Bragg might belong to the Army, but Smoke Bomb

Hill, the part of the post surrounding the John F. Kennedy Special Warfare Center, belonged to the green berets. Or, at least, they acted like it did. All of the men, even Benny, laughed.

"She's been inside Colonel Norton's house. I've asked her to give us her impressions of the room where the hostages are likely being held. Any time you're ready."

Avivah described the room as best she could, finishing with, "I've met all of the hostages. Would it help to know something about them?"

"Absolutely."

"Colonel Norton served since World War II; she's due to retire next month. Major Buckner did two tours in Vietnam, one at Chu Chi and one in Saigon. Captain Pepperhawk has done one tour. Does that help?"

"It helps a great deal. We know that they are experienced people, who are likely to keep their head in an emergency, and that loud noises aren't likely to send them into hysterics. Thank you." Across the room, Benny grinned at her, and gave her a *thumbs-up* sign.

A small voice inside her head said that she hadn't told the whole truth, just like Benny hadn't told her the whole truth. She tried to decide if any of the things she omitted mattered, or if what Benny hadn't told her mattered. She should have been kinder to him when he came back from Panama. She raised her hand.

"Captain Rosen."

"I left out some details. In spite of her years of service, Colonel Norton has never been close to combat. She's got a hang-up about that, and worries how she would behave in a close situation. Major Buckner is very uptight, like if you suddenly said 'boo' behind her, she'd shatter. Captain Pepperhawk . . ." she faltered.

Benny's finger traced the grain of the wood floor. "Captain Pepperhawk rolls with the punches better than she gives herself credit for, but she's one of those people who worries herself to death about whether she measures up or not."

Exactly, Avivah thought. Benny had Pepper pegged.

Captain Ortago nodded and looked at Avivah for a long, silent minute. "Gentlemen, Captain Rosen is going in with us."

Avivah caught the strangled "Me?" before it escaped her lips. Officers weren't supposed to sound baffled in front of sergeants.

"Colonel Tyler's brother reminded someone in the Pentagon, who reminded the post commander, who reminded Major Plauche, that, technically, none of us have the right to arrest Colonel Tyler."

Avivah started to ask, "So?" The "so" dawned on her. Somehow, Doctor Tyler had learned what she figured out on her own: that these so-called hostage-rescue specialists were neither military police nor from Fort Gordon. She'd respect their secret, but, if he didn't get his way, Doctor Tyler wouldn't.

"Why me?"

"Why not you?"

"I'm a woman."

"The post commander didn't specify a *male* military police officer when he gave me orders to add a military policeman to the team. You have the advantage of knowing the terrain and the people."

No big deal, Avivah thought. She would wait outside while the team entered the house. After they captured Tyler, she would step in and arrest him. If it were no big deal, why was her heart beating like a trip-hammer?

"Breszowski, you're her partner."

They stared at one another. She did not want the most junior member of the team as her partner and, from the look on his face, Sergeant Breszowski did not want her. He pressed his lips together. "Yes, sir."

"Captain, I'll be her partner." Avivah didn't have to turn. She knew Benny's voice. Her heart thumped so hard the front of her fatigue shirt must be vibrating.

"It's too late to change your assignment, Kirkpatrick. If she goes with you, she goes in the role you and your partner were assigned."

Benny stood. "Do I have time to run her through a practice?"

"Thirty minutes, no more."

Events had moved too fast for Avivah to think. She put her boots on. Someone handed her a rifle. Benny held the door for her. "You and I are the insertion team. We go right up the middle on this one."

Chapter 36

When Pepper entered the faintly-lit living room, she tried to look anywhere but at the other hostages. She felt embarrassed for the two senior officers, dressed only in their underpants and bras, sitting side-by-side on a sofa. Harlan Carter sat on a chair, wearing only boxer shorts. He had a thin scar running along one hairy leg. Had he been wounded when he earned his Silver Star? More important, why was he here and why didn't anyone know he was also a hostage?

Wood shavings surrounded two holes where huge metal screws had been forced into the polished wooden floor. Pepper remembered screws like that used as temporary hitching posts, driven into the pasture beside her aunt's farm.

A manacle held the women's ankles with a metal chain running between them. The middle of the chain fastened to the screw. Carter was manacled to a second screw. It made a kind of mad sense: semi-naked, manacled people did not escape easily. Tyler came prepared for two prisoners and had to improvise for three. Having to change his plans made him more dangerous.

Tyler, dressed in tan slacks and a golf shirt, constantly paced the same circuit around the room, talking to himself. "What I want is simple. I've done everything they wanted. If they want a bond, I'll give them a bond. No, let brother do it, he has money. That's good. Brother will give them a

363

bond." He stopped and pointed to a pile of clothes in the corner. "Take off your clothes, Elizabeth. You may keep your pants and bra. I'm not entirely without sensibilities."

For an instant, Pepper saw, not white uniforms, but piles of soft-sided combat boots and bloodstained fatigues, in the corner of the emergency room by the big fan. They stripped the patients naked, her on one side and a corpsman on the other, their huge scissors cutting up the sleeves and down to the boots.

Justice, she thought. She'd made other people naked, now someone had done it to her. She untied her shoelaces and kicked off her wet shoes, then her socks, and her dress. Even in the dim light, the rose sundress made a colorful slash across the pile of white clothes. With slow, deliberate movements, she opened the haversack. "I'm going to serve food."

She placed Styrofoam cups on the small table. Half a dozen sandwiches wrapped in foil. A thermos of soup. Another of coffee. Cookies. Sugar and powdered coffee creamer. Paper napkins.

She poured five cups of cream-of-tomato soup, and sipped it, while Tyler watched her. What would make him the least suspicious? Allow him to choose any cup he wanted? Give him the first one? Give him the last one? She decided to go in order of rank. The Army way. She handed the first cup to Colonel Norton, then picked up a second cup and tracked Tyler around the room. Surprisingly, he took the cup readily, pacing and talking now interspersed with sips of soup. She served Jane Buckner and Harlan Carter and drank from her own cup. The warm soup slid down her throat and she realized how cold she was.

In a few minutes, she dispensed sandwiches, making a little holder from the foil so Tyler could eat while walking.

"There's no pickle. Brother knows I must have a pickle with roast beef."

"He forgot. It's a good sandwich. Could you eat it this one time without a pickle?"

He took a bite.

"Coffee?"

Coffee, tea, or rescue?

Tyler motioned to a chair next to Harlan. "Sit down, Elizabeth."

She sat. Tyler took a key from his pocket, unlocked the second manacle attached to Carter's ankle, and fastened the cold metal around Pepper's ankle. While Tyler faced away from Jane Buckner, Pepper moved her hand in a small motion. Patience. Patience.

Avivah and Benny put an aluminum ladder down at the gate to Colonel Norton's back yard. Benny pointed to Avivah's weapon. She handed it to him and he checked to make sure it was loaded. Not, Avivah realized, because he didn't trust her, but because checking his partner's weapon was the way Benny worked. She pointed to his weapon. He handed it to her and she checked it for him. If they were going to be partners, they were going to be equal partners.

They stared at the soldier at the end of the alley. The soldier signaled *Go*. Benny tapped Avivah on her helmet. *Go*.

Their feet squished in the wet grass as they hurried with the ladder across the back yard. They placed it against a wall, under the partially-opened bedroom window that made this rescue possible. Avivah flattened herself against the wall while Benny went up the ladder. He drew a knife from his belt and made two quick cuts through the window screen, then reached inside and fully opened the window.

In less than a minute, he was inside and Avivah was on her way up the ladder.

She cleared the sill and rolled silently—she hoped—into the room. Minimal furniture: bed, clothes chest, chair. The chenille spread pulled taut over the single bed. A guest bedroom. On the other side of the room, Benny used a small can of oil from one of his voluminous pockets to lubricate door hinges. Avivah crouched, balanced, ready to move.

Slowly, Benny turned the knob and opened the door into the dark second floor. He moved into the hall, and she moved to the door to cover him. When they were both in the carpeted hall, Avivah could only see a small patch of wooden floor at the bottom of the steps. Just like in their hurried practice.

She strained to make out the words floating up from the living room, a rumbling man's voice with a Doppler effect. Tyler must be moving around the room. "Have to find the letter. Hagan thought he was so damned smart. Michael said he was too smart for his own good. Michael was stupid. After what happened in Laos, he was a basket case. He panicked when Hagan contacted me. Michael was stupid."

Pepper's voice. Calm. Soothing. The kind of voice Avivah imagined she would find comforting if she were sick. "Michael Fuller insisted on keeping the money with him?"

"He was scared to let it out of his sight. Carried it with him in a suitcase for two months. A hundred thousand dollars in a suitcase. I had to pry it out of his hand to give it to Hagan."

Benny and Avivah flattened themselves against the hall wall. Benny grinned and gave Avivah a *thumbs-up*. They were in position and, as a bonus, Pepper was distracting Tyler.

Colonel Norton's voice. "What happened to Michael Fuller?"

"Got run over by a bus in Saigon."

"No! That's what I saw." Jane Buckner's voice whispered, barely loud enough to be heard.

Avivah shivered. Benny moved down the stairs, stepping on the end of the stair closest to the wall, testing each step to make sure it didn't creak. None of the stairs in their practice house creaked. She followed three steps behind, hoping this house was in good repair, too.

"Michael collapsed before the bus hit him." Major Buckner's voice sounded frigid and Avivah realized she'd just figured out that she witnessed Michael Fuller's death.

Benny stopped halfway down the stairs. In another couple of steps he would be visible. Avivah remembered their short practice, part of which involved standing in the living room, watching two men pretending to be her and Benny come down the stairs, demonstrating how visible and vulnerable they would be on the last few steps. Benny had to risk being vulnerable. He had to reach the back door, oil the hinges, and open it silently for the rest of the team to enter the house. In the next few minutes, Benny could die.

The two of them bent down to rapidly catch a glimpse of the living room. Avivah had a fleeting glimpse of the living room. Four semi-naked people, manacled to the floor. Dark china cabinet. Tyler pacing the room. She felt like a photograph had been burned into her eyes. Benny signaled to her *four-not-three,* as if she couldn't see for herself that they had an unexpected fourth hostage to deal with.

"How do you know that? Ah yes, officers rented hideaways on that street. Is that where you and Michael went? That explains why he ran toward that street. I could never figure that out. His gook whore lived on the other side of town."

So, despite all her protests, Jane Buckner had slept with

Michael Fuller. Avivah wondered if Harlan Carter had just learned that Jane Buckner had two-timed him, or if he knew it all along.

Benny looked at Avivah. He made a fist. Avivah nodded. Now or never. He extended one, two, three fingers and moved.

"Bet you didn't know he had a gook woman in Saigon. We used to laugh at you, you know. You chased Michael so hard and all that time he had this mama-san on the side."

In an instant, Benny reached the back door. More oil on the hinges, then he opened the door and four more soldiers flowed inside, two covering Avivah and Benny and two behind the door from the dining room into the living room.

Pepper was amazed that she separated what happened into minuscule tableaus, each clearly visible, with spaces between them. The door to the dining room flew open. Benny's voice yelled, "Down." Harlan Carter grabbed her and pulled her to the floor, then lay on top of her. His hairy chest pushed into her back. The last thing Pepper saw before shots rang out were Benny and Avivah, dressed in identical battle gear, standing side-by-side, holding weapons.

Chapter 37

In late August, three exhausted people sat on a picnic table, watching a moving van negotiate the tight corner at the end of the alley. The air smelled hot, end-of-summer ripe.

Avivah pushed sweat-soaked hair out of her eyes. "Think I'll ever see my furniture again?"

Pepper shrugged. "They found my stuff, didn't they? After . . ." She ticked off on her fingers, "Seven weeks. Fort Belvoir, Virginia; Fort Bragg, North Carolina; they both begin with "B," they're both in the South. I understand how they sent it to the wrong post."

Benny wiped the sweat from his face with the green towel hung round his neck. "Look on the bright side, they didn't deliver it to you until you had a house to put it in."

Benny and Pepper now shared Lorraine's house. Lorraine and her boys had moved to Missouri, next-door to Benny's parents, in the house that had belonged to Benny's Granda. Lorraine planned to sell her house in a year, after Benny and Pepper left the Army.

Avivah smelled the front of her sweat-soaked T-shirt. "Shower." She attempted to stand, groaned, and sat back down.

Benny reached into the cooler and distributed cold drinks. "Let's order pizza."

"That's what Pembrook and I did the day I moved in."

Coming to a new post was more fun than watching other people leave. Pepper had been to a lot of farewell parties in the past month: the going-away party for Major Buckner before she left for Washington; Colonel Norton's retirement party; a private farewell David and Patsy threw for Harlan Carter.

Harlan Carter. Pepper tried not to think about the look on his face when Colonel Tyler rambled on about Jane Buckner and Michael Fuller. Something had gone out of him, something that had sustained him. When he threw himself over her to protect her, she knew he didn't care if he lived or not. She and David Willett had helped him start on a long road, convinced him to sign himself into an inpatient alcoholic treatment center. Pepper reminded herself to send him a card.

Benny shook his head. "I've seen some pretty dumb things, but I can't believe Boyd fell for Tyler's plan. Did he really believe that Tyler would let him live, and give him a thousand dollars for the orphans?"

Pepper held the cold drink against her chest, as if the cold would relieve her pain. "Boyd trusted people. He wasn't dumb, but Cody says he always believed the best of everyone. He saw a chance to get his friends off drugs and help the orphans."

"How's Sergeant Doan doing?"

"Giving the doctors at the Veterans' Administration hospital a hard time. He's been talking to other amputees, and he gave the docs a list of features he wants in his prosthesis."

"The doctors tell you that?"

Pepper blushed. "Doan did. We're sort of keeping in touch."

Avivah grinned. "Speaking of giving people hard times, Doctor Tyler is having daily telephone meetings with the Office of the Judge Advocate General, and flying up from

Atlanta once a week. Maybe we should send JAG a sympathy card or something."

"At least he's off Captain Delaney's—pardon me, Major Delaney's—back. The Army moves fast when they want to. A promotion for Delaney, orders for Vietnam for you."

Benny looked at Avivah. "Yeah, well, she trapped the post commander in a moment of weakness."

Pepper remembered that moment all too well. Colonel Tyler, sedated, had been taken away in an ambulance. The hostages were dressed. Pepper sipped hot coffee from one of Colonel Norton's china cups. People milled around all over the house, talking in small groups, trying to avoid the broken shards from the cabinet and the porcelain bowls that had been the only casualties of Tyler's shots. A voice boomed, "Attention."

Pepper put her coffee cup on the floor and stood straight, head erect, stomach tucked in, thumbs against the seams of her sundress. She had never stood to attention in civilian clothes before. It didn't feel right.

The post commander entered, flanked by two colonels and a major. They all wore fatigues. If your troops were in battle, you were in battle, Pepper thought. She pressed her lips together to keep from smiling.

The general automatically took off his cap as he entered the house. "Stand easy."

He shook Colonel Norton's hand and promised her that all would be made right in her house, then worked his way slowly through the room, speaking to everyone. He had been well briefed and knew what role each person played. When he came to Pepper he said, "Captain Pepperhawk," and took her proffered hand in a firm, dry handshake. He smelled like talcum powder and shaving lotion. "Well done, Captain. You showed great bravery."

371

A lump formed in her throat. "Thank you, sir."

He moved on to Avivah. "I've had an excellent report about you, Captain Rosen. If there is anything I can do for you, please don't hesitate to ask."

Avivah looked him in the eye. "I want to go to Vietnam, sir. I've volunteered several times and been turned down each time. I'd be very grateful if you could look into the matter."

"Colonel," he said, over his shoulder, to the man on his right. The colonel wrote something in a notebook, and the general moved to the next person. With that one word, Pepper felt her world changed. Avivah was going to Vietnam. Even at the memory, she put her sweaty arms around her equally dirty knees and fought back tears. "What do your parents think about you going to Vietnam?"

"My mother and aunt are hysterical. My father hasn't said anything yet, but I expect he will, in private."

"Would it help if I wrote your mother a letter?"

"Thanks. I think it would."

Benny offered, "I'll write her, too."

"No!" Avivah and Pepper shouted, in unison.

Avivah put her arm affectionately around Benny's shoulder. "Not that I don't appreciate the offer, but this is a woman-thing, okay?"

He grinned. "Okay. Besides I'll be busy packing for Panama."

Pepper's heart contracted. "You don't have to go back, you know. You've done your bit: two tours of Vietnam, the . . . other stuff. You could get a desk job."

"I'm a beret, Pepper. It's like being an old fire horse; the bell rings and I run for the traces."

"Well, I say it's a rotten deal, everyone going off and leaving me. I won't have any friends here."

Benny handed her a card from his wallet. "Call this number."

"Why?"

"Because Darby Baxter wants to discuss having supper with you."

Pepper took the card and fanned herself with it. "Did you tell him what I told you to tell him?"

"I said this nurse at Fort Bragg remembered him from Fort Sam Houston and had the hots for him."

"You didn't!"

"You'll just have to call Baxter and ask him."

Pepper squinted at the card. She didn't recognize the area code. "Where is he?"

"Fort Benning, Georgia. Not that far away, Pepper. He could show up here one day. I had him checked out. He's okay."

"What do you mean, *You had him checked out. He's okay?*"

"He's divorced, so he won't pull the geographic bachelor on you. Rumor says he doesn't have habits that are worse than the average beret. All I can say is *good luck.*"

Avivah struggled to her feet. "I really have to shower. My plane leaves for New York at 0730 tomorrow morning."

Pepper struggled to her feet. "Then what?"

"Ten days' leave, then the big bird. I should arrive in-country about the time Benny is cruising the tropical shirt shops in Panama City."

"I don't want you to go."

"Pepper, we've been all through this. You had your chance, now let me have mine. I'll be fine. It's a year, three hundred and sixty-five days. I'm going to Long Bien, not out in the boonies. I'll be doing the same things I do here: directing traffic, arresting drunks, doing drug busts."

"But you'll be doing it in Vietnam," Pepper said sorrowfully.

"But I'll be doing it in Vietnam," Avivah said gleefully.

Benny picked up the empty cooler. "Tell you what, you let us know when and where your freedom bird is going to land a year from now and Pepper and I will be there, holding up a big sign."

Avivah looked at them suspiciously. "What will the sign say?"

Benny and Pepper grinned at each other. *"Welcome Home,"* they said in unison.

About the Author

Sharon Wildwind, a native of Louisiana, is a former Army nurse. In the early 1970s, she served with the Seventy-first Evacuation Hospital in Pleiku and the Sixty-seventh Evacuation Hospital in Qui Nhon. She also served a year at Fort Bragg, North Carolina—the setting for *Some Welcome Home*—as a head nurse on an orthopedic unit.

This mystery came about as a result of a conversation Sharon had at a signing for her previous nonfiction book, *Dreams That Blister Sleep: A Nurse in Vietnam* (River Books, 2000). Someone in the audience asked what happened to her when she came back from Vietnam. In reality, the ten years after she returned—1971 to 1981—were pretty mundane: a year at Fort Bragg, marriage, two university degrees, three nursing jobs, divorce, and immigration to Canada. But what if . . . life had been a bit more exciting, and there had been a few bodies, and she'd kept up more with some of the people she served with on active duty? Enter Captain Elizabeth Pepperhawk, fresh from Vietnam, and Captain Avivah Rosen, desperate to go there. And, for good measure and a little excitement, Sharon threw in a green beret, Sergeant First Class Benjamin Kirkpatrick.

Sharon is now a Certified Gerontological Nurse, working with the elderly. She spends her time orbiting between her computer and quilting table because the colors and patterns help produce the words and vice versa. She also teaches mystery appreciation workshops and, through memoir-writing, encourages older women to write the true stories of their lives. She's never lost her interest in the military and is married to a military historian.

Some Welcome Home is the first in a planned five-book series, which features her three veterans as heroes and detectives. For them, adjusting to civilian life is murder.